KING OF THE DEAD:
THE SAGA OF MONELLA, VOLUME 3

Tarantula Tower: The Adventures of
Scarlet and Bradshaw, Volume 4

BY THEODORE ROSCOE

Henry Plays a Hunch: The Complete
Tales of Sheriff Henry, Volume 5

W.C. TUTTLE

Cave of the Blue Scorpion: The Adventures
of Peter the Brazen, Volume 5

LORING BRENT

The Monster of the Lagoon: The Complete
Adventures of Singapore Sammy, Volume 3

GEORGE F. WORTS

The Fourteen Points

ARTHUR B. REEVE

War Dragons: The Complete Adventures of
Cordie, Soldier of Fortune, Volume 4

W. WIRT

Shark Trail: The Complete Adventures
of Bellow Bill Williams, Volume 3

RALPH R. PERRY

Minions of the Shadow

WILLIAM GRAY BEYER

Rats of the Harbor: The Complete
Cases of Dirk and Baker

RAY CUMMINGS

KING OF THE DEAD

THE SAGA OF MONELLA, VOLUME 3

FRANK AUBREY

COVER ILLUSTRATION BY

LAWRENCE STERNE STEVENS

STEEGER BOOKS • 2021

CHAPTER I

PRESENTIMENTS

"**DEAR ARNOLD, DO** not press me for reasons; for I can give none. As well might you ask me to tell you why I admire yonder glowing clouds and the golden sunset; or why I should shiver and be filled with sadness were it all to be suddenly obscured by rolling masses of heavy sea fog. The one affects me pleasurably; the other unfavourably—but I cannot tell you why. Yet you know that such feelings are part of one's very nature. Well, so it is here—with this man. He affects me unfavourably, and therefore I instinctively shrink from him."

"But, Beryl! Is it fair to him—to any man—to condemn him thus arbitrarily, especially—"

"I condemn him? What a foolish idea, Arnold! I know nothing about him that would justify my forming any such opinion. Indeed, his kindness to you—"

"Exactly. That's just what I want to remind you of."

"Indeed, Arnold, I am not in any danger of forgetting it. You, yourself, are always dilating upon it, and—to a certain extent—I, of course, am compelled to admit it. But then, there are people who are sometimes kind for some motive of their own, perhaps an unworthy motive. I—"

"Beryl!"

"Well, I don't say that that is the case here. I only say that I have an intuitive distrust of your brilliant friend, and it urges me—oh so strongly, Arnold—to pray of you not to allow him to tempt you, or to persuade you, into joining him in any wild adventure."

The scene was Ryde, the time summer, and the speakers were Beryl Atherton and Arnold Neville, two young people who were lovers. One may say, indeed, very much lovers. They had been engaged for quite three months and had not had a single quarrel as yet; not even—as yet—so much as a difference of opinion or an argument. And now that a slight difference of opinion had arisen it took no form of jealousy, though it had been caused through another man. On the contrary, the occasion was merely that the lady obstinately declined to diagnose, in the character of a certain mutual friend, the claims to admiration and confidence which her lover enthusiastically insisted upon. Most likely, had it been the other way about—*i.e.* had the lady been foremost in assigning to the mutual friend such an attractive personality—her lover would have been torn by jealousy, and would have contemptuously pooh-poohed the proposition. Such is the inconsistency of young people in love.

Beryl Atherton was an orphan, living with a widowed aunt who had brought her up from childhood. This relative—Mrs Beresford by name—lived a somewhat retired life in a small cottage of her own called "Ivydene," one of the prettiest residences in the Isle of Wight. This home she scarcely ever left from year's end to year's end; and Beryl, in consequence, had grown up to what was now her twentieth year with but scant knowledge of the great world that lay outside that sunny island. A few visits, of no long duration, to distant and little known relatives, a month, once or twice, in London during the season, and a trip, one winter, to the South of France, for the benefit of her aunt's health, constituted the total of her travels from home. But she was a studious and intelligent reader, and her industry in this direction, and a curiously accurate, intuitive, natural perception, enabled her to make up in many respects for her real ignorance of the "world" and its ways.

But, if lacking in most of those doubtful accomplishments which usually mark the society belle, Beryl Atherton possessed other attractions in the form of beauty and grace such as are but rarely granted to even the most favoured of Eve's daughters. To a face and figure all but perfect, she added the charms of large, lustrous, grey-blue eyes, shining with the clear, unmistakable light of a pure woman's soul within, and a smile so sweet and so sunny that few who once saw it ever forgot it. Golden brown hair that glistened in the sunlight, well-marked eyebrows a little darker in shade, perfect teeth, exquisitely moulded hands and feet, and a stature neither short nor tall, complete the short description of one of Nature's fairest gifts to the earth, one of whom it had been said, by more than one, that she was "beautiful as a goddess, and as good as she was beautiful."

Now her *fiancé* Arnold Neville, was also an orphan; and perhaps that fact may have had something to do with the sympathy which had existed between the two from the moment of their first meeting. It had been a case of "love at first sight" on both sides. Not a surprising fact so far as the young man was concerned, for every young man fell in love with Beryl Atherton at first sight—or thought he did. But the fact that it was in this case mutual, was unexpected, especially by Beryl's guardian. That good dame had been so accustomed to her niece's attractions causing all and sundry to offer their adoration without the smallest symptom of corresponding feelings on her side, that she had come to look upon such an event as beyond the limit of everyday calculations. For, until Arnold's appearance upon the scene, the young girl had merely accepted the homage of her admirers as a sort of form of politeness, smiling kindly and cordially upon each in turn, but never giving to any the smallest encouragement. And this gratified her guardian, who seemed to think that no one beneath the rank of a nobleman was good enough for her beloved niece, and had quite fallen into a sort of belief that the girl thought the same, and was awaiting the advent of her Prince Charming.

The shock had been, therefore, somewhat severe when she woke up one day to the knowledge that Beryl had given her heart to young Neville, whom they had known but a year; and who was very far indeed from fulfilling her dream of an ideal husband for her darling—at least, so far as worldly prospects went.

For Neville—unlike Beryl—possessed no "blue-blooded" relations. If Beryl was an orphan, she not only knew who her relatives were, but could boast—if she had wished to boast—that she was very "well-connected" indeed. Her father had been sixth cousin to a Duke, whilst her mother had been the daughter of parents who had been closely related to an Earl.

But Arnold, so far from possessing ducal or lordly relatives, scarcely even knew his own name. That is to say, he had no relative that he knew of in the whole world, had never known his own father or mother, and had to take it on trust, so to speak, that his name was really Neville. Saved from a wreck in which both his parents had been drowned, he had been adopted and brought up by a kindly old couple who had educated him as an engineer, and finally died, leaving him just enough to live upon had he cared to be an idle man. Some linen in which he had been wrapped, when saved from the wrecked ship, had been marked "Arnold Neville," and this name had accordingly been bestowed upon him. Beyond that he knew nothing.

One thing, however, was certain—so far as appearance went, Neville might have claimed the best of descent. Fairly tall, and well built, with a face and head of a singularly refined, intellectual cast, there was something in his air and manner that denoted the polished gentleman almost before one had had time to perceive the pleasing character of the features, and the steady, searching gaze of the clear, grey eyes. Handsome he certainly was, and well-favoured beyond the common run of mankind; but the kindly expression, and the genial smile that were habitual to him, were more attractive, and formed a truer index to his real character, than even the manly beauty that was undoubtedly his. In temperament he was inclined to be somewhat of a dreamer; and he was an enthusiast in music and painting; but this was compensated by a natural mathematical bias which had been strengthened and fostered by the special education he had received as an engineer. He was fond, too, of outdoor sports, and was well skilled in athletic exercises—characteristics which served still further to balance the dreamy, poetical side of his nature. He had now reached, according to the only data be possessed, his twenty-fifth year, and the occasion had served to remind him that he had not as yet settled down to any fixed career. So far, he had passed his time, since leaving college, as an improver in the offices of two or three different firms, changing his ground with the object of gaining a more varied experience. Latterly, he had been seeking an opportunity of employment with some pioneer railway enterprise abroad, an occupation which would, he hoped, afford him still wider experience, combined with foreign travel and exploration, which latter had always had for him an almost irresistible fascination.

Hence it was that his *fiancée's* allusion to "wild adventure" fell somewhat unpleasantly on his ears. Beryl's ideas upon the subject, so far as she was able to judge, led her to oppose his accepting any post that would take him abroad, especially as it must, almost certainly, mean that they would be separated for a term. His argument was, however, that such a course was wisest in the end, though distasteful for the time being. He would in that way get a better position, earn more money, and thus be enabled to marry sooner than he could hope to do by staying at home and waiting for the slow promotion which would then be all he could hope for.

"I hardly see, Beryl," he said, in reply to her last remark, "that going abroad to take part in some engineering or mining enterprise deserves to be denounced as entering upon a 'wild adventure.' Look at my friend Leslie, for instance. He has been out for five years in South America, engaged in railway work. Beyond such adventures as are more or less incidental to travel and exploration, his occupation has been businesslike enough; and, as the upshot, he has not only made more money than he could possibly have earned by staying at home, but he is now qualified to take a position which he could not otherwise have hoped to gain for years to come. He is, moreover, so well pleased with his experiences, that he is ready and willing to go out again, as you know, and—"

"Ah yes; but he has been engaged in a legitimate business undertaking—not in (I must really repeat the words, Arnold) a wild adventure. For it seems to me to be nothing else that his friend, Don Lorenzo, now proposes to you. I have a sort of instinctive aversion to your going off on any such expedition with that man."

"But why, Beryl?"

Which question brought the two back precisely to the point from which the conversation had started. The talk had travelled in a circle; as, indeed, had happened more than once before, when the same subject had been under discussion.

This time, however, Beryl resolved to speak out more plainly.

"Well then, since you keep pressing me so, I will speak what is in my mind—so far as I can manage to frame it in words. For I admit, of course, that I have very little to guide me; it is all very shadowy and indistinct, to my perception. But then it is just that that impresses me with vague doubts and fears. You see we know, after all, very little—practically nothing—of this adventurer, who—"

"Beryl! You have been to Don Lorenzo's entertainments, cruised in his yacht, accepted his hospitality; you have been the recipient of innumerable and most flattering kindnesses from a man who can boast Royalty amongst his friends; and now you style him an adventurer!"

"Arnold, dear, listen to me for a moment. It is your safety, dear, that I have in my mind, and your future—our future—" Beryl answered, with a charming blush. "It is true, as you say, that this man has, or seems to have, very highly placed personages for his friends; but that only makes it the more surprising to me that he should seek such very quiet society as ours. But to go back to the point; what, after all, do we know of him? What, even, has he told us? Come now, let us put it plainly." Here she held up her hands as though counting on her fingers, and proceeded to mark *off* her points with an air of grave sedateness that was very pretty to look at. "This gentleman makes the acquaintance of your friend, Mr Leslie, somewhere in the wilds of the South American forests. He says he is a Brazilian—or rather he is supposed to be a Brazilian, for I do not know that he has actually declared it to be so. He says his name is Don Lorenzo, which sounds a very short, modest appellation for a Brazilian. He appears to be very rich—"

"What about Santos-Dumont, the inventor of the flying machine? Was not he a Brazilian and reputed to be rich? Are those things to be accounted crimes?"

"Very rich," Beryl repeated, ignoring the interruption. "He comes to England in a wonderful yacht; visits London, and becomes at once the lion of the season. He goes everywhere, seems to be courted by everybody—even, as you say, by Royalty. He gives lavishly to charities—"

"That, after all, is only the modern way to get into society, and to rub shoulders with Royalty, you know."

"—He is undoubtedly a very remarkable man. His personal beauty is admitted to be extraordinary—"

"*You* don't seem to admit it."

"But I *do*. No one can help acknowledging it He is a most accomplished gentleman—"

"H'm; you allow that, then?"

"—a brilliant talker; a master of an unknown number of languages; supposed to be a marvellously clever mechanician—"

"That he is I can declare."

"—An eloquent orator, a finished musician;—in short, a social wonder. A sort of brilliant social meteor, the like of which has hardly been known before."

"But is it not true?"

"Well; after a while, this wonderful being makes your acquaintance, and forthwith deserts all his brilliant circle of friends, at the very height of the season, to come down here to potter about in our little circle, apparently with no other object than to cultivate your society—"

"And yours—and Leslie's."

"—but *yours* in particular, as it has all along seemed to me. And then he suddenly remembers that he has an enterprise in hand or in view—a mysterious adventure, apparently—about which he seems to have forgotten until he met you. For no one else appears to have heard of it—not even Mr Leslie, who came over in his yacht, ever heard it spoken of during their long voyage. An enterprise for which he requires an assistant or lieutenant—a mysterious post, which, he declares, no one can fill but you."

"He did not say so, Beryl, dear. He paid me the flattering compliment of offering it to me before any one else; that's all."

"But the fact that he has so offered it to you is *prima facie* evidence that he considers that no one else but you can fill it. Is it not so? Out of all the people he met in London—dukes, marquises, earls, and the rest, with their younger sons and nephews and so on, who would have been but too eager to jump at such an offer—so we have heard—"

"And we know it to be true."

"Even his own friend—and your friend—Mr Leslie, the one with whom he travelled to Europe—all are passed over—altogether ignored—in your favour."

"And all this—which one would think ought to be considered the greatest possible compliment to myself, is, in your eyes, a sort of crime, I suppose."

"No, Arnold; not that It is a mystery; a most strange, most inexplicable mystery. And for that reason it has caused me misgivings, and imbued my mind with vague apprehensions of which I am very conscious, but which I am altogether unable to define in words to my own satisfaction?"

She paused, and gazed out dreamily at the scene before her. They were seated on a terrace in the garden attached to Mrs Beresford's residence, which stood on high ground overlooking the sea, with a view that extended across to Southsea and Portsmouth and the line of hills beyond. There were vessels of all sorts and kinds and sizes passing to and fro; busy passenger-steamers plying backwards and forwards from the island to the mainland; one or two Channel steamers of larger size were also within view, and two or three huge vessels-of-war riding majestically at their anchors. A torpedo-boat destroyer could be seen, too, boring its way along through the water at a terrific speed, and throwing up waves of its own that turned the twinkling ripples around into a tumbling, storm-tossed sea, threatening destruction to any small boat that lay near its path. And, not least, among the smaller craft, but most beautiful of all, were the yachts, with their wide spread of snow-white sails towering aloft, gliding in and out amongst all the rest with graceful, easy sweep, careening to the slight breeze. The whole scene was lighted up by the beams of the setting sun, slightly veiled, farther away, by a purple haze that softened the distant hills into the clouds which floated above them.

Beryl gazed out over the scene with eyes in which there seemed a great depth of tender longing. The view from that terrace had been familiar to her from childhood, but it always seemed to have a fresh charm. She loved it as she loved a very dear friend; loved it under all its aspects, in all its moods. In the summer daylight, when white-crested waves tripped merrily shorewards like rows of white-robed dancing children; at dusk, when, over the placid water, the guardian light at Selsey Bill waxed and waned in its ceaseless watch, now gleaming bright and clear, now fading slowly into nothingness, only to appear again as a tiny star that grey and grew till it became, once more, the flashing glare of a few minutes before; and in winter, when darkling skies and troubled waters and drifting sea-mists filled the scene, shutting out the opposite shores, and only showing a vessel here and there as a half-revealed, ghostly phantom;— under all these aspects, in all these moods, the outlook had seemed to her ever fresh, ever beautiful, ever fascinating. In its extent, in its quiet beauty, and its harmonious variety, there was, to her mind, a sense of restfulness that always soothed and comforted her.

She turned from it, and regarded her lover with eyes that were dimmed, ever so slightly, with tears.

"Dear Arnold," she said, softly taking his hand in hers, "it is my heart that speaks and that prays you to avoid this man's blandishments. My heart tells me there is something insincere in him. He is so cynical too; I like not his talk at times—"

"He is outspoken, certainly—especially against humbug, and cant, and hypocrisy."

"Not only against such as that; but against better things, lie sneers and rails at much that I, for one, respect and revere; and his words hurt me, at times, more than I can give you any idea of. Oh, Arnold, dear, be advised by me. It is a voice within me that speaks, that assures me there is about this man something inimical to your future good and to my own; something, I had almost said, uncanny, unholy. Listen to me, dear heart, in this one' matter. Avoid his persuasions, decline his tempting offers, and do not trust your future—our future—to his guidance, to his tender mercies. Promise me this, Arnold, *now*, before you have made any promise to him that might be irrevocable. I am more anxious about it than I can tell you—and—oh! I am so inexperienced in the world's ways, I cannot properly define my own fears—I can only beg and pray of you to yield to me in this. Will you, Arnold?"

"But what about your aunt, Beryl? She will be very much against my refusing his offers, or I am much mistaken. She will say I am recklessly throwing up a good thing when I have nothing else to choose from to put in its place. I feel sure, from many hints she has let fall, that she has quite made up her mind I am going out with the Don; and I should not be surprised if she were to show her disappointment in somewhat disagree-able fashion."

"You must leave that to me, dear. Since I shall be chiefly

responsible for the decision, I am quite prepared to share the blame. I will tell her it was my doing."

"She will be very vexed."

"I shall be sorry, but in this matter I feel so anxious, that I would rather bear almost anything than see you go away with this man. Dear Arnold, for my sake, for the sake of our love, for the sake of our future happiness—which is, I am sure, at stake,—make up your mind and give me the promise I so long to hear from your lips."

And Arnold, feeling that he could refuse nothing to such tender pleading, drew the almost trembling girl to him, and kissed her.

"Very well, Beryl; be reassured, my darling," he said. "I have now made my mind to do as you wish. Come what will, no matter what his offers may be, or what we may seem to lose by it, I have made up my mind I will not go away with him. Will that content you?"

Beryl gave a soft, satisfied sigh, and rested her bead lovingly upon his shoulder.

"Now I shall feel more at ease," she murmured. "I cannot tell you, Arnold, what a nightmare this haunting fear has been to me. Your promise has lifted a load from my heart."

A minute later she turned towards the house, as the sound of footsteps came along the path.

It was a servant.

"If you please, Miss," said the girl, "Mr Gordon Leslie has called, and wishes to speak at once to Mr Neville."

CHAPTER II

THE MESSAGE

A FEW MINUTES later Mr Gordon Leslie joined the two on the terrace; and since he takes a considerable part in the series of events that go to make up this strange tale, it may not be out of place to give a few lines to him, by way of introduction to the reader.

Mr Gordon Wentworth Leslie, to give him his name in full, was at this time some thirty years of age; he was tall and muscular in build, and fairly good-looking. His features were bronzed by exposure to a tropical sun, and this, with his black hair and brown eyes, made him somewhat dark in appearance compared with the average untravelled Englishman. His movements had in them a peculiar easy swing—perhaps be had unconsciously acquired some of the free grace of the Indians amongst whom much of his time during the last few years had been passed. His sojourn in South American wilds had made him hard and tough in constitution, and self-reliant and alert in action. In character he was somewhat contradictory, or appeared so to those who only knew him slightly, since he had at times a half-cynical, half-flippant, ultra-critical way of expressing himself which appeared to be at variance with the genial, hearty manner and blunt common-sense that characterised him at others. It was a little difficult to those who knew him but slightly to discover which was his true character; only, perhaps, by his "chum" Neville, and one or two other intimates, was he thoroughly understood. As to the rest, in addition to his qualifications for his profession—which were unquestioned—he delighted to dabble a little in science, and, in particular, in botany and natural history. On his return, six months or so previously, from the tropics, he had brought back with him a collection of specimens of tie fauna and flora of the countries he had visited, selected with such knowledge and skill that their sale had brought him a considerable sum.

Leslie's home had originally been on the wild western shores of Scotland, where he had been accustomed from boyhood to outdoor life with boat and gun; but after the death of his parents he had come to live in the Isle of Wight, where he met Arnold Neville, and the two had become henceforth the firmest of friends and the most devoted of chums. During the absence of Leslie in America a constant correspondence had been kept up, and so graphic had Leslie's letters been, and so detailed and eloquent his descriptions of his life and adventures, that Neville was wont to say he already seemed to know the country almost as well as if he had lived out there himself.

"I've come," said Leslie, after the few preliminary inquiries concerning health, and remarks about the weather, which form the indispensable introduction to more serious subjects in all civilised intercourse—"I've come to seek you, Arnold, by command of his excellency the Count—that latter-day Sphinx—"

"You mean Don Lorenzo, Mr Leslie, I suppose," said Beryl, with a smile.

"Exactly, Miss Atherton. That gentleman, so good, so wise that some have bestowed upon him the soubriquet of the human riddle."

"Oh, stow that, Gordon," Neville interrupted. "Do tell us what the message is."

"His excellency's message is that he will be very greatly and eternally indebted to you if you can do him the never-to-be-sufficiently-appreciated honour of paying him an early and not-too-long-delayed visit at the suite of rooms which he occupies at the hotel which he has favoured with his distinguished and very much-to-be-desired patronage."

"Good gracious, Gordon, man, don't be so ridiculous!" Arnold exclaimed, half in earnest, half laughing. "He means, dear," he went on, by way of explanation to Beryl, "that the 'Don' wants to see me."

"So I gathered," said Beryl, laughing at his expression of affected disgust at the other's circuitous way of giving the message. Then she became graver, and, turning to Leslie, said:

"Why is it so pressing, Mr Leslie? Have you any idea what his object is?"

Leslie nodded. "I believe," he answered, "that his excellency has received some news which has somewhat disturbed that lofty serenity which usually appears so unassailable. He talks of retiring, at an earlier date than at first intended, to his native fastnesses—wherever they may be located; and I apprehend, therefore, that he may desire to learn from his well-beloved friend here, whether he consents to accompany him. To give the precise message, he begs his dear and never-to-be-sufficient-ly-admired friend to go and see him at once—now."

"This evening?" said Beryl.

"Yes. It is only fair to his excellency to say that this somewhat peremptory-sounding request was accompanied by a string of most elegantly-worded apologies, so long, that were I to repeat the half of them his dear-and-well-beloved friend could not possibly arrive at the hotel before to-morrow morning. So I leave out all that part of the message, much as I should like to repeat it to you, if only out of admiration for its mellifluous and well-balanced phraseology."

"Oh! Do be sensible, Gordon; you are incorrigible," Arnold exclaimed, impatiently. "If I understand you aright, you believe he wishes to get a final decision from me; and if so it is too serious a matter to fool about with. Not, however," he added, more quietly, "that it requires much thought, for my mind is made up."

Something in Arnold's tone, as he said this, struck Leslie as unusual, and he opened his eyes and sat up in his chair.

"Your mind is made up, Arnold?" he said, with an entire change of manner. "And your answer is—?"

"No!"

Leslie gave a long, low whistle; and for a while there was dead silence. Then he looked at Beryl.

"You two have discussed this and made up your minds together, I can see," he observed. "May I ask—is it final?"

"Yes, Mr Leslie. Arnold has given me his promise, and that ends it," was Beryl's answer, given with quiet decision.

"The Don won't like it!"

"He has no claim upon Arnold, no right to insist upon his acceptance of his offer," said Beryl, with just a trace of annoyance in her tone. "Do you mean to say you think he will resent it? Would he dare—"

"No, no, Miss Beryl," Leslie put in hastily, smiling at the way in which the young lady had flushed up, and the indignant ring in her last words. "I was only thinking that he would be very disappointed; I feel sure he will."

"Well, he can get a very good substitute close at hand," Arnold remarked.

"You mean yourself?"

"Why, of course."

"Ah! I only wish he would transfer the offer to me!"

"What? Would you accept it?" Beryl inquired.

"Like a shot! But there—I feel assured there is no likelihood of his doing that."

"In that case it only adds to the mystery of the thing," said Beryl, meditatively. "I had had an idea that perhaps he had made you the offer at first, and that you had refused it, only you did not wish it to be known, thinking that if it were it might prejudice Arnold."

"No, Miss Atherton. He never seems to have so much as thought of me in such a connection."

"Yet you, with the experience you have already had out there would, one would have supposed, have been far better suited to him than Arnold. It is all a puzzle to me."

"Well, well, Beryl, dear, we have decided," said Arnold; "so why worry further about it? I think, if you don't mind, I'll trot along there now, and get if over. It won't take long; and I'd rather get it off my mind. Will you come with me, Gordon, or stay here and wait till I return?"

"I'll stay here and wait for you, with Miss Beryl's permission," said Leslie. "He won't want me there. But I should like to know what he says; so I will wait for you here—that is, if you will not be late."

"I shall certainly come back here to tell Beryl what transpires," Arnold returned; "so by all means wait for me." And with that he left them.

Beryl and Leslie, thus left alone, remained for some time silent; but presently the former exclaimed, half to herself and half to her companion:

"God grant that no harm may come of this! How I wish that man had never taken this strange fancy to Arnold!"

"It seems hard to say that, Miss Atherton," Leslie answered, warmly. He was fond of Arnold himself, and it seemed to him easy enough to understand why another man should feel the same way. "In selecting him, or wishing to select him, above all else, Don Lorenzo has but rated him at his true value; at least, so I would humbly submit the matter to you."

"Yes, yes; it is like you to say so. I know how true and loyal your friendship for dear Arnold is; and oh, I beg of you, Mr Leslie, I implore you to tell me truly—do you believe that Don Lorenzo will accept his 'No' quietly, and that no harm will come of it!"

"My dear Miss Beryl! What harm can possibly come of it?"

Beryl looked at him wistfully, as though wishing that she could read his secret thoughts. Then she gave a slight shiver.

"Mr Leslie," she said, in a tone so grave and serious that Leslie involuntarily gave a slight start of surprise, "why do you affect ignorance of what is in my mind—ay, and, for the matter of that, in your own mind—for I saw the grave expression that came into your face when Arnold told you that his answer would be 'No.' You felt then as I did. Immediately there flashed across your mind the question: 'How will he take this refusal?' and deep down in your heart you had a lurking fear that trouble would come of it I read it all in your face as clearly as I would read a book. Why did you have that fear, and what is the trouble that you instinctively foresaw?"

The girl was so earnest, so convinced of the reality of that of which she spoke, that Leslie felt himself in a difficulty how to make answer. Her searching gaze, telling so eloquently of the deep love and the tender concern that troubled her thoughts, conveyed to him, plainly enough, that she was not to be put off, like an inquisitive child, by empty phrases or conventional disclaimers. Her great love, he could not fail to perceive, had inspired her with a sort of exalted courage and a way of looking at things that were new in her—at least so far as regarded his own experience of her—and quite different to her usual quiet and simple manner.

He felt, in fact, to state his own thoughts about the matter at the moment, that he was "cornered," and that it would be useless to beat about the bush.

"Miss Beryl, I will not deny that you have correctly divined my thoughts. But of course there is no danger—"

"Dear friend—true friend of Arnold's as I know you to be,—do not play with me further; let us be frank. I fear this man's resentment; so do you. If it be the case that he is going away soon, then, if there is any harm coming it will come quickly. If there is anything to be done to avert it, we must take our precautions now—at once. There is no time for delay. This man is rich, powerful with all the power that an iron will and unscrupulous resolve, backed by great wealth, can give him. He has no ties here—will leave no hostages behind if he chooses to sail in his yacht and simply disappear. None can follow him, for no one knows whence he comes or whither he goes. Thus I read it; for I have given it much anxious thought; and so do you. Am I not right?"

"Partly; but—"

"Now, you know him better than we do. What form do you think his resentment is likely to take?"

"I cannot now say. I must have time to think. I declare to you I have never thought about it till a few minutes ago, for the simple reason that I never anticipated that Arnold would refuse so promising an opening."

"Then, Mr Leslie, you *will* think about it now, will you not? Promise me that you will give *all* your thought to it, as if our lives depended upon it, as indeed they do—mine does, for how could I live on if anything happened to Arnold!"

Her distress was so apparent, so real, that Leslie felt more deeply touched than he would have cared, perhaps, to own. Inwardly he made a vow to give his whole thoughts to this matter until the Brazilian had left the country.

"I will watch over Arnold day and night, Miss Atherton," he promised her, in a low but resolute tone. "The more anxiously in that, should any trouble arise, I should feel myself, in a measure, the cause of it, seeing that I was the means of introducing Lorenzo and Arnold to each other."

"No, no; you must not look at it so. But now do explain to me a little more clearly what you know about this man of mystery— for so I call him. You said just now that if he made you an offer you would accept it readily enough. If that is the case you must feel confidence in him?"

"I have confidence in him in this way, that I fully believe he possesses almost unlimited wealth; and if, therefore, he prom- ised me what would be to me a very liberal remuneration, I see no reason to doubt that he would keep his word. Moreover, you must not forget that he saved my life."

"Ah yes, of course; Arnold told me something of that; but I scarcely heard any details. Since you came down here, and this stranger with you, we seem to have lived in such a whirl, and Arnold has been so wrapped up in this new friend, as he considered him, and has regarded everything through such rose-coloured spectacles, as it were, that really I have only confused recollections of what you at first told us. Do you really owe your life to him?"

"Undoubtedly. It happened far away in the interior of Brazil, hundreds of miles from the nearest white settlement I was alone—that is to say, so far as white men were concerned—and for the first and only time in my experience I had, through over-confidence, allowed a party of treacherous Indians to steal a march upon me. They fell upon us in the night, murdered nearly all my attendants then and there, took away my arms, and tied me up to a tree, and the following day were about to kill me when this man rode into their midst. He was armed in the fashion usual in those parts, but he apparently disdained to unsling his rifle or so much as draw his revolver. He carried in his hand a heavy riding-whip, and with that he lashed right and left into the cowardly, murderous crew. They appeared thoroughly frightened, made only futile attempts at resistance, and finally dropped all their plunder—everything they had stolen from me—and slunk off like whipped curs. Yet they were a marauding band who had long been notorious in those parts for the robberies and massacres they had perpetrated."

"Could he have been in league with them, have been their real master?" Beryl queried, thoughtfully. "We have heard of such things."

"That crossed my mind, too. But it could not have been so, since he did not live in that part of the country, and was only passing through it. He, in fact, came on down to the coast with me, and offered me, as you know, a passage home in his yacht, which was waiting for him at Rio."

"Well, but who is he then? Who do you think he is?"

"Either a wealthy rancher who owns large properties far away in the interior of Brazil, or (more likely) one who has chanced upon some immensely rich gold or diamond mine, the secret of which he has managed to keep to himself."

"There is something more than that," Beryl said, dreamily, "some secret that you—we—have not yet guessed at. Riches can do a great deal, no doubt; but would you say in your own mind that this man is a 'mere millionaire'? We have seen millionaires before; they have been plentiful of late years; but we know fairly well what they are like—at all events, within certain limits. After all, they are only men with more money than usual, and, generally speaking, they only become noticeable as each in turn displays more vulgarity and ostentation than his predecessors. But there is something very different about *this* millionaire—or billionaire, or whatever he may be."

"I agree with that. Yet, so far as I can speak of him—and I lived with him on his yacht for some time, you know—I've had nothing to complain of with him."

"Nothing to complain of say you! Why, Mr Leslie, I cannot be in his company for half-an-hour without feeling that I dislike him—dread him."

"Dread him! Others speak of his marvellous attractiveness, of his magnetic influence, and his inexhaustible good nature and royal munificence."

"Yes; but does he not show his contempt for it all the time? He gives, it is true, ten thousand pounds in one lump to a charity to-day, and twenty thousand pounds to another to-morrow; but *you* know, well enough, the cynical humour with which he talks of it afterwards."

"I think a good deal of his cynicism is put on."

"It is not, Mr Leslie. He scoffs and laughs at everything that is good, everything that is pure and holy. He believes in nothing, reverences nothing. He avows it all to you, and you laugh at it, and affect not to believe he means what he says. But I *know* that he means it—every word of it. My heart tells me so; my instinct tells me so. And that is why I dread him, why I so dreaded the thought of Arnold going away with him. I tell you that this man, handsome—a demigod—as he is, in face and figure, fascinating as he may be to those who are too much dazzled by his splendour, or too careless to look below the surface—this man of many strange gifts and powers has a heart of stone! God help any of us who had to trust to his tender mercies! That is the final message that my heart has whispered to me. And my woman's instincts tell me that it is true."

Now this conversation had carried the two far into the evening, and at this point Beryl went into the house to seek her aunt and keep her company till supper-time. Leslie preferred to stay outside on the terrace, to smoke a cigar in the cool evening air, and ponder over all that had been said. For a long while he remained there, sometimes walking restlessly up and down, sometimes standing gazing out through the darkness at the lights that twinkled on the opposite shore, or at the regular waxing and waning of the revolving light. The moon rose, large and ruddy, and spread her soft light over land and sea; and still Arnold did not return.

Presently, however, just as Leslie, after many impatient glances at his watch, was about to go into the house, he heard a step coming along the path, and a moment later Arnold appeared and dropped, as though greatly fatigued, into a seat.

"Ah, here you are at last! What a time you have been," Leslie exclaimed. "How did you get on?"

"Gordon," said Arnold, in a low, awed tone, "that man is beyond my comprehension! He is most certainly no ordinary human being! I cannot make up my mind whether he is a god, a madman, or a devil!"

And Leslie, going up closer to him, saw, in the moonlight, an expression upon his friend's face that he had never seen there before. It was as though he had seen a ghost.

CHAPTER III

A MAN OF MYSTERY

WHEN ARNOLD NEVILLE left Mrs Beresford's house to call upon the Brazilian, he hurried along with only one idea uppermost in his mind, and that was to get the matter over as quickly as possible. He instinctively felt that the interview must, in any case, be an unpleasant one; but for that very reason he braced up his courage and determined to cut it short. As, however, he neared the hotel, at which the Count—as he was frequently styled—had taken up his temporary residence, his pace gradually slackened until his brisk walk had degenerated info a saunter, and a very slow one at that. He began to realise that the business before him might prove more difficult than he had at first considered it; and first one thought and then another came into his mind, suggesting points which he had for the moment left out of account, and which now made him wish that he had taken a little more time for consideration.

It was not so much that he had any fears—such as Beryl had confessed to—of the man's resentment. That he would be annoyed, and be likely to show it, was to be expected; for he was a man accustomed to have his own way and to consider solely his own will and pleasure. And when Arnold remembered his usual haughty and often disdainful manner towards others, and the terrible look that he had seen in his face once or twice when he had been crossed, he could not but confess that he shrank from the necessity that lay before him of bearding this lion in his own den. But alongside of these recollections came others of a softer character. They reminded him how this high and mighty individual had invariably softened in his manner towards himself; he thought of the many kindnesses he had received at his hands, kindnesses the more noticeable in that they had involved expenditure of time and trouble upon Lorenzo's part—a very different thing—with him—to the expenditure of money; of which he took no account.

There was another question that came to Arnold's mind, too; could he anyhow persuade the count to extend his offer to his friend Leslie instead of himself? If he could do that, it would be a good way out of it all. But in order that he might have a chance to accomplish it, it behoved him to be cautious, and to avoid, as far as possible, putting his refusal in such a fashion as to give even the slightest offence. And yet to manage all this, and still be firm in such refusal, would clearly not be an easy matter.

Thus did Neville cogitate; and by the time he arrived at the hotel he had come to the conclusion that he had before him a pretty hard nut to crack.

The moment he set foot inside the hotel door, an obsequious waiter, quickly followed by a still more obsequious manager, came forward to receive him. They knew him as the intimate and favoured friend of their illustrious Guest (they would have spelt the word with a very big G), and they almost got pains in their backs in their anxiety to bow low enough to do him homage.

"I believe that his excellency is in, Mr Neville," said the manager, rubbing his hands, and bowing two or three to the second. "Pray walk in here, sir, and be seated while I send word to his excellency's secretary. I've no doubt his excellency will see you immediately, sir. Very fine weather we're having, aren't we, sir? Very summery for the time of year, is it not, sir?"

The proprietors of the hotel had good reason for their attentions to their illustrious guest, and they naturally extended them to his friends, and to this one in particular, whom they knew to be on terms of especial intimacy. This millionaire had taken it into his head, during the last six weeks, to make the hotel his head-quarters, engaging the whole of the first and second floor, the first for the use of himself and his suite, and the floor above to keep it empty—such was his caprice—in order that no one should disturb him by stamping about or making other noises overhead. Which arrangement, by the way, was altogether supererogatory at that time of the year, seeing that the place never expected any visitors, to speak of, before the beginning of August—and it was not yet the end of July. Therefore this visitor, who paid so lavishly, and threw his money about in such royal fashion, had been a windfall indeed that year to the hotel proprietors; and it is not to be wondered at that both he and any friends who visited him received all the attention that the staff could bestow.

As to this notable visitor himself, giving his name as Don Lorenzo—which, as Beryl had remarked, was an unusually short and modest name for a Brazilian, and especially for such a man—he had been the wonder, the admiration, and the puzzle of London for some six months past. Arnold's friend Leslie had met him under the circumstances briefly related in the last chapter. The stranger was, he stated, on his way, with a large party of attendants, down to the coast where his yacht was awaiting him, when early one morning a fugitive Indian had burst into his camp declaring that his party had been set upon during the night and nearly all murdered, and that he believed the white man with whom they had been travelling was a prisoner and was likely also to be killed. Lorenzo had at once set off with the Indian to guide him without waiting for his armed followers, and had, single-handed, fearlessly attacked and scattered the bloodthirsty band, using only the riding-whip which he was accustomed to carry when mounted. Leslie, tied to a tree, looked on in amazement at the cool, contemptuous fashion in which this stranger drove off wild men who were known as the fiercest and most determined in that part of the country, never so much as drawing a revolver or unslinging his rifle. In describing the occurrence subsequently to Arnold he always declared that the man acted as though possessed of some magical power over the cut-throat crew. "The scoundrels would raise their rifles or pistols—they were well armed—and take aim, and seem to try to fire at him point blank," he declared, "or one would raise a cutlass, or another a dagger to cut him down or stab him in the back, but the firearm either refused to go off or missed him, if it did, in the most wonderful manner, while the steel never seemed to reach him. At last the whole cowardly crowd gave a great howl of fear and ran off with eyes starting from their heads, declaring that he was a devil Then his attendants came up and went after the flying wretches, shooting them down as they hunted them, while Lorenzo turned to me and, as he dismounted and cut the ropes that bound me, greeted me in English as quietly and unconcernedly as though we had just met in Pall Mall." Such had been Leslie's full description.

When the two came to talk, and Leslie had stated that he was on his way to Rio with the object of returning to Europe, Lorenzo replied that he was proceeding upon the same journey, and proposed that they should travel to the coast together. As Leslie had lost many of his attendants and horses he gladly acquiesced, and so well did they get on together that when the stranger afterwards offered him a passage home in his yacht, he cordially and gratefully accepted the proposal.

At the very first glance—even amid the excitement of his rescue—Leslie had been struck by the stranger's good looks. When he came to regard him more leisurely, this feeling was increased to wondering admiration. He was, to his mind, the most handsome, the most comely specimen of a man, white, red, or black, that he had ever seen. He appeared, in effect, perfect both in face and figure; and this verdict of Leslie's was subsequently universally confirmed by general opinion wherever the man afterwards appeared. Tall and commanding in stature, he was yet so exactly proportioned that he looked a little less than his real height; he was muscular without being stout, light and graceful in carriage without being thin. His voice had a charm of its own; once heard it was never forgotten. His clear-cut face was free from the slightest appearance of beard or moustaches, and what was very noticeable was that it had no appearance of having been shaven, as is generally the case with men with such dark hair and eyebrows—for these, like his eyes, were black, while his complexion was clear and smooth, almost like that of a fresh young English boy. The mouth was exquisitely carved and, in all his moods, very expressive; but when at rest its classic beauty was slightly marred, perhaps, by the smallest possible trace of cynicism. It was hardly noticeable; but it was of that kind that some natures—like Beryl. Atherton's, for instance—would intuitively *feel* rather than read, while the generality of folk would fail to notice it. But the most expressive features of all were the eyes—dark, luminous, large, and sparkling, with a gaze so steady, so penetrating, that few could long endure it without flinching. It had, too, that peculiar quality which is sometimes found amongst gypsies—that seems to look right through and beyond the person upon whom it is fixed. Leslie thought to himself, as he looked upon this stranger, that he had often heard and read of a "magnetic glance," but he had to admit to himself that he had never seen it realised before. Later on when, one day, he saw those eyes flash in anger, he understood a little better the overmastering influence that their owner had exercised over the Indians when he had appeared amongst them and attacked them in so sudden and so masterful a manner.

As they travelled together towards the coast, the stranger charmed his companion by his varied talk and captivating personality, surprised him by his extensive fund of information and familiarity with all the scientific subjects of the day, and amused and interested him by many curious contrivances and inventions which he carried with him, and which were different to anything the young Englishman had ever seen before.

As to his age, the Brazilian seemed to be between thirty and thirty-five, so far as appearance went, but Leslie told himself that in his surprising experience, and the intimate knowledge he exhibited of other countries of the world, and of all, even the most abstruse as well as the most recent, scientific researches, he conveyed the idea rather of acquirements such as only a man of great and advanced age could be expected to possess. Nor did he vouchsafe to Leslie any information as to his previous history, his native country, or his home. Upon all such matters he was absolutely dumb; and at the time of the opening of this story, Leslie knew no more about him than he had done a day or two after their first meeting.

When, at Rio, Leslie went on board the "Alloyah"—so the stranger's yacht was named,—his wonder and astonishment increased. Almost every contrivance on board differed from anything he had ever seen before, from the motive power to the smallest pulley block, from the shape and comparative size of the cabins to the furniture; and especially was he surprised at the number of novel inventions brought into use during the voyage to administer to their comfort or convenience.

The motive power was itself a mystery. That there were engines of some kind on board seemed evident from the fact that the boat moved without sails, and at great speed. A slight sound as of very smooth-working machinery was just audible when she was going full speed; but what the engines were like, or where they were situated, what was the motive power, or what the means of propulsion, he could not discover; and Lorenzo never told him. They took in no coal or other fuel, and there was no smoke, smell, or dust about the vessel, such as all machinery usually causes more or less. There was a funnel, but so far as the closest observation went, there was no smoke or fumes to escape by it The cabins were unusually large and spacious for the size of the vessel; this evidently being rendered easy to arrange from the fact that they occupied much of the space generally allotted in other vessels to machinery and coal. And in them the air was always maintained at an agreeable temperature, ever sweet and fresh under all conditions:—cool in a hot climate, warm in a cold one, and pure and bracing even when the ports had to be closed in heavy weather. But of how all this was managed Leslie was told nothing. His host avoided all questions and allusions with such perfect good breeding, and was ever so polished and courteous in his manner that his guest was completely baffled, without feeling that he had cause for complaint From the crew, too, he could learn nothing. Of these there were nearly twenty; but he could not so much as guess at their nationality. Their language was strange to him—though be knew something of most of those spoken on the South American continent—and they appeared not to understand English.

Thus Leslie landed in England with his mind full of wonder and unsatisfied curiosity, and full, too, it must be said, of admiration and liking for his new friend, piqued though he was at his refusal to explain to him the many marvels and mysteries of the vessel and her belongings.

Arrived at Southampton, Lorenzo left his yacht anchored in the river and proceeded to London, while Leslie went first to visit his mother and friends in the Isle of Wight Not long afterwards, however, he called upon the Brazilian in town, where he found that he had already established himself in a large furnished mansion in Belgravia, and had been introduced at court by the Brazilian Minister. Immediately, he seemed to be the rage in the highest circles, visiting during the winter at some of the most exclusive houses in the counties, and, later on, in the season, becoming the lion and the pet of London.

Just at the height of the season, at a time when invitations to splendid functions poured in thick and fast upon the "Lion," and his engagements multiplied as such things do at this time of the year, Arnold Neville went up to London. He went at Leslie's invitation to pass a few days with him before he returned to Ryde; and it was there that he was introduced to the man of whom he had already, by that time, heard so much.

The occasion of the meeting was a notable one, and proved remarkable both in itself and in its after results. It was at a very grand and exclusive function at a ducal mansion; more than one Royal personage, as well as Ministers of State, Ambassadors, and highly placed officials in the most gorgeous of uniforms, were there; and many who were amongst the *élite* of the nobility deemed themselves fortunate in being invited. To this brilliant assemblage Don Lorenzo sent Leslie tickets, one for himself, "and one for his friend," whom he did not yet know, but understood would be in London, with a polite instruction not to fail to seek him out and make his friend known to him during the evening. Arnold, who had never been to anything of the kind before, at first strenuously objected to going, but was overruled by Leslie, who pointed out to him that it would be an experience he might never meet with again. So they donned their "war-paint," arrived in due time at the mansion in Park Lane where the assemblage took place, and a few minutes later found themselves in the midst of the splendid throng.

They knew no one there—or saw no one they knew—but that did not matter; the place was too crowded for those around to notice them in particular, and they wandered on, interested and amused, till they reached the principal guest chamber. This was comparatively clear, being evidently reserved, by general consent, for the more illustrious guests. Here, surrounded by a brilliant circle, stood Don Lorenzo, who looked the very embodiment of manly grace and beauty, his figure admirably set off by a rich Portuguese court dress, with jewel-hilted sword by his side, and jewelled orders upon his breast.

To judge by the faces of those around him, he must have been talking with special eloquence upon some fascinating subject when he caught sight of Leslie and his friend, who had stopped just outside the open doorway. The brilliant talker looked at Leslie and, without interrupting his discourse, bowed and smiled ever so slightly; then his glance fell upon Arnold, and immediately it became fixed. He ceased abruptly what he was saying, stood for a space as though too much surprised to either move or speak, then, with merely a curt bow to those around him, he walked straight up to Leslie and shook hands.

"This must be your friend Mr Arnold, of whom I have so often heard you speak," said he. "Pray present me to him."

Leslie, much astonished, performed in some fashion the slight ceremony of introduction, whereupon Lorenzo took Arnold's hand and looked steadily and searchingly into his face. Then he turned and strolled along the gallery in which they were standing, motioning to the two to join him, and entered at once into a close conversation, asking many questions of Arnold, where he was staying, how long he proposed to remain in town, and so on. And all the time the two young men felt more confused than they afterwards cared to avow, for this open intimacy with one so well known, and more especially the manner of their meeting, created quite a stir in the crowded galleries, and caused all eyes to be turned upon them wherever they went.

Nor did their strange friend's attentions stop there. He insisted upon presenting the two to many of the most distinguished of the visitors, and finally took them back to their apartments in his own carriage.

During the rest of the time that the two remained in London, Lorenzo insisted that they should be his guests, and they therefore took up their abode for a week in his mansion.

At the end of that time they returned to Ryde, where they regaled and surprised their friends not a little with accounts of the magnificence in which they had lived and moved and had their being during that short week—for wherever the Brazilian had gone, there he had insisted upon the two going also.

Then, a few days after their return, they were all astonished, and the great world of London not less so—at the brilliant stranger's sudden appearance at Ryde, where he engaged rooms, as has been related, and anchored his matchless yacht off the pier. Ryde was handy, so he said, for some short trips he desired to make round the coast for the benefit of his health, which had suffered from too much gaiety in London; not, however, that he exhibited, to the ordinary observer, any signs of illness.

In these trips, Leslie, Neville, Mrs Beresford, and Beryl were always invited to join, though they did not always avail themselves of the invitation when, as often happened, some grand or eminent personage would come down from town for a short cruise. But he frequently invited the four alone, and on these occasions they had very pleasant outings; for the yacht and its belongings were a source of never-ending wonder and curiosity, and its owner was always a most accomplished and entertaining host.

And then it was that he had, at first tentatively, but subsequently more explicitly, unfolded to Neville the news that he had in view an enterprise or exploration—he never made it very clear as to what was the nature of the affair—in some remote part of South America, in the which he wanted an assistant who was possessed of engineering knowledge, and whom he was willing to remunerate on an extremely liberal scale. This post he offered to Arnold—very greatly, as has been already intimated, to the surprise of both himself and his *fiancée*. At first he had been very greatly inclined to assent, for he, too, had fallen under the extraordinary fascination that the stranger seemed to exercise over all those with whom he came in contact, whether rich or poor, noble or simple, male or female. All, that is to say, save Beryl Atherton. For her, alone, his attractive personality had no particular fascination, and she never fell under his spelt It was not exactly that she disliked him; on the contrary, she admired him almost as much as did others—but in a different way. Something there was, amidst all his seductive qualities, that jarred upon her, grated, as it were, against those purer, holier instincts which, in a true, good woman, are seldom found to be at fault, however simple and innocent her nature, however slight her knowledge of the world and of mankind. And, in her heart, this instinct had spoken against this stranger, and had given her courage, in her lover's supposed interest, and, as she thought, for his safety, to urge Arnold to reject his tempting offers and look with mistrust upon his professions of friendship.

But we have kept Arnold Neville waiting somewhat overlong in the hotel parlour. How he fared in his interview must be told in the next chapter.

CHAPTER IV

A STRANGE INTERVIEW

AT THE END of a short interval Arnold was waited upon by Don Lorenzo's secretary, one known as Moreaz.

This secretary was a well-known member of the Brazilian's *entourage;* indeed, it may be said that he was the only one amongst his suite who ever came directly into contact with the outside world, since he alone spoke English. All other employees of the "count," like the crew of the yacht, spoke to him and were spoken to in some language which no one but themselves was able to understand. Not even amongst the savants with whom "his excellency" frequently rubbed shoulders at a scientific *conversazione* or popular science lecture was there one who could guess at what this language might be. Señor Moreaz, however, as he was usually styled, was a rather notable character. He was indeed, in many respects, the very opposite of his master. In particular, he was so very far from possessing good looks that there were some cynically-minded folk, who, by way of a jest, were wont to say that he had been picked out by his employer as a foil to enhance his own superlative attractions.

From all which it will be gathered that the secretary was ill-favoured; but it was not so much that as that he scarcely seemed, as some put it, to have any looks at all. His face was absolutely expressionless; at no time had those who had observed him ever seen upon that impassive countenance any expression whatever, whether of pleasure or sorrow, anger or grief, or even recognition of another's presence. The man seemed a mere automaton.

He would answer questions truly according to his lights—by far the greater part of his replies consisted of "don't know's"—but never did he display interest, or animation, or even intelligence, beyond that which a wound-up lay figure might be supposed to exhibit "A treasure of a man for one so deep and secret as his master," some would say; but others shook their heads, and declared they could not understand "the creature": he seemed "uncanny," "hardly human," and so on.

In appearance the man was what is known as "washed out." His hair was thin, and of a nondescript, greyish brown; eyebrows he scarcely showed at all; while his face was always of a strange pallid, livid hue, that never betrayed a flush or the slightest trace of colour. Most noticeable of all, however, were the eyes, which were flat and staring; "like a cod-fish's," as the ill-natured ones sometimes put it.

However, though not well favoured, the secretary appeared to satisfy the Brazilian's requirements well enough; and he, naturally, had the most right to be considered.

The secretary, then, sought out Arnold, where he was waiting, and, with a short bow, and "This way, if you please, sir," showed him upstairs into Lorenzo's apartment, which was a large room on the first floor facing the pier and seafront.

Lorenzo, who had been engaged in perusing a book and smoking a cigar, came forward and extended to his visitor a very hearty welcome.

"This is indeed kind, my dear friend," he declared, with a warmth and animation in his manner such as be but rarely displayed. "You must have come immediately you received my message from Mr Leslie. How very good of you. It is an honour I deeply feel, my dear friend; and I shall interpret it as an omen that you wish to discuss with me the matter I spoke about in a like spirit to myself. Is it not so?"

He seemed so extremely pleased, and showed his satisfaction so openly, that Arnold could not summon up the courage to abruptly dissent then and there; and so for the moment he lost his opportunity.

"You will have a cigar? Yes? And a glass of wine; *my* wine, you know. I thought perhaps that you would come; so I ordered that some should be put out."

This referred to a very peculiar luscious wine which the Brazilian carried about wherever he went, but was wont to offer only to those guests whom he specially favoured. Usually, Arnold joined him in a glass, but to-day he declined. He, however, accepted a cigar, fearing to appear too *distrait* if he refused both.

"You have heard, doubtless," Lorenzo went on, "that I have received some news that will, I fear, hasten my departure from your shores? Yes; I received it this afternoon only. It has annoyed me very much, since it has, to some extent, disarranged my plans; and, as you know, I never like to have my plans disarranged."

Arnold condoled with him courteously, but somewhat list-lessly. Having lost, as he considered, his first chance of saying what he had come to say, he was now patiently waiting for some suitable opening.

"I suppose your news was from' the other side—from South America," he observed, by way of showing a polite interest, "a cable?"

Lorenzo laughed. For one who was "annoyed" he seemed to be in tolerably good humour.

"A cable!" he repeated, smiling. "Do you suppose I have ordinary 'cables' sent to me through the Post Office? No; I get all my messages direct, wherever I am; I thought you knew that. But now I think of it, I do not believe that I have ever explained my system to you. Not even to *you*, have I? I know I have not to your friend; no, I *know* I have not to him—or to anyone else over here. Eh?"

"I fancy not," Arnold answered, not, however, having any very clear idea what he was talking about.

"It is time, then, that I began to show you a thing or two."

He rose, and, going to an iron safe that stood in a corner of the room, he opened it, and brought out a small square box of polished wood, not unlike, as to size and appearance, the sort of box which holds the captain's chronometer on board ship.

This he placed on a side table which stood at hand, and then, moving the table out so as to come between them, sat down on the opposite side to Arnold. On the table were pen and ink, and some writing-paper.

"Now, Mr Neville," he said, "of course you understand the 'Morse' telegraph alphabet?"

Arnold nodded.

"When a message comes through you will be conscious of it in your left hand, if you will place it on mine. Then, with your right hand, write it down, yourself, on that piece of paper."

Beginning to feel curious, Arnold signified that he understood, and Lorenzo, opening the box, displayed within a complicated mechanism of wheels, cogs, springs, and levers.

He placed his hand upon a small lever, and immediately a faint but very melodious tinkling was heard. It was not unlike the ordinary telephone bell, but was much sweeter and softer.

For a while there was silence. The bell had ceased to tinkle, and nothing was heard. Presently, however, another tinkling became audible, and Lorenzo, saying, "Now," took Arnold's left hand and laid it upon his own left, which was already resting upon the instrument.

The moment Arnold's hand touched the other's, he felt a tingling sensation, as of a mild current from a small battery, followed, almost immediately, by sharper shocks, which, however, were by no means disagreeable.

"Write," said Lorenzo, curtly.

And then Arnold became aware that the little shocks that he felt were Morse signals, and he took a pen, dipped it in the ink, and wrote as the signals dictated.

"—*er reports state that the battle is over and the Government troops are beaten, Two other smaller risings are also reported, but I cannot verify them as yet. As to Government defeat, however, there can now be no doubt. Time, here, eleven thirty."*

"H'm, Government defeated in a pitched battle," Lorenzo commented, gravely, to himself. "The whole country thereabouts will be in a turmoil for months to come. That route *is* closed then."

He took his hand off the box and shut the lid. Then he addressed Arnold:

"Have you read the message, my friend?" he asked.

"Yes," Neville returned, in much surprise. "What battle is it? Where has war broken out then?"

The Brazilian gave one of his disdainful smiles.

"Only another petty South American revolution; this time in Venezuela," he answered. "That message is from my agent in Caracas. You will doubtless see the news in tomorrow's papers."

Arnold was now deeply interested, and showed some excitement.

"I presume, Count," he said, "this is a further message supplementing something that came on to you to-day? And I presume, also, that this is the news which has caused you annoyance, and shortened your stay here?"

"In part, yes. You missed some of the first word of the message. Of course you see that the complete word is 'Later.' I had the first message this afternoon. This insurrection has broken out very suddenly, or else they have somehow managed to keep it very dark till now. It will cause a flutter on your Stock Exchange to-morrow."

"Yes," Arnold assented, thoughtfully. "What money one could make if one had an instrument like this in a broker's office in the City. How is it done?"

"It is simple enough;—wireless telegraphy. It only carries out, practically, what your European inventors are still striving after. They have discovered the key—the principle—but cannot yet apply it practically, as I have done. That is all."

"Yes; I grasped that much—I inferred it; but it does not make it the less wonderful that—you—should have worked out this discovery to perfection, as I see is evidently the case here, and yet keep the whole thing to yourself in this way. Are none of those instruments what is called 'on the market'?"

"None. I keep their construction to myself, and my agents who use them for me abroad are bound to secrecy. Besides, there is a secret connected with it, without a knowledge of which the instrument itself is of no sort of use. And that secret I keep to myself."

"But it would bring you fame, fortune—" Arnold burst out, with enthusiasm. He was pulled up abruptly, however, in the midst of his exclamations, by the look upon the Brazilian's face.

"Boy," he said, rising from the table as if in great disgust, "you know not of what you talk. Fame! Fortune! Have I not fortune enough, do you suppose? Have I ever led you to suppose that I cared for fame?" His eyes flashed with scorn, and he spoke almost fiercely:

"What is such paltry nonsense to me? Do you, as yet then, know me—understand me—so little? Do you really suppose that amongst your array of paltry kickshaws called fame, honours, titles, you have anything that can tempt *me*, that *I* would stoop to covet?" He paced up and down the room, his hands behind him, his whole bearing one of inexpressible scorn and contempt.

"I have merely shown you here," he went on, slowly, but with emphasis on each word, "for the first time, one of my inventions—nay, not mine alone, mine and another's—but that does not matter. It is almost the least of any; one in which I have merely outstripped your latter-day scientists by—well, who can say?—a few years, a few months, or weeks, perhaps; what matter? 'Tis nothing; but a trifle! And you ask me why I have not sold it for—fame—fortune—"

"Nay, of course, I was wrong as to fortune," Arnold interrupted, deeply apologetic, and utterly awed by the unexpected outburst "But surely, if you are so rich that you can afford to give away such knowledge and forego its natural commercial reward, you would reap so much the more honour—"

The other turned on him impatiently.

"What! Again? If I wanted to get what you term a title, are there not plenty of ways, without taking so much trouble? With *my* wealth, a man has but to join a political party, to give more largely to charities than anyone before, or 'lend' money, in a delicate way, to the impecunious in high places! Pooh! Do you suppose I do not know?"

Arnold, not knowing exactly what further to say, judged it best to keep silent.

"But, my friend, all this is very much beside the mark," the other presently went on, more gently. "I have promised you that you shall come away with me and shall be a partaker of my fortunes, and this is but the least of the little mysteries that I could teach you. This, and many others, which you might consider even more wonderful, are to me but trifles, mere every-day conveniences—or luxuries if you will. But it shall be my part, my pleasure, my delight, to show you of greater things than any of these; of discoveries so eventful that your very brain shall reel, your senses become dizzy, as you realise whither they are lead-ing us. And as for all this empty show, this 'Vanity Fair' as some of the more sensible of your writers very aptly term it, you shall return to dabble in it if you will, only, as the *giver* of titles and honours, not the humble, easily-gratified recipient You shall *rule* over it all, lord it over the seething, struggling, fighting aspi-rants, as high above them and as mighty, as is the sun as he rises upon the whirling, battling morning mists, and suffers them, or disperses them at his royal will. Ay! I have said it! You shall have no equal on earth save myself, and I will be—your brother lord—older, stronger to lead and guide—but still your brother!"

The speaker's face, always so wonderful in its strange beauty, lighted up, and his eyes flashed with fire and exultation. And in his look, as he bent it upon his companion, there was a softness, a gentleness, such as Neville had never seen there before.

The man's good feeling, at least so far as outward semblance went, was so unmistakable, that Arnold felt himself carried away by the pictures he called up. For the moment he gave himself up to feelings of wonder and anticipation. But presently more sober counsels prevailed, and the hard, dry, sinister idea pushed itself slowly into his mind.

"This man must be mad!"

Surely, that must be the explanation of such wild talk! He was some great inventor—*that* much, evidently, could not be denied—whose discoveries and victories over science had been so many and so dazzling that, combined with unlimited wealth, they had at last turned his brain. And now the greatest triumphs of the most successful scientist, the powers lying within reach of boundless riches, were no longer sufficient to satisfy the cravings of his crazy brain. Instead of being content with what would already bring him fame beyond that of the greatest inventor or discoverer the world had yet known, he occupied himself with some most wild and impracticable fancy, some hallucination of ambition, the pursuit of some vague chimera of his own imagining, a soaring, daring phantasy, such as might fill the dreaming senses, not of a man, but of a demi-god; or rather—here Arnold paused, and, spite of himself, shivered, as the thought came to him—a devil who aspired to be a god!

Clearly, it would be best to appear to believe this madman. He was only mad, probably, upon this one point. At all events, in everything else, both his talk and his actions had always appeared sane enough. Nor could Arnold now forget the generous motives by which he seemed to be prompted towards himself.

"I do not know how to express myself, Count," he said, after a pause, "how to thank you for your kind intentions; but I ought not to leave you longer in doubt upon this matter. The fact is, I came here to—tell you—that is, to explain—" Arnold found himself hesitating and stumbling in a very confused and disagreeable fashion. Then he made an effort and almost jerked out the rest. "The fact is, I cannot accompany you to South America; I have made up my mind not to leave England."

Lorenzo turned first red and then white. His eyes seemed to flash, and his brows grew black and scowling.

"You—say—you—do not—intend—to—come—with—me?" he asked, every word coming from his mouth as though shot from a catapult.

"I cannot. I have come here to say so. I decided this afternoon that I cannot leave England."

This time the Brazilian made no reply. He only stood and gazed at his visitor as though speechless with anger and astonishment.

CHAPTER V

ON BOARD THE "ALLOYAH"

HAD A BOMBSHELL fallen into the room, Don Lorenzo could scarcely have appeared more utterly taken by surprise. Evidently, whatever else might have appeared uncertain in his view, it had never occurred to him that Neville would meet him with a point-blank refusal. The young fellow himself had always seemed to receive any suggestion bearing upon the subject so cordially, even eagerly, that he had, in the Brazilian's eyes, consented, so to speak, in advance. It had only, therefore, remained to arrange the terms; so he had looked upon it. Whatever his real reasons for desiring to engage Neville to accompany him, they were evidently very strong ones, judging by the effect that this refusal now produced. He was clearly bitterly disappointed, and seemed to be on the point of showing the Englishman, for the first time, the dark and angry side of his character.

Just, however, as the silence was becoming painful, and Arnold began to be conscious of a rising feeling of irritation on his own side at the other's visible anger, Lorenzo seemed to make a great effort. A sort of shiver passed over him; he clenched his hands, and bit his lip; then moved away and gazed out of the window. A few moments later he turned and faced his visitor again, speaking now in his usual voice, and with his ordinary look.

"You must pardon me," he said, noticing the rising light in Arnold's eye. "I meant not to show so much emotion; but the truth of the matter is that this decision is totally unlooked for.

I had expected quite otherwise. You have all along led me to expect otherwise," he continued, reproachfully.

"I am sorry; very sorry I should have appeared to do so."

"We had not as yet even touched upon the question of honorarium," Lorenzo returned. "Perhaps—"

Arnold held up his hand.

"No; say no more upon that point, Count It has nothing whatever to do with it. As far as remuneration goes—were I to come—I should ask for nothing above what I should expect from any firm who might require my services, say, upon railway work. Anything beyond that would rest entirely with yourself. But, tell me, why are you so bent upon my going, that you should feel disappointed? Are there not plenty more who would do equally well? There is my friend Leslie, for instance; why should not he take the post you offered to me? He has had experience out there already, while I have' as yet had none."

The Brazilian laughed. He seemed quite to have recovered his good humour.

"No, no," he answered, shaking his head. "You do not understand. Most of those in authority in this world seem to me to pass much of their time in putting round men, with most careful but exasperating perseverance, into square holes, and *vice versa*. Now, I never do that When I have a certain post to be filled, I look about for some one to fit it, and I know *at sight*—by my own instinct—exactly the man that *will* fit it And I know, too, that I shall certainly find him sooner or later if I but wait. But it is disappointing, when I have found the one I want, to be unable to win him over."

"But perhaps you have made a mistake, this time, Count," said Arnold, now also laughing. "You have seen but very little of me. I might, after-all, prove a sore disappointment if I went out with you. You cannot tell for certain."

For answer the Count seized hold of his arm, and led him to the window.

"Do you know anything of mesmerism, or hypnotism, as they now call it?" he asked.

"I do not know anything about it," Arnold replied, in surprise. "But so far as I have been able to form an opinion I am bound to say that I have no belief in it."

"So! Well, you did not know that I was a mesmerist, did you? I will show you."

He looked across the road, and to the right and the left Then he indicated some children playing about on the path on the other side.

"You see those children? Notice the boy on the right-hand side playing with a whip. He shall throw that whip into the road right under the wheels of the next vehicle that comes by."

They waited, and soon a cab drove past, whereupon the child, with no apparent object, threw the whip under the wheels, where it was caught and left broken on the road. He went and picked it up and began crying.

Arnold looked on with interest.

"That certainly was very curious," he admitted. "Still—"

"—it may have been a coincidence, you think? Tell me, what I shall influence him to do next?"

"Stand on his head," suggested Neville.

The words were scarcely out of his mouth when the child was seen making frantic attempts to stand on its head against the walk But, possibly because it had had no previous practice, it only succeeded in rolling over on the ground, to the very serious detriment of an extremely pretty suit of clothes. At this point a nursemaid came up, and taking the child in her arms, beat it for its performances, and carried it off, scolding and complaining.

Lorenzo turned away from the window.

"I merely showed you that little experiment in mesmerism," he now said, "to illustrate to you what I was talking of. I told you that I am a bit of a mesmerist; and you see that it is true. But I should tell you that that particular child was the one amongst that group over whom I had the most power. The others, children though they were, and to your eyes, no doubt, exactly like unto him, I could not have influenced nearly so readily."

"That is strange. Why is it?"

"That no man knows. It is one of the puzzles of a very obscure science. But I want also to point out to your notice that I *knew* at a glance which one I could influence the most easily. I made no mistake, you observe."

"No."

"Well, so it is here. I knew the very first moment my glance fell upon you that you were the one I was seeking, knew it as surely as I knew that that child was the one I could utilise as an illustration."

"Do you mean that you look upon me as an easy mesmeric subject?"

"Oh no; it is just the reverse. Else should I have won you to my will at once, without further trouble. Unfortunately for my purposes—I will admit to you frankly—you happen to be one of the few people in the world over whom I have no mesmeric power whatever. If I had, I should have used it without stopping to argue or entreat."

Arnold did not at all relish the "short method" of procedure suggested in this remark, or the cool matter-of-fact air with which it was spoken.

At this moment there was a knock at the door, and the secretary entered.

"The boat is waiting, your excellency," he announced.

"Ah! I will be there directly," Lorenzo answered. Then, turning to Arnold, he said:

"I have to go on board the yacht Do you mind accompanying me; we can talk there as well as here. The boat shall bring you back whenever you please."

Arnold would rather have excused himself and returned to his friends. But seeing that his host seemed to expect him to assent, and his curiosity having been strongly aroused by the turn the conversation had taken, he finally agreed.

A very few minutes sufficed to place them on board, for the vessel was anchored but a short distance from the shore.

They went at once to the main saloon, a large, sumptuously furnished apartment, where Lorenzo opened another safe. From this he took some papers and handed them to his secretary, who had accompanied them, and who took them and retired.

"To resume our talk," Lorenzo then began. "I essayed a little experiment to illustrate to you that I could tell at a glance which of those children I could influence and which I could not Mesmerists call this subtle connection between that child and myself, being *en rapport*. I suppose you know that?"

Arnold nodded affirmatively.

Lorenzo then went to a box standing in a corner, which he opened, displaying a set of musical glasses. Arnold knew them well, for the Brazilian was fond of playing on them, and could extract from them music of a surprisingly sweet, attractive character.

"I had the misfortune to break one of these glasses, yesterday," he observed. "Kindly look in that locker; there are a few spare ones kept there. Now, if we sound the note we want, the right glass will respond of itself, if it is there, and so save us a lot of trouble in hunting for it."

He touched a glass giving out a note above, and then one a note below, the one required; and then, in a powerful rich tone, sung out the required note itself. And Arnold, standing by the locker, heard one of the loose glasses stored therein give back the sound so unmistakably that he had no difficulty in picking it out and handing it to his host The latter took it, struck it to test it, put it in the place of the broken one, and shut up both the glasses in their case, and the locker.

"This, my friend, is another little illustration conveying the same lesson in another way. Here we wanted a glass which should give forth a certain note. You admit that no other glass than the particular one you handed to me would have fulfilled the exact requirements?"

"Certainly; that is obvious enough."

"And you also saw that there was a very simple and easy but sure method of picking out the right one from all the others?"

"Yes; I saw that."

"And so, my friend, it is easy to pick out the right man from all others if you only know how. And another man than yourself will no more fit the place I wanted you to fill, than would one of those other glasses have filled the place of the one I had broken."

To this Arnold made no reply; and Lorenzo continued, after a pause:

"You were very much interested just now in my wireless-telegraphy apparatus. I will now, if you like, show you one or two other little contrivances. They are nothing very wonderful; at least they no longer appear so to me. Is it not curious, by the way, how quickly the human mind becomes accustomed to what it at first regards as marvels? In your country, people are just becoming used to the telephone and phonograph; yet, by your grandfathers, such things would have been regarded as downright black magic."

"Yes; that is quite true."

"Well, so it is here. I could show you many inventions that I have on board this vessel which would appear to you marvellous enough; yet they are merely developments of other lesser inventions and discoveries that are perfectly familiar to you. What I have already perfected, your scientists will probably discover in a few years' time; and by the end of a hundred years they will have become common household necessities, and will appear to your great-great-grandchildren no more wonderful than they do to-day to me."

He then proceeded to close up carefully all the ports and doors, and opened another locker, taking from it two suits of thick seal fur. One of these he handed to his visitor.

"Put it on," he said. "We are going into a cold climate."

He drew forward a large, heavy metal box on castors, the lid of which he opened with a key, and then touched some spring or lever.

At once there was heard a hissing sound, though nothing could be seen. Within a second or two, however, the room had become perceptibly colder; a little later Arnold began to shiver even with the fur coat which he had put on, and was now glad to button up.

"Here are some gloves," said his host. "Better put them on, or your fingers may get frost-bitten." And he produced two pairs of gloves that looked like hairy bear's paws.

In a very short space of time hoar frost appeared upon some of the iron uprights and cross rods of the saloon, and Lorenzo pointed to a thermometer.

"It has fallen below zero," he observed. "Here comes the snow. However, you have had enough of this, no doubt" A mist was forming in the cabin which was, in fact, very fine snow.

He touched a lever, and the hissing ceased; then he crossed to the safe, took out a black box, and placed, it on the table. This also he opened with a key on his own chain, and so placed it that Arnold could only see the back of the raised lid. Then he touched another spring or switch, and a slight humming began which gradually grew louder. It soon became apparent that a light was growing up in the box, and since it was now getting dusk outside, it quickly began to light up the cabin. Brighter and brighter it grew, and the temperature commenced to rise. Soon, Arnold was glad to throw off his furs; and a minute or two later he would have liked to take off his jacket, thin as it was. And still the temperature rose till the thermometer marked 110°.

"I think 110° in the shade is enough," Lorenzo here observed. "I want you, however, before I turn it down, to observe the brilliancy of this light."

"It is marvellous," Arnold declared. "I have never seen anything like it before. It is not electric?"

"It is, and it isn't. It is a development or new form; just as are your X-rays. But it is so bright you cannot look direct at it;

it would injure your eyes. That is why I kept the lid of the box this way. The lid forms a reflector, and the rays thus thrown and focussed upon a human being, at anything up to a few hundred yards' distance, will destroy the eyesight completely, then and there."

Arnold gave an exclamation in which were mingled surprise and alarm.

"Yes," said the Brazilian, grimly. "I have tried it on some of my enemies. They will never see again."

He spoke so callously that Arnold felt an uncomfortable sensation as he looked upon the machine, and he instinctively covered his eyes to guard against an accident, until the cessation of the humming assured him that the light had gone.

In its place was now again heard the hissing of the larger box on wheels. His host had turned on the cold current to cool down the superabundant heat.

"This," Lorenzo observed, as he stood over the apparatus, and adjusted the supply of cold air, "is, as you have no doubt already guessed, a storage chamber for liquid air. Here, again, you see your inventors are not far behind. Your scientists have made the discovery some time since; only they have not yet brought it under control, and made it of everyday use, as you see has been done here. Now I have yet two more little inventions to show you; two that you will, I think, find even more interesting than those you have already seen."

CHAPTER VI

SOME MODERN MAGIC

WHILE ARNOLD SAT wondering what fresh surprises this modern magician was about to unfold to him, his host first turned on the ordinary electric light service, and then opened a chest, from which he took certain curious-looking garments, which he proceeded to hang upon a hat-peg fixed at one end of the cabin. When he had arranged them to his satisfaction he turned to his visitor:

"I have a particular reason for desiring that you should see my sword-and-bullet-proof armour," he said, smiling. "I have here hung up a coat; it is, in fact, a sort of coat-of-mail, formed out of a metal as yet unknown to the cleverest of your savants. The cap or helmet which I have put on the top is of the same material. Take one of those cutlasses over there; and see if you can pierce the coat or the helmet It looks but a very light, flimsy affair—and so, in fact, it is—but you will find it difficult to drill a hole in it."

He had placed a cutlass and a rapier upon the table, and Arnold, greatly wondering, took up the latter, and, walking carelessly up to the coat, made as though to stab it.

To his surprise, the sword somehow slipped to one side, and missed the garment. Slightly annoyed, he made another and more determined dig at it; but the weapon again sheered off as though from some invisible steel fence or barrier. He turned, and looked at Lorenzo in questioning astonishment.

"What does it mean?" he asked.

"Try a cutlass," the Brazilian suggested. "See what a cut or a slash will do."

And Arnold tried, but the result was the same. Some invisible force seemed to meet the blows and turn them aside.

"Try bullets," Lorenzo now suggested; and he opened a locker from which he took out a revolver. "This is loaded; try if you can send a bullet through the coat or the cap. You need not mind firing, as they are used to it about here. I often indulge in a little pistol practice; and the panel against which I have hung the coat is wood with an iron backing. A bullet or two lodging in it will do no harm. My fellows will cover up the marks to-morrow."

Arnold had at first hesitated to fire against the painted panel; but, on hearing this, took up and cocked a pistol, and fired at the provoking garment. To take aim seemed scarcely necessary; however, he missed, and the bullet lodged in the wood by the side. He therefore took a very careful aim with the next shot, and finally emptied the pistol; but the coat still remained untouched, while the woodwork on either side showed where the bullets had lodged.

Arnold threw down the revolver in disgust.

"It's no use," he exclaimed, in a tone that expressed both chagrin and amaze. "If you were not so ready always with sweetly-simple scientific explanation, I should be inclined to declare that this, at any rate, is real, downright, unblushing magic."

"Yet the explanation *is* a very simple one—when you become accustomed to the thing," Lorenzo observed, as he proceeded quietly to replace the wonderful garments in the chest from which he had taken them. "The dress is made from a new metal at present unknown to your inventors. It is extraordinarily light—by far the lightest metal yet discovered—and it lends itself easily to the manufacture of the kind of network of which these garments are made. Its most remarkable feature, however, is that it can, by a certain process, be endued with a quality which I may, perhaps, best explain by the expression 'anti-magnetic' For just as a metal that has been magnetised will *attract* certain other metals, so does this material *repel* other metals. It will not, in fact, allow another metal to touch it, but brings into play a curious and powerful repulsive force. This suggested the idea of using it in the way you see here, as material for bullet-proof—or rather bullet-and-steel-deflecting—shields."

"I see," Arnold returned, thoughtfully. As a matter of fact, he did not see or understand either; but he made use of the conventional expression. "I suppose," he went on, "that you were wearing those clothes beneath others when you first met Leslie and drove off his captors."

"Certainly. I always wear them out there."

"Then that explains what has so puzzled us both," Arnold commented, nodding his head thoughtfully. "I have been inclined to think, sometimes, that Leslie was either drawing the long bow, or that the Indians had given him such a fright that he was ready to look upon you as a god, coming in such timely fashion to his rescue; and that he fancied things that were not."

The Brazilian smiled, but made no further answer. He had again dived into his safe, and this time he brought forth what looked like a large opera-glass of very beautiful workmanship. It was made of gold and ivory, decorated with floral designs worked in precious stones that sparkled and scintillated in the rays of the electric light. He offered it to Neville.

"Take this, and look into it attentively," he requested, "and tell me what you see. Please be seated, and give me your whole attention."

Arnold seated himself accordingly, took the instrument, and looked gravely into it for nearly a minute.

"I see nothing," he said.

Lorenzo came and stood by him, laying one hand on the top of his head. Then he touched a spring at the side of the instrument, and immediately the interior became lighted up.

"I see a light," said Arnold.

"Look steadily and be patient," was the answer.

Arnold heard Lorenzo take a long breath, and felt his hand

press upon his head with a trembling sensation, as though its owner were bracing himself to some great effort, or to bear some immense strain. And simultaneously, images, at first vague and shadowy, began to form before his vision, very much like a dissolving view that is gradually becoming more sharply defined. Presently, he exclaimed:

"I see a wide river; the banks are covered with a thick vegetation, amongst which are many high trees that, I suppose, are palms."

"That is the great Essequibo River in British Guiana," returned his companion. "Do you see any canoes?"

"No;—oh yes, I see some now. They are coming nearer. They are full of Indians, and they go alongside a landing-place where several people are waiting for them. Two, by their dress, I should say, are white men, but their faces are turned away and I cannot see them."

"Do you know them?"

"I am not sure. Something about them seems familiar, but they keep their faces turned away."

"Watch them. What do they do next?"

"They load a lot of goods and stores on the canoes, and all start off together. Now they are out in the middle of the stream."

"How wide is the river?"

"Quite seven or eight miles. Now the scene has suddenly changed. The river is much narrower; not above two to three miles wide. They are approaching some rapids. The river is divided into several channels, and the water comes rushing down in a foaming current. It is as much as they can do to make headway against it I see an immense alligator near one of the canoes; it will overturn it—no—it has just missed upsetting it—I think—"

"What do you see now?"

"Ah! it has all changed again. The river has narrowed to a quarter of a mile. Some distance ahead I can see waterfalls, with a cloud of mist hanging above them on which the sun makes a glittering rainbow. The travellers cannot pass up the falls, so they are landing and dragging their canoes ashore."

Many other scenes passed before his eyes in this strange fashion, Lorenzo, at many points, bidding him take particular note as to the direction in which the route was continued, or enjoining him to impress certain conspicuous landmarks upon his memory. At last the curious panorama—such it had, in a sense, been—came to an abrupt termination, and Arnold raised his head from the glass and sat confusedly rubbing his eyes; for at first everything around him appeared misty and undefined.

During the whole time that he had been looking into the glass, the Brazilian had kept his hand upon the young man's bead. He now took it away, and seated himself on a chair a short distance off, and remained silent. When, presently, Arnold had regained his normal eyesight, and came to regard his host more attentively, the Brazilian gave him the idea of one who had undergone some severe strain—either physical or mental, or perhaps a mixture of both—and was but slowly recovering from it.

After a while he addressed his guest in a low hut clear tone, which had in it a measure of gravity approaching almost to solemnity, and a touch of sadness.

"In showing you these things, Mr Neville," he began, "I am, as you are aware, doing more than I have ever done for your friend, or even, I may tell you, for any one of the many whose acquaintance I have made since I came over to this country. I would prefer that you should respect my confidence—though, you will observe, I exacted no promise—and not lightly chatter of it to other persons. But I leave that to your own sense of what is fitting. You are, I have always found, what is called (though many people misemploy the term) a true gentleman, and, knowing that, I am satisfied that you will not, when you leave me, go and recklessly blab to the world that which you can see—from my reticence even with your friend—I desire to keep secret.

"With regard to what I am about to say, however, I wish to

impose upon you a solemn promise that you will keep it absolutely to yourself. Will you give me such a promise?"

Arnold considered. He never had much liked the idea of
being mixed up in mysterious secrets—especially other people's.
His nature was naturally honest and open. A self-respecting reticence was one thing; the burden of carrying secrets which one
might want to make use of, and yet be prevented from utilising
by promises, was quite another.

"Why thrust upon me a confidence that I do not wish for,
Count?" he presently asked. "Whatever you choose to tell me I
shall be glad to listen to if it so pleases you; but I do not seek it.
If, having said this much, you still desire to proceed with your
statement, I will say this;—I will respect your wishes, and your
secret will be as safe as though I had sworn the most binding
of oaths. But the promise must be conditional. Circumstances
might arise which would make it incumbent upon me, in my
own judgment as a gentleman, to tell to some other friend,
whom I could trust, what you had told to me."

Lorenzo made no immediate reply, and seemed to be reflecting. Arnold's tone had been perfectly courteous and friendly, but
there had also been a firmness in it which warned the listener
that he was not likely to shake his resolution. Besides, a conversation had taken place between them upon the subject of giving
promises, only a few days previously, during which Arnold had
been very outspoken, expressing his views very much as he had
now explained them.

"Very well," Lorenzo said, after a while, though still displaying some hesitation, "we will leave it so. After all, I would rather
accept your promise, given in those terms, than the solemn oaths
of many other men."

"Still—let me say again before you begin—I seek to know
none of your secrets. Why, therefore, thrust them upon me?"

"No matter, for the present, why. You will understand my
reasons later on. Now listen, then, to what I wish to say:

"I have this evening exhibited to you two or three little inventions or contrivances which have, as I can see, caused you a good deal of surprise and some wonder. I knew—I felt sure—that they would interest you; yet they are as trifles compared with what I could unfold to you if I chose. On board this vessel alone, I could show you many more just as wonderful, all quite new to your ideas—some of them, perhaps, far more marvellous in your eyes than those you have seen. But having seen what you have, you will no doubt be willing to take my word for the others; is it not so?"

Arnold made a sign of assent; and his host proceeded:

"Why, then, have I opened so much to your view? you ask yourself. It is, my friend, that when I come to speak of marvels of quite a different character you may believe me.

"What I am now about to unfold to you is as true as that which I have already laid open to you. To you it will appear marvellous, incredible, perhaps, simply because it is new. To me it is matter of everyday knowledge, and therefore it does not appear anything out of the way.

"People call me a Brazilian, and suppose my name to be Lorenzo, that being the name that I have chosen to assume. It is true that I was born upon territory which is included within the limits of that which is to-day called Brazil; but I am not on that account necessarily a Brazilian; for I come from a country unknown as yet to your modern geographers, and one which does not recognise or bow to the rule of the Brazilian or any other of the known governments of the World."

"How can that be, Count?" Arnold asked. "I never heard of any separate or semi-independent state within the Brazilian empire. Do you mean a native Indian state?"

"Certainly not. But you have to remember that the country called Brazil covers a very large area—an area so extensive that it has never yet been by any means fully explored. It is the fifth largest territory in the world. Roughly speaking, I suppose it is about thirty-six times as large as your little country of Great

Britain. It includes nearly half of the whole South American continent; it has an area of over three million square miles."

"Yes, yes; I know."

"Ah! but what you do not know, or, at least, what you people over here do not seem to realise, is, that of that three millions of square miles, at least one million are to-day altogether unexplored. They constitute, in fact, an unknown land. There is a far greater extent of territory, untravelled and unexplored, to-day, in South America, than on the continent of Africa."

"So I have understood."

"But the people over here are very far from understanding it. For instance, here is an expression of opinion that I cut out of one of your leading papers the other day. The writer, half-seriously, half-quizzically, laments that the 'novel of adventure' is 'about played out,' because, he says, 'the blank spaces on the map of Africa having been pretty well filled in, writers have no longer any land wherein their characters can discover an unknown city with any air of plausibility.' Now, the man who wrote that has evidently never read up his geography so far as regards the South American continent Does he think, I wonder, that it has been all surveyed and mapped out like the Isle of Wight, and that you can buy a map of Brazil's three million square miles upon a six-inch scale?

"Well, to come to actual facts, the true state of the case is that, as I have said, fully a million square miles are an utterly unknown land. And it is there, in a part of the world that has never, so far as is known to your geographers, been visited by any white traveller, that my people are living to-day."

"Your people!"

"Yes; my people. The remnant of a once proud, dominant, conquering race. A remnant of the great *white* race that once ruled the whole of America, both North and South. Thousands of years before Columbus 'discovered' the country—as you term it—my people held the whole of it from what is now Alaska to Cape Horn. This is shown by our ancient archives, our sculptures, and our traditions. And at that time—a time coeval with the most ancient Egyptian records—this race was far more advanced in what you term civilisation than Egypt or any other country of the world. Had you embraced my offer, and returned with me, I would have shown you all this, shown you the proofs. I would have proved something else also; and that is, that we have kept ahead of the rest of the world ever since. You people over here boast of your progress in the sciences. Bah! I could show you things that would make your greatest scientists turn green with envy, and cause your cleverest inventors to kill themselves with chagrin!"

"But how comes it, then, that all this is not known to us?"

"My people, for their own reasons, have kept strictly to themselves. We have no sympathy with the rest of the world, no wish to intermingle, until"—here the speaker's face brightened with a great light—"until we come forth to be again the conquerors and rulers we once were."

"How can that be?"

"It is written in our ancient prophecies, it is our tradition, our belief, our religion. It is that for which we have worked, and toiled, and invented, through countless generations. Our old prophecies declare that we shall be greater in the future than we ever were in the past; that we are to be the ruling race, and our empire the greatest the earth has yet seen. And the head of that race, the Chief, the King—the descendant of a line longer, older, and more honourable than the oldest of your mushroom dynasties of to-day is—myself!"

"Yourself!" Arnold repeated after him. He scarcely knew what comment to make on so wildly improbable a tale.

"But," he said, after a moment's thought, "you must be comparatively few in numbers."

"Certainly—at present."

"How, then, can you rule the world?"

"Firstly, by our superior knowledge of the sciences and of the powers of nature; for we know more than you have ever even dreamed of. Secondly, by our numbers; for when the time comes—and our prophecies tell us that it is now near at hand—we shall pour forth in countless millions, innumerable as the sands of the sea, as the ants of the forest and plain."

"But how can that be; if the time is to be soon, and you are now but few?"

"That, my dear friend, is a secret—one that I must keep back from you. Had you thrown in your lot with me—were you now to change your mind and say you will do so—I would tell you everything. Otherwise, beyond what I have now told you, my mouth is sealed."

After a few minutes' silence, Lorenzo rose and spoke briskly, and with his usual manner.

"And now my boat shall put you ashore. I, myself, sleep on board to-night I shall remain here for a little while, so I hope to see you again shortly. Think well over what I have said; and, should you alter your mind, there will still be time."

And Arnold left him and went back to seek Leslie, hardly knowing, so confused were his ideas, whether he was on his head or his feet.

CHAPTER VII

GONE!

BERYL ATHERTON SAT at work on the terrace in the garden at Ivydene busying herself with some fancy embroidery, while Mrs Beresford, seated a little way from her, under the shade of an overhanging tree, alternately dozed for a few minutes, and then woke up and read, or pretended to read, diligently, from a book she held in her hand.

It was a sultry morning. The July sun was pouring down upon the garden walk, upon the flower-beds, upon the shore, and upon the sea. Light, very light, fleecy clouds, so brilliantly white that they dazzled the eyes, floated in a sky of deep blue; while even the broad expanse of sea that stretched across to the opposite shore threw back the sun's rays with a steely brightness that had in it nothing soothing for the tired and wandering gaze that sought some relief from the oppressive glare. The distant hills were shimmering in the waves of heat that seemed to be ever rising through the air, and there was no wind to cause so much as a ripple on the surface of the sluggish tide. On the sea the little island forts, and a fishing-boat here and there, were all that could be seen. Even the passenger steamers, and those indefatigable sailers, the yachts, seemed, for the time, to have yielded to the influence of the hour, and to be indulging in a *siesta*.

Mrs Beresford, presently growing tired of her many vain attempts to concentrate her mind upon her book, put it down with a scarcely-stifled yawn, and addressed her niece:

"You seem very pre-occupied this morning, Beryl," she said; "what is it you are thinking of so deeply?"

The young girl turned her glance upon her questioner, and in her look and smile there was a world of affection and tenderness. That look alone spoke more eloquently than many words could have done of the affection with which she regarded her aunt.

And, indeed, it seldom happens that an orphan left to the charge of a relative, as Beryl had been from early childhood, is fortunate enough to find in her guardian so perfect a substitute for the lost mother. Mrs Beresford was not only kindly and good-hearted, she possessed that rare gift of true sympathy with those younger than herself—those, that is, to whom she gave her complete love and confidence. She bad been a widow cow many years, and had had no family to bring up—her only child had died in infancy—hence she had centred all her affection upon her niece. She was still a strong, active—some thought a rather strong-minded—woman, somewhat thin, with dark hair, and usually a brisk, bustling manner.

In former days she had travelled abroad with her husband. Early in their married life he had been appointed to the management of a plantation in Mexico, and frequently had business errands that caused him to make journeys further south. In many of these she had accompanied him, and thus she had seen far more of the world than an occasional visitor to her house nowadays would have had any idea of. When, however, her husband fell into bad health, necessitating their removal to England, they took up their abode at Ivydene—which had been left to him by his father—and she had now lived in it so long, and her former life seemed so far away, that she herself almost forgot it, unless something happened to put her in mind of it.

"If I am unusually quiet this morning, auntie, dear," Beryl presently said, "I am sure you are not less so. It is rare, indeed, to see you in the daytime so lazy as you seem to be this morning. I actually saw your eyes closed."

"It is the heat, I suppose," Mrs Beresford returned, "and being up so late last night Whatever made those two young men stay so late? I fell asleep over my book, or I should have sent them off long before. Really, my dear, I ought to scold you. It is not exactly the thing, you know. We shall have Mrs Grundy—"

"Oh, never mind Mrs Grundy, auntie, dear. It was no ordinary matter that we were discussing, I assure you. Arnold had been to see the Count, as you know, and he kept him rather late to begin with. Then, when he came in, he had a lot to tell me—both of us—for he wished Mr Leslie to hear it too."

"He did not wish *me* to hear it too, apparently," commented Mrs. Beresford. "I think you must have been particularly careful not to wake me, or I should not have slept so long. What did the great news consist of?"

"There is no great news, auntie," said Beryl, "but there might have been. The news might have been that Arnold was going away with the Count, who, as I told you last evening, expects to return to his own country very shortly. He made Arnold a sort of formal offer, and asked him for a definite reply—yes or no—and Arnold—"

"Well, child?" said her aunt, seeing that Beryl hesitated. "When do they start?"

"They don't start, auntie," was the unexpected reply, given with evident apprehension of what was to come—"that is, Arnold will not start, because—he declined the offer."

If Mrs Beresford had appeared lazy or sleepy before, this unexpected announcement proved a very efficient awakener. She sat bolt upright, and the book tumbled to the ground.

"Declined! Why, what do you mean, child? What are you saying? Did, then, the Count offer such poor terms? That would not be like him—after all his open-handed liberality too—"

Beryl shook her head. "No, auntie, I do not think that anything of that nature stood in the way, though I do not know that actual figures were mentioned. However, it is all the same; Arnold declined, and there the matter has ended."

This last Beryl brought out with a sort of rush, evidently

wishful to get the murder out. She knew her aunt well enough to be aware that she would be sure to blame Arnold for what looked like a wilful throwing away of a splendid opportunity. For though Mrs Beresford was kindness itself wherever her sympathy had been fully given, this had never been altogether the case with regard to Arnold—or, at any rate, since her niece's engagement to him. Towards Arnold, himself, Mrs Beresford was very well disposed; she would very likely, even, have been fond of him had he *not* become engaged to her niece. But directly he aspired to that high destiny, she viewed him through altogether different glasses; and these particular spectacles showed her only a very commonplace, struggling young man, without fortune, family, or influence, who was hopelessly beneath the ideal she had heretofore set up for herself, one quite unworthy to be the husband of her darling ward.

Just lately, however, Mrs Beresford had seemed to put aside her dislike to the match, and had shown herself quite complacent towards the young engineer. Fortune, it seemed to her, was evidently inclined to smile upon him; this brilliant stranger had taken him up and offered to provide a splendid opening for him in his own country. The young man's fortune, she therefore considered, was as good as made, and—well, well, after all, she had always liked him; he was a very personable young man and—it might have been worse.

And now she was suddenly given to understand that this house of cards had tumbled incontinently to the ground; not only that, but the young gentleman himself had been the cause of the collapse; the sole, the disappointing, the exasperating cause. What in the name of common-sense could be the meaning of it? Had these two young people taken leave of their senses? Was the world coming to an end?

So Beryl experienced what our neighbours across the channel term *un mauvais quart d'heure* with her aunt that morning. It is not necessary to give a full account of the scene; suffice to say that it turned out far worse than poor Beryl had in any way deemed possible. It proved, in fact, the greatest upset she had ever had with her usually fond guardian; and it ended in her seeking her room, and shutting herself up alone with sorrow and tears and burning of heart.

Thus it came about that Arnold received a pitiful little tear-stained note, informing him that auntie was in a terrible rage with both her dutiful niece and her would-be nephew, and that it might be as well for the latter to remain *perdu* for a few days until the storm had had time to blow over. Further bulletins would be issued, the note intimated, as circumstances might render necessary.

Then Arnold sought out his friend Leslie, who condoled with him, as became a loyal chum. In his ready sympathy, indeed, the latter took it so much to heart that he grew? almost as miserable as Arnold himself. And, looking upon the Brazilian as the indirect cause of their trouble, they both tacitly avoided his society.

On Beryl's side, this enforced temporary separation greatly added to her trouble and anxiety, since it prevented her from watching over her lover's safety as her fears had led her to resolve to do. For though Arnold's account of his interview had made it appear that Lorenzo had taken his refusal in good part, and shown no signs of resentment, yet Beryl's anxiety would not allow her to trust too much to such appearances. She sent pressing notes to Leslie, reminding him of the promise he had made to look after his friend, and urging him to take every possible precaution against any unexpected action upon the part of the Brazilian. And Leslie, on his part, sent her comforting messages in reply, assuring her that he was carefully, but unostentatiously, doing everything that was possible' to fulfil the promise. He also kept her informed, from day to day, of all that took place, and especially how they were avoiding the Don, and keeping away from every place where they were likely to run against him.

On the morning of the third day, however, a letter arrived for Arnold which caused him surprise—considerable surprise. It was from a firm of solicitors in London, stating they had been desired to communicate with him respecting a very important matter, which they were unable to go fully into in writing, and requesting him to be good enough, if he could possibly make it convenient, to come up to London to see them personally.

This letter caused him surprise, because the names of the writers—Adamson & Hynton—were unknown to him; and also some concern, because he felt very averse to going to town in answer to the summons, without first discussing the matter with his *fiancée*.

There, however, he found Leslie against him.

"It's just as well, Arnold," he said, decidedly. "Tell you what, I'll run up with you. It'll be a good excuse for keeping out of the way both of Mrs Beresford and the Don, for a while, without appearing to have done it intentionally. And by the rime we get back, things will have settled down into something like their old groove. Send a note to Miss Atherton at once and explain; say I am going with you, and tell bearer to wait for an answer. You will find she will take the same view that I do."

And when the answer came back—not so tear-stained this time, and a little more cheerfully worded—it turned out that Leslie had prophesied aright. So the two packed a bag apiece, and started off that same day.

The business with Messrs Adamson & Hynton occupied more time than either Neville or Leslie expected, and kept them waiting about from day to day. They had put up at the Inns of Court Hotel, in order to be near the lawyers' office, which was in Lincoln's Inn Fields—hard by—but the move, though apparently good in theory, had not turned out satisfactory in practice. They passed most of their time oscillating between the hotel and the offices, "And we could have done no worse if we had gone to an hotel further west, and then we should at least have had a walk for our trouble, and seen more of the town," Leslie said.

As to the business the lawyers wished to see Arnold about, however, it tended somewhat to raise his drooping spirits. It was intimated that there was a tidy little sum in Chancery going a-begging until such time as someone of the name of Neville— that is, of course, the right Neville—should prove his claim to it Matters looked hopeful, it seemed, for Arnold in this respect, that the missing heir, one George Neville, was stated to have sailed from America in the "Bluebell," which was the vessel from which Arnold had been rescued. Hence it appeared a reasonable inference that his father had been the heir, and that he himself was now the next-of-kin.

Every day's investigation seemed to render the matter more' promising, and Arnold, albeit he grew each day more anxious to return, could hardly shut his eyes to the obvious fact that he was probably doing far more good for himself in a worldly sense by remaining in town than he could do by returning to Ryde. Nor could he doubt but that his reception from Mrs Beresford was likely to be very different, if he succeeded in taking back with him some such news as he was waiting for.

Every morning, too, he received a letter from Beryl giving him full particulars of all that took place during his absence. Amongst other items of news, he learned that the Brazilian had been two or three times to call upon her aunt Then, one day, she mentioned that they were both going, the following day, for a short cruise with a small party in the Count's yacht.

"I am very vexed that auntie has promised," Beryl wrote, "and I tried all I could to get out of it, as I do not at all like the idea of going without you; but auntie is in such a disagreeable mood with me these days, that I am frightened a the idea of doing anything that may displease her further; so I have promised to go. I do so wish you could bring or send some good news such as you are hoping for, and put an end to the present state of affairs. Yet, you must not be too hard on auntie. I am all she has in the world, you know, and we can scarcely be angry with her for feeling very anxious about my future, can we?"

"The disagreeable old woman," Arnold commented, after reading this out to Leslie. "And to compel her to go gadding about with a lot of people in the Don's yacht, too, just when I am away! I think Beryl ought to have refused, point-blank."

"I am afraid things must be quite disagreeable enough as

they are—judging by the way she writes—without incurring her aunt's further displeasure by crossing her about so small a matter," Leslie observed.

"I don't know. I don't see that he has any right to ask her, or to expect her to go while I am away," Arnold grumbled. "In fact, Gordon, I feel sure she ought not to have gone. Something tells me so. I've a great mind to wire to her and absolutely forbid her to go."

"Stuff and nonsense, man; everybody will be laughing at you. They've been out with him often enough before."

"Yes; but never without us. However, I tell you what it is;—I don't like it, and there shall be no more of it I go back to-morrow, whether I have any definite news to take with me or not We can easily run up again in a week or two if need be."

"No; that you cannot; because you have to remember that the vacation will have commenced, when all good lawyers flit away from their London dens to parts unknown."

"Then we can leave it till after the holiday season. I've had enough of hanging about in town."

"Very well; I am quite agreeable. We will tell these lawyer chaps your decision to-day, and, in the morning, pack up and be off."

But when, in the morning, the two met at breakfast, Arnold found no letter from Beryl, as he had expected, but, instead, a letter in a handwriting which he did not at first recognise. In his disappointment he did not hurry to open it but sat looking at it, not really scanning it, but busy with thoughts of Beryl, and speculations as to why she had not written.

"That's from the Count, by the look of it," Leslie observed, after glancing at the envelope.

"H'mph! I wonder what *he* is writing about?" said Arnold, as he took it up and opened it.

But as he read it, he first turned very white, then let the letter fall to the ground, and buried his head in his hands.

"My God!" he gasped. "The scoundrel! He has run off with her!"

Leslie, in amaze, picked up the letter and looked at it, and this is what he read:—

Dear Brother,

I have offered you my friendship, asked you to be my brother, and you have refused. I am a man accustomed to have my own way, and I do not like anyone to cross me, especially when I mean them well. Therefore, since you will not come with me of your own accord, I take the means that appear to me to be the best and the surest to compel you to follow me. When you get this, your fiancée and her worthy aunt will be far away upon the sea with me—on the road to my home. Thus, I take with me the lodestar, knowing that you cannot choose but follow. Now, do not give way to passion, when you hear this news, but act like the sensible man I know you can be if you choose. Call on Messrs Cranstone & Sons, solicitors, of New Inn, close by where you are staying, and they will hand you the sum of £5,000, which I beg you to utilise for the necessary 'expenses of your journey; then make your preparations as speedily as possible and follow us. I pledge you my word that no sort of harm or trouble shall come to your friends, apart from such discomfort as may be inseparable from a long and difficult journey; and money and my own ingenuity shall reduce even this to a minimum. They shall not be unduly hurried, nor shall their liberty in any way be interfered with. Indeed, Mrs Beresford is already reconciled to the idea, and quite looks forward to an exciting adventure. She declares that she will be delighted to see the sunny south once more. And as to Miss Atherton, though she is at present a little depressed at the prospect of a temporary separation from you, yet she understands that she has nothing to fear, and that the length of that separation will depend greatly upon the diligence you display in following us. I have said her liberty shall not be interfered with; and this shall be the case. For she is not likely to run away from us, knowing that you will have left England and be somewhere en route—where, of course, she could not tell, and therefore would find it hopeless to try to meet you. And she would not care to go wandering about alone in a strange land. Moreover, I have solemnly assured her, that if she comes with me without giving trouble, no harm shall come either to you or to her.

Now, as to your journey. Make for Carácas, where further instruc-
tions shall reach you. There you shall have full details how to make
your way up the Essequibo river. Call to mind what passed before
your eyes when looking into the 'magic glasses' in my cabin. That was
a forecast of what your actual journey will be; and you will under-
stand now why I particularly wished you to impress the scenes and
many of the landmarks upon your memory. At the end of each stage,
fresh instructions and, if necessary, supplies, shall reach you; so that
you cannot fail to find your way. But do not attempt to intercept us
or catch us up, or to travel faster than I wish, for I warn you that any
attempt to do so will result disastrously for both you and your friends.
Come in peace, and trust to my good intentions, and you shall not be
disappointed. Au revoir! For the nonce I sign myself as before. My
true name you will learn in my own country.

Lorenzo.

"The villain! I won't touch a penny of his accursed money!"
Arnold burst out.

But Leslie was more practical "Oh yes, you will," he quickly
decided. "We'll go and draw it at once, and set off as soon as we
can. This is no time for crying over spilt milk, or for fastidious
scruples. We must up and after them."

CHAPTER VIII

THE HAUNTED MOUNTAIN

SOME FOUR MONTHS later than the events recorded in the last chapter, Arnold Neville and his chum, Gordon Leslie, after a tedious and toilsome journey, found themselves encamped in the wilds of British Guiana, a country that, since the days of Sir Walter Raleigh, has teemed with stories of fascinating romance, strange legends, and vague suggestions of exciting mysteries.

And it remains, to-day, very much what it was in Sir Walter's days, a region of wondrous possibilities in regard to exploration and discovery; for though a few white men have penetrated into the interior, some of whom have written books thereon, yet vast tracts of its forest and mountain land are still altogether unexplored.

There are still, to-day, as in Sir Walter's time, no roads of any sort or kind into the interior, the only means of travel being the waterways—those great rivers, such as the Essequibo and Orinoco, which take their rise in the mountainous districts on the vague and ill-defined boundary line between British Guiana, on the one side, and Brazil and Venezuela upon two other sides respectively.

This region embraces some of the wildest and most savage districts of any to be found upon the whole South American continent. Here Nature can be seen under her grandest, most sublime aspects. Situated but a few degrees from the line of the equator, the tropical vegetation, alone, forms a sight that almost passes imagination, that certainly defies all attempts at description, and that can only be adequately understood by those who have actually gazed upon its wondrous developments.

It was in such a region, with towering mountains, and thundering, foaming cascades around them, at a spot where the ground was carpeted with begonias, gloxinias, and other gorgeous tropical flowers, and the trees festooned with orchids such as would delight the heart and arouse the admiring astonishment and envy of even the wealthiest European collectors,* that the two young engineers had encamped.

They had just had their breakfast, and the dawn was breaking, for in tropical countries the sun rises and sets all the year round at much the same time, and there is but little variation between winter and summer. Travellers, therefore, who desire to make the most of the day, usually get up and breakfast before daylight— *i.e.* about six to half-past six o'clock. At no time of the year is it light at three or four in the morning, or until eight or nine at

---

* That such a statement is no exaggeration is evidenced by the following quotation from the writings of the naturalist, Richard Schomburgk (brother of Sir Robert Schomburgk, formerly Governor of British Guiana), one of the few white men who have penetrated to this little-known but most fascinating region. He says of it, in his book, "Reisen in British Guiana" (Leipzig) vol. ii., p. 216: "From the crevices in the strata sprang various orchids; and besides these, the rosy-flowered *Marcetia taxifolia* had established itself in the fissures—a plant which I had not before seen, and which, from a distance, I mistook for an *Erica*.... On reaching the declivity, a breeze from the north came loaded with a delicious scent, and our astonished eyes were attracted by innumerable items of white, violet, and purple flowers, which waved about the surrounding bush. These were groups of superb *Sabralias;* and amongst them *S. Elizabetha* rose tallest of all. I found flowering stems of from five to six feet high. ... But not only these orchids, but the shrubs and low trees still dripping with dew, were unknown to me. Every shrub, herb, and tree was new to me, if not as to its family, yet as to species. I stood on the border of an unknown plant zone full of wondrous forms which lay, as if by magic, before me. I once again felt the same delightful surprise which had overpowered me when I first landed on the South American continent, but I now seemed to be transported to a new quarter of the globe amongst the *Proleacea* of Africa and New Holland, and the *Melalencea* of the East Indies and Australia. The leathery, stiff leaves, the curiously coiled branches, the strange, large flowers of various forms, the dazzling colour of these—all were essentially different in character from all vegetation that I had before seen. I did not know whether to look at the wax-like, gay flowers of certain species of *Thibandia Befaria* and *Archytaeat* or whether at the large, camellia-like flowers of a *Bonnetia,* or whether to fasten my eyes on the flower-loaded plants of various kinds of *Melastoma, Abolboday Vockysia, Ternstromia, Andromeda, Clusia, Kielmeyera,* or on the various new forms of *Sobralia, Oncidium, Cattleya, Odontoglossum,* and *Epidendron,* which covered the blocks of soft sandstone—and there were many plants not at the time in flower. ... Every step revealed something new."

night, as in the case of a European summer. On the other hand, it may be truly said there is neither winter nor spring. A large proportion of the vegetation is perpetually in leaf and in flower, for some trees, or shrubs, or flowers, are always just budding and coming out as others are beginning their rest time; and so far as is noticeable, therefore, there is no general fall of the leaf, no "dead" season for either flowers or foliage, as in the winter time in northern latitudes.

"Shall we never reach the end of this awful journey, Gordon?" Arnold asked, with a sigh. "Shall we never run down to his native haunts the elusive will-o'-the-wisp we have been following up through so many weary months? What is the end of it all to be? We know no more to-day as to where we are going to, how far it is, or the identity of the man we are hunting, than the day we started from Southampton."

"We must struggle on, Arnold," Gordon made answer. "'Tis useless to make matters worse by worrying so. We want all our strength for what is still before us, if we may judge of it by what we have already passed through."

"Strength! How can one husband one's strength in such a country, living on such food, tormented, ever, by such harassing doubts and anxieties? And how can I help fearing the worst when I think of that poor girl being dragged through all that we have passed through? What about *her* strength, Gordon? It maddens me only to think about it all! The inhuman cruelty of the thing! If this callous-hearted monster was so set upon dragging me out here, why not have kidnapped *me?* That would not have presented any great difficulty. But to coolly carry off a delicate, helpless girl, as a mere bait to catch me, as reckless of what she would have to go through as is the fisherman of the suffering of the worm with which he baits his hook! And then to declare,—to keep on declaring, in every message we receive from him in such mysterious fashion,—that it is all for my good, as parents tells their little children! Bah! it makes me sick!"

Arnold laughed bitterly, and his chin sank upon his hands as he sat on the ground beside the camp fire. With his knees closely drawn up, and his elbows resting upon them, he sat silent and gloomy, huddled up in Indian fashion, staring vacantly at the ashes that had cooked their early breakfast. And Gordon, who was smoking his morning pipe, puffed away with a contemplative air, evidently at a loss what to say to cheer his chum.

"I am in hopes," he presently answered, "that what Lorenzo says in his messages may have some foundation of truth—I mean, as to his studying the comfort of the ladies. In fact, we have, as you know, come upon many signs which point that way. And, after all, though the journey has been tiresome and arduous to us, we have really travelled very slowly—by very easy stages; and, with the resources he undoubtedly has at his disposal, he may have managed to make it fairly comfortable. He declares that that is the case; and I am willing to hope it may be so. It would be some consolation for the long waits and delays we have been compelled to put up with, to think that they had been in the interests of the comfort of his prisoners."

To this Arnold only replied by a dissatisfied grunt; and Gordon, hoping to turn his thoughts into a less gloomy channel, went on, after a pause:

"Apropos, I suppose we are in for another wait here; and, that being so, I propose that we start on a little exploring expedition to yonder 'haunted mountain,' as the Indians insist on calling it."

"I don't care to go, Gordon. I don't suppose we should find it differ much from other mountains we have already come across. These Indians seem to have one or two fresh legends or special superstitions for each separate mountain we pass. There was the one near which we camped the night before last—let me see—it was something about people who are fish by day and men and women by night, wasn't it?"

"Yes; but—"

"I thought it was. I can hardly understand the Indian lingo yet, but I managed to make out that much amidst their chatter."

"But their legends or beliefs about that flat-topped mountain over yonder, opposite to us, which they call Maraima, beat all the rest put together as specimens of weird imagination. That Macusi Indian who has been with us all along—Lenaka—and who seems to have taken a real liking to us—or to you, at any rate—was telling me a lot about it last night after you were asleep. He declares that the belt of forest which surrounds the lower slopes is haunted by terrible creatures or beings, who are placed there specially to guard the wood against intruders by some strange, unknown people who live at the top. It is true, as you say, that the Indians have tales more or less weird about most of their mountains; but there struck me as being something unusually picturesque and circumstantial in what they say about this particular hill—Maraima. In that respect—viz. wealth of legendary and mystic lore—it is second only, it seems, to the highest and most mysterious of all, the far-famed Roraima, which lies not very far away. For Maraima's woods, says Lenaka, are haunted by many fearsome and awful creatures, amongst which perhaps the most striking is a great white puma, very fierce and terrible and uncanny—a sort of werewolf, in fact Then there is a beautiful woman, a witch apparently, sometimes to be seen, who reigns there as the queen of the place, and is styled by the Indians the 'Lady of the Mountain.' It's rather an interesting fable that, it struck me."

"It has the merit of novelty, certainly. It is different from the ordinary run of their superstitious ideas."

"Just what struck me. But there also are other stories much more gruesome, One relates to what they term the 'Didi,' or wild man of the woods, a species of gigantic ape, bigger and more terrible than the African gorilla; while another is a particularly disagreeable tale about a hideous, monstrous 'camoodi' or serpent, called the 'Kragi,' or 'Kao.'; This terrible creature (a creature of the imagination only, let us hope), being of a very sluggish nature, would never get a good square meal, probably, from year's end to year's end, were it not that it has a diabolical attendant goblin in the shape of a beautiful bird called the 'Kalon,' or 'Kao-Kalon.' This attendant, it is declared, entices victims into the neighbourhood of the spot where the monster is lurking, so that it may seize them without trouble or exertion; the beautiful bird-fiend being afterwards rewarded for its disreputable share in the shady business by being allowed to pick out the victim's eyes and other tit-bits, before the dead body is swallowed by the reptile."

"Ugh! That's a gruesome idea."

"Yes; especially when it is added that the bird's song is so wonderfully sweet that it charms all who hear it, and lays them under a sort of spell while the crawling brute creeps up to them."

"Altogether, 'very like a whale,' as we used to say at school."

"It is curious, though," said Leslie, thoughtfully, "that this country has many queer instances of the oddest sort of cooperation amongst animals and insects—and even plants. I have, myself, met with examples. I have seen a small tunnel on the ground, a mile in length, which, when we came to examine it, proved to be formed of small winged creatures—flies of some sort—which had tangled themselves together of set purpose—what do you think for? Simply to form a shade for a journeying column of friendly ants which dislike the light! Again, I once came upon an eel lying across a small brooklet while millions of ants made a bridge of his body to cross the stream by. I at first thought the ants had killed him, and wondered that they had not eaten him. I wondered a little, too, how they had managed to arrange the body to so exactly suit their purpose; so I moved one end of it with my stick, to see if they could replace it; whereupon the beast swam off like a flash of light, being, as it appeared, very much alive! That seemed strange enough; for ants on the march kill almost everything they come across; even big snakes and tiger-cats flee in a panic before them. Yet here was this eel untouched! But my surprise at what I had thus seen was nothing to my utter astonishment when, happening to return the same way an hour later, I saw the eel back in his old place again, as still and stiff as a wooden bridge, but evidently quite contented and happy, and the ants swarming over him as before, hurrying and scurrying to reach the other side of the stream!"

"Well!" exclaimed Arnold, rousing up a little, "that 'beats cock-fighting,' I think."

"Take another example—one that is well known to botanists. You have heard of the leaf-cutting ants?"

"Yes."

"They destroy great numbers of trees in some parts, climbing the trunks and stripping off every particle of foliage. But some trees seem to be safe from them. Why? They somehow encourage certain kinds of plants to grow round their roots, plants which exude sweet juices of which certain ants of *another* kind—a very warlike race—are excessively fond. These ants, attracted by the agreeable nectar, in their turn also make their abode in the vicinity, and fight and drive off the leaf-cutting species whenever they attempt to rob the trees.

"I cite yet another instance, which has been recorded by several travellers, though it has not come under my own observation, and that is the remarkable alliance that exists, in some places, between certain wild bees and wasps, and the black-and-yellow mocking-birds. These are often found living in colonies, banded together for mutual protection and support. The birds refrain from eating the insects, and the latter, in return, guard the birds' nests during their absence. Woe to any unlucky creature that ventures near those nests intent on filching the eggs or young birds! The bees or wasps attack him in such swarms, and with such viciousness, that he is fortunate if he escapes alive, whatever or whoever the intending thief may be, tiger-cat, or serpent, or man himself.* In fact, all the other creatures of the woods seem to be aware of the existence of this compact, and prefer to give the nests a wide berth rather than face the risks which an attack upon them invariably entails."

"Having these curious examples—which I know to be true—in my mind, I look with a special feeling of interest, upon this serpent and bird story, which, after all, may possibly be founded

---

* These curious facts have been attested by many well-known travellers in these regions, notably, Sir Robert Schomburgk, Mr Barrington Brown, and others.

upon some actual fact in natural history bearing a family resemblance to those I have quoted, but which has not yet come under the cognisance of any reliable authority. And I feel, too, specially curious about this particular mountain. Won't you, then, come with me and investigate?"

But Arnold, who had made a passing show of interest during his friend's quasi-scientific discourse, now relapsed! once more into gloomy silence, and merely shook his head.

Gordon regarded him with an expression half-quizzical, half-anxious.

"Well!" he said, in a tone of disappointment, "here have I been cudgelling my memory to rub up all the extraordinary facts I could think of in order to give you an entertaining lecture in natural history, and you show about as much interest in it as though I had merely been repeating nursery rhymes."

Arnold looked up with one of his old bright smiles.

"Are you quite sure, Gordon," he said, slyly, "that they are not fairy tales?"

"Now I call that too bad! However, I have one shaft still left in my quiver that I have not yet made use of. We saw some mysterious lights last night on yonder mountain side."

"You did! What sort of lights?"

"That, of course, is difficult to say. But Lenaka and I both saw them. They were somewhat such as one would expect to see if there were a party of people with lanterns going to and fro, backward and forward, as persons might if they were looking or hunting for something. We watched them for a long time until they at last disappeared one by one to the east. Now, won't *that* fetch you?"

Arnold smiled, but again shook his head.

"No," he answered, quietly. "You go off on your little exploring trip, if you wish to, and I will stay in camp. One of us had better remain to keep an eye on our belongings, for, somehow, I don't feel altogether sure of our Indian friends. They have shown signs of restlessness and home-sickness the last few days, or so I have fancied; and we had better be on our guard."

"I have had a vague idea of the sort, too, but I think it arises from superstitious fears. We are getting into a country which is strange and almost unknown even to them. Of course, you can understand that very likely they do not greatly care to trust themselves in a neighbourhood of which such queer tales are told. After all, you cannot blame the poor devils; they are brought up from childhood to believe these wild fancies, and know no better."

"Well, so-long, then. Beware the werewolf, and the spell of the goblin-bird; and, above all, do not fall a victim to the fascinations of any beautiful lady of the mountain."

"I think I'm proof against feminine charms, Arnold. I've never yet seen the woman who could attract me. You ought to know that by this time. And least of all is it probable I should fall a victim to the sort of dusky beauty likely to be met with in this primitive wilderness."

And with that Leslie turned and disappeared down the slope of the hill in the direction of the mysterious mountain.

CHAPTER IX

THE WHITE PUMA

BEFORE FOLLOWING MR Gordon Leslie in the enterprise upon which he set out so cheerfully—a little expedition destined to be more adventurous and fateful than he or his friend had any idea of—it may be as well to give the reader a brief retrospect of the main incidents of their journey up to the point at which the two travellers had now arrived.

In the first place, on leaving England, they had made for the capital of Venezuela, Carácas, as directed in the eccentric Brazilian's letter. Various vague plans of intercepting his yacht by telegraphing to the British Consul in Carácas had been thought out and considered, only to be abandoned as the practical difficulties in the way were reluctantly recognised. Leslie, as the more practical and experienced of the two, pointed out that since Lorenzo (as they were already aware) had agents in Carácas, those agents would be likely enough to get wind of any such attempt in time to warn him; in which case his anger might be visited upon the defenceless ladies he had at his mercy. It would also, in any case, probably be futile; as the yacht would be more likely, he thought, to keep clear of Carácas altogether.

In the end, they had reluctantly to recognise that they were so completely in the hands of this determined man, as to have no alternative but to follow out his instructions and hope for the best.

At the hotel at which they put up at Caracas, a letter was mysteriously delivered to them, on the very evening of their arrival, in which they were informed that the party they were following was then already on its way up the Essequibo River. And Leslie knew that, if that were so, they were now altogether beyond the reach of any civil power, and that they, the pursuers, had again no other course before them than to follow as speedily as might be. As to their means of transport, the letter informed them that all arrangements had been made, and that a party of Indians, with canoes and all requisite stores, would be found awaiting them at the old "Penal Settlement," where the local steamer touched, inside the mouth of the Essequibo River. This is the usual place of arrival and departure for most of the parties of Indians in British Guiana who corns at intervals to the coast to do a little trading with the whites, lay in stocks of gunpowder and other stores, and then disappear again into the wilds of the interior.

Here, sure enough, the two travellers found a party of Indians awaiting them. They were Macusis, and the leader, an old "Buck," who rejoiced in the name of Captain Jim, could speak a fair amount of English. As a matter of fact, Leslie had once passed some time at Georgetown, the capital of British Guiana, and, while there, having made two or three long excursions, had acquired a very fair smattering of the Indian tongues most commonly in use; but he arranged now with Arnold, for reasons of his own, to affect to be a stranger to the country. Within a short time of their arrival the whole party were on their way up the great river, which forms the chief highway from the coast into the interior of the country.

This first stage—the navigation of the Essequibo—occupied them nearly a month. It was toilsome, and at times dangerous, especially where rapids had to be negotiated. The whole time they were paddling against the stream, exposed all day to the fierce rays of the tropical sun which beat down upon the voyagers with pitiless persistency hour after hour. Attempts to rig up a sort of canopy or shade proved but partially successful, and when one which afforded some kind of shelter had at last been constructed, it was carried away in the first storm of

rain and wind that they encountered. The banks, the whole
way, were impenetrable forest or swamp, and nothing could be
seen beyond the margin. After some time, they left the Essequibo, and branched off into one of its tributaries, where they
encountered waterfalls, which could only be passed by carrying everything, canoes included, round from the river below to
the stream above the falls. Then came further long stretches of
river, always becoming narrower, where the continuous struggle
against the current, with the monotonous swish, swash of the
paddles, was varied by exciting scenes at the rapids, which were
now of a more difficult character than those they had first met
with, and where many a hair-breadth escape befell them. Several
of their canoes, in fact, got upset; and one was actually lost, with
all the stores it contained. Thus several weeks passed, at the end
of which they came to the point where the navigation became
so difficult and dangerous, that the river and canoes had to be
abandoned altogether.

The second stage consisted of forest travel, and the two
Englishmen soon found that this part was far more arduous
than even the slow struggle against the stream, and the fights
with the rapids. Before this second start could be made, however,
there had been a long halt, caused by the necessity of waiting for
the arrival of another party of Indians; for some of those who
had accompanied them thus far returned with the canoes to
their own village, which had been passed on the way. The fresh
party were mostly of the Arecuna tribe, and they turned out to
be far less agreeable company than the river Indians who had left
them. Captain Jim, however, and another Indian named Lenaka,
a Macusi, and a fine specimen of the native hunter, to whom
Arnold had taken a great fancy, which the Indian evidently
reciprocated, stuck to them. As it turned out it was well that they
did, for the newcomers were anything but easy to manage. On
this part of their expedition—and indeed all the time henceforth—everything had to be carried. There was no proper road,
the so-called Indian path being altogether bewildering to a
white man; and fresh meat was unattainable in consequence

of the denseness of the forest, which rendered it impossible to hunt for game. This necessitated occasional detours, and long halts, in order to beat up some Indian village in a forest clearing, and so procure supplies of cassava, which is the native food of the country, and without which the Indians could not get on.

But the worst part of this stage of the journey was the irresistible feeling of depression inspired by the sombre gloom of the forest. At all times, in all parts of the world, whether in Africa, or India, or America, travellers through forest regions have testified to the reality and intensity of this feeling. It affects the bravest, the strongest, and the gayest, as well as the timid or weak. And the longer one remains within the forest depths, the more powerful, the more irresistible does the feeling become, until it grows into a veritable nightmare. The Indians are just as much a prey to this feeling as white men, indeed they are even more susceptible to its influence, seeing that they are more superstitious, and have so many fabled terrors of the woods to scare them.

But, in time, a fourth stage was reached. The travellers emerged from the gloom of the forest to find themselves upon the swelling uplands, the glorious savannahs, of the higher ground.

And then they experienced a change indeed. The air was fresh, bracing, exhilarating. The sense of light and freedom came to the weary, depressed travellers like liberty to the prisoner. They felt their pulses bound, their blood leap in their veins, as they pressed the elastic greensward under their feet, and met the cool prairie breezes fanning their cheeks. They took long breaths of the invigorating air; and in a few hours became different men.

Here, at last, they could hunt and fish, and had more opportunities of studying the natural wonders amidst which they were journeying. In the boats, or in the forest path, they had had no chance of properly observing what went on around them. Now they could deviate at will to the right or to the left, and follow up whatever attracted their attention or aroused their curiosity. For the first time since placing his foot on the South American

Continent, Arnold began to realise the full meaning of tropical life, of tropical fauna and flora; and a wonderful fairyland he found it. Even to Leslie it was a wonderland; and the farther they advanced the more novel and strange the surroundings became. For though his experience of South America had been considerable, yet he had never penetrated so far into unknown and unexplored fastnesses as they were now doing. Hence he soon began to exhibit nearly as much surprise and astonishment as Arnold, who had never before seen, never imagined, anything even remotely resembling the scenes and sights that were daily, hourly, unfolded before their eyes.

But though some parts of the journey had been through a land altogether new to him, yet Leslie's general knowledge of South American travel, and of Indian life, naturally stood them in good stead, and served to mitigate, in no small degree, the trials of the enterprise. Moreover, in times of danger or difficulty he showed a resourcefulness, a courage and energy, combined with unfailing good-humour, that exhibited him in an entirely new light to his inexperienced chum. And the quiet, unassuming care with which he watched over his friend, and sought by every means in his power, to lighten his share of their troubles and inconveniences, daily increased the admiration with which Arnold regarded him, and served to continually cement the strong friendship that existed between the two.

At intervals their journey had been temporarily suspended, and they had been compelled to put up, as best they could, with spells of enforced idleness varying from two or three days to a week. These breaks were consequent upon messages or commands which reached the Indians from the enigmatical being in whose wake they were following. Sometimes these communications were confined to their Indian guides; but at others they included a message or even a brief note from Lorenzo to Arnold, conveying renewed assurances that the ladies were well, and that no harm was intended either to him or to them. Usually, however, alongside these friendly assurances, there were warnings against any attempt to depart from or to disobey the instructions and directions from time to time given, and especially as to hurrying their movements with the idea of catching up with the objects of their pursuit.

All endeavours to extract information from their Indian attendants by direct questioning had proved useless; and the two had no alternative but to struggle blindly on when progress was permitted; or halt and await fresh directions whenever their guides declared it to be so ordered. No persuasions, no coaxing, or offers of bribes on the part of either Arnold or Leslie—even in the case of the Indian Lenaka, who had shown unusual friendliness—had succeeded in drawing from them any information worth mentioning, or any explanation worth consideration.

In respect to one point—his acquaintance with the Indians' language and customs—Leslie had, as has been stated, concealed the extent of his knowledge; and this, as it turned out, had bean a politic course, and had put them in possession of a good deal that their attendants had endeavoured to conceal from them. He had been astute enough to divine that the Indians sent to guide them would be instructed by their clever employer, the Brazilian, to give them misleading information, and prevent their discovering the true meaning of much that occurred in the course of their progress. Of course, it was not probable that these poor natives were in Lorenzo's secrets, but still they were in his pay, and doubtless they knew more of him than they chose to tell; and something of this Leslie had managed to learn by judiciously pretending ignorance of their language and silently listening to their talk whenever opportunity offered. Thus he had come to know that the party they were following were not far ahead of them; and he had more than once discovered the exact spots at which they had encamped. From the signs thus observed and understood he gathered that Lorenzo had with him a much larger party than their own; and that they had also beasts of burden, not horses or mules, which were of no use in such a country, but probably llamas from the region of the Andes. From this he inferred that the two ladies were probably not making the journey on foot, as he and Neville were doing, but were riding in easy stages.

More than once, too, his observant eyes had discovered a few small articles that had been dropped or thrown away, no doubt by careless Indian attendants when their master's eye did not happen to be watching them. These various observations, taken together, gave him good reason for the opinion he had expressed to Arnold that Mrs Beresford and her niece were probably making the journey much more comfortably than they themselves were; a conclusion that gave them both no small consolation.

He did not, indeed, take quite the same gloomy view of the whole affair that Arnold's anxious fears led him to do; at least, so far as the actual journey was concerned. Having thus good reason for the hope that both the ladies were travelling in comparative comfort and good health, he was inclined to believe that, as regards Beryl, the excitement and novelty of the affair and the knowledge—which she would doubtless possess—that her lover was not far behind them, would enable her to keep up her health and spirits fairly well until they reached their destination. Of what was to happen afterwards—well, of course, he could form no idea. They could only hope for the best. He was not, however, inclined to take a pessimistic view even as to that. The eccentric Lorenzo had apparently taken a fancy to Arnold, and might, as he professed, mean well by him; and altogether, if he could only have felt quite sure that the ladies' health would not suffer, Leslie, for his part, would rather have enjoyed the whole affair, if only from pure love of adventure and curiosity as to what it all meant.

Such was Leslie's state of mind as he made his way towards a rocky eminence which he had noted from their camping ground, and from which he hoped to be able to get a better view of the mountain he was bent on visiting, and also some idea of the easiest and quickest way of getting there.

In a short time he reached the bluff he had been making for, and sat down to rest awhile, and gaze upon the extensive view there spread out before him.

On all sides he could discern an endless sea of mountain-tops rising and falling in billowy fashion, until they grew dim and blue in the extreme distance. Mountains and valleys, greensward and rock, dense masses of forest, alternating with smooth, velvet-like stretches of open savannah; wild gorges and deep vales, foaming torrents and glittering cascades, towering precipices sinking into sombre, dimly-revealed ravines suggestive of the unknown and unfathomable—these were all lying before him, mapped out with greater or less distinctness according to the distance, the floating haze, or the mysterious shadows thrown by the soaring masses of the higher mountains. And everywhere, in all directions, everything spoke of solitude; solitude the most intense, the most vast, the most overwhelming. It was a solitude that overshadowed the senses, that bewildered the mind, and that overwhelmed and oppressed the very brain. The solitude that impresses the soul of man with something near to a true sense of his utter insignificance beside the vastness, the mightiness, the majestic gloriousness of nature.

"To think," Leslie said, to himself, "that all this goes on for ever, totally irrespective of puny mankind! These mighty, roaring torrents, these thundering waterfalls, this wonderful play of light and shade—all goes on ever the same as the years follow each other, while, far away, men and women are being born, and buried, and forgotten! To think of all this going on everlastingly in these mountain solitudes, while the centuries roll by, and new nations arise, and have their season and vanish—is it not enough to overturn the poor little tottering brain of that insignificant, crawling earthworm called man?"

Such were the thoughts that passed through Leslie's mind as he stood gazing at the view before him. Even his nature—ordinarily so sage and practical—could not but feel the strange, awe-inspiring influence of the scene; and for awhile he lay down on the soft sward, and gave himself up to the dreamy fascination of the hour.

Presently, looking across towards the large mass of "the haunted mountain," that towered up in dim shadow right against the sun, he occupied himself for a while in speculations as to the meaning of some of the vague outlines which were all he could now make out in the murky depths of the shade in which it was enwrapped. As his eyes became more accustomed to piercing the gloom, he sought to discover, from his present point of observation, something that might account for the lights he had seen the night before; the lights which had so frightened their superstitious Indian guide. But failing in this, he resumed his walk in the direction of the mountain.

The intervening distance proved to be greater than he had supposed; but after much climbing up and down, and many detours to avoid awkward precipices or streams that could not be forded, he arrived at the slope of the mountain base. Ascending this, he finally reached the skirts of the forest belt which, according to the Indians, was haunted by the fearful creatures which rendered it impassable to mortal man or, at least, to all save those who were in league with them.

Now that the sun was no longer in his eyes, Leslie could get a better view of this mysterious belt of forest, and he felt bound to admit to himself, as he came close to it, that it was about as forbidding and uninviting a piece of woodland as he had ever looked upon even in those remote wilds. Nor could he, for a while, discern any point at which it seemed likely to be possible to penetrate even a short distance into its sombre depths. In search of some such opening, he walked first in one direction, then in the other, till, by-and-by, he perceived a stream issuing from the wood. Hastening his steps, he soon came to an opening, a sort of glade, in the centre of which ran the daintiest of little streams, broad, clear, translucent as crystal, blue as the sky above, running over a bed of golden sand, with here and there a rocky boulder bright with brilliant-hued mosses and ferns.

Leslie sat down upon a convenient piece of rock, and looked up the glade. The spot was beautifully sheltered and cool, and the trickling and plash of the water sounded musically in his ears. He followed with his eye the broad, shallow stream, till be saw that it came gently tumbling from a sort of terrace a few hundred yards farther into the wood. In fact, from where he sat, he could see that there was a succession of such dams, one behind the other, as the ground rose, until the farthest was lost in the gloom of the overhanging trees. There was something in this arrangement which appealed pleasantly to Leslie's senses, though he would have found it difficult to define precisely what it was. Of streams, and cascades, and rocks, and waterfalls he had seen many—plenty and to spare. But they had been wild, rough, fierce-looking. This was so quiet, so shallow; so mild and gentle, so to speak, and withal, so extremely pleasing in its richness of colouring and suggestiveness of soothing, restful coolness, that his mind went back to English woods and meadows, and plash- ing brooks, and he could almost have fancied himself in some quiet, peaceful nook in the New Forest.

Suddenly he heard a slight rustling, and, like a flash, a small deer bounded out of the undergrowth a hundred yards or so away, ran a little distance by the side of the stream, and then plunged back into the wood. Gordon had his rifle with him, but it was slung at his back, and, rather annoyed at having lost the chance of a shot, he now unslung it and laid: it across his knees. But no more deer came along, and his attention was drawn off, for a few moments, by the curious metallic call of a bell-bird which seemed to be not far away. Strain his eyes as he would, however, he failed to discover it amid the surrounding foliage, and his glance wandered back to the place at which the deer had appeared. And then he gave a great start!

There, upon the sand, quietly watching him with a steady fixed stare, was an immense white puma! As he turned he saw it clearly and distinctly, sharply outlined against the dark back- ground, its tail slowly swaying from side to side.

But ere he had well caught sight of it, and before he could catch up the rifle lying across his knees, the apparition sprang high over some bushes and disappeared, like a silent ghost, into the forest.

CHAPTER X

THE LADY OF THE MOUNTAIN

LESLIE RUBBED HIS eyes, then stared blankly at the place where the animal had stood. So large had it looked, so sudden, so unexpected had been the sight he had had of it, and so quickly and noiselessly had it vanished, that he was half inclined to doubt the evidence of his senses. Surely he had imagined it! He had had the Indian's tale in his thoughts, and it had so influenced his imagination that it had played him a trick; for, of a surety— putting aside the colour—there could not be an animal of such proportions in that part of the world! Why, it had loomed up as large as a lioness! For some time he sat silent and motionless, hoping that it might reappear; but after a long wait his patience gave out, and he rose and went quietly and cautiously forward till he came to the place where he had seen it—or thought he had seen it—standing. But the ground was hard, and he could find no tracks. He peered into the wood, and searched all around, but without any success; and finally, greatly puzzled and perplexed, he strolled further along the sandy margin of the stream, keeping a sharp-look out in all directions till, all of a sudden, he once more stood and stared in speechless astonishment.

There, in the damp sand at the very edge of the stream, was the impress of a woman's shoe!

Robinson Crusoe, when he came upon the black man's footprint on the sand of the shore of his lonely island, was scarcely more startled than was Leslie at sight of this.

He looked about for other footmarks, but for a while could

see none. The surrounding sand was too dry to leave such a mark; it was only at the very edge of the stream that it was sufficiently soft, and just there some pieces of rock lay across the bed of the little river in such a manner as to suggest that they might be used as stepping-stones for crossing. Then the idea came into Leslie's mind that the owner of the shoe must have gone across the water in that wise. At once he went across himself, and, on reaching the other side, found that his surmise had been correct; there, sure enough, were several similar footmarks, and, the sand being less dry on that side, he was able to follow them for some distance. They led him on into the forest, still, however, following the windings of the stream, and mounting a succession of slight terraces or shallow dams—evidently, at some time or other, the work of beavers—over which the water now gently fell with a pleasing splash and soothing murmur.

As he went on, the footsteps became plainer, the sand, under the cool shade of the trees, being moister, and here began other marks, the sight of which gave him a shock of surprise, mingled now with vague apprehension. They were the pugs of some very large animal, probably of the leopard or jaguar tribe. Then it flashed upon him that they were the footmarks of the big white puma, and that the beast—which had probably at first been hunting the deer he had seen—had come upon these shoe-tracks, and, guided by its scent; was now following up their owner in place of the deer which he had lost!

He followed the footprints thus blended in such curious and ominous fashion, for some distance, till presently he was still more startled to see the pugs of yet another animal. They bore a close family resemblance to the first ones; pausing to observe them more closely, however, he noticed some minor differences, and they were certainly smaller, but both animals were evidently large beasts of the feline species. And now he hurried on, for, to his mind, the story told by these tracks was only too plain.

Here was, evidently, some woman, *a white woman*—for it was absurd to imagine an Indian woman with shoes—alone in this remote wilderness, making her way up the bank of the stream;

and, upon her track, two large beasts of prey steadily following with all the cruel, relentless patience of the cat tribe upon
the hunt. How or why it came about that, any woman could
be alone in such a country, so far even from the nearest Indian
village, was a puzzle that he need not then waste time in trying
to solve. A moment's brief guess that Beryl Atherton might
have escaped, or strayed from the party ahead, and got lost, was
quickly dismissed as hardly probable. But he would not stop to
speculate as to who it might be. It was sufficient that she was
probably in danger, and it behoved him to hasten to render the
assistance of which she must be sorely in need.

Sorely in need! Ah! but perhaps it was already too late! With
two such fierce enemies thus hunting her with all the bloodthirsty pertinacity of their kind, what chance would the lonely
wanderer have?

As these thoughts rose up in his mind, a cold shiver ran
through his whole frame, and, after a brief stoppage to look at
the sights of his rifle, and loosen his revolver in his belt, he took
up the track at a run.

The footmarks now left the side of the stream, and seemed
to strike across as though to cut off a bend, following a tolerably wide and well-defined path with thick bush on either side
and a sandy bed—evidently the course, at present dry, of some
smaller rivulet that in the rainy season ran into and fed the main
watercourse. Suddenly he stopped, and gazed horror-struck
upon the sandy path, which now revealed further testimony as
to what had gone before.

For there were marks as of some sort of struggle having
taken place, the bushes were broken and pushed aside as by the
hasty and violent passage of some heavy body; but the tracks
still continued, only now there were bloodstains as well. Then
they turned abruptly into a narrow side-path where the ground
became first stony and dry, then grassy; and there all further
trace of them was lost.

For some time Leslie vainly searched about to recover the

lost tracks, and after a while succeeded in finding traces of blood upon the grass, and upon the leaves and reeds which had been brushed against by those he was following. Then he became aware, by the increased light ahead of him, that the slight path led out into some open space or clearing.

And here, stopping to peer cautiously through the bushes before leaving their shelter, he was gradually making out the main details of a rather extensive clearing or glade, when his eyes fell upon a sight which froze the very blood in his veins, and, for a space, rendered him incapable of further action.

The opening spread from left to right apparently for some considerable distance, but it did not appear to be more than sixty to seventy yards wide. At any rate, the view on the side opposite to where he stood was shut in at that distance by a low wall or ridge of rocks, that rose abruptly from the general level of the glade to a height of some fifteen or twenty feet. And at the foot of these rocks was lying a motionless female form, while beside it was a large, white animal, clearly the white puma of which he had had so brief a glimpse. The figure lay with its back towards him so that he could not see the face, but from the general contour he was impressed at once with the conviction that it was the figure of a young girl. Beside it lay the form of the animal, with its head in his direction, engaged in licking its paws, which were red with blood, while similar stains could be seen upon other parts of its snow-white coat.

To Leslie's horrified senses the story thus told seemed clear enough. The cruel beast had evidently run down and killed the girl, and was now taking a short rest to lick the blood from its paws before proceeding further with its horrible repast. As to the second animal of which he had seen the pugs, no sign of it was to be seen; but Leslie, looking at the marks upon the body of the beast before him, concluded that the two had fought over their victim, and that the one he now saw had proved the victor— though not without itself receiving some nasty wounds—and had finally driven the other one away. So he had arrived too late!

He felt sick and giddy, as the meaning of it all came home to him. Great Heavens! If he had been but a few minutes earlier!

He determined, however, that the bloodthirsty monster should not enjoy its horrid triumph. As he saw the graceful form of the innocent victim lying so still, a murderous rage against the savage brute which had killed her rose up in his heart, and he slowly raised and levelled his rifle.

But at the very moment he was about to fire—when his finger was already pressing the trigger—the recumbent figure turned slightly and raised a hand, which, to his utter astonishment, was laid, as though caressingly, upon the great head of the animal. It was too late to refrain from firing—or at least it so seemed to him—but he involuntarily jerked up the rifle, and the bullet flew high over its intended mark and struck the rock beyond.

At the report the animal started to its feet with a loud roar, and then bounded, with open jaws, in the direction of the firer of the shot. But before it had got far, or Leslie had had time to raise his rifle again to defend himself, the girl had turned and seen him, and called to the animal, with the result that it instantly stayed its rush and slowly retreated to its former place. All the while, however, it kept looking over its shoulder, growling, and breaking at intervals into a loud roar of defiance.

Meantime, the figure on the ground sat up, and brought into suggestive prominence a rifle which had been lying on the grass beside her.

Leslie advanced into the glade, and then stood staring in astonishment at the two before him; while the young girl returned his inquiring gaze in very similar fashion.

Truly, for a brief space, he again half fancied that he must be dreaming, or that he was the victim of some extraordinary hallucination, so inexplicable did the whole affair now appear. Was the mountain really haunted by uncanny beings after all? he wondered.

He saw before him a girl who seemed to be about twenty to twenty-two years of age, and of wondrous, most surpassing beauty, who looked at him with dark eyes of indescribable depth and brilliancy that had in them an expression—or rather, a mixture of expressions—that held him fascinated in a maze of wonder, doubt, and admiration. At first she had raised her rifle half-threateningly, but as she continued to look at him, and noted his glances of astonishment, she let it sink slowly into her lap, and there came into her features a look that gradually betrayed more and more of amusement, until her wondrous eyes fairly sparkled with merriment. All the time, she had one hand upon the neck of her body-guard—for so it presently appeared the animal beside her really was—holding it back and softly patting it, as one would a too demonstrative lap-dog.

Owing to her position he could not see her dress more than to make out that she appeared to be attired in a sort of hunting costume of light green, with brown leather belts and straps, and a wide-brimmed hat of a darker shade.

Leslie's utter astonishment at last found vent in an involuntary exclamation:

"Who in the world are you, and how do you come here?" he burst out.

There was a silvery laugh, and then the lady answered, in perfect English:

"I might ask you the same, Mr Englishman—for such I perceive you to be—and with more reason, for *I* am upon my own territory, whereas you are—Oh dear!"

A spasm of pain passed over the beautiful features, and the speech was left unfinished. At the same time the speaker's hand left the rifle, and was placed upon her right foot.

"You are hurt," Leslie exclaimed, and made a start to rush forward to her assistance, but stopped abruptly upon hearing a particularly savage admonitory growl from the big puma.

"I have hurt my foot; sprained my ankle," she replied. "I had almost forgotten it for the moment, in the surprise of seeing you. But now, when I moved, it reminded me very sharply that I am chained to this spot, helpless—as I have been all night."

"All night!"

"Yes, all night."

"Why—I wonder you are not half dead! You seem to take it very coolly!"

"It was no good doing otherwise. It did not pain me so long as I did not attempt to walk, and the air has not been cold, you know. For the rest, I am accustomed to roughing it, and it is no hardship for me to pass a night in the woods. I have only been troubled with thirst—since my flask was emptied and the sun began to get hot."

"Shall I bring you some water? Or, here is my flask. It contains brandy—"

"Thanks, no; I have brandy with me; I always carry a little in case of accidents. But you may bring me some water if you will. I am almost dying for a good draught of nice, cool water. But it hurt me so much every time I moved, that I had to give up the attempt to crawl to the stream yonder."

Following with his eyes the direction she indicated, Leslie perceived that he was again within a few hundred yards of the stream which he had been following; and, without more ado, he started off and quickly returned with a flask filled with the welcome fluid. This visit to the stream had to be repeated two or three times before the lady's thirst was satisfied. When that was accomplished she turned to him, and said quietly:

"Now sit down, and tell me who you are and all about yourself."

"First, are you not hungry?"

"No, thank you. I had food with me, for I had been upon a little journey when this accident befell me, and I brought some food with me on my return."

She had induced her leonine guard to lie down and resume its former occupation of licking its paws and wounds. But it cast a suspicious glance now and again at the stranger, who, upon his side, kept a watch upon it out of the corner of one eye, so to speak, while ostensibly giving all his attention to his questioner.

He gave a very brief account of himself and his friend Arnold, without, however, going into particulars of the real reason of their presence in that part of the world. He left it to be inferred, for the moment, that they were there for the sake of travelling and exploring. He was the more anxious to hurry over his own explanation in that he was dying with curiosity to know more about his strange companion.

"And now," he presently said, "pray answer me in turn. Who are you, what is your name, do you live about here, and, if so, where? And, if not, where *do* you live, when you are at home? How did you manage to sprain your ankle, and how did you come to have such a strange body-guard? What *is* the animal? Can I trust it? and what is the meaning of the blood upon it? I thought it had killed you, and I was going to kill it in revenge. If you had not moved when you did I should have shot it."

"Shot it!" exclaimed the fair one, in evident agitation.

"Shot my white puma! my lovely, beautiful, faithful pet! my loyal, brave guardian! Poor Myllio! What a narrow escape she has had, then!"

"She has indeed. I am more glad than I can tell you (now I understand the truth about her) that I missed. You raised your hand just at the very moment, and threw out my aim. Else I had killed her, sure enough. I thought the beast had killed you, and that you were lying dead, and I determined it should not survive the crime. Can you wonder? I tracked you both all the way up by the side of the stream. I saw your footprints first, and then, afterwards, I also saw the pugs off some animal which I conceived must be following you with evil intent. So you can understand my horror and rage when I saw you, as I thought, lying dead, and believed that I had come up with you too late."

"Ah! I begin to understand now. I did not think of it in that way."

"But I saw the prints of the feet of another beast that must have been also on your track, I fancy."

"Oh yes; a great brute of a jaguar. I heard its cry, and guessed that something of the kind was afoot. Now *that* animal did really follow me, as you put it, with evil intent. And when I met with the accident, and had to lie out all night, I suppose the brute had marked me down for an easy prey."

"I expect so."

"Yes; and it would have been a nasty beast to have to tackle lying here in the dark, unable to move or to see where to shoot."

"You are right; it would! Were you not in fear?"

"Not in the least. The cowardly brute reckoned without Myllio here, as it quickly discovered to its cost. For my faithful pet soon settled its business. Not, however," she added, patting the animal affectionately, "without a nasty fight for it, or without receiving some ugly scratches, as you can see. Judging by the noise they made, they must have had a pretty lively scrimmage; it lasted some time, too."

"Were you not in fear for the result?"

The stranger shook her head, and laughed merrily.

"Not for a moment. There's no jaguar in America that can stand up to Myllio. She tackles them and bowls them over like a good fighting cat would a rat. She's killed dozens of them. I guess you'll find the carcass of the brute somewhere at hand if you trot around and have a look. Myllio seldom lets them get away alive, once she comes to close quarters with them."

"I see. That explains much that has been puzzling me. But I saw your wonderful pet, less than an hour since, just within the wood. I fancy she was on the track of a deer which passed the same place a minute or so before I caught sight of her. Indeed, it was seeing her as I did which led me to the place where I first caught sight of your footstep. Apparently your faithful guard must have forsaken you for a while."

The other laughed. "Oh yes; she knew I was safe enough by daylight, and went off to get her breakfast. But when she caught sight of you, I expect she thought it best to return to look after me. I was wondering what had brought her back so soon; the mystery is explained now. But it also makes it clear that she has had no breakfast, for she must have abandoned the deer to come back to me. The faithful Myllio! She must be hungry."

"I hope she won't let her hunger lead her to try to make a meal off me," said Leslie, looking at the animal with a comical mixture of admiration and suspicion. "Can I trust her, do you think?" And he put out his hand, half inclined, but half afraid, to stroke her.

"That," said her mistress, archly, "depends upon whether you and I are going to be friends. She loves all those who are friends of mine, and they are quite safe with her. Otherwise—"

"But you will have me for a friend, will you not?" Gordon interrupted.

She did not answer immediately, but looked steadily at him with a searching gaze that seemed as if it could read almost his very thoughts. Then, as though satisfied with the result of her scrutiny, her face lost its earnest, eager look, and softened into a very sweet, captivating expression; and she flushed a little as she replied, simply:

"Yes; I think—I hope—that we shall be good friends."

CHAPTER XI

RHELMA'S WARNING

"AND NOW, PRAY, tell me something about yourself," said Gordon, after a pause of a few moments. In that brief space a great deal had passed through his mind as he noted the expression that had accompanied his companion's answer to his last question. He had found time to admit to himself that he had put the query with a feeling of vague anxiety for which he could not exactly account, and had heard the reply with sensible relief. Why had that been? Never before had he hung upon the answer to a like question from any living woman. Yet here he had to acknowledge to himself—and he made the acknowledgment with a feeling of strangeness that amounted almost to awe—that his spirits would have dropped down to something near "aero" had the answer been "no." That being so, it was not perhaps surprising that the "yes" had imbued him with a sense of exhilaration.

"And instruct me in what I am to do to help you in your present predicament," he added.

This brought them both back to the difficulties of the situation, and she sighed and looked troubled.

"Indeed, I scarce know what is best to be done," was the reply. "I was in hopes my people would have found me before this. They are no doubt out searching, and I think it will not be long before they trace me. But rather foolishly tried an unusual route last night, and that is the reason no doubt. It is my own fault, so I cannot complain."

"Do you know," said Gordon, seating himself comfortably on the grass, "that reminds me that we saw lights moving about last night on this mountain, as though a lot of people. Were out searching for something with lanterns. That was the very idea that occurred to me as I watched the lights."

"Ah! That would be my friends looking for me, no doubt. But your shot will perhaps guide them now, if one of them should be near enough to hear it."

"I wonder you did not think of that and fire some shots yourself," observed Leslie.

"I did, you may be sure. In fact, I have expended all the ammunition I had with me except two or three charges, which I reserved in case of emergency. But this place, where we now are, is a very secluded ravine, and the sound of a report is muffled by the surrounding wood, and does not travel far."

"I must say, again, that you seem to take matters very coolly!" Leslie exclaimed. "You surprise me more and more. The more we talk, the more do I wonder at finding you alone in such wild regions."

"I am, really, not so very far from my home, as I am accustomed to regard it, if only I had the use of my feet. My father—"

"Your father!"

"Yes; my father lives upon this mountain, where we have lived together now for some years. He is a man given over to study and to some kind of scientific research—I scarcely know exactly what, or why he should choose such a place in which to carry it on. I lived with my mother, who was an Englishwoman, in England, till her death. That took place when I was about fifteen. Then my father came and fetched me away. I had never seen him till then, though I knew he was alive, and that he was living somewhere out here. But my mother never spoke of him; nor do I remember that he ever came to see her. He brought me here, where I found that he was living alone—so far as white companionship is concerned—surrounded by a small Indian tribe who are devoted to him body and soul, and look upon him as a sort of god. And from that day to this I have scarcely set eyes upon any other white man."

This statement was made with a frank, straightforward simplicity which greatly charmed her listener who, every moment, showed in his manner increased surprise, and interest.

In reply to further queries the fair unknown proceeded to give him some more details:

"My father's name," she went on, "is Manzoni; I am called Rhelma, which was my mother's name. When I first came here I found it very lonely and was thoroughly miserable, but I have become used to it, and now I enjoy the wild freedom of the life we live."

"But do you, then, always go about alone in this fashion?"

She shook her head, and laughed.

"No; and my father will give me a terrible scolding when I get back—that is," she added, gravely, "after he has recovered from the anxiety it will have caused him, for which I am more sorry than I can tell you; for I know how he will fret. Usually I am not allowed to stir abroad without a bodyguard of our faithful Indians."

"And very sensible, too."

She gave another ringing laugh.

"I suppose it *was* very wilful and wrong of me, but I do get so tired, at times, of their grandmotherly care. And now, sir, tell me more of yourself, for you have not told me much as yet. It is a most unheard of thing to meet a white man in this part—at least—" here she checked herself, and spoke hesitatingly, "except the one or two who sometimes come to see my father."

"Then white men *do* come to and fro here? I had no idea that any—" then he paused in his turn, as he thought of the man they were following,—"that is," he went on, slowly, "I suppose there must be at least *one* who knows this part fairly well, because he is somewhere in the district now. It is he, in fact, who is the cause of our being here. We are following in his wake, so to speak."

The girl gave a startled exclamation, and looked up quickly, with an entirely new expression on her face.

"Who is he? What is his name?" she demanded, with evident anxiety.

"Goodness knows what his real cognomen may be in his own country. So far as we are concerned we only know that he calls himself by the not very uncommon appellation of Don Lorenzo."

"Don Lorenzo! Great Heavens!"

It was impossible to mistake the meaning of the tone in which these words were spoken. Fear, and intense anxiety, were mingled with a sort of horrified surprise.

"Don Lorenzo!" she repeated. "*That* is the man who brought you here! You are following him, you say! What can his object be?"

Leslie gazed at the girl in astonishment Her emotion was so strong that he feared she was about to faint. She turned first white, then a dangerous-looking red overspread her face, and this was followed again by a deadly paleness. Then she rocked herself to and fro as if in pain.

"My dear friend," Leslie exclaimed, in distress, "what—what can be the matter? Are you—are you ill? Shall I bring you some more water?"

He started up, and was about to rush off to the stream, but the sudden movement aroused the suspicion of the puma, who gave a warning growl.

The girl put one hand on the head of her too zealous pet, and with the other signed to Leslie to remain quiet. He sat down again and waited in silence until she was more composed.

Presently she spoke, but with evident difficulty, and in a voice that sounded half-choked and trembling.

"You call—me your—friend—" she gasped out. "I am—that is—wish to be. But if—you believe me—when I say so—then by all you—hold dear in this world—and—and—the next—*turn back*. Oh! turn back! turn back! Go no farther upon such a quest.

Follow that man no farther, but—go back at once—now—ere it be too late!"

Gradually she recovered control of herself, and now her words poured forth rapidly, in rising tones of passionate entreaty, her eyes seeming to blaze with energy, and her arm extended, with finger pointing in the direction in which he had come.

"My dear young lady," Leslie answered, vaguely alarmed and bewildered at her wild words, "pray tell me what you mean! I know nothing! I do not know even who this man is. Tell me—what is there to fear from him?"

"You do not know who he is? Then why follow him?"

"Because—because—oh, it is a long story. I cannot explain all in a minute. But for pity's sake tell me more. Who is he? What is he? What is the danger? Let me hear it that we may know what we have to face."

She shook her head, and went on vehemently.

"You do not know who he is? Then what—what are you doing here with him?"

"We are not here with him—that is, we are—" Leslie broke off, confusedly. He knew not how to make the situation clear to her without waiting to tell the whole history. And all the while, as he sought blindly, as it were, for words, there rose up in his mind a great sickening dread and horror inspired by his informant's ominous talk. If Lorenzo's company was dangerous to Arnold and himself, what about the two helpless women he had in his power?

"You do not understand," he tried to explain. "We are not free to go back; we are bound to go on. We have no choice."

She looked strangely at him, and asked, in a voice that sounded almost stern in its intense eagerness.

"Why?"

"Because—because—well, the fact is, to put it shortly, this man Lorenzo, or whoever he is, has carried off—is now carrying along with him—two ladies, friends of ours. One is an elderly lady, the other a young one—my friend's betrothed. And we are following him in the hope that we may be able to rescue—to bring them back."

This statement evidently upset the girl still more. She clasped her hands and stared at him in horrified amazement. "Great Heavens!" she murmured, as though to herself, "Lyostrah carrying off two ladies! What can it mean?"

"Lorenzo; I said Lorenzo," Gordon explained.

"Do you not know that his true name is Lyostrah?" she asked.

"How should we? He never told us. We know nothing, I tell you. For heaven's sake, explain. What is this Lyostrah, as you call him? Who is he, where does he live? What does it mean?"

"Lyostrah," said the girl, slowly, looking at Leslie with eyes in which fear and terror seemed struggling with an overmastering horror, "is Lorenzo's real name, and amongst the Indians it is said to signify 'King of the Dead'!"

"King of the dead!" Leslie repeated after her. "But what does *that* mean? It conveys nothing to my mind, beyond a vague idea of some fresh form of Indian superstitious belief. Some new dismal fable, I suppose. If we have no more than Indian folly to go upon—"

"They declare," she interrupted, "that there is a dread significance in the title. But I may not tell you more about him. I have given my promise that I would never tell what I know of him to a living soul I may, however, say two things more to warn you, since you wonder at my speaking so strongly. The first is that Lyostrah—or Lorenzo—is now with us—with my father, or was yesterday."

"With your father?"

"Yes; he comes sometimes to see him. What about I do not know; but I do not like him." She shivered, and paused a moment; then went on: "That's the reason I am here alone. I stole off in such a way that no one should know where I had gone and so be able to follow me and bring me back while he is there; and I did it to get away from him, for I fear and dread him more than I can give you any idea of." She shuddered again.

"I cannot exactly tell you why I dread him so. The feeling is not the effect of the tales I have heard. It is something beyond that; a sort of instinct which I cannot define or control."

"That is very singular," said Leslie, musingly. He was thinking of poor Beryl's instinctive fear and dislike of the man. She had used almost the same words. It was certainly a singular coincidence.

"What is the other thing you referred to, Miss Rhelma?" he presently asked, finding that she remained silent.

"It is this," she answered, in a low, awe-struck tone. "I have heard it said, again and again, by my Indians, that though some are believed to have journeyed to the city where Lyostrah reigns, no white man has ever been known to come back!"

CHAPTER XII

HUNTING WITH LIONS

GORDON LESLIE MADE no comment upon the suggestive statement made to him by his new acquaintance, but remained for some time silent and abstracted, turning the ominous words over in his mind. Once or twice he seemed about to speak, but checked himself and relapsed again into reverie. He was sorely puzzled what construction to put upon the information he had heard—whether to regard it as a serious and timely warning, or to treat it as fantastic fable gathered by this young girl in her intercourse with her Indian attendants.

That she believed what she stated, and had implicit faith in its absolute truth, he did not for a moment doubt. Her painful emotion and very evident anxiety had quite satisfied him upon that point. But then she was young and impressionable; and she doubtless had lived so much in the companionship of the superstitious natives as to have imbibed a certain amount of belief in their wild notions. Yet—she clearly knew this Lorenzo,—Lyostrah, as it seemed he was really called—and certainly she knew a great deal more about him than either he or Arnold did. True, they knew sufficient of him to be aware that he was likely enough to Use his powers to make himself an object of mystery and fear to the natives around his dwelling-place. And who could do so more easily than the man they had known as Don Lorenzo, that astonishing inventor, that modern scientific magician? How easy for such a man to make himself appear as a sort of demon-god to these ignorant, superstitious children of the forest and savannah, and so to guard against both their enmity and their too-inquisitive interest by surrounding himself with a halo of such mystery and fear that they would not dare to seek to penetrate it?

Musing thus, Leslie presently turned his gaze from the distant water, at which he had been vacantly staring, to his companion, intending to question her further. He saw, however, at the first glance, that she had now something else to say. She, too, had been silent and preoccupied; but she seemed now to have made up her mind, and spoke quickly, but with a certain quiet decision:

"I have been thinking what is best to be done; how best I can help you," she began. "I, indeed, can do little, but I have been thinking that if you—if I—could interest my father in your favour, he would know better what to advise. I will endeavour to do so. It will not be easy. He is so wrapped up in his studies and his experiments, so lost, apparently, to ordinary worldly interests, that it is difficult to secure his attention to everyday matters. Moreover, there is some bond or connection between him and Lyostrah of a kind that I do not altogether understand. I don't *think* it is an intercourse altogether satisfactory or pleasing to my father—though that is only my idea—I have nothing tangible to go upon. Still—I think—that he *might*—be induced to assist you against Lyostrah—supposing—" here she paused and blushed charmingly—"supposing that—I were to declare to him I felt—interested in the matter. That is, you know—if I were to entreat it as a favour. I should have to ask it for myself, I fear. He is so fond of me he would not be likely to refuse me if—I—declared it was a matter of personal interest."

She had hesitated a good deal at the last and evidently felt embarrassed, but though she coloured up, she looked at the young engineer with a glance that was frank and open, and full of friendly interest.

"I see your meaning—and your difficulty, my dear friend—for such I feel sure you wish to be—and I thank you with all my heart on behalf not only of myself and my friend, but of those poor ladies, who, if what you fear is true, may be in some danger. If you can aid them in any way, directly or indirectly, you will be rendering the greatest possible service to all of us. They will be deeply grateful; and so shall I."

Having thus lessened her embarrassment by putting the matter upon more general grounds, Leslie returned to the question of the moment.

"But all this is, after all, less important just now," he said, "than the question of how we are to get you to your home. I confess I do not see—"

She waved her hand as though to brush that matter aside.

"Do not trouble now as to that," she said, "My friends may come for me at any moment—in any case I feel confident they will not be long. They can only reach this part of the mountain by a very circuitous route, and I expect that they are now on their way here and will soon be searching the neighbourhood. Let us arrange our plans for the future before they come. It is as well they should not see you here." She had returned now to her former decisive, self-possessed tone, and spoke somewhat rapidly.

"Why, Miss Rhelma?" Leslie asked, in surprise.

"Have I not already said that this man, Lyostrah, is on a visit to my father? He was to have been gone by the time I expected to reach home last night; but he may have stayed longer. He *might* therefore, accompany our people in the search; and, if so, it were better he did not see you. You see that?"

"I suppose so," Leslie returned, somewhat doubtfully, "if you think so. Though, for my part, I should have preferred to see him face to face. Then I could insist upon an explanation, and refuse to let him go without—"

"It is but folly to talk thus!" Rhelma exclaimed, impatiently. "You know not the man with whom you have to deal. You have only seen him over in England, where he doubtless appears in another guise, poses as an ordinary gentleman, much as other men—"

"No; he could never appear quite that."

"But you know what I mean. He seems quiet and harmless enough. But out here he is a king; ay, 'every inch a king,' as you will find out, and he is not accustomed to bandy words, or allow others to argue with him. He is lord of the lives of all who surround him, and if you dare to cross him or rouse his wrath your life would not be worth five minutes' purchase."

Leslie reflected. Evidently it would not be either wise or safe to fall out with such a man upon his own ground, and surrounded, as he would certainly he, by his own people.

"What, then, do you advise?" he asked.

"It is only a possibility that I have suggested," she answered. "I expect he has gone before this; but even so, it were better that none of our people saw you until I have had time to confer with my father. Lyostrah has a long arm. He has his secret agents and emissaries everywhere, even, perhaps, amongst my father's people; and it were better he should not get to hear of your having met me. Let me tell you this, which I can clearly see, such a chance as has actually happened—this meeting with myself— is something which never entered into his calculations, and we should do wisely not to let him know of it if we can help it; at least, until I have consulted my father."

"I see—and I begin to understand your drift. Yes! I see that your precaution is a wise one."

"Very well; now, listen! Go away at once. Go back by the way you came, and be here again at the same time the day after to-morrow. Someone I can trust shall meet you here with a message from me, telling you what my father advises. Possibly—I only mention it as a possibility—my father may wish you to go and see him, in which case you could not get back to your camp the same night. So arrange accordingly with your friend. But be careful, in coming here, that you are not watched and followed."

"Thank you. I am very grateful for your thoughtfulness and for your promised help."

"I did not promise help," Rhelma interrupted, with a sigh. "Would that I could. I only said you should have my father's advice if I can prevail upon him to interest himself sufficiently to give it."

"Advice *is* help—in our present helpless situation. But—I am not going away thus. How do you suppose I can leave you here, lying on the ground—"

"Hark!"

The girl suddenly put up her hand, and her face grew pale again.

"I feared it; it is too late! They are coming, and the pack with them," she exclaimed, in anxious tones. "Oh, what is to be done? I feel more certain than ever that they *must* not see you here!"

Leslie listened, but heard nothing.

"Who is coming?" he asked. "I cannot—"

But even as he spoke, a faint far-off cry was heard. It came borne upon the breeze, a strange, wailing cry, that rose and fell and died away, and then rose again upon the air. Then came another similar cry, but pitched in a different key; then two or three together. Then deeper sounds, roars and growlings, still faint, but slowly growing louder. Soon these mingled sounds began to swell into a chorus, a wild weird chorus as of a troop of great beasts of prey roaring and howling through the forest.

"What on earth is it?" Leslie exclaimed, "Sounds like a whole menagerie of wild beasts!"

The white puma now seemed to think it time to take her part, and, springing to her feet, sent back an answering roar that almost shook the ground upon which they stood. The girl caught the animal's mouth with both hands and closed it.

"Quick, quick! Listen to me!" she cried to Leslie. "Run to the stream, walk into it and up its bed in the water. It is not deep. A short distance up you will see a little island in the middle—a mere sand-bank, but with a thick, bushy mango tree growing out of it. Climb into it, and hide till we have all gone away. My father has a pack of pumas—he uses them as you in England use packs of dogs for hunting—and he is hunting with them for me. We call them our 'hunting lions' and very fine hunters they are, I can tell you. They will not, however, follow your track into the water, and you will be safe in the tree if you keep well hidden and quite quiet. When we have all been gone a good hour—not before—get down, and make your way back to your camp, and be here as arranged the day after to-morrow. Quick! You have not a moment to lose; I will hold Myllio."

With some misgivings, Leslie turned and ran towards the stream. He could not help glancing back to make sure that the great puma was not following him, but, true to her promise, the girl was holding it fast, both her arms being round its neck. He reached the water and stepped into it without hesitation. It was not more than a few inches in depth at first, but grew rather deeper as he went on. However, the sandy bottom was firm and smooth; and he had no difficulty in wading to the little island, which he soon saw straight before him, with an immense and very thick mango tree growing out of its midst. In two or three minutes more he was safely ensconced in a hollow amongst its branches. Here he found himself completely concealed, yet able to peep out in the direction in which he had come and keep an eye on the bank from which he had stepped off into the water. But he could not see beyond the banks on either side.

The hubbub in the forest gradually grew louder and louder, then he heard two shots close at hand, evidently fired by the girl he had just left, as a signal to her friends. They were answered at once by two shots a little farther away and an increased chorus of roars and howls that became almost demoniacal in its savage intensity. And with the roars were now plainly to be distinguished the voices of men calling excitedly to one another, and wild Indian whoops.

The outcries grew louder and louder, and rose, all at once, into an indescribable clamour; then suddenly dropped to a low, confused murmur. It was clear the searchers had found the object of their hunt.

Leslie wondered what was going on, and wished his hiding-place commanded a view of the meeting, that he night have some idea of the nature of the proceedings and the sort of company there gathered together. However, that could not be; all he could do was to wait as patiently as might be until they had cleared off and left a way open for his return to the camp. As he had been warned to let at least an hour elapse after their departure before he left his place of concealment, he had evidently a good long wait before him. So he settled himself as comfortably as circumstances permitted in his hollow, keeping a sharp look-out on the banks of the stream at the point where he had entered the water.

Presently a large animal of a greyish-brown hue, running with nose to the ground, came into view round the trees upon the bank he had lately quitted. It stopped, threw up its head, and glanced about, then put its nose down again and went on to the water. After stopping a moment to drink, it began running to and fro, sniffing the ground and whimpering, much as would a dog that had lost the scent, but stopping now and again to utter a loud roar. In a minute or two it was joined by first one and then another of its companions, who all in turn went through a similar performance, until there were more than a dozen large beasts, evidently of the puma tribe, who ran to and fro, or climbed into and thoroughly searched the adjacent trees, evidently seeking for his broken trail, but baffled by his having entered the water.

Some of these animals were almost white, others were streaked with greyish markings upon a fawn ground, while others, again, were of the uniform colour that one generally associates with the puma. All, however, were unusually large, fine-grown specimens. Evidently they were some special strain, bred and trained for hunting purposes as are foxhounds in England.

Into the midst of this roaring, growling, howling pack, there now stepped a tall commanding figure, who cracked a long whip, driving them from him right and left. He stayed perhaps two or three minutes, looking intently up and down the stream and scanning the banks, and the keen glance he cast at the little island and its single tree, was longer and more searching than Leslie altogether liked.

However, it gave the latter the opportunity of observing the stranger, and he peered at him, as well as he could through the intervening leaves and branches, with a lively curiosity that grew in interest the longer he looked. He saw before him a white man with a tanned and wrinkled visage, somewhat old—for he had grizzled hair and beard—yet tall and stalwart as a sturdy giant, and exhibiting, in his every movement and attitude, evidence of strength and great muscular development. There was, moreover, an easy grace in the swing of his limbs, and in each separate pose, that called up in the mind of the unseen watcher feelings of ungrudging admiration, causing him to wonder who the stranger could be. Then some Indians came to the waterside, all of whom, in turn, looked searchingly at every foot of the banks and at the mango tree; but in the end they all turned and disappeared in the direction from which they had come, calling off the noisy pack and driving them before them as they went.

For some little time Leslie could hear the party, though none of them came again into sight; but eventually the sounds grew fainter, and finally died away.

Then he took out his pipe, lighted it, and fell into a reverie, going over in his mind his strange meeting with "the Lady of the Mountain," his thoughts running at one moment upon her enchanting beauty, and the next upon the purport of the warning words she had uttered.

CHAPTER XIII

A LETTER FROM BERYL

IT WAS WELL on into the afternoon when Leslie drew near to the camp. Just before he got in sight of the ridge upon which it was placed, he came upon Arnold, who was evidently on the look-out for him. At the first glance, and before a word had been said, he saw that his chum had something of importance to communicate. His listless manner of the morning had given place to what was almost gaiety by comparison. His face had in it a light such as Gordon had not seen for a long time, and he rushed forward with eagerness to meet him.

"Where have you been, Gordon?" he began. "I've been hunting around, first in one direction and then in another, and wondering what had become of you."

"Why, what's up?" Leslie asked, quietly. "You did not seem so particularly anxious, when I left you this morning, to have me back soon. I thought you were rather glad to get rid of me."

"Such news, Gordon! Guess!"

But Gordon only shook his head. "I'm not good at guess-work," he returned. "But I'll guess that your news is not more important than mine. I've met with a most surprising adventure. When I tell you—"

"Never mind your adventure now, old man. See what I have here!" And he held a sheet of paper up in the air. "A letter from Beryl!"

"Sakes alive! A letter!" exclaimed Gordon.

"Yes! And from Beryl! She is well, and writes quite cheerfully.

Says, too, that she is told our journey is nearly over and that she may expect to see me very shortly!"

Arnold poured all this out volubly, fluttering the letter in his hand as he did so, as though he were shaking a sort of trophy. He could scarcely stand still, and seemed ready to dance with excitement.

"Sit down, and I will read you what she says," Arnold continued, and was about to seat himself upon the greensward when his companion stopped him.

"Let us walk a little farther away," Gordon advised. "If walls have ears, so, sometimes, have trees, and bushes, and shrubs."

He led the way out on to a grassy expanse where, at a distance of a few hundred yards, was a small clump of two or three trees standing alone. Having carefully inspected the upper branches of these trees, to make quite sure that no lurking listener was concealed in them, he seated himself at their feet on the shady side, and motioned to Arnold—who had regarded his manoeuvres with impatience, and some wondering surprise—to do the same.

"I think this will be safe," Leslie observed. "I have had an object lesson to-day, teaching how easy it is to hide in an innocent-looking tree. Now, old fellow, tell me all about it."

"Captain Jim gave me this letter about two hours ago. He said an Indian had brought it, and was waiting for an answer. After I had read it, I scribbled a few lines on a sheet or two of paper, as I was told the messenger was in a hurry, and sent him back with it. Now listen. I will tell you what Beryl says."

He then proceeded to read extracts, picking out such parts here and there as he thought likely to interest his listener. The letter was a long one, and was, in places, a little prolix and disjointed, being interspersed with a great deal that was natural enough in the circumstances, and quite usual in communications between lovers, but hardly interesting to a third party. Consequently the reader would break off abruptly now and again, in the midst of a passage, and then take up a fresh paragraph, which rather spoiled the general effect and produced the impression of a somewhat incoherent epistle. But it was full of matter that they were glad to hear.

Beryl began by saying that Don Lorenzo had promised, on his honour, that her missive should not be read either by himself or others. She was to seal it up securely, and it should remain absolutely secret to everyone until it passed into Arnold's hands. So, she said, she was able to write freely; but it was easy, reading between the lines, to perceive that she had not been able to altogether overcome her doubt as to this point, and had consequently, notwithstanding her declaration of confidence in Lorenzo's assurance, exercised a certain amount of cautious reserve.

That being allowed for, as regards a few points here and there, it was nevertheless clear that she felt she could write freely upon others, and did so, apparently in the best of spirits. She confirmed, in every respect, the truth of the messages which Lorenzo had from time to time sent to Neville, as to his having done everything in his power to lessen the inconveniences and discomforts of the journey. As to these points the writer said:

"I am bound, in fairness to Don Lorenzo, to tell you that he has done everything humanly possible to make our journey as comfortable as circumstances would allow. I see I have written 'humanly'; I think I ought almost to say that much that he has done for us would rather appear 'superhuman' to ordinary people. I am sure it would to me, except for the many ways in which I had already been prepared to be astonished at nothing that this wonderful magician does. His inventiveness and ingenuity seem absolutely unlimited; and they are exhibited daily in little things as well as great. Thus we have suffered scarcely at all from the heat. Our tents have been as cool, both by day and night, as though we were travelling in England. We have all kinds of luxuries, even to ices and soda-water; and we have no walking, except now and again by way of a change. We ride on pack animals in a sort of miniature howdah, so ingeniously constructed that the motion is deliciously easy. We have been wonderfully free, too,

from mosquitoes, sandflies, 'jiggers,' and the rest of the numerous army of little torments which abound in this land where,
according to Sydney Smith of blessed memory, everything with
life in it 'bites, or stings, or teases.' We have seen no snakes—my
special horror—and only one big spider, auntie is charmed with
the 'holiday,' as she calls it, and has assumed quite a jaunty and
juvenile air, as compared with her former usual sedate demeanour.

"... We are both in good health, and have been all the time;
our jailer—as auntie sometimes playfully calls the Don—has
really been most gentlemanly, and I cannot say that—putting
aside his one astonishing act—bringing us away in the manner
he did—we have had anything whatever to complain of. And
at most frequent intervals—almost every day or so, in fact—
he has given me news of you, telling me exactly how you were
getting on, and reporting as to your health and the progress of
your journey.

"... I cannot write exactly all I feel, or give you full details of
everything that has taken place. Nor can I, of course, repeat at
length all the conversations and arguments I have had with this
most mysterious, most incomprehensible man. I cannot pretend
that I understand him now any more than ever I did, but may
go so far as to admit that I like him a little better. Or, let me put
it another way, and say that I do not dislike him or distrust him
quite so much. He has certainly softened somewhat, and altered
a little in his bearing and perhaps I should like him still more
were it not that he professes such strange dogmas. He holds
beliefs that are repugnant to my very nature, and seems to have
aspirations and expectations which, to my mind, are incompat-
ible with any truly reverent ideas of religion, of heaven, of our
future existence, or of a great, beneficent, overruling Creator.
He seems to hanker and hunger after earthly power and domi-
nation, talks vaguely, but with evident enthusiasm, of a near
future in which he is to be a sort of Lord of the Earth, another
Alexander, Caesar, or Napoleon; but greater than any of them.
And in these dreams he persists in mixing *you* up, declaring that

you are to be 'his brother lord,' and so on. Still more curiously, when, on one occasion, I ventured to remind him that life is but short at the most, and that all these wonders, even were they to come true, would be but transient glories, passing away like a brief dream, he smiled indulgently, as though I were a child who did not know what the was talking about, and replied, 'If that were indeed so, then I admit the end would not be worth the trouble for the space of an ordinary life. But you do not under-stand'—and there he broke off and walked away as though he were afraid he might be led into saying more than he intended. What can he mean? Is he a modern example of that visionary band, the alchemists of old—an-up-to-date, twentieth-century alchemist—who believes he can find, or has already discovered, the grand Elixir, the secret of perpetual life? Or is he... But I may not say here, perhaps, all that is in my mind.

"... Well, we are told that our journey is near its end; and that I shall soon see you again. How strange it will seem!... At least we shall be together, and can help and advise and support one another.... But, whate'er betides, we are in the hands of One greater than this latter-day enchanter. I do not fear; I keep my faith and my hope firmly fixed where they have ever been. Be firm also, dear heart, for be sure that I am steadfast, even as I know you would wish me to be."

"It is a brave, courageous, cheering letter; one such as could only come from a good, true woman," was Leslie's comment at the end. "I fear, however, that she has more misgiving—that she really feels more anxious—than she there cares to admit. In any case, it is the letter of a plucky little woman."

"Yes, Gordon, she is all that and more," Neville assented, thoughtfully. "Her letter does not throw much light upon the future, but it is such a relief to know, from her own statement, that she is well and in fairly good spirits. It has cheered me up more than I can give you any idea of."

Much talk naturally followed upon the subject of this letter, Arnold, apparently, never tiring of discussing it and re-reading it. He seemed to have quite forgotten what his friend had said about having met with an adventure. At any rate, he showed no curiosity to hear the particulars, and this gave Gordon time to consider how much or how little he should tell him of what had taken place.

In particular, he hesitated to repeat what his new acquaintance, the "Lady of the Mountain," had said about Lorenzo. It seemed cruel, now, at the very moment when Arnold was in better spirits than had been the case at any time since they left England, to raise up again in his mind those grim spectres of doubt and anxiety which Beryl's letter had temporarily laid to rest. And, after all, he asked himself, was it worth while, was it necessary, in view of the very vague and shadowy nature of the information that had been given him? What was there to go upon as matters stood? Merely that this young lady knew Lorenzo and disliked him, even as did Beryl; and that her Indian attendants regarded him with awe and superstitious dread, and had made for themselves a fantastic and meaningless interpretation of his true name! What was there, in all this, of reliable evidence? Very little, Leslie persuaded himself; and he finally decided not to refer, for the present, to that part of his experiences.

Thus it came about that when, after several attempts, he succeeded in securing Arnold's attention to his story, he told him nothing of what he had learned concerning Lorenzo, beyond the fact that his true name was Lyostrah, and that he was an occasional visitor at the dwelling-place of the people who lived upon the "haunted mountain."

Of Rhelma's warnings he said no word.

"At any rate, for their stories about this mountain the native chaps seem to have had more foundation than is usually the case with them," was Arnold's comment—"there actually *is* a white puma, and a fair lady to boot! It is wonderful, though, to meet with anyone like that living in such a wilderness. It is not so very surprising that the fanciful Indians should invent weird tales about it all. And what a quaint idea to have a pack of trained pumas to hunt with; I should like to see a good hunt of that sort Fancy hunting with animals that can climb into every tree and search it thoroughly for your game! It gives one a new idea as to sport and its possibilities, but what an awful thing to be hunted by such a pack! I should like to see such a hunt; that is, if one could look on in safety."

"The puma is a singular creature, a bit of a puzzle," Leslie observed, thoughtfully. "Out on the pampas in La Plata the Gauchos have a most curious appellation for it, they call it 'Amigo del Cristiano'—the friend of man—and believe that it has a mysterious sympathy with man, so that it not only never attacks human beings itself, but will even defend them when they are wounded, unarmed, or otherwise helpless, against other wild animals, even against the powerful and dreaded jaguar. They declare that there is no authenticated instance in that country of a puma having attacked man, woman, or child, by day or by night; and they have many stories and legends of wounded men lying out in the forest at night having been watched over and protected by pumas.* And they always act upon this belief when camping out at night, by never troubling to light fires to keep off wild animals, if they have reason to believe that pumas are about. Yet is the puma most ferocious and bloodthirsty in its dealings with all other animals. From all which one can readily understand that it might be comparatively easy to tame it and so train it as to develop its hunting instincts to the best advantage in the service of its master."

When the two came to discuss the question of the rendez-vous that had been appointed for the next day but one, Arnold showed himself so dubious about it, that a somewhat warm discussion took place.

"It will never do to trust yourself alone amongst this strange lot," Arnold argued. "Of course, I shall come too."

"But I was expressly warned that one of us must stay to look after the camp, and, in particular, to see that I am not watched

---

* This remarkable characteristic of the South American puma is described at considerable length by Mr W.H. Hudson in his fascinating work, "The Naturalist in La Plata." He refers to it as "the mysterious, gentle instinct of a most ungentle species."

and followed by any of the Indians of our party," Gordon pointed out.

"It is easy to see that that may be put forward as a means of trapping you the more easily. This white woman—white witch, the Indians call her—may be in league with some enemies, some hostile tribe of Indians, who may have their own reasons for wishing to secure one of us as a prisoner. She is a stranger; we know nothing of her, and—"

But this Gordon would not listen to. He broke out into such a warm defence of the fair stranger, declaring that he would trust her with his life, and asserting that "anyone could see, at a glance, that she was in every respect trustworthy, and altogether above suspicion," with so much more to the same effect, that presently Arnold, after staring for some time in the greatest surprise, ended by bursting into laughter.

Then Leslie pulled up abruptly, and, greatly offended, demanded of his chum what he was laughing at.

"Why," Arnold returned, laughing more heartily than ever, as he noted his companion's highly indignant manner, "I am laughing because—I—really do believe you have fallen in love."

At this astonishing suggestion, Gordon—who would scarcely have felt more surprised and indignant if he had been seriously told he was an escaped lunatic—got up and stalked off in high dudgeon towards the camp, followed at a little distance by the still laughing and unrepentant Neville.

CHAPTER XIV

MANZONI

ON THE SECOND day after the adventure recorded in the last chapter, Leslie found himself again in the wood where his meeting with the fair unknown had taken place.

Nothing further of note had happened meantime to the two travellers. Captain Jim, the leader of their Indians, had informed them that their stay in their present halting-place was likely to extend over some days more. There was nothing, therefore, to prevent Leslie from keeping the appointment he had made save certain natural doubts and objections to his venturing alone, put forward by his friend, and these he over-ruled. He pointed out that he had been expressly enjoined to keep the matter a secret from the rest of their party; and to do this it was obviously necessary that Arnold should remain in camp to keep the Indians together, and see, as far as possible, that they did not follow him. And in this course Arnold finally concurred.

So Leslie had stolen out just before dawn, purposely taking a very roundabout route, and adopting every possible precaution his experience and ingenuity could suggest to make sure that he was not being followed. And when he had gained the wood, and entered upon the track beside the little stream, he congratulated himself upon having made absolutely certain that his movements had been unobserved.

As he arrived at the edge of the clearing for which he was bound, he paused a moment to look through the bushes, and saw a tall figure just entering the glade from the other side.

He recognised the man he had seen on the river bank amongst the throng of noisy animals, and at once stepped out and advanced towards him. They met almost upon the spot where the puma and her mistress had been lying; and the stranger was the first to speak.

"You, young sir, are, I presume, the one my daughter desired me to meet here, the one who gave his name, if I remember aright, as Leslie—Gordon Leslie?" And as Gordon made an affirmative gesture, the speaker proceeded, "Allow me to express my thanks for the services you rendered to my daughter, and the courtesy she met with at your hands."

He spoke with an old-fashioned, old-world sort of accent, but his voice was clear and sonorous, and Gordon thought it peculiarly musical and pleasing.

"Rather, sir," he answered, smiling, "you should say, I think, the services I was desirous of rendering. I was very anxious, I assure you, to do something to assist the young lady in her painful and unpleasant situation; but it seemed that all I could do was to keep her company for a little while, until she heard you in the distance, and knew that stronger aid was at hand. Then she dismissed me, and bade me disappear promptly, else I should have remained to meet you, to see whether I could not really be of some assistance."

"Ay, ay. Just so, just so," the other returned, quietly. "Still, you found time to make a good impression on my daughter, else she would not so have urged me to come to meet you to see if I can be of service to you in turn."

During this brief colloquy, the stranger had been eyeing the young man with a keen, searching glance that had in it, at first, something of doubt and sternness, mixed with considerable hauteur. But gradually this relaxed, as he noted the frank, open look that met him in return, and marked the manly bearing of the young Englishman. By degrees it softened still further into an expression of friendly interest.

Meanwhile, Gordon, on his side, was regarding the stranger

with close attention. He had been curiously attracted by this man when he had first seen him, imperfect as his view of him had then been. An indefinite something in the man's carriage had struck him; and now that he could observe him more clearly, his first impressions were not only strengthened and deepened, but they began to take more definite shape.

All that he now saw and noted increased both his liking and his interest, and even roused his admiration. For he thought he had never seen a more handsome figure, or met with a being so thoroughly the personification of royal dignity and manly power. But for the grizzled hair and beard, and the deep lines of the face, one would have supposed him to be in the very prime of life. It was easy to see that he was still full of vigour, for every movement, every pose, was suggestive of latent energy and strength. His head and features were noble, and his eyes large, bright, and piercing; their very glance commanded respect, and at the same time inspired confidence. There shone in their depths, not merely great dignity and high courage, but a look, that could not be mistaken, of kindly, human sympathy. The face that was so lined seemed to bear the mark of suffering rather than of age; but it was a suffering that had left as its heritage, not sourness, but fellow-feeling for others.

And while he gazed upon him, Gordon could not help, somehow, thinking of the man who had been the cause of their long journey—the mysterious Lorenzo.

As the image of the latter rose in his mind, Gordon, at first wondering why it should just then present itself, was conscious of a certain vague resemblance between the two. Yet even as he tried to discern wherein the similarity lay, the likeness, if there were any, eluded him and vanished. Certainly, the two were alike in this, that they were each remarkably handsome specimens of manly form and beauty, allowing, of course, for the difference of age. But they were not alike in features or in build, so far as he could perceive; and still more did they differ in the "impression" that each produced upon his consciousness. Lorenzo's fine features excited admiration, indeed; but their general expression was proud, haughty, and unsympathetic. And at times, as has been said, there lurked in the eyes and the corners of the delicately-chiselled mouth that subtle suggestion of hardness and cruelty, that was, perhaps, felt, rather than actually expressed. But in the face of the man before him, Gordon could clearly read that which filled him at once with trust and faith. Indeed, the feeling passed through his mind that he would rather trust himself to this man, even if he were angry, than to Lorenzo in his best humour. And yet—through it all—there was that shadowy, elusive likeness which made itself felt for a second, every now and then, but always vanished the moment he tried to seize it so as to identify it.

"I hope, sir," said Gordon, at the end of a brief pause, "that the young lady's hurt is not serious, and that she is better."

The stranger bowed his head, with an air of courtly grace, as he made answer:

"Thank you; she is already nearly well. In these parts we have learned to so treat a sprain that its effects very quickly pass off. Tell me, have you taken any precautions against your being followed?"

"I did all I could, and I have made endeavours in several ways to make sure, on my way here, that no one was following me. I think, from the care and precaution I have observed, that no one knows of my coming here, save, of course, my chum, Mr Neville."

"We had better make sure. I understand my daughter told you my name—Manzoni—and you also heard from her of our troop of hunting pumas."

"I saw—" Gordon began, and then suddenly checked himself.

"Ah, you saw one; Rhelma's—a white one. That is my daughter's particular pet; but we have many others. You will not, then, be afraid to be amongst them if I promise you they will not harm you?"

Without waiting for Gordon's reply, the speaker put a whistle to his lips and blew a shrill blast upon it. Immediately the whole forest around seemed to be alive with wild beasts, if one might judge by the cries that broke forth. Roars, growls, squeals, and snarls burst out on all sides of them—so it seemed to the amazed listener—and then, through the bushes, there sprang into the clearing the troop of pumas he had seen two days before. Leaping, bounding, tumbling over one another in their eagerness, came the great animals, like a pack of yelping, boisterous dogs, eager to crowd round their master, and receive a caress, or a pat, or a word of recognition. Of Gordon—to his great relief, be it said—they took scarcely any notice; all their attention was centred upon their master. Gradually the din died down, and the animals stood around, expectantly awaiting the signal that should indicate what was required of them.

Behind them came a dozen Indians who took up positions close by, evidently also awaiting orders.

To the latter Manzoni spoke a few words in some strange language which Gordon did not understand. Then he waved his hand.

In an instant all had silently disappeared! Gordon gazed round in bewilderment. So quickly had they gone that he had had no time to do more than just catch sight of a few tails disappearing into the bushes. There was no sound, no noise, not so much as the crackling of a dry stick to be heard. The whole noisy troop had become as quiet as a cat stalking a mouse, and vanished into the wood without making a single sound to betray their whereabouts or their movements.

Gordon turned to Manzoni, and was about to express his admiration and surprise, when there came from a distance the sound of a faint whimper, followed by a deep growl and then a loud roar.

"Hark!" Manzoni exclaimed, in low tones, holding up his hand. "That's Tresca. He's caught someone. Come with me."

He led the way through into the wood, and in a few moments Gordon found himself in the path along which he had come. After traversing this for a short distance, they came to a place where it turned abruptly and then opened out somewhat, and here, in a small clearing, there was an immense tree, the branches of which sprang out from the stem only a few feet from the ground. At the foot of the tree a large, greyish-white puma was crouched, his gleaming eyes glaring up into the thick foliage. At that moment four or five Indians of their party, and a couple more pumas, came stealing, noiselessly as shadows, out of the surrounding dense wood.

Then Manzoni called out in a loud, commanding voice, as though addressing someone concealed in the tree. What he said Gordon could not understand, but almost immediately a voice above cried out an answer; there was a rustling sound, and down the trunk of the tree, one after the other, there came three strange Indians. Each, as he touched the ground, threw himself upon his knees and bowed his head till it nearly touched the earth, gabbling all the time something which Gordon could not interpret. Manzoni had called off the pumas by a wave of the hand, and addressing the kneeling men in stem accents, signed to his Indian followers. These stepped forward at once, and tightly bound the arms of the strangers, and also tied their feet and legs in such a way that they could walk but not run. Then, at a sign from their master, the pumas bounded up the tree and explored every branch, high and low, to make sure that there was no one else concealed there. But they came down after awhile, one by one, without having made any further discovery. Manzoni then led the whole party back to their starting-place.

"You thought you had made sure that you were not followed," he observed, to Leslie. "But you see you were mistaken."

"Why—were these Indians following me? I do not know them. They are not any of our party."

"No; none of your Indians would venture into this wood. These are another lot sent specially to watch you and report. But never mind about that now. We have caught them; that is the main thing."

Leslie felt not a little mortified at this proof that all his precautions against being watched had been in vain. The incident furnished an illustration of the superior craft of the Indian in all that appertains to hunting. However, he only asked:

"What are you going to do with them?"

"Keep them as prisoners, for the present, at any rate. Later on—we shall see. In this case spying upon you means spying upon me, and those who spy upon me very seldom do it a second time. We must wait a little while here to see if there are any more discoveries, though I do not suppose there will be. My animals will hunt out every corner, on the ground, in the ground, and above the ground."

"They work admirably! They seem to be wonderfully trained! But how is it they were so quiet? They made no sound over their work, whereas, the other day, I heard them a long way off."

"Yes; noise then did not matter; indeed, it was rather an advantage in the quest in which we were engaged. To-day we had Indians to deal with, and the conditions were different. It depends upon what game is afoot."

"How was it the animals did not mount the tree after the Indians concealed there?"

"They never touch a human being. When they come upon a stranger they merely stand guard over him till we come up. That is, unless he attempts to run away. In that case they would knock him over and hold him down; but still without hurting him."

During a somewhat protracted halt which followed, Gordon asked many more questions and learned a good deal more about the "lions," * as he called them, and their methods of hunting. He also began tentatively to make friends with some of them, and was agreeably surprised to find how tame and friendly and playful they showed themselves to be.

After a time the rest of the party came straggling back, all empty-handed, and reporting that there was no trace of any further spies.

"Now we can go. I want you to accompany me home,"

---

* As is generally well known, the puma is called "the American lion." In different parts it bears slightly different distinctive titles, as "the forest lion," "the mountain lion," etc.

Manzoni explained to Gordon. "It is some distance, and you will have to stay all night. Are you willing to trust yourself with strangers?"

"I am quite ready to trust myself with you," he said, heartily.

"Then come along," was the answer. "You will not regret it."

CHAPTER XV

A MYSTERIOUS PLANT

THE JOURNEY ROUND the mountain to Manzoni's home proved to be longer than Leslie had expected. The route taken was circuitous, seemed to zig-zag a good deal, and, in places, involved some rather stiff climbing.

Towards the afternoon they reached a place about half-way up the hill, but on the opposite side from that from which they had started. Here they came to a sort of terrace or tableland that ran back, as it were, towards the centre of the mountain.

At intervals on their way up, Gordon had caught views of the surrounding country of so enchanting a character that he would fain have lingered awhile to gaze upon them. But Manzoni, while smiling indulgently at his display of admiration, had hurried him on, saying that the time at their disposal was not too much for what they had to do. When, however, they reached this terrace, there was such a glorious panorama spread out at their feet, that Leslie could scarcely bring himself to turn from it to follow the road, which now led them away between over-hanging, gloomy-looking rocks into a retired valley shut in on ail sides by frowning precipices. Passing through this, and leaving it by an extremely narrow outlet, they came to yet another valley, or plain, of considerable extent, with a stream of water running through it that came down in a great fall from rocky heights at the farther end.

Here Gordon was surprised to see a number of huts, and what at first sight seemed to be many large and imposing buildings;

these, however, as they came up to them, turned out to be but ruins. All, that is, save one, which had been so far restored as to form a very comfortable-looking residence. This, it turned out, was the house in which Manzoni and his daughter resided; and the huts were those of his Indian followers.

Manzoni led the way through a doorway, so exquisitely carved that it would have been looked upon with wonder and admiration by any European antiquarian, into a large hall similarly decorated. Here he opened another door, and ushered his guest into a roomy apartment, where he found the young lady of the glade reclining on a couch, and busily engaged in some kind of sewing work.

On seeing who had entered, she sat up and extended her hand.

"Welcome to our mountain home," she said, with a winning smile. "I am glad indeed that my father has been good enough to bring you. I had some fears about it, for"—here she glanced at her parent with a roguish smile—"he does not encourage strangers. And he can be a terrible ogre, when he chooses, to everybody—except myself."

Manzoni went up to her, and kissed her with evident affection.

"Your wish went a good way in deciding me," he said, gravely. "Our young friend's own personality did the rest."

There was further talk while an Indian attendant prepared the table for a meal, and then, for a few moments, Manzoni and his daughter engaged in a chat between themselves upon some matters appertaining to their domestic concerns; which gave Leslie an opportunity of looking at his surroundings.

It was a large room, furnished amply and comfortably, albeit the furniture was plain and evidently old. Still, there was a general air of homeliness about it, strange, indeed, in such a situation. But the decorations of the apartment were very curious and interesting. There were frescoes, still quite vivid in their colouring, and in good preservation as to general details; but they represented scenes and people different to anything he had ever before seen, and were descriptive, apparently, of a past age unknown to modern research. And, amongst the furniture, or hung against the walls, he noted many articles of curious and unfamiliar shape, whereof he could not guess the use or the meaning, unless they were old relics hung or placed about as one would ancient weapons, armour, and such-like curios.

There was, indeed, everywhere around him an odd combination of the known and the unknown, of the bizarre and the commonplace, such as raised in his mind feelings of the most vivid wonder and curiosity.

And these words—let it here be said—would fairly describe his state of mind during the whole time that his visit lasted. Turn which way he would, as his host conducted him round his domains, whether he looked upon his right hand or upon his left, there was ever to be seen "something new and strange," something to puzzle and mystify him, until he grew weary and a little ashamed of asking questions, and ended by passing without comment all except what his host chose voluntarily to explain.

For these reasons it is not possible, nor would it be to the purpose, to give here a full account of all that took place at this—to Leslie—memorable visit It will suffice to relate only those matters and incidents which are material to the elucidation of our story.

Manzoni, when he had offered his guest refreshment—very welcome after the labour of the ascent,—showed him the extent of the settlement, the Indians' huts, the land they had under cultivation, the flocks and herds they kept to supply their needs, and what he called his menagerie, a collection of cages in which were kept the troop of pumas and many other animals. On all sides there were signs that the present inhabitants were not the first occupiers. Many ancient ruins—some of magnificent proportions and great extent—showed that a large and flourishing city must have existed there at some time in the distant past. But speculations as to who or what they were, were crowded out of Leslie's mind by the interest aroused by the present.

In particular, his attention was attracted towards one of the slopes which shut in the north side of the valley. A portion of this slope, several acres in extent, was glistening and sparkling just as ripples upon water glisten and shimmer in the sun's rays. The effect was dazzling, and puzzling to the observer, who strove in vain to account for the phenomenon. The whole shining mass seemed to be in motion, quivering, trembling, and swaying, yet he could not in any wise distinguish *what* it was that was thus moving; and he turned at last a perplexed look of inquiry upon his companion.

"What you see yonder," Manzoni explained, interpreting his look, "is a small plantation of what I consider the most wonderful plant in the world. It comes from the region towards which you are journeying, and has never been grown anywhere else, until I accidentally discovered that it could be cultivated successfully in the soil of this valley. Its foliage is unique in the botanical world, each leaf being like burnished gold on the upper side and polished silver underneath. But the leaves are extremely fine and delicate—resembling, indeed, rather the tracery of the most exquisite lace-work than ordinary foliage—and they are ever quivering and shivering with a motion of their own, which produces the curious effect you see."

"What is its name?" Leslie asked.

"*We* call it Mylondos, which is a word signifying lightning, electric energy, life itself; just as you would say 'Electricity is the Life.' The exact translation of the name is a little difficult. It might be rendered 'lightning plant;' or 'plant,' or 'tree,' of life. The only botanical product I have ever heard of that can in any way be compared with it is the so-called 'electric plant' of India. You may have heard of that?"

"Yes; I remember reading a description in the English publication called *Nature.*" *

---

* The following is the description of this plant which appeared in *Nature:* "The hand which breaks a leaf from it receives immediately a shock equal to that which is produced by the conductor of an induction coil. At a distance of eighteen feet a magnetic needle is affected by it, and it will become deranged if brought near. The energy of this singu-

"Well, that might be termed a sort of distant cousin to this one. But it would be but a very distant relation."

As they approached the plantation Leslie became aware of a peculiar impression that made itself felt throughout his whole body. Every muscle, every nerve, began to tingle with a feeling analogous to what is known as 'needles and pins'; and as they drew nearer he felt as though a mild current were being passed through his body from an electric battery. Yet was there a something beyond; a curious sensation as of increased strength accompanied by a feeling of elation. When they reached the nearest specimen he perceived that the leaves were slender as the finest gold and silver wire, and from their points minute sparks played constantly in and out, giving off the while a sharp crackling sound which, in the mass, swelled into a considerable volume of noise.

"It is like a burning bush that is not consumed," Leslie presently said, in astonishment. "Is it safe to touch it?"

"It depends upon the amount of electricity your system can bear," was the answer. "It will give you a sharp shock, but the strength varies from one hour to another, and is much stronger at night than by day, and in the morning than in the afternoon. Also, if you touch it, it is better to select an isolated specimen; otherwise you receive the combined force of several."

"On consideration, I think I will leave it alone," Leslie decided.

"Perhaps it is wiser to do so," Manzoni returned, with a scarcely perceptible smile. "I shall have more to tell you about this tree; you shall hear it later. By the way, have you ever been on the Andes?"

"Oh yes. And I expect I can guess what you are thinking of—the curious electrical condition people sometimes get into there at the higher altitudes. I have seen a man literally ablaze with light, as though he were on fire all over the surface of his

_____

lar influence varies with the hour of the day.... One never by any chance sees a bird or insect alight on the electric plant. An instinct seems to warm them that they would find sudden death."

body. And when I touched him—or rather, when I was about to do so, and before I actually touched him—a long spark shot out from him to me and gave me a shock like a miniature flash of lightning. I was told that such phenomena are quite common in those parts."

"Yes; that is so. And the same thing obtains here, in the vicinity of these trees. Some people, when brought into their neighbourhood, seem to become gradually impregnated, as it were, with the electric fluid, and often they can throw off sparks and flashes exactly as you have described. But I will explain more to you this evening."

When they returned to the house and re-entered the room in which he had seen Rhelma, Leslie found that she had disappeared. Manzoni noted the look that he cast round the apartment, and answered his unspoken thought:

"My daughter will rejoin us later on," he observed. "I wish you now to give me a full account of the events which have brought you into this country. Please be exact, and tell me every detail you can remember. And be sure that my object in asking for the information is not idle curiosity. I am disposed to do what I can to advise, and, if need be, assist you."

Thus encouraged, Leslie entered upon a detailed narrative of all that had occurred from his first meeting with the man who called himself Don Lorenzo, down to the letter received two days previously from Miss Atherton. He described minutely everything that had taken place at the last interview between Lorenzo and Arnold. For Neville had naturally considered that what had since occurred had entirely released him from the conditional pledge of secrecy which he had been asked to give. Everything that had taken place, therefore, had been told to Leslie, and had been discussed between them over and over again.

Manzoni listened with grave attention, nodding his head from time to time, but making no remark, save to put a brief query, here and there, to elucidate some point that was not quite clear to him.

Before the story was finished evening had come on, and it had grown dark. Manzoni bad then interrupted his guest for a few moments, while he went to a corner of the room and touched a switch, which immediately flooded the place with a brilliant light.

When, finally, everything had been told that Leslie could recall, and he had come to the end of his narrative, his host still made no comment, but sat for some time silent and absorbed, as though in deep reflection.

Suddenly he rose, and saying, abruptly, "Come with me," led the way out of the house.

Outside, as Leslie quickly became aware, no lantern was required to guide their steps. There was light enough to see fairly well just around them, for, farther away, the sky was lighted up in lurid fashion as from the glare of a large fire. Following his host for a short distance, they came, all at once, in view of the cause of this illumination: the whole of one side of the valley seemed to be on fire.

"What is it?" Leslie asked, in surprise. "Has the grass caught fire?" Yet he perceived, even ere he had spoken the question, that such an ordinary cause would by no means explain what he saw before him.

"It is no fire," Manzoni answered, quietly. "It is but the plantation of 'Mylondos' that you saw by daylight. This is its normal aspect when seen at night."

As they came close to it Leslie's wonder increased every moment. Innumerable little flashes like mimic lightnings were darting to and fro in all directions amongst the foliage, which everywhere kept up the same ceaseless swaying and shivering movement that he had seen by daylight, giving now the aspect of a restless, rolling sea of fire. Yet he noticed that there was little or no heat given off; it was possible to stand close to it without becoming sensible of any additional warmth. But always there was that feeling of a current from an electrical or galvanic battery pervading every muscle and nerve of his body.

"You will see, if you look closely," Manzoni observed, "that the sparks given off are of two colours, violet and red."

"Yes; I can see that. What does it signify?"

"The violet ray is that usually exhibited by what you term the electric light; but the red ray is something entirely unknown to your scientific men. It is not only far more powerful than the violet ray, but has characteristics of its own, as have the so-called X-rays which your savants have lately discovered. But these red rays possess subtle qualities and powers surpassing anything hitherto known or dreamed of. Come now with me into my laboratory, and I will show you some experiments that will probably surprise and interest you more than anything you have yet seen."

CHAPTER XVI

THE RED RAY

RETURNING TO THE house, Leslie's strange host led the way through several wide corridors, and then, across an open court, to a detached structure which stood, dark and gloomy, at a short distance from the main building. Here, drawing forth a key, he unlocked a door, shut it behind them, touched a button on the wall, and immediately bright lights shone out on all sides.

Leslie gazed about him with surprise and interest. He was in an immense hall, so large and so filled with all sorts of queer-looking articles as to remind him, at first sight, of an exhibition. No doubt, as Manzoni had led him to expect, the place was a laboratory. It had all the usual litter of chemical apparatus; queer-shaped glass retorts, metal stands, bottles and jars of many and various sorts, sizes, and colours, being scattered about in most admired confusion. There was also that peculiar smell or mixture of smells well known to all laboratory students. To Leslie most of these were familiar enough, though he felt no small surprise at meeting with them in such a place. But beyond these he again noted many objects which were entirely new to him, and of which he could not conjecture the use. There were mysterious-looking instruments and machines, some with long levers reaching up almost to the domed roof, others with wheels so heavy as to lead him to cast about for engines with which to work them. But he saw nothing that seemed familiar in such a connection until he caught sight of a little electric motor. It was but a small affair—a mere toy—and he wondered somewhat at seeing it there amongst such surroundings. His glance, however, rested on it with a sense almost of relief; it was like the face of a friend seen suddenly and unexpectedly amongst a crowd of uncouth and doubtful-looking strangers.

"Where are your engines to work all these machines?" he asked of Manzoni, who, for answer, pointed to the little motor. "But," Leslie objected, "surely that little thing cannot be of any use for such ponderous machinery as you have here?"

"Strength does not necessarily mean bulk," was the reply. "If a man had the strength of a flea in proportion to his own size, it has been estimated that he could leap something near five hundred feet into the air; and, similarly, if he had the proportionate strength of a limpet, he would be able to lift several tons. The muscle of a flea, therefore, must be capable of exerting a force nearly a hundred times as great as the human muscle. Can you explain that? Can you even say that in the muscle of a flea you have reached finality as regards relative power? May it not be quite possible that something may exist in nature more powerful still?"

"I suppose so," Leslie admitted. "When you put it that way, almost anything may be possible."

"The power exerted by a muscle," Manzoni went on, "depends not so much upon the size of the muscle as upon the nervous force which moves it. That is what we call the 'Will.' Given two men of equal size and equal muscular development, that one will be able to exert the greatest power who has the most nervous force—in other words, the stronger 'Will.' You have heard that a madman will, in an access of insane fury, sometimes exert a strength equal to that of ten or twelve men. And the statement is true; it is not a mere figure of speech. Yet the man's muscles remain the same; it is only the Will force that varies.

"I could interest you here, doubtless, for a long time, explaining to you the meaning and uses of my various mechanical contrivances. But just now I shall confine myself to two or three experiments which are pertinent to the matter we have to keep in view."

"All this reminds me of the interview which my friend Neville had with Lorenzo, and of which I have just given you the particulars," observed Leslie. "Are you, then, another wonderful scientific magician? And, if so, are you a rival or a colleague?"

"You shall know before you leave me. Now, look at this machine. It is a reservoir, so to speak, in which I store up the red ray."

"Analogous, I suppose, to the contrivance we call an electric accumulator?"

"Precisely; but of different construction. You observe I take from it this rod. It is a small accumulator in itself. It has taken up, or absorbed, as it were, a certain amount of the fluid *or* force stored in that machine."

"A rod in pickle, in fact," Leslie could not help suggesting.

It was a sort of wand, about five feet in length, of polished metal of a deep, red-gold hue. At two or three places the metal was covered, for a space of a few inches, with some material that might have been silk tightly bound round it. In handling it, Manzoni put his hand, Leslie noticed, upon one of these covered places.

"Upon the ground before you," Manzoni then said, "are some heavy weights. Try to lift that one to the right."

Leslie essayed the task, and did his utmost, but was only able, by using both hands, to drag the weight a few inches along the floor.

Manzoni went up to the weight and lifted it with ease with one hand; at which Leslie uttered an exclamation of astonishment. But his host went on:

"Take this rod—hold it in your left hand, as I did—so. Good; that is right. Now, try to lift the weight with your right."

But no sooner did Leslie's hand close on the mysterious rod than a most curious sensation came over him. Up his arm and through his body there began to creep a delightful glow, a most agreeable tingling, that brought with it a sense of exquisite exhilaration. It was like a gentle, liquid fire running through his veins and nerves; a feeling as though he had absorbed into his system some wonderful, powerful elixir, that was gradually permeating and exciting, in a most enjoyable fashion, every muscle, every separate fibre of his body. With it there came a great sense of power and irresistible energy. He felt three or four times stronger than before taking the rod into his hand. It seemed a veritable fairy wand, imparting new life and strength to the one who held it.

Then he took up the weight, and swung it easily in one hand.

"It is wonderful! Marvellous!" he cried, in an ecstasy of admiration and astonishment. "Why, I feel a veritable giant! a Hercules!"

"Yet," observed Manzoni, "your muscles are the same as they were a few minutes ago. It is only the nervous power—the 'will-force'—in your body that has been increased. In the madman of whom we spoke just now, a sudden rush of nervous force—or sudden access of Will power—gives to his muscular system a strength ten times greater than it had previously seemed capable of exerting; and if he could but keep up the supply of 'Will,' he would remain always ten times stronger than usual. But he cannot maintain the necessary supply; there is reaction, followed by prostration and proportionate weakness. Here, you will find, there is no reaction, no feeling of exhaustion. So long as that rod continues its supply of 'the Red Ray' to your system, so long will you rejoice in the abnormal strength that the madman exerted. Only here you will be none the worse for it afterwards; on the contrary, you will feel its beneficial effects for some days to come. You see there is no miracle, no magic about it. The explanation is quite simple."

"That is so; but to me it is not the less astonishing," Leslie answered.

He surrendered the wonderful wand to his instructor, and when he had done so was agreeably surprised to find that the virtues it had imparted did not by any means depart with it. They remained behind, inspiring him with feelings, thoughts, ideas, different to anything he had experienced before in his whole life. He found, too, that he could still pick up the great weight, though not so easily as before. His excited comments, however, were cut short by Manzoni, who bade him follow him, and then led the way into another chamber.

Here Leslie could not repress a slight start. The place seemed to be a museum, and was filled with a somewhat gruesome collection of stuffed animals, skeletons, and such like specimens. The change of ideas that the sight of them brought was sudden and somewhat unpleasant. But his conductor proceeded to explain:

"Here you have some frameworks, if one may use the expression, of what were once living creatures. Some are mummified bodies, others articulated skeletons. Those bodies that are mummified are complete in their organisation, as would be the case if they had been but just killed—by drowning or suffocation, let us say. What, then, do they require to give them a semblance of life? Merely nervous force—'Will' force—to move their stiffened muscles. Just as in the anatomical schools the lecturer sometimes, by way of experiment or illustration, makes the limbs of a corpse move by applying to it a galvanic current. Have you ever seen that experiment?"

Leslie made a gesture of repugnance.

"No; I have never seen it; but I know it is often done. I have both heard and read of it."

"But the current that you get from a galvanic battery is not 'the Red Ray,' the true 'Will' force. It is but a poor imitation. See, here is the preserved body of a mouse, and beside it that of a cat. I will touch them with this rod, and you will witness the result."

He touched the mouse with one end of the rod, and almost immediately the creature scurried off as if alive, racing round and round the room as though seeking for an outlet, or for a hole in which to conceal itself. Then he touched the cat, which stretched itself, looked about it, and then, apparently catching sight of the mouse, raced after it, chasing it in and out amongst the contents of the museum.

"I chose the mouse and cat to experiment upon, not only to illustrate what I have been speaking of, but to demonstrate another and still more curious discovery I have made. It is this, that a creature thus vivified behaves itself, I have invariably found, according to its instincts when alive. Thus the cat, you observe, chased the mouse; and the mouse, on its side, ran away from us and sought for a hole in which to hide. Yet the cat does not now require food, and therefore does not want the mouse to eat."

"It does not? Cannot it eat?"

"No. The necessary force for performing its present movements is now derived from the outside; it is not from within, as in the living cat. Therefore, it requires no food; and, the brain being quiescent, there is no sense or will to direct its movements. There is left to it only a vague instinct—which prompts it, in this instance, to chase a mouse. I find it the same in every case. Thus, if I were to touch that preserved jaguar yonder it would chase *us* round the place as the cat did the mouse."

"Then please leave that experiment out," Leslie observed. "I will take your word for it instead."

"Even a skeleton can be acted upon in somewhat similar fashion, though in a lesser degree," Manzoni continued. "Here is an articulated skeleton of an Indian, in which a carefully-planned system of springs takes the place of muscles. It is just as amenable to the action of 'the Red Ray.' Note the effect in this case."

He touched the skeleton with the magic wand, and, to Leslie's horror, it began to move, shuffling about in most ghastly fashion, running to and fro, kneeling down, and making strange motions with its bony arms and hands.

"He was a hunter," Manzoni explained, as quietly as though lecturing upon the most ordinary of subjects, "and his native instinct is directing his actions. He is going through the motions of shooting with a bow and arrow. Why he should do this, or why the cat should chase the mouse, when it no longer requires food, constitutes a curious psychological puzzle—"

But Leslie had hurried away and left him standing alone. The exhibition appealed to him in a different fashion from the purely scientific view which was the one the other evidently took of it. He hastened out of the room; nor did he look behind him to see how the experiments ended. He shuddered, and, for a moment or two, felt quite sick.

Manzoni soon joined him, and conducted him back to the room he had first entered on their arrival at the house in the afternoon.

Here further refreshment was awaiting them, served at a table over which Rhelma presided. Beside her was the white puma, which the girl was affectionately caressing. It was clear she had nearly recovered, for she could now walk fairly well; and her beauty and bright conversation won upon Leslie's heart, and affected him as no woman had ever done before. Ere the evening ended, he was well on his way to being over head and ears in love, though, perhaps, he scarcely realised it himself, and would probably have very indignantly repudiated such an idea had anyone then suggested it to him.

As to Manzoni, he took little or no part in the talk between the two; he scarcely seemed, indeed, to be aware of it, but sat apart, evidently plunged in deep reflections. Yet, now and again, his glance would rest upon his visitor, when he would watch him for a while with a look of keen interest, and then fall again into his reveries.

Eventually, Rhelma bade him good-night, and retired; whereupon Manzoni roused himself from his self-absorption.

"I will now, my friend," he said, "explain to you some further matters with which it is as well you should become acquainted. They constitute a strange story, one of which the great outer world knows and suspects nothing. No word of it has been told before to any being beyond our own circle; nor should I confide it to you now, were it not that I perceive that a crisis in our affairs is approaching. Listen carefully to what I have to tell; and do not ridicule or disbelieve that which may appear to you incredible merely because it is unexpected or unusual. You will have proofs enough and to spare by-and-by."

And with that he proceeded to impart to his visitor the narra-tive given in the next chapter.

CHAPTER XVII

THE STORY OF LYOSTRAH AND THE HIDDEN CITY

"THE ONE YOU know as Don Lorenzo," Manzoni commenced, "belongs to the same race as myself, a people related neither to the Brazilian nor any other modern people, but to one whose origin is lost in the mists of antiquity. Long ages ago they lived and ruled in this continent, and its adjacent islands. Our country was called Myrvonia, and its inhabitants, our ancestors, were a conquering race who had subdued and absorbed first one and then another smaller nation, until their sway extended over the whole continent. That much, however, you have already heard; Lorenzo (or Lyostrah, to give him his true name) said as much in his talk with your friend."

"Then," exclaimed Leslie, in surprise, "Lorenzo—or, rather, Lyostrah—is—"

"A kinsman of mine, you are thinking? Yes; you have rightly inferred. And up to a certain time, now some years ago, we lived together in the closest friendship, fellow-rulers over the small remnant that remains to-day of our ancient race, fellow-workers, fellow-inventors, fellow-seekers after knowledge, fellow-believers in a high destiny that, as we conceived, was reserved for our people in the future history of the world. In those days I had ambition, very much like that which rules Lyostrah to-day; though I do not think, looking back now, that it was ever so great or so deep-seated as his. He has allowed it to take entire possession of his whole being. It is to him life itself. I verily believe that if he were convinced that his dreams were never destined to be realised, he would—well, well, there is no saying what effect it might have upon him. Certainly it would be a terrible, an overwhelming disappointment, and one that, I feel assured, he would not care to survive.

"Our nation, after centuries of rule, fell upon evil times, and gradually lost ground. Little by little they lost a province here, a territory there, until even their original country became over-run by invaders, and little was left to them save the memory of their former glory. They had, however, a fastness in the midst of the almost impenetrable forests (which, then as now, covered so great a portion of this continent) their Royal City, the very birthplace and cradle of their race. Hidden away, much as it is to-day, it had formed the nursery-ground in which they long remained unknown, and from which they burst forth as rulers and conquerors. It was called, as I have said, Myrvonia, and to it were carried, in the time of their triumphs, all the richest and choicest of the splendid spoils of the nations they vanquished. It was, in fact, their Sacred City, their Mecca, and, it may be added, their secret storehouse. It was also their great burying-place. In those days the dead were always embalmed, and with the Myrvonians it was considered a point of honour and of religion to be buried in their Sacred City, in every case in which it was in any way possible. No matter how far away a Myrvonian might be at the time of his death, his family, or his heirs, or friends, regarded it as a solemn duty to send his embalmed body to find a final resting-place in the catacombs of the Sacred City. No question of cost or trouble was ever allowed to stand in the way, at least in the case of those of wealth and position. Doubtless, amongst the poorer classes it could not always be accomplished. It is, however, said that the custom was carried out in the case even of common soldiers who died on the field of battle; the duty, in that case, being religiously undertaken by the State.

"At the same time, this Sacred City was scrupulously reserved for their own citizens. No strangers, no foreigners, were ever allowed to enter it. The nominal capital of the country, the mili-tary and commercial centre, was on the coast. There all the business of the Government of the country and its dependencies was carried on, and to foreigners and citizens not of their race, the Sacred City of Myrvonia was unknown save by repute, and existed, probably, only as a sort of half-mystic, half-real creation. Surrounded by the dense primaeval forest, there was but one road, tradition avers, by which it could be approached, and that was most jealously guarded. When, therefore, a fugitive remnant of this once great people finally took refuge in their mysterious city, very little trouble was required on their part to cover up all traces of the whereabouts of their refuge. One knows how quickly vegetation will spring up in this climate and eliminate all traces of roads that are not purposely kept open; and it is easy, therefore, to understand that the refugees became lost to the rest of the dwellers upon the continent, and that in time their very existence was unsuspected,—by all, that is (perhaps we ought to say), except the wandering Indian tribes of the interior. Amongst these the tradition of the former existence of this wonderful and wealthy hidden city, and a belief in its continued existence, have always survived, even up to the present day."

"Yes," Leslie assented; "that is well known. I must say, however, that I was always very sceptical, and am not a little astonished to hear the truth of the belief so positively and circumstantially asserted."

"You may add, 'and confirmed,' my friend; for I, who talk to you, am one of that race, and was born in that strange old city. And so also was Lyostrah."

"But how, then, have you managed to keep its existence a secret all these years? And why?"

"As to the first query, it has not, as it happens, been very difficult. Practically no serious attempt has been made to explore this particular tract of country by any but the wandering tribes of Indians before mentioned, and them we have easily frightened away."

"Ay, ay, I can understand. Still—why?"

"It has been so commanded to us through hundreds—thousands—of years. Fathers have enjoined it upon the sons, through successive generations, as a religious duty to be strictly enforced until—"

"Until—" Leslie repeated, as the other paused.

"Ah! that is the question. There are traditions, old prophecies, which declare that a time will come when the ancient glories of this people shall be revived, when they will issue forth once more as a conquering nation, subduing everything and everybody that may stand in their way. In that day—so the prophecy runs—two men shall arise who are to jointly rule over the remnant, and lead them forth to victory. Now Lyostrah believes that that time has come, and that he is one of the men marked out by destiny for a mighty ruler."

"And the other? Who, then, was to be the other?" Leslie asked, with an awakened sense of interest.

"He believed it was myself. We were, indeed, both brought up in that belief. Our fathers taught it to us as something that was not merely a possibility, but an actual event that would most certainly occur. And I believed in it also, and worked cordially with Lyostrah, until—"

Manzoni paused and hesitated. His voice had gradually assumed a tone of intense sadness, and his eyes a dreamy, half-vacant expression. He sighed deeply, and passed his hand over his face, as if he would shut out something unpleasant from his view.

Leslie made no comment, but patiently awaited his pleasure.

"Until," he presently resumed, "something—something—came between us. Then I refused to be associated further with him in his plans. We parted, and I came away. I discovered this place—evidently the site of one of our own ancient cities. Here I brought the contents of my workshops and laboratories, and a small tribe of Indians with whom I had made friends; and here I have lived and laboured ever since."

Manzoni stopped, and seemed to have finished. It was clear that for some reason he was deeply affected, and his emotion, and the deep musical tones of his voice, quivering with half-suppressed sadness, greatly impressed his listener.

Leslie also sat silent for some time; then he asked, in a quiet, respectful tone:

"May I ask, sir, what it is you have worked at—are still working for, seeking for?"

"Why do you think I am seeking something?"

"A sort of instinctive idea of mine. Perhaps it was suggested in your voice, in your manner. I think you seek something and have been so far disappointed—deeply disappointed; is it not so, sir?"

Manzoni looked at the young man, with a gaze that strangely impressed him, there was in it such profound, wistful longing.

"My son," he answered, with a kindly, emphasis that sounded almost affectionate, "truly there is something I should like to find before I die; there *were* two things, but I think I have found one. The other is yet to seek; perhaps, one day, you may like to join me in the search."

This was said half as a statement, half interrogatively, but before Leslie could reply, he resumed, speaking now almost mournfully:

"A voice within me tells me that we are drawing near to a crisis in our affairs, and I may have need of one to work with me, even as to-day you stand in need of my advice. I feel inclined to confide more to you than I had at first intended. Tell me, can I trust to your honour?"

The steady eyes, with their strange mixture of commanding dignity and wistful regard, were bent upon Leslie, who answered their appeal with a look which was full of sympathy and manly, honest resolve.

"Indeed, sir," he exclaimed, earnestly, "whatever you confide to me I shall regard as sacred—and as an honour. I feel already more honoured by your confidence than I can find words to tell you."

"So be it," Manzoni answered, with a sigh that seemed to have in it an expression of satisfaction and relief. "If we are to help your friend to free himself and this ill-used young lady from their present entanglement we shall need all our resources, all our brains, all our courage, and, I may add, absolute mutual trust and reliance. Now listen to what I have further to tell:

"Lyostrah and I are both direct descendants of the old dynasty that once reigned over this ancient people. He is, to-day, the hereditary Chief of the Priests, who has always been co-equal with the King, and I am the last representative of their Royal House. That is to say, were there a kingdom to-day to rule over, I should be the king; and though, for many generations, we have dropped the actual title, I am still regarded by the people as their king—or I was so regarded before I seceded from the community."

"One moment, sir," Leslie interrupted. "How many of you are there now left?"

"About five thousand."

"But that amounts, in point of numbers, to nothing at all! What then is the meaning of this Lyostrah's wild dreams—"

"You shall hear—all, at least, that I know. Lyostrah is, then, the Chief Priest, a being looked up to in that simple-minded, old-world community, with reverential awe. He is literally lord of their lives. He is a man of extraordinary capacity, of iron will, and a wonderful worker."

"All that I can well believe."

'And until he got this fixed idea into his mind he was in no wise a man to be feared. *Once* he was good-hearted, and of a kindly, well-disposed nature. *Now* the canker of a restless, boundless ambition has eaten into his heart, or rather, has enveloped it, hardening it, blunting his better instincts until he has become, to-day, a man of remorseless, relentless will, ready to sacrifice anything, anybody, even—if need be—his dearest friends, to the advancement of his soaring ambition.

This change was brought about in a curious way. When we were quite young men, a slight earthquake—the country is subject to earthquakes, I must tell you—a slight shock one day occurred which opened a gap in a rock and revealed an ancient vault, a sort of secret temple. It was of most curious construction, and contained an immense, a fabulous treasure, in the shape of gold and precious stones. But beyond this there was an altar upon which was a gold urn hermetically sealed, which, on being opened, was found to hold merely a packet of seeds and a scroll. The scroll had upon it writing in a language something like our own, yet so unlike that it caused us a great deal of study and guessing before we could make out its message. By dint of perseverance, however, we finally deciphered the meaning. It was to the effect that whoever was Chief Priest at the time of the opening of the vault was to be deemed the legal possessor of the treasure it contained; and, further, he was instructed to sow, in a certain manner, the seeds which had been placed in the urn and from which he would be enabled to rear the true Mylondos, or Plant of Life. Finally, if he employed the virtues of the plant with wisdom and prudence, he would have it in his power to become—well, a very great man. The exact interpretation of the last words is doubtful; one may read them two or three ways. They may be rendered either as 'the greatest man the world has ever known,' or 'the greatest benefactor to his race'—or something analogous thereto.

"Our sages had, about this time, been talking much about the old prophecies, declaring that; according to all the signs, the time of what they called our Second Empire was near at hand; and Lyostrah's father being dead, he was already, though a young man, Chief Priest. From that time he became more than ever imbued with the fixed idea that he was destined to be the man, or one of the men, to restore the old status of our nation in the world; and he set to work to prepare himself for the position. I must confess he worked hard and zealously. First he called together our Council of Elders and pointed out that it was necessary he should go out into the world to learn its ways, study its methods, become acquainted with its sciences. At first the proposal was received with fierce opposition, for never had one of the community been given permission to go beyond its

boundaries. There were ugly tales about that now and again one
or two had stolen away, but it was darkly hinted that they had
never reached the outer world. But Lyostrah's eloquence and
enthusiasm prevailed, and he was given permission to travel, a
permission which was subsequently extended to myself. I had
no wish to go, but he prevailed upon me to accompany him.
We started off together. We travelled about for many years; we
had practically unlimited wealth, for he insisted upon my sharing his newly-found treasure, and we went everywhere, saw
everything that was to be seen, learned all that it was possible
to learn. But the experience had a totally opposite effect upon
him to that which it produced upon myself. We found that, as
far as scientific knowledge and discovery were concerned, we
had scarcely anything to learn. Our own knowledge, handed
down from the remote past, imperfect perhaps as it is to-day
compared with what it once was, was yet, we found, ahead in
a great many respects of the latest so-called triumphs of your
scientists and inventors. But in other matters we were behind
you; in many things, for example, relating to the arts. From
time to time we returned to our own country to report upon
what we had learned, and to establish schools for instruction in
those branches of knowledge wherein we deemed our people
to be deficient. The last time I visited Europe in company with
Lyostrah, something happened which I will for the present
pass over. I will only now say that I returned to my home with
different views; and when, after a while, he would have had me
go abroad with him again, I not only refused to go, but, seeing
reason to believe we were not likely to agree well together in
the future, I retired altogether from the community and came
here to live, as I have already explained. That is many years ago.
Since then I know very little, comparatively speaking, of what
Lyostrah has been doing. I know, however, that, as regards his
visits to Europe, he has had some sort of apprenticeship, so to
speak, to almost everything. Whatever he deemed worth learning he threw himself into with his characteristic energy, and,
with his genius, quickly became proficient. Painting, music,

soldiering, and a host of other studies he took up in turn. He served with the Turkish army against the Russians, and actually became one of their most successful generals—the *most* successful, perhaps, I ought to say. If I were to tell you the name under which he served, you would recognise it at once."

"But—you amaze me! How can that be? His age—"

"Wait. I give you all these details to show you the sort of man with whom we have to deal."

"How came you to disagree?"

"That I cannot now fully explain. But I may say that matters of religion had something to do with it."

"Religion!"

"Yes. Our experiences affected us differently. They fanned his ambition, and at the same time rendered him proud and cynical. He now looks upon the whole world with contempt, with a great disdain, as only fit to be his plaything. Certainly he is a great character; he is a genius, a wonder. But he thinks himself a god. While I—"

"While you—?"

Manzoni had paused as though hesitating to tell what was in his mind.

"Well, I," he at last said, slowly, "I returned from my contact with the great world with the burden of a heavy grief upon me, saddened and horrified at what I had seen, and what I had gone through. My people profess an ancient religion, which, though it is not Christianity, is yet founded upon a high moral code. And we are not Atheists. Though we do not profess so much as your Christian sects, we have always lived in peace, amity, and goodwill one with another, and hypocrisy and self-righteousness are unknown amongst us. I returned shocked at the turmoil of crawling selfishness, self-seeking, and mean hypocrisy which was revealed on every side, amongst every class in the outer world. The memory of it all, and of what I suffered, still haunts me. Lyostrah had not my unfortunate experience, and that, no doubt, made a great difference. Still, he took a very different view of the world to mine. What we saw excited in him only contempt and disgust. 'These worthless, arrogant, self-righteous humbugs,' he used to say to me, 'deserve only to be made use of, to be my creatures, to be ruled with a rod of iron.'"

"But that is scarcely a fair estimate. There are good and bad in every class—" Leslie objected.

"Yes; but you see it is their professing so much that excites his disdain. They are so *very* self-righteous. Your Christian religion (he says) sets such a very high standard that mere mortals can never hope to attain to it. But for that very reason, they should be the humblest-minded of all dwellers upon earth. Instead, they are the most puffed up with spiritual pride. They strut about, and say by their manner, 'Behold how very pious we are. See what a very, very good religion we profess; think, then, and wonder! Think how good we *must* be!' And all the while—"

"Are you not somewhat uncharitable?"

"They are Lyostrah's words, my friend; not mine. I do not judge. I, too, saw the evils that were everywhere apparent—too glaring to be hidden; and amidst it all I saw the suffering! Ah, the suffering! What awful misery had I seen alongside all your parade, and pomp, and boastful pride. I wished to try to relieve some of the misery I saw, but, alas! I had to give up the attempt in despair, appalled, overwhelmed by its immensity. Then an idea came to me. This Mylondos, the 'Plant of Life,' what did that name mean? In your account of the Garden of Eden it is said that there was a Tree of Life, of the fruit of which, if any man partook, he would become immortal like unto the gods. But to make a man immortal would be to abolish pain—or nearly so, since there would then be no disease. Also, the scroll declared that the man who used aright the virtues of this plant would become a great benefactor to his race. That—as regards myself—I interpret to mean that if I could but extract those virtues,' and learn how to employ them, I might discover the one great remedy which should abolish for ever all disease, and consequently nearly all pain and physical suffering from our planet. That, then, is my ambition! Providence has, haply, placed in my hands the key to this great mystery, and given me the opportunity to solve it, to accomplish for suffering humanity this one supreme benefit! That is what I have devoted myself to for so many years. Is it not worth all the work, all the energy, all the knowledge one can bring to bear upon it?"

Manzoni's face, as he spoke, was lighted up with enthusiasm, his eyes almost seemed to blaze, and Leslie thought that never in his life had he seen an expression of such nobility upon any man's countenance. He gazed at him in wonder and admiration, and again there rose up in his mind the picture of Lyostrah's face, so exquisite in its beauty, yet so wanting in its human sympathy. He could not help reflecting upon the great gap that now separated these two men, upon the remarkable difference in the effects which their sojourns in the great outer world had respectively produced upon them. Starting together, under precisely similar conditions, upon their experience of a—till then—unknown world, the one had only seen that which excited his contempt, exalted his own pride and ambition, and confirmed him in his craving for earthly power and worldy dominion. The other had returned softened, saddened, and sympathetic, weeping for those who wept, for getting his former ambitions and rejecting his equal share in the destiny of his soaring friend, conscious now of but one desire—to humbly contribute to removing or lessening the sum of human pain!

"But, after all—of course, Lyostrah is young, and—"

He spoke this thought unconsciously; but Manzoni caught the words, and answered them in a way that amazed his companion almost more than anything he had yet heard:

"Lyostrah young, say you?" Manzoni exclaimed. "Know, then, that he and I are of exactly the same age!"

CHAPTER XVIII

WHAT IS LYOSTRAH'S SECRET?

LESLIE STARED AT his host, in amazement too great for words.

"Surely, surely," he cried, "you cannot be serious!"

"Do I, then, look so much older than Lyostrah?" Manzoni asked, with a quiet smile.

"I think, sir, if I read aright, that many of the lines upon your face have been caused by suffering rather than age. I thought so at first sight," answered Leslie, evading a direct answer. "Yet, even allowing for that, I should never have imagined that you and he were anything like the same age."

"Lyostrah and I were foster-brothers. We were brought up together, we studied together, we pursued our youthful sports together. We have lived our lives together, I may say, until some twenty years ago. What he has been doing during those twenty years I do not know. I have seen him occasionally. He sometimes pays me a visit; has continued to do so ever since our separation. At first he used to make endeavours to shake my resolution; tried to induce me to return to our native city and join with him upon the old conditions. But gradually he became convinced that his efforts were vain, and thereafter he came less often, and grew much less communicative about himself and his doings. On my side, I never cared to evince curiosity; so have heard practically nothing from him. I think his visits, for some years past, have been made chiefly with a view to finding out what I am doing, what progress I am making in research, and so on. Once or twice I have thought that he seemed to show more interest in my daughter than—well, than I cared to encourage. But, whatever his real object as regards me or mine, he is silent concerning himself and his own doings. I feel convinced, however, from his disdainful glances at what I show him, that he must have made some discoveries very much in advance of what I have been able to accomplish. From himself I can get no inkling of what they are; but rumour—"

"Rumour!" Leslie repeated.

"Well, yes—Indian rumour. For some reason of his own, Lyostrah has modified our traditional attitude towards some of the Indian tribes living nearest to him. There are among them two or three very warlike races. These he has taken into his pay, and he makes use of them to further his purposes—whatever they may be. Some of their chiefs and principal men are allowed to visit the city; and my Indians have heard from them strange tales—very strange tales indeed.

"But let me go back a little.

"Lyostrah and I, as I have already said, were fellow-workers and fellow-inventors. Many of the inventions you have seen were our joint work, or joint discoveries. We worked hand-in-hand, having no secrets, telling each other, day by day, all our thoughts, theories, or speculations concerning whatever work we had in hand. From this you will perceive I can guess the lines upon which, in all probability, he has been working, and the direction his investigations have most likely taken since we parted. As you are by this time well aware, he has an extraordinarily brilliant intellect; he is nothing less than a gifted genius in his aptitude for research and invention. In all such matters his powers are far in excess of mine. I did not always recognise it when we were working together; but I have realised it since. It is more than probable then, that, working upon the same foundation, and following out, no doubt, somewhat similar theories, he has outstripped me in the race, and has arrived at that which I am still labouriously seeking.

"There is another point to be borne in mind. Lyostrah, though extremely practical in his scientific work, is yet something of a dreamer, a mystic. He has some sort of belief in the reality of what is usually termed occult science. And he undoubtedly possesses the hypnotic or mesmeric power in a very high degree. Now what is mesmeric power but 'Will-force'? When we separated we had just discovered the Red Ray, and were investigating its marvellous properties; and I remember his remarking that it ought to assist him to increase his natural mesmeric gift. Now can you begin to understand the form his latest discoveries have probably taken?"

"I can scarcely say that I do. Yet a dim idea, a very vague, shadowy impression, seems to be forming in my mind."

"But there is one other factor, and a very powerful one, to be considered. Alloyah, the Chief Priestess—"

"Alloyah!—the name of his yacht!"

"Yes; his yacht—our yacht, I may say, for I helped to design and build her—was named after Alloyah, the Chief Priestess, a woman almost as remarkable, in her way, as Lyostrah in his. In our country we have priestesses as well as priests, and the headship in each case is hereditary. Alloyah's mother was also a woman out of the common. She was reputed—with what amount of truth I cannot say—to be deeply versed in all kinds of occult mysteries; and she is said to have imparted all her dark secrets and hidden knowledge to her daughter. It is further believed that Alloyah has not only proved herself an apt pupil, but has even attained to more than her mother ever knew. She is a woman of great beauty, though to my mind it is of somewhat too sensuous a character. Through her beautiful features I cannot help seeing the fiery passions, the restless ambition, and the inflexible will that lie beneath; and—well, she is not a woman into whose hands I should care to trust myself. Yet is she of most fascinating, captivating powers, a very queen of beauteous grace, of exquisite symmetry of form—born to bewitch all upon whom she chooses to exercise her subtle charms, and to drive many to madness. This enchantress, as one may truly term her, this sorceress—as she is reputed to be—is enamoured of Lyostrah!"

"Ah! And he?"

"He—there is the puzzle! I cannot tell how he regards her; I never could understand in what light he looks upon her. It was understood, at one time, that he would wed her; but for some reason the union was postponed again and again—until—I know not how matters now stand. Only this I know, that she still exerts a very powerful influence over him. She supports him in his wild projects, fans his ambitions, and encourages him in his plans. Standing alone, I would, personally, not fear Lyostrah so much—but acting under her influence, at her instigation, or urged on by her, he is one to be dreaded, for he is then capable of anything!"

"Altogether, our outlook can scarcely be termed cheerful," Leslie commented.

"We must hope for the best I will aid you in every way that I can, though it will mean, in my case, departing from the attitude I have taken up now for nearly twenty years."

"You observed just now," said Leslie, thoughtfully, "that you fancied Lyostrah must have made some discovery of which you are ignorant It seems to me also that it must be so; else much of what he said to my friend Neville would appear to be but the ravings of a crazy lunatic. You have seen him lately—within the the last few days, I believe; tell me, did he appear to you to be crazy?"

"Not at all."

"To you he seemed quite as usual; as sane and sensible as he has always appeared?"

"Decidedly."

"Yet either what he said must be the wildest sort of loose talk, or else he must have something up his sleeve, as we say, of which you are ignorant?"

"That would appear to be a fair statement of the case. It crystallises, so to speak, the thoughts that have been running in my own mind."

"And you can make no guess at the nature of this great discovery, or invention, or whatever it is?"

"I did not say that," Manzoni answered, slowly. "I have, as I told you, heard tales—"

"What tales?" Leslie asked, with quiet persistence.

"I scarcely care to repeat them to you until I know something more definite."

"They are too wild, too improbable?"

"Well, yes. They are very wild, very fantastic, highly improbable stories. Weird, far-fetched ideas that may be mere rubbish—"

"Such as your daughter hinted to me?"

"Possibly. However, to leave out for the time these unreliable rumours, let me speak now of one thing which, apart from all the rest, seems to me within the bounds of possibility." Manzoni paused, and then added, in a low tone, rather as if to himself than to his companion; "Indeed it must be so—there is no other explanation possible."

"What is that, sir?"

"It is this. You know that I am engaged upon a quest—you said just now that you had guessed it—and you can now guess what it is I am seeking."

"A universal medicine, a panacea for all diseases, I gathered."

"Y—es. But—what, then, hangs on to it?"

"I confess I do not follow you."

Manzoni rose from the chair on which he had been seated, walked over to Leslie, and laid his hand impressively upon his shoulder.

"Can you not see," he said, "that the effect of such a medicine would be to prolong life far beyond the present average length—almost indefinitely?"

A light began to break in upon Leslie's speculations.

"You mean," he exclaimed, "that it would be a sort of Elixir—the old mythical Elixir of Life!"

"Exactly. Tantamount to that."

"But," Leslie objected, "you referred just now to tales too wild to repeat, and yet you speak seriously of a thing like this as being possible?"

"Probable was my word. I have long believed that something of the kind lay behind the name of Plant of Life? In my case I sought, as I say, only a medicine—one that should relieve and reduce the sum of human pain and suffering. But Lyostrah, if he discovered anything of the kind, would see in it but one use, would endeavour to apply it to but one purpose—the prolongation of his own life."

"Ah! I begin to understand."

"My good friend, you may feel assured that I am right. I have suspected it, believed it, felt convinced of it for a long time. Lyostrah has discovered this Grand Secret! He has found in the Plant of Life the secret of eternal youth—or something very like it!"

"It takes one's breath away!"

"No other explanation is possible; no other theory will fit in with the facts as they are known to me."

"You must know best, sir," said Leslie, who felt altogether bewildered. "To me it comes as a surprise, and I confess—"

"For years past now Lyostrah has puzzled me by the evident fact that he has shown none of the usual signs of advancing age. So far from that, he has actually become continually younger-looking, until he appears now as I remember him when he was about thirty-five years of age."

"That is what I—everybody—would take him for."

"It also explains a subtle change that I have remarked in his character and disposition. He used to be fiery and impatient, spoke often of the comparative shortness of man's ordinary life compared with the immensity of the task that lay before us. He does not talk thus now; he is completely changed. The old impatient temperament has disappeared, and has given place to a quiet, dignified repose, which is somewhat of a new feature in his character."

"I—all who come in contact with him—have remarked it. I have heard some speak of him as 'the man who is never in a hurry.'"

"And on those rare occasions when he has referred to the future, lately, he has—unconsciously, I fancy—spoken with a sort of god-like patience, as might one who was assured he would live for centuries, and could afford to wait indefinitely for the fulfilment of his desires."

"I, too, have noticed something of that, and I confess I have, at times, felt puzzled by it. Still—he has said nothing direct to you?"

"Nothing. But, as I said just now, no other explanation fits in exactly with all the circumstances. Even in Miss Atherton's letter to your friend, as you have quoted from it to me, I see an indirect reference to this subject. He admitted to her that his aims and expectations could not be fulfilled within the space of an ordinary life. What could that mean except that he believed his life would extend beyond the ordinary span?"

Leslie made no further comment He felt so astounded at the possibilities thus opened before him that—as he himself afterwards described it—all his ideas seemed to have got into a tangle.

"We are certainly getting on," he presently said, in the half-comic, half-serious manner that he sometimes affected. "The Elixir of Life; a beautiful Sorceress, a sort of past-mistress in occult mysteries; and your wonderful Red Ray. Yes; we are getting on. I shall get to that state, shortly, when I shall be ready to believe almost anything at sight. But—those millions of your race—I think he said—of whom he spoke to Arnold, who were to pour forth from your fastness like a devouring torrent, and overrun the world at his call—where are these to come from? At present you say he has about five thousand subjects, all told, and possibly a few thousand. Indians might be brought in to make up a little army. Where, then, are the millions? Is the air truly peopled with spirits, and can he harness them to his chariot-wheels?"

"I cannot wonder, my friend, that these dreams—as they naturally seem to you—should excite your ridicule rather than your—"

"Not at all, sir. I beg your pardon if my frivolous talk jars upon you. I am given to it at times, even in the most serious circumstances; and these *are* serious—I admit that. How we shall ever extricate ourselves, and those unfortunate ladies, from such a strange crowd, is a question serious enough in all conscience. I confess I do not see my way at present. It would perhaps serve to help one a little if one knew what this Lyostrah's real object is in thus dancing us over here. Can you give a guess as to that? It all began in his taking a strange fancy to my friend Neville. That is at the root of all this mischief. Now, what on earth can he want with Neville that should render it worth his while to make all this fuss over it? Can you help me with a guess as to that?"

"I confess I do not understand it. But, as I have said, Lyostrah is somewhat of a mystic, and he indulges at times in the most extraordinary dreams. He believes in destiny and, in particular, he believes that he is destined to rule the world conjointly with another man. The old prophecies all clearly and unmistakably point to the fact that there are to be *two*. So long as I was joined with him, this all seemed clear enough. I am one of the ancient dynasty which formerly ruled over our people. *That* was quite satisfactory from Lyostrah's point of view. But since I withdrew matters are different He is assailed with doubts—so I read his thoughts; for if he undertakes all that he dreams of single-handed, the prophecies are not being fulfilled, and he cannot hope for success. To put it another way, the predictions would evidently not apply to him at all—they must point to some other two yet to be born; and so the very foundation of his castle-in-the-air is destroyed, and it all crumbles to nothing. Thus he reasons. Do you understand me?"

"I think I do. His desire to find another to take your place is prompted by an idea that he will thus be able to get round the old prophecy and make everything fit in with it, ship-shape and comfortable. Yes; there is method in it. It is a long-headed sort of idea. Still, to come now to the last nut we have to crack—Why, with all the world to choose from, should he select my friend?"

"Though there be all the world to choose from, only one can be chosen. You might ask the same question in the case of any other."

"Yes, of course, that is true," Leslie admitted, with a perplexed air. "Still, I cannot form a guess as to why his choice should fall upon my friend in particular."

"I have not seen him, so I cannot judge. But you must not look upon Lyostrah as an ordinary man and be surprised that he does not do everything in an ordinary way. If you do, you will, I expect, go on being surprised and puzzled to the end of the chapter. He has, at times, strange mystical ideas, and amongst them is a theory about certain minds being *en rapport,* as he terms it, with one another. You may be sure that he discovered—or fancied that he discovered—something in your friend which answered precisely to what he considered he wanted. Having made up his mind to that, he would not care who or what he was; and you may be sure he would move heaven and earth, if necessary, to win him over. He may, in addition, have some other hidden reason, at which neither you nor I can give any guess. But, whatever the motive, we have to deal now with the fact that he has made up his mind, and taken very efficient means for carrying out his resolve. Your friend has a sweetheart in England, and refuses to leave her, 'Very well,' Lyostrah said to himself, 'we will bring sweetheart and all.' And he has done so—in his own fashion.

"But you have the proverb, 'One man can lead a horse to the water but ten men cannot make him drink.' The question is, will your friend submit? Will he accept the destiny which Lyostrah desires to force upon him?"

"True. And as to that, one cannot, after all, form any idea, until one knows a little more of what the conditions are likely to be. I should so very much like to know—if you will not deem the desire impertinent—more of the reasons which caused you to so firmly refuse?"

Manzoni turned his glance upon his questioner before reply-ing, and there came into his face an expression of unutterable sadness mingled with wistful longing. And when presently he spoke, his words were uttered, dreamily, and his eyes gradually assumed a far-away look:

"My son, there came into my life a great sorrow, a burden that seemed, at one time, almost too heavy, too cruel for mortal man to bear. When such a grief enters into any man's life, it never leaves him as it finds him. It invariably marks a parting of the ways, the point at which he finds that two roads lie before him of which he must take one. Those roads diverge, and their direc-tions lie ever farther and farther apart; they never again meet, and whichever of the two the man then enters upon, that one must he henceforth follow. To put it another way, after such a blow, he becomes either a better man, or a very much worse one. Either it opens his eyes to the suffering and misery that exist around him—of which, till then, probably, he had seen nothing, very likely had even suspected nothing—and fills his heart with sympathy, and a desire to help others who are fellow-sufferers; or it drives him to drown the haunting memories of his troubles in worldly distractions or ambitions. In the former case he finds his best remedy in working for the good of others, and in pursuit of that solace he can scarcely fail to rise in the spiritual plane, for 'work is prayer, and prayer is work'; in the latter, his worldly appetites and ambitions grow upon him, he hardens his heart to the troubles of others, and gives himself up to selfish dreams. Do you follow my meaning?"

"Certainly," said Leslie, deferentially. "And I think I can see now why you chose the first road."

"No, no; say not 'chose,' my son, say not 'chose,'" returned Manzoni, with a sigh. "That were to impute merit; whereas, in my case, it was rather forced upon me, I think. The grief that fell upon me opened my eyes to the true value of all those earthly 'prizes' for which men strive so madly, for which they struggle and fight, and push others under that they may stand upon their bruised and suffering bodies. No; there is no merit in not seeking what one no longer values. Rather should one be humbly grateful for the shock that has opened his vision and chased away his blindness.

"It was only then that I suddenly realised the full meaning of the path we two—Lyostrah and myself—had entered upon. Till then that path had appeared a sunny road indeed, a road strewn with the flowers and all the delights of life. But I realised in time that it would be covered in due course with the bodies of those slain in the wars that our ambition would bring about; that we should have to wade through a dismal flood of pain and sorrow, of bloodshed and misery, all directly caused by our hunger for worldly glory. Then it was that I drew back, and refused to go farther with Lyostrah upon such a road. I preferred, instead, to retire from the world, and to devote myself to work, the work of research; humbly hoping that the results may be something that shall benefit mankind.

"It seems to me, however, that I am called upon to abandon my work temporarily, to come out for a space from my retirement. In your intercourse with Lyostrah and Alloyah you will have need of a friend. You may leave me with the assurance that when the time comes I shall not be far away."

Leslie essayed to thank him, but he waved his hand, and continued:

"This is my advice to you and to your friends: Be vigilant, be courageous, be faithful to the right. You will meet with many wonders, but do not be led away by them. Do not let your better instincts be drowned in new ambitions, however tempting or dazzling; do not be frightened from doing what you believe right by any dangers, however appalling they may appear. It may be you will be sorely tried and have need of all your steadfastness, but remember that in the hour of greatest trial support is always forthcoming to them who have deserved it. Of your visit to me, be careful that you let no hint escape you; else may you put it out of my power to aid you. The Indians who traced you will remain with me as close prisoners until I deem it prudent to release them. And, when we next meet, give no sign that I am known to you unless I first intimate that you can do so."

Such were the chief counsels given to Leslie by his new friend. There was further converse before they separated; but it added little to his information. Next morning he passed, however, two or three hours in the society of the charming Rhelma, who had now quite recovered, and who insisted upon conducting him around their domain, explaining everything to him afresh, with running comments and bright sallies of her own. He was introduced to each of her many pets; and she came with her father to see him well upon his road back to the camp. Finally, he left them and went his way, his mind full of the most delightful memories of his brief visit, albeit allied, only too closely, with gloomy presentiments as to the future.

CHAPTER XIX

A SURPRISE

ON THE SECOND morning following Leslie's return from his visit to the "Lord of the Mountain"—as he had come to call Manzoni—a party of strange Indians arrived at the camp. They were henceforth to be their guides, one of them, who spoke a little English, stated. They brought a note from Lyostrah as their authority, and an hour later the Indians who had accompanied them thus far left, and the two Englishmen shortly afterwards set out with the new arrivals. They were very loth to part with Lenaka and Captain Jim, both of whom had become attached to them. They had, however, no choice in the matter, and could do no other than acquiesce in the arrangement.

Naturally, there had been much talk between the two friends upon the subject of the eventful visit, and everything that had occurred; every word that had been spoken by Manzoni in the way of information, advice, or warning, was not only discussed over and over again, but forced itself into the mind of each as matter for deep thought and meditation. It was as well, perhaps, that the order to resume their journey had come when it did, since, in the face of what they now knew, further inaction would have become almost intolerable, and might possibly have driven one of them, at least, to attempt something imprudent.

With the bustle and excitement of travel, and the constant change of scene, however, to divert their attention from anxious broodings to the events of the moment, their spirits rose somewhat, and they stepped out with comparative vivacity. At least, as Arnold remarked, they had the satisfaction of knowing that they were approaching the end of their long journey.

"We shall soon know the worst now, I take it," he said, with a praiseworthy attempt at cheerfulness. "We shall then be face to face with whatever we have to deal with. Anything is better than groping along blindly in the dark, or being treated like children in leading-strings, as though we were not old enough to take care of ourselves. Don't you think so, Gordon?"

"H'm! I suppose so," answered Gordon, somewhat dubiously. "I've heard somewhere—perhaps it was in a copy-book at school—a disagreeable saying about getting out of the frying-pan into the fire. I hope to goodness it does not apply to our fortunes in the immediate future. I guess we shall want all our wits about us—all we can manage to pump up. We've got to deal with the very deuce here, by all accounts. I'm not thinking so much of the 'party by the name of' Lyostrah, as of t'other."

"Who?"

"Who? Why, who should it be but this modern Circe—"

"Miss Rhelma?" Arnold asked, mischievously.

But at this, Gordon showed himself highly indignant.

"I was thinking of the mysterious Arch-priestess. Pray do not couple them together, Arnold," he replied, in an aggrieved tone.

"You forget I have not seen either of the ladies," Neville rejoined. "But, to be serious, why should we fear her in particular?"

"I hardly know—but—somehow, I don't at all like this last development—one which brings a scheming, plotting, ambitious woman into the business. It gives a different complexion to it altogether. For of Lyostrah—as it seems we must henceforth call him—I do not feel so much fear; in fact, I must confess to feeling, rather, a little sneaking sort of admiration."

"Admiration!" Arnold exclaimed, bitterly. "So far from feeling admiration," he went on, between his teeth, "if I had my way I would—"

"You don't quite see it from my point of view, old man," Leslie interrupted, soothingly. "Don't get excited over it. I was only going to say that I cannot refuse to yield him a certain meed of admiration—or, appreciation, perhaps, is the better word. After all, he's a fine fellow, handsome as a god, clever as a genius, filled with the fire of a great purpose, a character in which, at least, there is nothing mean, or paltry, or narrow-minded, or hypocritical. Such a man I could follow—on conditions. It would be a wonderful experience—a revelation—to be in his confidence, to know all the workings of such a mind, to join in his work, his discoveries, his triumphs!"

Arnold regarded his chum in surprise and dismay.

"Are *you* going to fall down and worship him?" he cried. "Is it possible that you too have fallen under the spell of this man!"

"Nay," replied Leslie, composedly; "I had not finished. I say all this would be very interesting to me, very entertaining. But before I gave him my allegiance, I should want to know whither it all tended. He says he means well by you, and he has invited you to share his fortunes—not a small thing, coming from such a man!"

"God knows, Gordon," Arnold answered, with a perplexed, almost despairing, ring in his voice. "Sometimes I think one way, sometimes the other. Would to heaven I knew that he is to be trusted! Then should I be relieved of some of this torturing anxiety."

"Manzoni said that he would not fear Lyostrah so much if it were not for that woman's influence over him. And, thinking it all over, and despite the trick he played us, I can't help feeling somewhat the same way. That was my meaning."

"But that is only to say," Arnold rejoined, gloomily, "that we have now before us another probable complication—a danger, or an enemy, greater even than we had suspected. I do not see that there is anything consoling in that."

"Very far from consoling, I'm thinking," was Leslie's reply. "That's just it. And I am puzzling my poor brains wondering what this woman will prove to be like, and what on earth we can do to counteract her influence over Lyostrah, if she should elect to use it against us."

These speculations, however, carried them no further, and therefore appeared to be but a waste of time. But such thoughts continued to suggest themselves again and again as they journeyed, initiating discussions, of which the above is but a sample, and always leading to some similarly lame and unsatisfactory conclusion.

Meantime their route lay through a country which seemed, if such a thing were possible, to grow in savage grandeur. Gloomy gorges and stupendous precipices, mighty torrents and magnificent waterfalls, were now intermingled with stretches of forest so tangled that the toil of making their way through it was greatly increased. Finally, on the third day after leaving the camping-ground where they had made their last long halt, they entered a forest region more sombre, more dense, more impressive than anything they had yet seen.

Here they struggled forward with difficulty, and the oppressive gloom and silence began to affect the spirits of the whole party in a very marked manner. They made their way almost without a word, and with many distrustful and doubting glances around them. Every now and then the brooding stillness was broken by some sudden sound that came echoing through the woods, startling them and bringing them all to a halt as with one accord, listening and trying to make out its cause. Sometimes it was but the death-cry of some unlucky creature pounced upon by a tiger-cat, or seized by a serpent. At others the call of a bell-bird, or the sudden, startling roar of the howling apes. Anon, it would be the sound of a mighty crash that came reverberating through the whole forest, perhaps caused by the fall of a giant limb of some towering arborial monarch, or of a mass of rock. Or, suddenly, there would rise on the air that weird, blood-curdling wail, "so full of hopeless agony and fear," of which the origin has never been discovered, and which is called by the superstitious Indian? "the cry of a lost soul." It has been heard again and again by travellers in South American forests, and described by many pens, but by none, perhaps, more aptly than the American poet Whittier, who calls it "The long despairing moan of solitude."

Besides these things, however, there were very real dangers to be faced or risked. The forest was inhabited, to an unusual extent, by reptiles of a formidable character. The bush-master—or Lord of the Woods, as the Indians not inaptly call it—a large, brilliantly-coloured venomous snake of savage and aggressive disposition, found there a congenial lurking-place. This is, perhaps, the most dangerous snake in the world. Its bite is certain death within the hour; it can move faster than any human being, and, instead of scuttling out of the way when disturbed, as most serpents do, it rushes forward to the attack with extraordinary ferocity. Then there were gigantic anacondas, and the streams were infested, in places, with monstrous alligators, and giant specimens of that vicious, supernaturally ugly reptile, the snapping turtle.

They passed one night in this horrible wilderness in a small clearing. Here sleep was rendered impossible, partly by the mosquitoes, and partly by the heat from the fires they felt compelled to keep up as a protection from the wild beasts, whose howls and roars resounded on all sides throughout the night. In the morning, the two friends looked at each other with inquiring glances.

"I can't stand much more of this," said Arnold, with dismay in his tones. "Try to find out how far we have to go through this inferno."

Though it was long past dawn there was but a sort of twilight where they then were. The dense masses of foliage overhead shut out nearly all the sun's light, and seemed to make the very air oppressive. There was no refreshing morning breeze; and the whole atmosphere was stagnant and heavy, and laden with miasma.

"Have we been led on so far, to be abandoned and left to die in this awful place?" Arnold continued, fretfully. "Is that man a fiend that he should serve us like this?"

But nothing clear or satisfactory could be got from the Indians; and naturally the fact that they were now in the hands of strange guides did not tend to reassure the two despondent young men.

"I feel inclined to make a stand and refuse to go any further into this dismal swamp," Arnold exclaimed, doggedly.

After some further talk with the Indians, however, the march was resumed, under protest, as it were, and for two or three hours the party slowly made their way through difficulties that seemed to multiply as they advanced. Fallen trunks, great boulders, yawning chasms, had continually to be "negotiated," either by climbing, or tedious circuits, until, just when Arnold's patience was utterly exhausted, and he was on the point of making a more determined protest, they arrived at a place where all further progress seemed to be finally barred by a wide river.

They came out on to a clearing upon the bank of a stream which spread out, just opposite to them, into a wide and smooth sheet of water. Above and below this large pool the current was broken, and ran swiftly amongst great scattered masses of rock that everywhere started up out of the river bed. At the sides, save just at the clearing, the high banks were so rocky and precipitous as to be impassable, while the forest around, to right and left of the open space, closed in in such dense fashion as to render hopeless any attempt to advance in either direction.

The clearing was of sufficient extent to allow the rays of the sun to peep through and play upon the broken water to the right of the party, which foamed and tumbled among the jagged rocks, throwing, in places, little clouds of spray into the air. Upon all this the sunlight fell here and there, causing it to glisten with thousands of many-hued sparkling points of light, like tiny diamonds dancing and romping on the surface of the stream.

To Leslie and Neville, who had seen no actual daylight since they entered the forest nearly two days before, the sudden glare was so dazzling that for a minute or two they could not take in the details of the scene.

When, however, their eyes had become a little accustomed to the brilliancy of the light reflected from the water, their attention was attracted by other flashes of light, that came from their left; and looking round in that direction, they saw something which fairly took away their breath with surprise, and caused them to break out into simultaneous exclamations of astonishment.

The flashes which had attracted their notice, came from a group of three or four tall, fine-looking men, who were lounging on the river bank. They wore swords, and appeared to be officers, being attired in handsome uniforms of purple and gold, with shining helmets, epaulets, and glittering coats of mail. A short distance away, a file of soldiers was drawn up, dressed in a fashion somewhat similar, and only a little less resplendent. They carried, by way of arms, short swords and spears of a peculiar, novel form. But beyond these was something more wonderful and unexpected still, considering the place and the circumstances. Beside the bank, resting lightly and easily upon the water, was a large, roomy boat, or, rather, a sort of State barge, of beautiful design and workmanship, and most sumptuously fitted and decorated. The bow was a serpent with many-coloured, metallic scales, the head thrown high in the air, with open mouth and forked tongue. The whole of the after-part was taken up by a saloon with open windows, through which could be seen a table spread as for a meal. A single, slender mast carried a square, purple banner upon which, amongst much gold embroidery was, upon one side, the word LYOSTRAH in English capitals; while, on the reverse side, appeared something which might have been the equivalent of the word in a different language and lettering. In the fore-part of the vessel, a few men in white costumes lounged over the bulwarks.

As the party of travellers emerged from the wood into the open space, the officers stood up, drew their swords, and saluted; while the rank and file stood to attention.

Then there advanced a curious, ungainly figure, in a handsome black velvet dress of a very quaint fashion, in whom our two bewildered travellers had some difficulty in recognising the secretary—Moreaz.

Except for the dress, however, this strange being was evidently just the same as of old. Upon his expressionless face there beamed no smile of welcome, and from his tongue came only words as from a talking automaton; just what he had been instructed to say, and no more.

Singling out Arnold, who was a little behind his friend, he bowed, and merely saying, "This is from his highness," he presented a sealed letter.

Arnold took it, and opened it. It contained two enclosures, one of them being another but smaller letter also carefully sealed. Recognising the handwriting upon the latter, he impatiently broke it open first. It was from Beryl, and ran somewhat thus:

> *Have arrived safely; Auntie and self both well, and now await your arrival with eagerness. We are both very kindly treated, and Auntie is in ecstasies of delight. Certainly we find ourselves in a perfect wonderland, and—but it is all too strange and too astonishing to describe in a brief note. Come on to us as quickly as you can.*

This is but an extract, and is by no means all that the missive contained. But it represents the essential part of the contents.

The other epistle enclosed was from their singular friend himself. It was thus worded:

> *My dear friend and brother—as I hope you will be,—*
> *I send my own, boat to bring you the remainder of your journey. And also, to do you honour, some of my own Guard, and Maylion, the Commander of my soldiers, Okabi, the Chamberlain of my household, and my Secretary, who is known to you. The two first-named can speak a little English, and will have pleasure, I feel sure, in conversing with you during your short voyage. I trust to soon see you in good health and spirits, and to receive you as my guest amongst my own people.*
>
>

Your friend and brother,
Not Lorenzo, but Lyostrah.

When Arnold had made Leslie acquainted with the contents of these notes, the secretary, with much ceremony, presented the two officers whose names had been given, and a third named Gaylia, the son, as it appeared, of Maylion.

Maylion and Okabi were tall, stately, grave-looking men of handsome face and figure, and of, perhaps, some fifty years of age. They were dark and swarthy, as though tanned by exposure to the sun, slow and dignified in movement, and deliberate in speech. The other, Gaylia, was a young fellow scarcely twenty years old, probably, with light, fresh complexion, brown hair, and clear grey eyes that had in them a marked expression of good humour and high spirits. All were clean shaven, and wore their hair cut short.

After a few formal remarks, the secretary suggested to Arnold that he and his friend would probably like to step on board and partake of some of the refreshment awaiting them; and this they very gladly did. They found the table invitingly laid out, with white tablecloth, plates, knives and forks, glasses, etc., all much as one would have expected in a well-appointed houseboat at Henley Regatta. And this description applied also, as they soon discovered, to the eatables. As to these, however, there were, in addition to what was familiar, some dishes, and notably some delicious fruits, that were altogether strange. Nor were cooling drinks, wines, and ices wanting to this unexpected repast, all the more enjoyable for being so unlooked for. Only those who have travelled for months in such a country can imagine how grateful to the weary, toil-worn travellers was such a feast.

The secretary, assisted by two servitors in a sort of livery, attended on them in his queer, automaton-like fashion, seldom speaking, his eyes and features a perfect blank, so far as expression went. The others remained upon the river bank, standing deferentially a short distance away, and conversing at times with one another in low tones.

When the two had satisfied their appetite, the servants cleared the table, leaving upon it only cigars and wine, and packing everything else away in a small after-cabin.

"I suppose," said Gordon, in an aside to his chum, "you ought now to invite those fellows to join us, eh? What do you suppose the etiquette of the country requires?"

"Good!" said Arnold; "thank you for the hint."

It turned out that that was good advice, for just then Moreaz came to inquire whether "his excellency"—meaning Arnold—was ready to start.

"His excellency," said Gordon, gravely, taking it upon himself to answer the inquiry, "desires me to say that he will be delighted if those gentlemen will do him the honour to join him in smoking the pipe of peace, or, in its place, some of the very excellent-looking cigars which I perceive your master has been thoughtful enough to send us. Further, he is quite agreeable to your starting as soon as you please."

The solemn-looking officers bowed their acceptance of the invitation with grave, stately courtesy, came on board, and ceremoniously took seats at the table. The Indians followed and stowed themselves away somewhere in the bow, then came the soldiers, who ranged themselves in two rows near the centre.

Moreaz blew a whistle as a signal, the men in white loosed the mooring-ropes, and the vessel majestically, smoothly, noiselessly glided out from the bank, and proceeded slowly up the rushing river.

CHAPTER XX

THE CITY OF MYRVONIA

THE "MYRVONIA" (SO the craft, it presently appeared, was named), moved slowly up the stream, in spite of the strong current, the dangerous-looking rocks, and the foaming rapids with which she had to contend. What the motive power was neither Arnold nor his friend could make out; but that was a matter which caused them no surprise. What most interested them was the masterly manner in which she was steered and manoeuvred through the difficulties and dangers of the stream. Evidently, somewhere amid this seeming chaos of boulders and shallows and rushing rapids, there existed a safe, practicable channel, but how anyone could hit it off, as it were, with such exactitude, seemed little short of marvellous. It was clear, as they went on, that the slightest deviation, the most trifling error, would have brought them inevitably to grief a dozen times over. Indeed, so absorbed did the two become in watching this feat of navigation, and marking their many hairbreadth escapes from what every now and then looked like certain destruction, that they almost forgot the presence of their new companions; and the conversation was, consequently, of a most meagre and intermittent character.

This fight with the stream—for such it really was—occupied some hours, but as the afternoon drew on the river became deeper and smoother, and the speed then increased. The banks, the whole way, were either precipitous rocks, dense, impenetrable forest, or reeking, seething swamps, in which could be seen many huge, crawling forms of which they could not make out the name or species. Presently the attendants came and closed up the sides of the saloon with sliding metal shutters, while a stir amongst the soldiers suggested that preparations were about to be made to resist a possible attack.

These precautions, it presently appeared, were rendered necessary by reason of the fact that the stretch of river they were coming to was infested with water-snakes, some of them very large and of a venomous and deadly description. And, as they steadily pursued their course, more than one terrible-looking head was reared above the bulwarks, rivalling in size and ugliness their own figurehead, and threatening with open jaws those on board. These, however, the soldiers succeeded in beating off, and no actual casualty occurred, though there were two or three narrow escapes.

Towards evening a stupendous precipice suddenly loomed up in front of them, partially shutting out the light, and absolutely barring all further progress. It towered up, almost in a plumb-line, for quite two thousand feet; on either side the banks were also sheer smooth rock; and no possible outlet or landing-place could be seen. Yet the stream came down against them as though it poured out of the solid rock itself.

Just, however, as the anxious watchers thought they would certainly crash into this mighty wall, a great mass rolled slowly on one side, like a sliding panel, and showed a clear passageway into a dark and very uninviting-looking tunnel. A minute later, and the voyagers had glided through the gloomy entrance, and the door of massive rock had closed behind them with a sullen rumble, shutting them into inky blackness.

A light now flashed out from the open jaws of the serpent's head in the bow, and the whole interior became illuminated. It was then apparent that they were going through a rocky tunnel in which nothing could be seen but the arched roof and perpendicular sides, and the dark stream that now flowed quietly and sluggishly past them. But it seemed that vigilant eyes must have been observing their progress, for when, after a short interval, they came to a second great stone door that filled the whole space in front of them from the roof to below the water level, it rolled quietly back, and allowed them to pass, closing in behind them as the first had done. This happened a third time, and then they became aware of a confused murmur which grew as they advanced; the roof became gradually higher, and the waterway wider, until it stretched out into an underground lake or dock, surrounded by lighted quays. Here many people were bustling to and fro, and sounds could be distinguished, above the general hum, as of workmen's hammers.

Their conductors, however, took no heed of these things, but held straight on across the middle of the sheet of water, evidently making for an outlet which could be seen ahead. When they had entered the tunnel at the other end, the shades of night had seemed to be falling, but this had been chiefly due to the effect of the overhanging cliffs and the dense wood upon the banks. Here, daylight evidently still lingered outside, for, as they advanced, the opening in front of them grew brighter as well as larger, until, a little later, they emerged into the fresh air.

Then such a scene burst upon the view of the two young men as once more called forth from them expressions of astonishment and delight. The vessel now glided quietly along a beautiful river that stretched away before them, winding in and out amid a landscape so enchanting that it would be difficult indeed to find words to do it justice. There were smiling groves and meadows, noble mansions with terraced gardens reaching to the waterside, then noble buildings that towered into the air, and again, at another bend, the clear blue water reflected giant colonnades, or a fairy-like bridge. To right and to left the ground rose till, in the distance, it reached to rocky heights that shut in the whole plain.

Upon these heights, on one side of the valley, the red rays of the fast setting sun were just lingering, while overhead was an expanse of ethereal sky flecked with glowing clouds of rose and gold.

Then the light faded, and the twilight, as is always the case in these latitudes, died almost suddenly into the shades and darkness of night.

But twinkling lights quickly showed themselves upon all sides, shining in quivering lines deep down into the water. These increased in number, and first one and then another building emerged again from the shadows, until the whole extent within view was lighted up as though showing forth special illuminations in honour of the newly-arrived visitors.

Finally, they approached a pile of buildings, larger and more stately than any they had yet seen, occupying' an eminence that rose from the river side. Rising terrace upon terrace, it was ablaze with light, each terrace being studded with braziers upon which lambent flames leaped and flared.

From these rose columns of light vapour which floated upwards, wrapping the whole in a haze, and forming a scene that led the observers to almost doubt whether what they saw were substantial buildings or the effects of some strange mirage.

Leslie, who had visited Lake Titicaca, recognised, in the general plan and design here apparent, a striking likeness to the wonderful ruins that have there come down to us from an unknown past; and the idea thus suggested afforded him much food for after speculation.

Meantime, it soon became evident that this was their destination. The boat approached the bank at a point just beneath the towering palace, and ran quietly beside a landing-stage, where it was quickly secured.

During their voyage but little conversation had taken place between the two young men and their conductors. Either the latter's knowledge of the English tongue was very limited, or they were disinclined to impart information. At any rate, the two travellers were not much the wiser for such talk as had taken place.

As the vessel stopped, Maylion turned to Arnold, and addressed him:

"Here, your excellency, is the palace of our great and good lord and ruler, the gracious Lyostrah. For the present, having guarded you thus far, my mission is ended. I hand you over now to the care of our worthy chamberlain, who will be responsible for, and look after, your future comfort and convenience, until our great Chief is ready to receive you."

With this speech the official turned away, and stood at the head of his men, now drawn up in line, while the two landed, Neville escorted by Okabi, and Leslie following after with Gaylia.

Gordon found that his companion grew more talkative now that he was free from the immediate proximity of his elders. He spoke English well, and Gordon complimented him upon it, expressing his surprise-thereat.

"Our wise and illustrious ruler, Lyostrah," returned the young man, "has told us that in the great world outside, a large number of different languages are spoken, but that what is called English is destined, in his opinion, to be the language of the whole world in the future. For that reason he has; not only ordered it to be taught in all our schools, but has directed that it is to be accorded first place after our own, and used in daily converse, so that all may become accustomed to it You will find even the children here understand it."

"And what other languages, then, do you teach in your schools?" Leslie asked.

"Portuguese, Spanish, French, German, and Russian."

"A pretty comprehensive programme," Leslie remarked. "But these languages cannot be of much use to you, shut off from the world as you are."

"No; not at present But they will be required when our day comes," was the quiet reply, delivered in tones of firm conviction.

"Again the same strange notion," thought Leslie. "Clearly, Lyostrah is educating his followers up to his own ideas." But he kept his thoughts to himself, and turned his attention to what was going on around him.

On all sides were groups of people, very richly dressed, in costumes that reminded one, as Leslie remarked, rather of ancient Greece than the present day. Amongst them, drawn up in respectful attention, were servants in brilliant liveries. All saluted the strangers quietly and deferentially as they passed.

After landing, they first ascended flights of steps, from terrace to terrace, till they entered a wide corridor, from which they emerged into a courtyard where cool, plashing fountains played amidst ornamental plants and statuary. Passing through this, they made their way along halls, galleries, and passages, all brilliantly lighted and most beautifully furnished and decorated, until they came to an apartment overlooking the place where they had just landed. Here Okabi paused.

"This and the adjoining apartments have been prepared for your excellency's occupation," he informed Neville. "Beyond, are bed and bath chambers. Refreshments await you in the room you see to the left But you may prefer first to bathe and change your apparel."

"As to apparel," Gaylia put in, "you will find all sorts awaiting your selection in the ante-chamber which I will show you. Would you like something of the kind you are accustomed to in your own country, or would you prefer to dress as we do?"

This was rather an awkward question for the two young men. To say that their own clothes were travel-stained, was to put the matter somewhat mildly. They were, as a matter of fact, almost in tatters. All that they had brought with them in the shape of spare garments had been used up long since; and latterly they had been compelled to patch up, as best they could, many a rent torn by unsympathetic thorns in what were their very last suits.

An inspection of the wardrobe laid out for them to choose from rather added to their perplexity than otherwise. There were some English suits, of sorts; but what young English gentleman cares to dress himself in "ready-made clothes"; especially when the assortment he has to choose from is so limited as to render it extremely unlikely that he would be able to pick out "a good fit." On the other hand, the costumes of the country were, to their minds, bizarre to a degree, and the suggestion that they should array themselves in anything of the kind came upon them with a sort of shock.

"It's like going back to the times of ancient Greece," Leslie again declared, as he handled some of the resplendent dresses in very gingerly fashion, as though half-afraid of them. "I could never deck myself out in that style, Arnold. Could you?"

Arnold could not resist a smile, as he saw the perplexed and rueful expression upon his chum's face.

"It is likely enough," he observed, "that we should appear, to the people here, less outlandishly dressed in the clothes they are used to than in our own. All the same, however, I mean to content myself with a plain tweed suit if I can find one, and I think I see yonder something about my size."

"Then I will certainly do the same," Gordon declared, with evident relief in his tone.

And, in the result, they found themselves arrayed in better style than they had, at a first glance, ventured to hope for.

Previously to this, however, their new friends had withdrawn, after stating that Lyostrah would be ready to receive them, if agreeable, in an hour's time; and instructing them how to summon attendance if required.

When the two were left alone, Leslie sat down upon a luxurious-looking couch, leaned back, stretched out his arms and legs, and gave a long whistle.

"Well!" he exclaimed. "If this don't beat cock-fighting, then I'm a Dutchman! Our journey is ended at last; and what an ending to it! I never dreamed of anything like this! Did you?"

Arnold shook his head.

"I cannot understand it," he declared. "I am puzzled and bewildered."

"You are 'his excellency' here, it seems," Gordon went on, with a humorous twinkle in his eyes. "It's almost worth all we've gone through to be treated like this, and styled 'your excellency.' They don't 'your excellency' *me*. You noticed that?"

Arnold said he had not remarked it.

"Oh yes, you did; you couldn't help noticing. It means that—well, I guess it's a sort of hint that *you* are the invited guest, and that I am—one who came uninvited, and whose company is not particularly wanted."

"Don't be absurd, Gordon! you always will persist in putting in some of your flippant talk."

"Not at all, dear boy. I'm serious; very serious. All the same, they'll find it difficult to get rid of me till I feel quite sure that you and your friends are safe here. I must say, up to now, there is nothing to complain of so far as appearances go; you have had a very cordial welcome, are treated *en grand Seigneur*, 'with vassals and serfs at your call.' And all this being thusly, I am rather interested to know how you are going to treat our respected friend Lyostrah, when you meet him. Are you going to 'give him a bit of your mind,' to tell him all the plain home-truths about himself that you have been saving up during these few months for this especial occasion? Or are you and he going to fall upon each other's necks, and declare, with brotherly embraces, that all is forgiven and forgotten?"

But to this bantering address Arnold gave no reply. Truth to tell, he had no definite answer to give, for the same questions had for some little time been running through his own mind; and the more he thought about it all the more puzzled and bewildered he felt at the unlooked-for nature of the events of the last few hours.

"It only once more proves," was Leslie's final comment, "the truth of the saying that 'nothing is certain except the unforeseen.'"

CHAPTER XXI

IN LYOSTRAH'S PALACE

PUNCTUAL TO THE time that had been named, came the two officials, Okabi and Maylion, and with them the young officer of the King's Guard, Gaylia.

They bowed ceremoniously to the two Englishmen, and after inquiring if their comfort and requirements had been properly attended to, the former, addressing Neville, said:

"His highness is now in the Hall of Reception, and will be delighted to receive your excellency and your excellency's friend if it be your esteemed pleasure to meet him."

Arnold signified that his esteemed pleasure tended in the direction suggested, whereupon Okabi led the way with him, the others following.

And then the strangers perceived that the portions of the palace through which they had previously passed were almost poor in comparison with those they were now traversing.

Marbles of many and varied hues and character, wonderful mosaics, columns of jasper and alabaster; gold and silver ornaments in, profusion, many of them studded with precious stones; curtains and hangings of costly silks and satins, superb frescoes, paintings, statues, and adornments—these and a thousand other items caught their eyes; while other senses were charmed by exquisite perfumes which filled the atmosphere, or enchanting strains of music that floated upon the cool, refreshing air. Everyone they encountered drew respectfully aside to make way for them, ranks of soldiers saluted, rows of liveried servants bowed,

as they passed through the various corridors and apartments,
up and down broad flights of stairs, along a route so filled with
wonders that each in turn seemed more surprising than that
which had gone before.

They came at last to an ante-chamber in which were a few
splendidly-dressed people apparently awaiting permission to
enter a room beyond. From within came the sound of music,
but the folding-doors dividing the apartments were closed, anti
were guarded by officials in specially handsome uniforms. Okabi
stayed but for a word with one of these, and then, at a sign from
the officer in charge, the doors were thrown open, and the two
Englishmen were ushered into a spacious reception room, amid
a blaze of light and splendour that fairly took their breath-away,
and caused them involuntarily to put up their hands for a few
moments to shade their eyes.

They found themselves in a lofty hall of light-coloured
marble, ornamented above and below with designs in mosaic
formed with costly material that sparkled and glistened in the
brilliant light. These enclosed panels, upon which were paintings, some representing battle scenes on land and on sea, the
vessels shown being of very primitive and ancient design; others
portrayed tented fields, or palace interiors depicting a king
surrounded by his ministers of state, a general receiving the
submission of his vanquished enemy, and others of the kind that
we should term historical. However, these the newcomers did
not notice at the time, their whole attention being attracted by a
dazzling blaze of moving lights with which the whole place was
filled. The roof was supported upon columns, which apparently
were of glass or some other transparent material. Within them
moved spirals formed of myriads of tiny lights, each brilliant as
a diamond, which travelled ever upwards inside the columns,
till they reached the roof, where they spread out in hundreds of
branches that met, and crossed, and interlaced. While, therefore, the columns were like pillars of fire perpetually ascending
towards the roof, the latter was itself one great glowing design

of sparkling, fiery chains, which met and twined in and out, and finally disappeared no one could say whither.

Turning their bewildered eyes from this dazzling sight, the two young men saw, at the end of the hall, Lyostrah seated upon a throne of ivory and gold, placed upon a raised dais approached by half-a-dozen steps running nearly the width of the hall. Overhead was a canopy, and beneath it, behind and above the occupant of the throne, gleamed an immense star formed of fifty or more rays of dazzling light ever in motion like the fiery columns, only that in this case the sparkling chains started from the centre and disappeared at the extremities of the rays. They moved in a succession of waves, in a sort of rhythm, or pulsation, which had a weird, startling effect upon the spectator.

And there, beside Lyostrah, Neville, with a beating heart, beheld the beauteous Beryl, her face lighted up with love and happiness, and smiling what was to him the most enchanting welcome that even his ardent hopes could have imagined. Close beside her—an empty seat only separating them—he perceived Mrs Beresford, who also smiled at him in kindly fashion; and a vague wonder came into his mind as to whether the vacant seat between them had been purposely reserved for him.

As they entered this Hall of Light, Lyostrah held up his hand, and at once the music ceased, and there fell a dead silence. It was a silence that was somewhat embarrassing to the two strangers, who could not but feel the difference between all this magnificence and the homely fashion in which they were attired.

Every one turned to look at them, every eye was upon them, and, in the hush, one could have heard the proverbial pin drop—supposing that one had been loosened at the moment.

The pause was, however, but momentary. Then Lyostrah rose, and, extending his hand, cried in a voice that was heard all over the great hall:

"Welcome my friends; welcome to Lyostrah's home."

Obeying his beckoning hand, the two advanced across the floor and up the steps of the throne.

Lyostrah took Neville's hand, as he came up, in his own right, and turned him round so as to face the assembled concourse; and Leslie he ranged in like manner on his left. Then, holding one of their hands in each of his own, he exclaimed in ringing tones, addressing all those present:

"Behold! my children, the two friends I have been expecting. Let them know that you all extend to them the same greeting, the same warm welcome, that I do!"

The chorus of acclamation which followed this address, as all present rose to their feet, was almost deafening; nor did it die down immediately. Two or three times it rose and fell, seeming to die away, but breaking out each time afresh before it had actually ceased.

Without, however, waiting for silence, Lyostrah then turned to Neville:

"There, my friend," he said, indicating the vacant seat beside Beryl, "is your place. Go now, and greet the one who has so impatiently awaited your arrival."

Whatever ideas or intentions Arnold might have had as to the manner in which he would meet the man who had forced him, in such a strange fashion, to journey from the other side of the globe, or what he would say to him, he had now no word, no thought but for Beryl. Certainly, he would have preferred that their first meeting should have been a private one, and not taken place thus before so many eyes. There was, however, no help for it; and he obeyed Lyostrah by taking first her hand, then Mrs Beresford's, and afterwards seating himself between them. Thereupon the rest of the company resumed their seats, and the buzz of general conversation which ensued was welcome to the two lovers as putting an end to the somewhat awkward situation.

Meantime, Lyostrah had requested Leslie to take a seat on his left hand just vacated by some grandee of the place, who had stepped down to join a neighbouring group.

Lyostrah began talking to Leslie as he might have done to any friend who was in the habit of visiting him at intervals, and had now come for another stay very much as usual. There was no trace of embarrassment in his manner; no sign that he felt any lengthy explanation to be necessary. And so gracious and cordial was he, so courteous and so friendly, that Leslie could not hut feel pleased and gratified with his reception. There was no suggestion of his being what he had called himself in his talk with Arnold, "an uninvited guest."

"I do not forget, Mr Leslie—I shall not forget, in our future intercourse—that it was my act which, as it were, compelled you to come out here," Lyostrah said. "Your devotion to your friends was such that you had not any choice in the matter. Since, then, it is my doing that you are here, I feel it a personal duty to make you as comfortable as I can amongst us, and to endeavour to compensate you, as far as may be in my power, for what you left behind—for what you gave up in coming here against your will."

This was said with such polished delicacy, and in such kindly tones, that Leslie was quite won over. Any lingering feeling of resentment was entirely chased away.

"I am bound to say, sir," he answered, "that if I thought, up to yesterday, that I had any ground for complaint, the kindly welcome I have met with at your hands, and at the hands of everyone thus far, has effectually removed it. I feel, indeed, that you are conferring a favour in receiving thus one who has come amongst you without waiting to be asked. Therein, of course, I stand on a different footing from my friend—"

"Nay, nay. You must not think that way," Lyostrah returned, smiling. "You are my guest; presently, as I hope, you will be one of my bands of workers. For we are all workers here, I assure you. There are no drones in Myrvonia. To-night we are making holiday in honour of your arrival; but to-morrow you will find we are a hive of very busy bees indeed. And to work well it is necessary that one's heart should be in one's work. Now, if I remember aright, you did not see anyone during your visit to England who made any such impression upon you as to render it a hardship to have to leave her behind you, eh?"

He had reverted to his old manner in talking to Leslie—the fashion that had marked their intercourse previous to his meeting with Neville. During the time that Gordon and he had been travelling to England together, there had naturally been much friendly talk. Gordon had told him everything about himself, about his prospects, his hopes, and his ambitions; and the other accordingly knew that he was rather inclined to boast of the invulnerability of his nature to the charms and attractions of the fair sex.

In reply to the last remark, therefore, Gordon smiled, and shook his head.

"No," he said; "I did not leave my heart behind me in England."

"That is well," Lyostrah returned; "and *now* it cannot be said that your friend has either. So neither of you has any reason of that kind for hankering to get back to England. He has here all the friends he needs trouble about; and we will endeavour to make the same remark applicable in the future to yourself. Then you can throw your heart into our work and become one of us—is it not so?"

Just then a vision of Rhelma's lovely face rose in Gordon's mind, and, spite of himself, he coloured under Lyostrah's keen gaze. However, the latter showed no consciousness of his slight confusion, and continued, in the same kindly tones:

"Let me then say at once that I want you to make yourself thoroughly at home with us. That is to say, I wish you to look upon it that our country is to be your future home. In our former journey to England, and in the whole of our subsequent intercourse, you and I were always good friends. There is no reason why we should not remain so to the end of the chapter. And now you would, I daresay, like to speak a word or two to Mrs Beresford and her niece. Your friend has already brightened up under their influence. He looks in better spirits, and shows far less signs of his long journey, than he did when he entered yonder door." He paused, as his eyes rested upon the two lovers, and marked

Arnold's face, and the glow of modest love and pride that looked forth from Beryl's sweet eyes. When he turned again to speak to Leslie, there was a shadow on his brow, and a scarcely perceptible sigh escaped him.

"Afterwards," he added, "we will show you how we amuse ourselves here in our 'hours of ease'!"

The greeting Leslie met with from Mrs Beresford and her gentle niece was as warm as his heart could wish. And so glad were the four to be together again that they paid but small heed to what went on around them. They saw, therefore, but little of the amusements that followed, though, during the evening, there was much in the dancing and the various entertainments that, at another time, would have aroused all their interest, and excited their keenest attention.

CHAPTER XXII

HAPPY HOURS

"**AND NOW, DEAR** Arnold, that we are alone, and can speak freely, tell me all that has happened to you since we parted that day, that seems now—oh, ages and ages ago! Think! I have not seen you since that evening at Ivydene—dear old Ivydene—when you told us about the long interview you had had with the 'Don,' as we called him, and spoke of all the wonderful things he had shown you!"

"Nay, tell me first about yourself, Beryl; tell me how you have fared. How did you manage to survive all the hardships of such a journey? You can never guess the half of what I have suffered in thinking about you! All that has happened to us I pictured to myself as occurring to you; and, in my anxiety, I felt full of anger against the man who had caused you to undergo it all. I vowed all sorts of vengeance against him; and yet now," Arnold added, a little shamefacedly, "I have passed it all over, and said nothing. I don't know what you will think of me!"

"Think of you, dear Arnold?" exclaimed Beryl, her sweet face lighting up with a bright smile, "why, naturally, none the worse for your having shown yourself good-natured and forgiving. Though, truly, dear, I suppose we ought to think—as *he* does, I know—that there is nothing to forgive. His argument is that he has merely brought us out here to 'make our fortunes' in spite of ourselves. We would never have come voluntarily; so he compelled us to against our wills, for our own good. Thus he argues; and I cannot help thinking he is sincere—or believes himself to be sincere."

"That is a curious reservation, darling," said Arnold, looking at her tenderly. "As to *your* forgiving him—well, of course, knowing you as I do, there is nothing to be surprised at in that. Only—"

"But, Arnold, indeed, there has been nothing to forgive, save that one thing—the taking us off so suddenly from you. I cannot tell you how wonderfully kind and thoughtful he has been, how solicitous for our safety and our comfort, down to even the smallest detail. Nor can I readily express my appreciation of his great delicacy and consideration. He is always a gentleman; a true gentleman, through and through. Even in the midst of our many arguments, and when, in my bitterness, I have said some very hard things to him—even through it all, he has never been other than a model of all that a gentleman should be."

"Oh well," said Arnold, "if *you* have said a few 'hard things' to him, and put his conduct before him in its proper light, why, then, I don't regret having been so forgiving myself."

Whereat they both burst out laughing.

It was the day after Arnold's arrival in the place. He and Beryl had started out for a walk together, but, at her suggestion, they had taken one of the canoes that were lying beside the landing-stage, and paddled off up the river till they found a shady resting-place beneath the shadow of some trees that overhung the water.

"I cannot tell you," Beryl went on, "what a wonderful place this is—or how lovely! Of course, we have only been here a few days ourselves; but we have been able to look round a little. They say that this table-land lies thousands of feet above the level of the sea, and that the climate is that of a moderately warm English summer all the year round. There are no snakes or reptiles here, and no wild animals; and, what is still more welcome news, none of the ordinary pests of tropical countries, such as mosquitoes, jiggers, scorpions, and so on. The river is charming! At every bend you get a fresh ravishing picture! And at sunset the effects of the sun's beams upon the heights around us are beyond belief. The place is turned into a veritable fairy-land!"

"I saw something of that as we came out of the tunnel last evening," Arnold assented.

"And then the people! They seem so unaffected, so simple, so kindly-disposed! Though, at their *fêtes,* as last night, they put on the grandest of grand dresses—keeping up the fashions, they tell me, of their people ages and ages and ages ago—yet during the daytime they go about in most homely fashion, very plainly dressed, and all, apparently, busy—ever quietly and content-edly busy."

"Sounds like an earthly paradise—a sort of Utopia," commented Arnold, "if that be so I wonder that friend Lyostrah is not content to quietly dwell in it altogether. Some people do not seem to know when they are well off. A very hackneyed saying, yet one that seems to apply very aptly in this case—if all be really as it appears to you. Here is a man, a sort of king of a small but delightful realm, with a people devoted to him—one can easily see that,—with everything, one would think, to render life happy—yet he must needs go seek after other adventures in a world which he professes to despise."

"Yes, truly," Beryl answered, with a sigh, "And so I have told him—told him over and over again. You cannot think what battles, what arguments we have had over it all' And some-times—sometimes"—here she spoke hesitatingly, dreamily, her eyes seeking vacantly a distant towering cliff that reached high into the azure above them—"sometimes I have thought I had made an impression upon him. And then—then—"

"Then—what?" Arnold asked, as she again paused.

"Then," she went on, in the same slow, dreamy fashion, "he has caused me to pity him!"

"Pity him!" Arnold repeated.

"Ah yes! Pity him! And so would you, if you had seen the awful look that came into his face just those two or three times."

"How do you mean, Beryl? I don't understand! Why 'awful' look?"

"Ay, 'awful' look, Arnold, dear! Oh!" she shivered, and glanced up into the sky with an expression of tender pity and concern upon her innocent features that made her appear, in Arnold's eyes, like some sweet saint pleading before heaven for a lost soul. "God grant, Arnold," she presently continued, "that I may never see such a look upon your face! It was the mute expression of utter, hopeless, helpless despair! A look such as a man might wear when he suddenly finds himself slipping upon the edge of a precipice of the existence; of which he had had no suspicion, and knowing that the discovery had come too late to save himself!"

"Beryl? What foolishness are you talking? I declare you look quite white over it!"

As indeed she did. Carried away by her thoughts, the situation she had pictured had appeared so vividly before her mental vision that she was frightened at her own imaginings. But she recovered herself quickly, and turned her eyes from the sky above to meet her lover's glance, and as she did so he saw in them both smiles and tears.

"What queer fancies you do have, Beryl," he said, after a pause. "You always had strange fears or presentiments about this man! Do you remember? It was your fanciful presentiments that caused you to make me promise to refuse all his offers. See what has come of that! You are here yourself!"

"Ah! But how much better, if you were to come here, that I should be here too! Has it not all turned out for the best?"

"Let us hope so, at any rate, dearest, and be thankful for it," said Arnold, devoutly.

"And now tell me all your adventures—everything—from the time I last saw you," Beryl asked.

But at that moment they heard a hail, and, looking round, saw Leslie standing upon the bank on the opposite side of the river.

As it was impossible to hear what he was shouting, Arnold paddled across to him.

"I saw you two from over yonder," he said, as they came within speaking distance. "I was walking with our friend Gaylia. But he has some duties to attend to, and we were just turning back when I caught sight of you and thought you might not mind my joining you for a short time. Then our friend is going to trot me round, and show me more of the place."

"Come along, Mr Gordon. You won't be *de trop,"* Beryl declared, laughingly. "Arnold was just going to begin his account of all your adventures. You will be able to check his statements and see that be leaves nothing out."

"All right; let him fire away," returned Gordon, as he made himself comfortable in the bow. "I'll dot his i's and cross his t's for him."

"And you'll be able to tell all your own part yourself," Arnold put in, slyly. "All about the young lady whose name was Rhelma, and the love-making that went on. I couldn't recount all that as I wasn't there."

"Dear me!" exclaimed Beryl; and, as she looked at Gordon, and noted the colour that rose in his face, a mischievous light came into her eyes. "This is indeed something to listen to! A young lady! And—what did you say her name was?"

"Rhelma," Arnold told her again, and, to make sure that she understood he spelt it for her. "She is the lady of the haunted mountain, and goes about guarded by a white lion—or lioness,—and her father's another wonderful magician, and did all sorts of marvellous things, and he's a relative of Lyostrah. There! There should be the making of a good story in all that; don't you think so, Beryl? In fact, all that there is worth the telling in our adventures, as you call them, happened to Leslie while he was off 'on his own.' My own experiences have been mere prosy, humdrum commonplaces by comparison."

"I am going to settle myself down with the idea of listening to a new version of the Arabian Nights' Entertainment," Beryl then declared. "If it be as you say, Arnold, you had better begin, and let the dull part come first."

"Quite so," Leslie assented. "Silence, please, for the dull part. It is called 'Ye doleful journey of ye tearful lover and his sympathetic friend.'"

Arnold disdained to take any notice of this pleasantry, and commenced his recital without further preface. Beryl listened to it attentively and almost in silence, making only a brief comment here and there.

He stopped when he came to their arrival at the camping ground opposite the haunted mountain.

"It is very curious," Beryl then observed, thoughtfully, "how all that corresponds with what you saw in the magic glasses, as we called them, that night on board the yacht. It seems to suggest that Lyostrah was then, in that mysterious fashion, foreshadowing to you what your own adventures were to be."

"Just what Leslie and I have said many times," Arnold agreed.

"But then—he must have thought it all out, planned, and made up his mind about the whole affair—about carrying off my aunt and myself and all—just in that short space of time while he was talking to you, and showing you his wonderful inventions."

"Just so. No doubt he did. Little did I then suspect what was passing in his mind all the time that he affected to be so easily reconciled to the disappointment I had sprung upon him, and while he talked so glibly! Yet even of his talk every word was chosen, spoken with an object."

"Y—es. One can see that now," Beryl declared.

"And, in regard to what he showed Arnold," Leslie put in, "we have since perceived that each subject was chosen for some particular reason."

"How so?"

"The demonstrations concerning the production of artificial heat and cold, and so on, were intended to ease Arnold's mind subsequently in regard to the journey as it affected yourself, Miss Beryl Then the other matters, the telegraphic communication with his agent at Caracas, and the magic, bulletproof garments, were shown to demonstrate to Arnold, in advance, the futility of endeavouring to intercept the yacht, or to attack him *en route.* They were all 'trotted out' with an object?"

"How quickly, then, he must have planned and decided!" Beryl said again. "It shows, once more, that he must have an extraordinary brain. But, do you know, I don't think his busy brain work stopped even there. I have wondered several times whether the lawyers' letter that drew you up to town was not a sort—you know—"

"A ruse to get us out of the way!" exclaimed Leslie, slapping his knee. "Why, of course! What fools we have been not to see that before. Don't you see it now, Arnold? That our journey was a mere wild-goose chase, planned out for us by our dear, scheming friend?"

At this Arnold made a lugubrious face. "It never occurred to either of us that we were being made fools of, Beryl," he said; "but I think there is not much room for doubt about it, once you look at it as possible. The outrageous—"

"Nay, nay, dear Arnold," Beryl objected, holding up her hand and checking his outburst. "We have forgiven, have we not? Do not worry about it any more. Now, please, I am impatient to hear the rest of the story—about Mr Gordon's young lady, you know," she concluded, demurely.

"Gordon's young lady! Hoorooh! You've hit it exactly, Beryl," Arnold exclaimed, with sudden vivacity. "Drive ahead, Gordon. This part of the story, Beryl, is entitled, 'Ye journey of ye knight-errant Sir Gordon to ye haunted mountain; and how he rescued ye lovely young damsel and nearly shot her faithful lioness guard by mistake. And how he then performed prodigies of valour, for he did run away and hide in ye convenient tree—'"

But Beryl laughingly put her hand over his mouth; and Leslie, after a preliminary remark expressive of his great and scathing contempt for the other's weak attempt at drollery, plunged at once into an exact, true, and particular account of his meeting, with Rhelma, and his subsequent visit to her father.

As he proceeded, Beryl grew more and more interested, and at its conclusion drew a long breath.

"How very extraordinary it all sounds! How strange that you should have met with these people! But for the accident that befell her, and the chance that led you in that direction just at that very time, and induced you to follow the puma and so come upon her footsteps in the sand, we should not have suspected their existence. But, there," she broke off; "I do not believe in chance; there is no such thing. The question now is, What does all this portend? What is it to lead up to? Is it a warning? and ought we to try to read its import? or what does it mean? Somehow, do you know, I fancy this is all much more important than you seem to have deemed it."

"I don't know that we have been disposed to underrate its importance, Miss Beryl," Leslie explained to her. "But, you see, events have moved so fast since that we could scarcely keep up with them. For my own part, my thoughts have been so taken up with the panorama of fresh scenes passing before me, that I have, as yet, had no time to think these matters out properly. One requires a pause, a breathing time, as it were, in which one can sit down and have a good 'think' undisturbed, before one can satisfactorily appraise all that has happened, and try to fit each part into its proper place in the puzzle."

"Yes; that is quite true," Beryl agreed, with a contemplative air. "But now that we all three of us seem likely to have such a breathing time, we must put our heads together and see what we can make of it. Like you, Mr Gordon, I dislike this new complication, this priestess coming on the scene."

"I thought you would," Leslie answered. "However, she does not appear to be on the scene yet, judging by last night. Have you heard anything of her?"

"Yes—a little. I have heard Lyostrah speak of her—but nothing much. I have also heard her name mentioned by others since I have been here. She does not seem to be about much. Keeps to herself, I fancy, in her own domain."

"Sulks in her tent, to put it another way," commented Gordon. "I like that less still. It is all a mystery; and the one who holds all the threads in his hands is as inscrutable as the sphinx. By the way, that reminds me;—I watched our friend very carefully last night, and I am persuaded that what you said in your letter is correct. There *is* a change in him. The question is, is it for the better?"

"I think," Beryl answered, falling again into the dreamy manner of a little while back, as though striving to read her answer in her own inner consciousness, "I think that he seems, somehow, softened, more gentle."

"Yes," Leslie assented, but with a doubtful sound in his tone. "I saw that, and I admit it; and, so far, that would be to the good. But I also fancied I saw something else which, as I fear, would not tend to our advantage. I thought, at times, there was a shadow upon his face, a look as of doubt and perplexity."

"But why," Arnold asked, "should that affect us, either one way or the other?"

"Only in this way:—The Lorenzo that I knew, a year or so ago, was a man of iron resolution, absolutely self-reliant, never allowing the slightest doubt to interfere between himself and any course to which he had once made up his mind. If, then, the Lyostrah of to-day, as we know him, admits into his mind doubts and hesitations—I will not go so far as to suggest fears— it becomes a matter of probable inference that something has happened recently for which he was not prepared, and which is upsetting, or is likely to upset, his calculations. For such a man, to even doubt at all is a wonder in itself. Where, then, is the cause? What has happened to disturb the godlike calm, the colossal self-esteem, the sublime self-belief of this egoist? It cannot be any small thing. It must be what *we* should consider some- thing important—more likely a grave danger. And anything that would be a danger to him, would in all probability be a danger to us. Thus I read the riddle—so far as we can guess at it at present."

"I see," Arnold replied, gravely. "Yes; I can see that your argument is a good one."

"At the same time," Beryl observed, "let me suggest that the air of doubt and uncertainty you speak of may possibly—I only say possibly—arise from a different cause to the one you have indicated. We have had many long arguments upon religious and spiritual matters, and I do hope and believe that I may have made some impression upon him. When I first knew him he seemed to be a very pagan at heart, and spoke so cynically of everything connected with our religion that it hurt me deeply to listen to him. He used to sneer and gibe at everything that is holy and good. He appeared to believe that there was not one single soul to be found in the whole world who was a sincere, pure-hearted believer in our religion. You cannot think how his cruel, cutting sarcasms used to hurt me! It was chiefly on that account that I did not like him, and that I dreaded that you, Arnold, should fall under the influence of his cynical nature. But latterly he has been less sceptical, less obstinately unbelieving in his talk. He does not openly scoff at that which is sacred, or declare that true piety is non-existent He actually, the other day, went so far as to admit to me that he believed there might be found in the world *one* honest soul, following our religion in simple, unworldly faith and devotion. Now, that is a great step for *him!* And, that step once taken, who can say how much farther upon the right path his newly-found doubts as to his own infallibility may carry him? So, you see, what you have noticed may arise from a different cause to that which you have suggested. But what I have said does not explain the mystery of how this change has been brought about; and I have asked myself and wondered, many times, what can have happened to him to have wrought even so small a change as that, within the last few months?"

Neither Neville nor Leslie made any answer, but the thoughts of each ran in the same groove. *They* found no difficulty in tracing any such change for the better to Lyostrah's having passed "the last few months" in the constant society of that "one sincere, pure-hearted believer," whose existence he now admitted.

THIS WAS the first of many happy days which the re-united friends spent together; days that quickly grew into weeks and months. Beryl's first impressions of the country and its people, and the opinions and anticipations she had expressed, were fully borne out by their subsequent experience. The climate proved to be delightful, the people amiable and friendly, and Lyostrah showed himself a courteous and hospitable host. After the trials and troubles of their long travels their present surroundings seemed a veritable Elysium, and hey made the most of the fleeting happy hours, little dreaming of the sombre shadows and direful mysteries that were slowly but surely creeping across their path.

CHAPTER XXIII

THE TEMPLE OF DORNANDA

DURING A PERIOD of some three months, matters continued to run along—or drift along—with Arnold Neville and his friends, amid their new surroundings, very much in the same groove as at their first arrival. They found the climate so enjoyable, the people so hospitable and sociable—and they had had, be it remembered, such a rough time of it during the many months to which the duration of their journey to the place had extended—that they thoroughly enjoyed the long and pleasant rest that these three months represented.

By the end of the period they had come to know the whole country—with certain exceptions hereafter noted—thoroughly; and had formed many agreeable friendships among its people.

As to the country, they soon came to understand its situation, and the knowledge served to explain how it had happened that its existence, with its ancient City, its considerable population, and its busy workshops, had remained undiscovered, unsuspected by the world in general; and even by their neighbours—comparatively speaking—the Government and people of Brazil.

The territory consisted of a vast plain or basin, forming a table-land, and lying at an elevation of something like twelve thousand feet above the level of the sea. This plain was enclosed and shut in on all sides by cliffs, which rose still higher. These were jagged and castellated, running into a thousand picturesque pinnacles and fantastic peaks. On the outer side they rose sheer, in the form of a mighty, perpendicular, rocky wall, from

an impenetrable maze of forest and swamp, and fierce, rushing, unnavigable torrents and rivers. This tangle of impassable
swamp and wood extended for two or three days' journey on all
sides, and no traveller, in the ordinary sense of the word, had
ever passed beyond its outer fringe.

The existence, in its midst, therefore, of this great rectan-
gular wall of rock and the country it encloses, has, as stated,
remained entirely unknown to the white man. And though some
of the tribes of Indians that wander about the district have long
told their marvellous tales* of a wonderful City hidden away
somewhere in the inhospitable tract, their talk has never been
regarded as sufficiently reliable to induce any explorer to face
the difficulties of search in such a region. Nor is there a probability that if anyone had essayed the task his enterprise would
have been successful; enough has been revealed in the manner
in which Neville and his friend were guided thither, to show the
hopelessness of attempting the feat without the special knowledge and appliances by which they were aided.

A curious feature of the country consisted in the fact that
within this large plain, thus enclosed in a natural wall of precipitous cliffs, lay another much smaller area, similarly enclosed,
and forming a small model, as it were, of the whole; analogous
to a citadel within a fortress. This curious area lay at one end
of the larger plain, where perpendicular walls suddenly rose to
a height of a thousand feet or so, enclosing within their limits
another smaller basin, about two square miles in extent, and,
roughly speaking, a quadrangle in shape.

The lowest part of the space thus enclosed was fully five
hundred feet above the level of the larger plain, and was stated
to contain a small lake which, in fact, fed the river which mean-
dered through the latter. This river issued from an opening or

---

* It is the fact that similar tales of mysterious lost cities, tenanted by still-living
remnants of ancient races, are common amongst the Indian tribes of Central and South
America, especially those of Mexico, Brazil, Argentina, and Peru. And the extensive
ruins which, even now, frequently reward a search in the depths of some of the vast
tangled forests, tend to show that in some cases, at least, these tales may have had, in
the past, some solid foundation.

tunnel in the solid rock, similar to that from which the travellers had emerged on their arrival, and which lay on the opposite
side of the territory.

The whole area thus detached, as it were, was called Maviena,
which might be interpreted in two or three ways—*e.g.,* "The
Sacred Land," or "City," or "City of the Dead." The whole of
the face of the rock from which the river issued had been carved
into a temple, so designed that the pinnacles that towered up a
thousand feet into the air, were made to represent turrets, towers,
or spires, all exquisitely and most elaborately carved and sculptured. Below these were arches, hanging terraces, staircases,
balconies, colonnades, all carved in the solid rock upon a Titanic
scale. Viewed from a distance the whole had the appearance of a
colossal temple, from eight hundred to a thousand feet high, and
nearly a mile in width. Every portion of this extensive surface
was delicately chiselled, and in many parts decorated in colours
which had withstood the test of time and were still bright and
glowing. These decorations sometimes took the form of intricate
patterns and fanciful designs; at others they consisted of figures
of serpents, alligators, birds, animals, etc., boldly executed upon
an immense scale.

Either the rock naturally contained some shining substances
embedded in its mass, or something of the kind had been
worked into the decorations, for, under the rays of the sun, the
whole mass glistened and sparkled, and was, in places, irides-
cent, dazzling the eyes to look upon it. At sunset, effects were
often seen that are fairly indescribable; at other times, again,
the mountain mists would descend and rest in layers across the
front, causing the parts in shadow below to take on an aspect
of terrible, frowning grandeur, while the upper portions were
shimmering and dancing in the sunlight.

This temple was dedicated to a god or spirit called Dornanda,
supposed to be the special protecting deity of the Myrvonian
people. It was understood that the two square miles or so of
enclosed, high-lying land at the back of the temple, were laid
out principally in groves and gardens reserved exclusively for

the priests and priestesses and their particular attendants. Very few outside the priestly circle were permitted to so much as look upon this "forbidden land," as it was often called amongst the people. Another name for it was the "Sacred Gardens."

But, underneath this land, again, the solid rock was hewn out into miles upon miles of galleries and subterranean chambers, forming extensive catacombs, wherein reposed the embalmed bodies of countless generations of dead and gone Myrvonians, comprising, as Manzoni had explained, not only those who died in the country, but numberless others who had died abroad.

Upon this subject Leslie managed to pick up information from Gaylia, who, being a privileged individual, had been allowed to view some of these galleries. He confided to Leslie, with whom he had gradually become very friendly and confidential, a graphic description of what he had seen, and Leslie, in turn, repeated it, one day, to the wondering ears of Arnold and Beryl; and these are a few of the particulars:

"Gaylia said that what impresses you most," Leslie commenced, "is the wonderfully life-like appearance of these mummies. They are not dried up, as are the mummies of Egypt and other parts of the world. Therefore, it would appear, the process here employed must be one entirely unknown elsewhere. It is now a lost art even here. It is hundreds of years, at least, since the secret was lost.

"In any case, and however it was done, the effect, Gaylia affirms, is most surprising. The dead appear as though actually alive; they seem to be sleeping, or, as it were, temporarily stupefied. And they are not laid in coffins, as was usually the case in ancient Egypt and Etruria; they are placed about in positions such as they might naturally assume if they were alive. Thus you may see soldiers, fully dressed, and equipped with complete arms and armour, standing in long rows, their officers beside them, as though on parade. In the case of high personages—kings, princes, generals, priests of high rank, and so on—you can see them arranged in groups, the king on his throne, and his courtiers or officers and attendants around him, all dressed as they were in life. I should have explained, by the way, that they are all placed in vaulted chambers beside the galleries, with glass walls on one side, so that, as you pass along the passages, you look through the glass and see them as if you were looking through windows. These chambers are hermetically sealed, which partly accounts, no doubt, for the fact that the mummies are still in such a wonderful state of preservation. But, allowing for all that has been suggested, there is still something very extraordinary about it all, unless there is anything in the idea that there is some preservative property about the rock in which these catacombs have been made. If that were so, it might also help to account for the undoubted fanatical anxiety of those who died away from the place to be brought here to be—we can't in this case say 'buried,' so I suppose we must substitute—'preserved.' You can understand that they would argue that it was of little use to go to the expense and trouble of being embalmed (embalming was always an expensive luxury, you know) unless there was reasonable ground for believing that they would thereby be 'preserved' until the appointed time."

"How do you mean?" Beryl inquired. "What appointed time?"

"The Egyptians believed that at the end of a certain cycle of time—some put it at two thousand years, some as high as ten thousand—they would live again; and the object of embalming, consequently, was to 'preserve' their bodies uninjured, and in as perfect a state as possible, against that resurrection. No doubt the object here would be the same; which points to a certain identity or similarity of religious belief."

"I see. But about those vaults, in which you say are to be seen groups, such as a king surrounded by his courtiers, what does that import? Were they, do you suppose, the bodies of those who had been his actual courtiers or attendants, during life, or others dressed up to represent them? And if the former—how could it be managed—unless—"

"I believe I can fill in that question for you," said Leslie, as Beryl hesitated to put into words the idea that had presented itself. "Did they, you would ask, when a king or great man died, kill off his officers and attendants and so on, so as to be able to bury them all together? I think it quite possible that they might have done so. It is the custom to-day, as we know, among many savage races, to kill off a dead king's servants and dogs and horses, that they may be at hand to wait upon him in his future existence."

"What a ghastly idea!" Arnold exclaimed, with a shudder.

"It is. Yet, seeing that it still survives in some parts at the present time, it is likely enough to have been the rule here in the pre-historic days in which these old johnnies flourished.

"It is a curious fact," he went on, "that so far as history takes us back—which, by-the-by, is only a few hundred years at the most,—America was always notable for the extraordinary number of human victims sacrificed in the religious rites of the Inhabitants. Prescott estimates, from reliable data, that, at the time the Spaniards first invaded Mexico, the number of human beings thus immolated in that country alone was not less than fifty thousand a year. Think of that! A thousand victims a week; or more than one hundred and forty a day!"

"Horrible! Almost incredible! But there is one thing to be said," Arnold answered; "if human sacrifice was ever a part of the religious rites of these people amongst whom we are now living, it has not survived to the present day."

"Perhaps not—but—how can we say?" was Leslie's enigmatic answer, given in a very dry tone.

"Great heavens, Mr Gordon!" exclaimed Beryl, turning visibly paler, "how can you say that! Why, of *course* there's nothing of the kind going on here now."

"Possibly not, as I said. But you can scarcely say we *know*, because we may not have been here long enough to find out. Such practices, if indulged in at all, are usually reserved for certain festivals, and these may occur but once in six months, or once a year."

"To go back to these catacombs," Arnold put in; "are they on view now? Could we see them?"

"It appears not. They have been closed to the public, as we should say at home, for the last few years. Someone strayed away, and got lost in them, and died raving mad. That, or something of the sort, was the alleged reason."

"Enough to send anyone mad, to be lost in such a terrible place," Beryl declared, with a shudder. "But are the galleries really so extensive as all that?"

"Gaylia declares that they extend for miles and miles. The whole of the miles of rock lying beneath the 'Sacred Gardens' is honeycombed with galleries running to and fro, one beside the other and one above the other, as close as they could be made with safety. He says that the mummies there are known to amount to something like seven or eight millions."

"Surely that must be an exaggeration!"

"I don't know," Leslie answered, thoughtfully. "The mummies in some of the burying-places of Egypt were probably as numerous. There were labyrinths in the Nile valley that extended, as these do, for many miles. And, to take another case, there is the well-known cemetery at Rome. It is credibly computed that over six million people have been buried in it. They were not mummies, it is true; but that does not affect the question of numbers. Then, again, there are the catacombs underneath Paris. Altogether, I see nothing impossible in Gaylia's statement."

These comments of Leslie's were then regarded by his hearers as mere fanciful speculations. But the time was at hand when they were to assume a new and sinister, almost prophetic, meaning.

CHAPTER XXIV

GATHERING SHADOWS

IT HAS BEEN said that the three months which Neville and his friends had spent in the country of Myrvonia had "drifted" by—that is, perhaps, the best term that could be used in the circumstances. Arnold and Beryl, engrossed in each other, as lovers are apt to be, took no heed of the flight of time. Mrs Beresford was quietly satisfied with everything, and saw no reason to trouble herself concerning the future. She was treated, as Beryl would sometimes tell her with a merry laugh, "like a dowager princess," and apparently found the life much more to her taste than the dull existence she had been passing in the Isle of Wight.

Leslie was the only one of the four who experienced any feeling of uneasiness or doubt In one sense, certainly, he had every reason to be satisfied with the way in which he was treated; but that was just one of the things that troubled him. He had been left free to do much as he pleased, and he would have preferred to be appointed to a post, or given some definite, active employment.

It was quite true, as Lyostrah had said, that they were all workers there. Decidedly there appeared to be no idlers; but what they all worked at Leslie could not find out There were busy workshops and factories, but what they were making in them he could not tell. Some, apparently, were manufacturing arms, so he thought; but he had no proof of it; and the articles themselves were of a design so strange that he could not guess their use or application, and those who made them were no wiser. It was the same everywhere He had expected, when he first came, to be able to watch the manufacture of some of Lyostrah's many surprising inventions; and learn their secrets. He had been able to do the first; but not the last. He could witness only the manufacture of the respective parts. These were made to exact drawings and instructions; but how they were to be fitted together, or what they would form when so fitted, not even those knew who laboured upon them day after day.

It had been the same as regards Arnold. Lyostrah had said nothing, done nothing, in the direction of explaining why he had been so anxious to bring him all the way from England. He had given him no appointment, no recognised position. He laughingly said, on two or three occasions, that he thought that after their toilsome journey both the young men required and deserved a good long holiday; and with that vague suggestion as to the cause of the delay, they had, perforce, to be content. Lyostrah was not one to be questioned when he did not choose to speak; and the two friends, therefore, had no alternative but to exercise patience.

Arnold did not much trouble about all this. He said they must await their patron's own time, and that, for his part, he was content to do so. But Leslie was less patient. The inaction was irksome to him; he chafed and fretted against it, and, of course, be it remembered, he had not his friend's reasons for being satisfied with things as they were.

So while Arnold and Beryl, with or without Mrs Beresford, and others with whom they had made friends, passed their time in rowing upon the river, or little picnics, music, and other harmless amusements, Leslie wandered aimlessly about, seeking wherewithal to occupy himself, but finding not that which he sought. By way of a distraction, he had taken up the study of the language of the country, and had worked at it to such good purpose that he could now understand and speak it with fluency and ease.

Perhaps his thoughts reverted a little too often to the fascinating Rhelma; and this may have been partly to blame for his feelings of vague dissatisfaction and uneasiness. Certain it is that he often found himself wondering what Manzoni and his fair daughter were doing, and whether, or when, he should see them again. Manzoni had given promises which led Leslie to think that he might expect some day to meet them, or hear of them—but when? Perhaps this partly explained his outbursts of impatience.

Then there was Lyostrah; he puzzled himself about him, too. Whatever the cause, it was clear to Leslie that there was some change going on in him. They did not see much of him, it was true; he was most of the time invisible, supposed to be deeply engaged in his scientific or mechanical studies and experiments. It was also believed that a good deal of his time was passed in the Temple of Dornanda, why, none could say; and as the place—and even its vicinity—was forbidden ground to the general public, save when they were specially bidden to attend some religious function, no one knew anything certain about it.

Whatever Lyostrah's secret occupations, however, the fact remained that, to Leslie's eyes, he was visibly changing from week to week. Each time he came amongst them, the cloud which Leslie had noted upon his face the first night of his arrival—and which he had never seen there before—was more perceptible, and its shadow was deeper. The look of sublime self-reliance and dignified repose would frequently now give place to an irritable restlessness, shown by a biting of the lip, or a constant change of pose; and this again would be succeeded by fits of deep abstraction, in which, even in the midst of the gaieties over which he was presiding, he would appear to have entirely forgotten everybody and everything around him.

Something, Leslie decided, was worrying him; something was not going precisely as it should do; and, whatever it was, Leslie believed he could see that it was growing worse at an accelerated pace.

This conviction caused him to keep a sharp look-out upon all sides; and from those of the inhabitants with whom he came in contact he concealed his growing familiarity with their language, in order that they might deem it safe to talk amongst themselves in his hearing. There was little difficulty in doing this, since, as Gaylia had told him at first, almost every child understood English.

And this strategy was successful. By degrees he had heard hints, rumours, vague murmurs, which satisfied him that things were not going on satisfactorily in the country. What was the matter he could not yet discover; the people whose talk he overheard did not themselves appear to know. But by piecing together scraps heard here, and hints picked up there, he gradually became convinced that there was abroad amongst these kindly, well-disposed folk, a vague, undefined sense of coming danger, a lurking dread of some unseen evil, a brooding, shapeless sense of terror and apprehension. Up to the present he had kept this knowledge, such as it was, to himself. He had no clear evidence to put before anyone; and he shrank from disturbing the innocent happiness of his friends upon the strength of what might, after all, prove to be but a false alarm. He was not one to cry "wolf," until he was quite sure there *was* a wolf. Therefore, not even to Arnold, and still less to Gaylia—who had now become quite a close friend and companion—did he speak any word, or give any sign of the fears that were troubling him. But he redoubled his vigilance and watchfulness; and especially did he endeavour to mount guard over the safety of his friends without their knowledge, and without exciting their suspicions. On many a night he passed long hours watching from his window, looking out over the sleeping landscape—especially on moonlight nights—watching for he knew not what; or pacing noiselessly up and down the corridor outside the suite of apartments occupied by Mrs Beresford and her niece.

Somehow, he associated his fears with the mysterious, still invisible, arch-priestess, Alloyah. Since they had come to the country she had never appeared in public, and they had never seen her. This in itself was not, perhaps, conclusive, since it seemed that she had frequently before hidden herself from public view in similar fashion for months, and even a year at a time. Still, he had ascertained that she had presided at many "functions" previous to their arrival; why, then, had she suddenly shut herself up when they came? Why, if she had such a regard for Lyostrah as Manzoni had spoken of, had she not welcomed his friends, as everyone else in the country had done? Did it not look as though she regarded with disfavour the fact of his having brought those friends into the country? As though for that reason they had in her an enemy? Perhaps this was the cause of Lyostrah's strange behaviour. Perhaps his delay in doing or saying anything definite in regard to Arnold and himself had been caused by her opposition; and he was waiting in the hope that he might overcome it, or that it might die down of itself. But against this suggestion Leslie could not but recognise that Lyostrah was not a man likely to be turned from his fixed purpose by a woman's caprice. No; he must seek further yet.

Then an idea flashed across his mind. What if Lyostrah's arrival, after his long absence, in the company of two ladies, had roused this woman's jealousy? It was quite possible she might believe that Lyostrah was himself in love with Beryl, and that his ostensible interest in Neville had been assumed as a blind to his real feelings and designs. In that case, Lyostrah's apparent "cooling off" as regards Arnold might seem, to her eyes, to favour her idea, and serve to fan her smouldering jealous suspicions. If so—then—ah, then—what?

Leslie's blood seemed to turn cold, and a shiver passed over his senses as these ominous thoughts thrust themselves across his consciousness. For who could say what terrible vengeance such a woman might be preparing; what plots she might be hatching? And how could they contend with such a danger? how guard against such a silent, unseen enemy, brooding over a fancied injury, and planning revenge? How defend themselves against one armed, as she was, with all the opportunities that her peculiar position gave her, and backed, it was everywhere believed, by darker, hidden powers?

And yet—this again would not explain that feeling of dread

that was abroad amongst the people themselves. What had now occurred to him might only too possibly be actually the case; but there was yet something beyond, which affected the whole community as well as the four strangers. What, then, could it be?

Such were the real but unavowed reasons which had influenced him when he had reminded Beryl and Arnold, in such dry tones, that they had not yet been long enough in the country to justify them in taking for granted that all was just as it appeared to be on the surface.

It was a few days after this conversation that Lyostrah suddenly announced that he was about to set out upon a journey, and that he would consequently be absent from the country for a short time—perhaps (he said) for a week or two, possibly for a longer period.

This news fell on Leslie's ears with a sense of coming trouble. He could not but feel that, inexplicable as Lyostrah's behaviour was in his eyes, he was most certainly their one and only friend in the place upon whose protection they could—they had a right to—rely.

If his (Leslie's) distrust of the unseen Alloyah was in any way justified (and the more he pondered upon it, the more he came to believe that his fears were well-founded), then he felt persuaded that it would be during Lyostrah's absence that she would be likely to make whatever move she had been planning.

Obviously it behoved him to be more alert, more watchful than ever. Ought he not now, too, to take Arnold into his confidence, and warn him? But, if Arnold, then also Beryl and Mrs Beresford; and he shrank from doing this just yet. They were so innocently happy in their paradise—as it seemed to them—so unsuspicious of danger, of the darkening thunderclouds that he fancied he could distinguish lowering above their heads. Ought he to take any step which might suddenly change their happiness to vague apprehensions and alarms? Or ought he not rather to wait until he had, at least, something more tangible to go upon than mere undefined surmise?

How he wished, at this time, for a friend amongst those around them in whom he could confide! How he longed for one like Manzoni, who knew the people and their ways, and knew Alloyah too, and could weigh his shapeless fears, and advise him!

Strangely enough, one morning, a few days after Lyostrah's departure, as Leslie was brooding in the above vein, his friend Gaylia came to him and spoke words that seemed like a response to his unuttered wish.

"I have been seeking you, friend Leslie," he said. "I wish to speak to you upon a private matter. Can we go together to your own room?"

"Certainly, friend Gaylia," Leslie readily responded. "It is odd, but I was just thinking I would like to consult you upon a private matter of my own. Can it be, I wonder, that the two things have any connection?"

"Now, by Dornanda! that is strange! And yet not altogether so unexpected as you might suppose. For, do you know, I have thought several times of late that you looked as though you had something on your mind which you were on the point of telling me, and yet were afraid to venture."

"You have divined aright," said Leslie, linking his arm through Gaylia's. "I am more pleased at this than I can well tell you; the more especially that your esteemed Ruler's absence has accentuated the difficulty in which I have found myself, and increased my desire to seek the advice of someone in whose friendship I could trust."

"That is precisely why I came to you," returned Gaylia.

"I believe there is need for us to take counsel together, and advise, and, if need be, help each other."

CHAPTER XXV

THE HORROR IN THE LAND

"**AND NOW, MY** friend," said Leslie, when they were safely ensconced in an inner "sanctum," and quite secure against any danger of being overheard, "now tell me what it was you came to seek me about, and then you shall hear all that is in my own mind."

"I sought you," answered Gaylia, speaking slowly, and seeming to weigh every word, "because there are strange things, strange rumours abroad, and, what is worse; strange—foul doings in the land!"

Leslie looked at him for a moment or two in surprise. Then he said, gravely:

"Foul doings! That is serious news indeed! Queer rumours, undefined fears, unspoken dread, I have known of, but—"

"Ha! You have known that much? And you said nothing to me!"

"I said nothing to you, my dear friend, because—well, precisely because they *were* undefined, and, consequently, there seemed nothing to go upon, nothing to justify my troubling you. Moreover, my own fears have been rather of a personal nature; they have concerned, that is, ourselves—my friends who came with me here."

"So! I knew not of that!"

"You know of nothing that should cause us any special fear on our own account?"

"No. Do you, then?"

Leslie paused, and looked keenly at his companion. He still hesitated whether to give him his full confidence. But after a minute's reflection he went on:

"Then you know of nothing pointing to any special danger to one of our party—the young lady—"

"By Dornanda, no!" exclaimed Gaylia, with such sudden vehemence, that Leslie was taken altogether aback. But, taking no notice of his evident surprise, the young man went on, excitedly:

"Tell me, my friend Leslie, tell me, I pray you, is it so? Is there any danger threatening that good, beautiful, angelic lady? Let me know it at once! Can I be of any help? Make use of me in any way, every way, you think proper. I would give my life rather than anything should happen, in our country, to that innocent, lovable being!"

This outburst fairly astonished Leslie. But as he listened a great light burst in upon him, and he understood its real import. He saw that this good-hearted youth had fallen in love with the unconscious Beryl, and he perceived, too, that this formed the secret—the worthy, honourable secret—of the friendly disposition he had shown towards both Arnold and himself.... Arnold had been too much wrapped up in his *fiancée* to notice or profit by it; but to Leslie the friendship thus proffered had been, as we have seen, very acceptable, though he had been far from suspecting its real origin.

He was filled now with feelings of mingled pity and admiration—pity for the youth's hopeless love, and admiration of his manly way of showing it.

He deemed it, however, better not to appear to have divined his secret; so he replied quietly:

"I thank you from the bottom of my heart for your expressions of kindly concern and offer of help if help is required. At present, I am glad to be able to say, I know of no definite danger; it is, rather, a curious sort of uneasiness, or what is termed presentiment, that has forced itself upon my thoughts, than any actual sign of coming trouble. So let me hear what you have to say first. Perhaps the one may throw some light upon the other."

"My news is bad—about as bad as it can well be; indeed, for several reasons, it is worse than anyone would have imagined, for it savours not of open, honest danger, such as every soldier expects to have to face, and is, therefore, always ready to meet, but dangers that are secret, hidden, uncanny. We have here, apparently, to deal, not with enemies who come out into the light of day to meet us face to face, but with mysterious, prowling beings of the night, that lurk in shadows, and whose deeds—as it seems, for it has now come to deeds—are deeds of darkness and of honour!"

"Prowling beings! Deeds of darkness!" exclaimed Leslie. "What mean you? Tell me—pray tell me plainly what you mean?"

"Listen! my friend Leslie. For some time ugly stories have been floating about of strange beings of uncouth appearance, so far as could be made out in the shadows, which they evidently prefer, prowling about during the night when nearly everyone, save the men of our watch service, is asleep. For a long time past these stories have been rife—"

"Before our arrival here?"

"Oh yes; long before that. For a long time, I say, these stories have been floating about, spoken of shamefacedly, talked of in whispers, as it were, as children speak in hushed tones of ghosts and goblins. But for a while there was nothing tangible, nothing definite, about them, and we—that is, those in authority—I myself, for instance—treated such statements just as one *would* treat children's goblin tales.

"Latterly, however, these vague assertions of something uncanny going forward have begun to assume more precise forms. There is one thing in particular, for instance, that has been credibly asserted by several trustworthy witnesses. It is that a large black canoe, paddled, by a ghastly, spectral crew, of horrible shapes, half-men, half-goblins, has been seen at night upon our river."

"Ah!" Leslie started, and uttered the one word, and then checked himself.

"What! Do you then know anything of it?"

"I have seen it," Leslie replied, gravely, "or something like it— something of which that would be no unfair description. But it was a long way off—I was looking out of my window at night; there was a moon, but what I saw crept along in the shadows, so that I could not make it out distinctly. I have seen it twice."

"So! And what did you judge it to be?"

"A party of Indians. It did not strike me at the time as anything out of the way. You have a few Indians here, and I thought it likely enough that they were patrolling the stream by order, though I remember wondering why. They also seemed to me to be an unusually ugly, ill-formed lot."

"They were not Indians, my friend. They could not be. No Indians are allowed to prowl about at night here, either in canoes or out of them. They are confined to their own quarters, and every evening the roll is called, and guards are set for the night to make sure that they do not leave those quarters. Moreover, it happens to be part of my special duties to see that these regulations are strictly observed. To say, therefore, that the Indians who are with us can get out at night and amuse themselves paddling about in canoes, or in any other manner, is to cast a reflection upon my vigilance, and to suggest that I am careless, or allow the men under me to neglect their duties."

"Nay, my dear friend, I *was* very far—"

"I know you did not understand it so. But these beings are not Indians. They do not, I am assured, resemble Indians, save, perhaps, when seen from a distance and in a bad light, as in your case. Nor would such Indians be likely to chase any of our people who chanced to be about, as these have done. They would not dare to. And, again, why should they?"

"Chase people! How do you mean?"

"Complaints have reached us, during some time past, of mysterious beings who darted out of the shadows and made attacks upon individuals who happened to be about alone in the dark. Not upon our soldiers or any of the watch; they seem too artful to attempt that. But persons compelled to be out during the night in lonely places, looking after our cattle, and so on, have declared that they have been attacked and chased by beings whose very appearance frightened them nearly out of their senses."

"Can that be true?"

"For long we ourselves have pooh-poohed these tales; but latterly we have been compelled to regard them more seriously, because some of our people have undoubtedly disappeared—"

"Disappeared!"

"Ay; of that there seems to be little doubt. The story goes that this canoe with its strange crew has been seen at intervals of a month—always about the time of the full of the moon—for some time past, and that its advent has invariably been followed by the disappearance of at least one—sometimes more—of our people. But, as no trace could be found pointing to the actual cause of their disappearance, we still remained doubtful and uncertain what to think, till this morning."

"Till this morning! And now—?"

"Now, my friend," Gaylia answered, solemnly, "we have found the body of one of our citizens not only dead—evidently foully murdered—but half-eaten!"

"Half-eaten? Why, surely—some wild beast—"

Gaylia sorrowfully shook his head.

"There are, as you know, no wild beasts in our country; besides—I have not finished. The body was lying on the bank of the river, and beside it, in the soft sand, were footmarks—not of wild beasts—but the prints of naked feet, and those the feet of a human being!"

Leslie was silent. The whole affair was so surprising, so utterly different to anything he had expected to hear, that he really knew not what to say. He wanted time to collect his ideas, and to think out such an extraordinary statement Thought followed thought in his mind, and he recalled all that he himself had heard or suspected, and reviewed it by the aid of this new and lurid light. He could now, at any rate, understand the feelings of vague, undefined fear and dread that he knew had been abroad in the land. Clearly, he had been right in his surmises as to that; but this explanation of the puzzle was a terrible revelation indeed.

"Surely it cannot be true," he murmured, more to himself than to his companion.

"I can hardly believe it myself," Gaylia declared; "but there is the horrible evidence. What I want to know is, whom have we here to deal with? Human beings, or—"

He paused, and looked at Leslie in blank perplexity, evidently hesitating to fill in the end of his own speech, afraid to speak what was in his mind. Presently he continued:

"It is a dreadful affair, not merely in itself—and it is repulsive; ghastly enough, even if it stood alone—but in the panic it has created. The relatives of those who have disappeared are running frantically up and down crying out that the missing ones must have been treated in the same way, only that in their case no traces were left; and one does not know what to say to pacify them.

"Our Ruler is away, and we know not how to act. Never in our history, for many a long year, has so foul a deed been committed. We have no murderers, no criminals here; there has, till all this began, been perfect confidence between man and man. Our citizens are peaceful, quiet-loving folk, and a single murder would be sufficient to scare them out of all their accustomed equanimity; but a series, as we have but too good reason to suspect here—!"

"One madman—say a crazy, bloodthirstily-inclined Indian, combining an Indian's craft with the madman's proverbial cunning, might do a lot of mischief before he was hunted down," Leslie ventured, by way of suggesting a possible solution.

Gaylia shook his head.

"No," he said, with decision; "one Indian might go mad, and turn into a sort of man-wolf; but not a whole crowd of them."

"One really does not know what to say on the spur of the moment," Leslie observed. "That sounds weak, I know, but:—"

"But it is frank, my friend, though, to us, a little disappointing. We were in hopes that you might be able to assist or advise us. We know nothing here of the great world outside, nor do we know where our Ruler has gone, or how long he is likely to be absent. Since, however, he has brought you here, and shown that he considers you as his friend, we thought you might be in his confidence, and so be able to tell us—"

It was Leslie's turn now to shake his head; nor could he resist a slight smile at the other's simplicity in supposing that he and Arnold were in Lyostrah's confidence.

"Your master," he replied, "is not a man, I fancy, much given to taking people into his confidence."

"I know that—at least, as regards ourselves. But with you we hoped it might be otherwise. If he were here, he would, of course, take this affair in hand himself. As it is, we are in doubt as to what we ought to do."

Leslie pondered awhile, turning matters rapidly over in his mind.

"I'll tell you what I would suggest," he said at last. "If you think well, I would propose that you and I take this matter, for the present, into our own hands. Keep your own counsel; say nothing to anyone; but to-night meet me outside the palace at ten o'clock, and let us go together and watch for this mysterious canoe and its cannibalistic crew. We will see if we cannot hunt them down by ourselves."

After a few minutes' consideration, Gaylia agreed.

"Good," he said. "We will, as you say, hunt them down together; or, at least, we will find out whether they are men or devils!"

And, after a little further talk, the two separated, to meet again at night and start upon their adventurous mission.

CHAPTER XXVI

BERYL'S DREAM

THE SURPRISES OF that morning for Gordon Leslie were not, however, yet over, for he had not long parted from his friend Gaylia, and was still sitting thinking over the story that had been told him, when Arnold came hastily into the room.

At the first glance Leslie saw that something was amiss, and a dull apprehension fell upon him of new troubles, relating this time—he somehow felt sure—to Beryl.

"Why, Arnold, what is the matter?" he asked, before the other, who was evidently excited, could speak.

"Beryl is unwell—ill—upset; I hardly know how to describe it," was the reply. "She wishes to see you. Can you come round there?"

"Certainly; I will come at once. But, pray, tell me what is the trouble. We can talk as we go along."

"The fact is," said Arnold, as they passed through the corridor towards Mrs Beresford's suite of apartments, "Beryl has had a terrible dream."

"A dream!" Leslie repeated. "Thank Heaven it is nothing more. I feared from your manner—and—well—I fancy I have been a little nervous myself, lately. I feared it was something serious."

"But anything is serious that makes her ill!"

"True. Forgive me. I—feel rather out of sorts this morning. Pray, tell me all about it."

"That is just what I cannot yet do; she has not even told her aunt. It must, however, have been a very nasty, very vivid dream, to upset her so. You know that, as a rule, she is neither nervous nor timid."

"Far from it; I have always marvelled that one so delicate and sensitive should be so plucky. As you say, it can have been no ordinary sort of dream that could so disturb her."

"Mrs Beresford says that she is still quite ill, and that, early this morning, she was seriously concerned about her. She would answer no questions, but lay and moaned, as if in pain, and every now and then screamed out, as though at the memory of some sight too dreadful to bear. She was trembling like one who had been badly frightened, or received some terrible shock; her eyes, Mrs Beresford says, were wild and terrified, like those of a hunted hare, and the glances she kept casting on all sides were pitiful in their expression of extreme fear. She seems more composed now, and has been able to get up; and she says she wishes to tell her dream to you and me together, if you will indulge her foolish fancies. Do you mind, old man?"

"Mind? I should think not, Arnold! I am more sorry than I can possibly say, and, coming just now, everything may be of importance."

"Why 'just now'? However, here we are."

Mrs Beresford came to them in an outer room, and, in answer to their inquiries, said that Beryl was rather more composed, but appeared to be still very weak.

"I cannot think what can have happened," said the good lady, in tones of mingled anxiety and perplexity. "Knowing her as I do, it seems absurd to suppose that a mere dream, however disagreeable, can have affected her like this! Up to yesterday I know that she herself would have been the first to scout such an idea as childish. It is very strange."

"What *was* the dream?" Leslie asked.

"Why, that's just what she obstinately refuses to tell me," returned Mrs Beresford, with some vexation in her tone. "She says it would upset me too much—*me!*" she repeated, almost scornfully, "as though I were some child who might afterwards be too frightened to sleep alone. But there it is. She will not tell me anything till she has told you two; then, it seems, if you choose to confide it to me, I am to be allowed to listen to it at second hand. However, the poor child is too weak and ill to be worried. I suppose I must indulge her fancy," concluded the good-natured dame; "so I will take you in to her, and then take myself off till she sends me further orders."

They found Beryl really very ill. Though what they had heard had in some measure prepared them, they were both surprised and grieved at her appearance. A stranger might have supposed that she was just recovering from some enfeebling sickness. She was visibly thinner than when they had last seen her; her cheeks looked almost hollow; she was deadly pale, and there were dark circles round her eyes.

She smiled feebly, as she greeted her visitors, and, after many preliminary questions and answers on both sides, Mrs Beresford left the three together, and Beryl commenced the relation of the dream that had so affected her.

"Last night," she began, "towards bedtime, I grew singularly restless and excited. When I went into my bedroom, I decided at once that it would be useless to go to bed, for I knew that I should not be able to sleep, so I took up a book—one of the two or three old favourites I was permitted to bring with me—and essayed to read. But, try as I would, I could not fix my mind upon the page before me. I felt terribly uneasy and anxious. It was just such a feeling as one sometimes experiences before a coming storm, when the air is heavy and oppressive, and one is filled with a kind of dread of what is going to happen. Presently I threw down the book, opened the window, and looked out. It was a lovely, an enchanting night! The moon was nearly full, and the river and all the country around lay before my eyes, tranquilly sleeping in the glorious moonlight. I sat, I may truly say, entranced, and the peaceful beauty of the scene had a deliciously soothing effect upon my excited feelings. I grew drowsy, dreamy, and gave myself up to all kinds of strange thoughts and fancies that came crowding into my mind. How long I sat thus, I cannot tell. It must have been a good while; then I seemed to have fallen asleep and woke up again. Anyway, I came to myself with a start as I became conscious that I was gazing at something, as yet far away, floating down the river towards me. At first I could not make out at all what it was. There seemed to be just a spot of light, like a twinkling silver star, that was coming each moment nearer, and gradually growing-larger. Then it slowly took shape, and I could see that it was the figure of a woman, all luminous, as it were, from head to foot. But she was not walking or floating on the water, as I had at first fancied, for I presently made out the shape of a large black canoe."

"The black canoe!" murmured Leslie, involuntarily.

He felt very vexed with himself a moment after, as he saw the looks the other two turned on him. However, he said nothing more, but signified by a sign that he wished Beryl to continue. Henceforth, his interest increased, and he became an eagerly attentive listener.

"The canoe was paddled by a party of dark figures," Beryl went on; "and that was all I could make out, if, indeed, it was paddled at all, for it rather seemed to me as if it moved along of its own accord, or floated on the stream. Yet its motion was too swift for that to be the case. Evidently it must have been travelling rapidly, for it grew in size very quickly, so that I soon began to be able to distinguish more of the details."

She shuddered, and passed her hand over her eyes. Her hearers were too deeply interested to interrupt her by making any comments, and she proceeded:

"Just, however, as the canoe was getting near enough for me to make out with some distinctness the several figures, its progress was stayed, and the dark crew turned and began to paddle the other way, so that the craft retreated in the direction from which it had come. Only the white, shining figure of the woman remained facing me, and her hand was slowly raised as though to beckon me.

"At the same time there floated up to me the sound of singing, a sort of chant, in a rhythm that rose and fell in accord with the strokes of the paddles. It was such a strange, wild chant, such weird music! Never have I heard the like of it before; never do I wish to hear it again! It was sweet, oh, so deliciously, delightfully sweet!—yet it was repellent, terrible, heart-rending! It was soothing and seductive, enchanting; yet, in its wild, thrilling cadences, one could seem to hear shrieks and moans, as of beings in mortal agony! It was ravishing, inspiring, intoxicating—and yet it was agonising, despairing, horror-laden! Yes; ah yes! All these attributes had this unearthly music; it rent the heart even while it entranced the senses; pierced the very soul, while fascinating the whole nature!

"How long I listened thus, I cannot say. I was as one spellbound; but suddenly I found myself out in the moonlight How I got there, I have no idea. Whether I went through the open window, or left the palace in the ordinary way, I do not recollect; but I found myself outside, following the siren canoe. I followed it swiftly, so that, rapid as its motion was, I gained upon it Very quickly it drew near to the great temple of Dornanda, and approached the sombre portals of the tunnel from which the river issues. I had never before been near enough to the temple to see it clearly, and I felt a terrible dread of it when I found myself in its shadow as it loomed up in frowning majesty against the moonlit sky; and then it was that I felt myself drawn near enough to the canoe to plainly see all the figures. I seemed now to be in the boat itself; the music ceased, and then my head swam and my heart nearly ceased to beat with the terror that seized upon me!"

Here Beryl paused, and pressed her hand to her side. The listeners saw that she was violently trembling, and Arnold moved as though to go to her assistance, but she signed to him with her hand to keep his seat; and after a few moments she mastered her emotion, and continued:

"The woman was tall and, of a certainty, of noble appearance. There was that in her air of command that held me at the first glance, and compelled my unwilling admiration along with my submission, for I had no power to resist. Try as I would, fight against it as I would, I felt that I was utterly, absolutely in this woman's power, subject to her will, obedient to her spell.

"As to her personal appearance, never have I beheld such wonderful beauty; but, like the music, it frightened and repelled, even while it fascinated. Such a face! so grand in its own consciousness of loveliness and power! Yet so hard, so cruel—oh, so terribly, awfully, relentlessly cruel! And when she smiled, as later on she did, it was as the smiles of a devil and an angel mingled in one.

"She stood erect, her shining eyes still fixed on me, her whole body luminous, or rather enveloped in a halo, through which darted flashes of light like St Elmo's fires. She was dressed in white, flowing robes, and her hair hung in luxuriant tresses around her shoulders, falling from under a crown in which glittered, like a star, the light that had first attracted my gaze while still far away. She spoke no word, but her fixed expression changed a little, and I thought I could read in it a savage, exulting triumph. This change in her gaze seemed to release the spell which had till then held my eyes enchained, and I turned with a feeling of relief—as I at first thought—to look at the dark forms who were wielding the paddles; and then it was that I was seized with renewed terror. Never, surely, has mortal seen or imagined, even in fevered dreams or hateful nightmare, such grim, uncouth beings. What they were, who they were, it passed my wits to conceive. They seemed to me to belong neither to the living nor the dead, but to some dread midway state. If one could imagine a ghostly land of horrors, in which certain of the dead are fated to roam, masquerading in the guise of the living, being actually neither the one nor the other, then I should have said that these belong to such a region. Or, again, if one could conceive those hideous mummies that one sees at the British Museum suddenly animated by a sort of spurious life, so as to become for a time the counterfeit presentments of the human beings they once were—a sort of galvanised automatons—

then these might have been some of them. Dried up, shrivelled forms had they; with shrunken faces, on which the tight-drawn, leather-like skin barely concealed the skull and bones beneath; with expressions—ah! such as might well befit those lost souls doomed to wander for ever midway between the kingdoms of the living and the dead!

"I gazed at these creatures with a feeling that was a curious blend of deepest pity and intolerable loathing, but if they saw me in return they gave no sign of having done so. They continued their monotonous strokes with the paddles, staring with glassy, vacuous eyes into the distance as though ever seeking for something that they yet knew it was hopeless to try to find.

"And still the canoe continued its course, and presently entered the tunnel, through great gates that swung open to admit us as if of their own accord. Presently we came to what looked like a landing-place, and the canoe drew up beside it.

"Suddenly something grated against the keel of the boat, and a moment later we were lifted up, canoe and all, clear of the water. I felt that we were mounting quickly in the air, carried, in a sort of cage, through a great shaft that opened above our heads. Finally, we stopped beside a platform. No word was uttered, no order given, but, as if moved by one common purpose, all landed and passed up a flight of steps, in a sort of procession, in which I followed, compelled by the force against which my will struggled and rebelled in vain. Up many steps, and through many passages and galleries, we passed, till we came into an immense hall, larger and more lofty than any in this palace. It had high, arched doors, opening upon an outer terrace, and barred windows, which looked out, as I afterwards found, over extensive groves and gardens. I could see, through these windows, in the distance, clouds of thin smoke or vapour floating upwards, illuminated by a lurid light, amidst which I caught sight of many figures moving fantastically, while the air was filled with a low murmuring hum and occasional cries, as of a distant crowd disporting in revelry.

"But now my attention was directed by the power that controlled my will to my immediate surroundings. The place was illuminated somewhat after the fashion of Lyostrah's great Reception Hall; but, in place of the columns and spirals of light, there were here, on every side, serpents of fire that writhed and intertwined in every possible form and combination, above and around. At one end was a wonderful throne, of which the arras were also serpents, and these raised their fiery heads and forked tongues above and overhung it.

"There were many couches or divans around, very richly adorned, the prevailing tint being a deep, sombre red. Before the throne was a sort of altar, upon which there glowed a single light, also of a deep red, which kept continually changing, taking all manner of strange and unexpected forms.

"Again we started, as by a mutual impulse, in a procession, and passed along an interior passage or gallery, and thence into others, all lighted by a weird, ruddy glare. And now I perceived what caused yet another thrill of horror—we were traversing the galleries of the Catacombs—the place of which Mr Leslie told us a little while ago—"

"And which description has made you nervous, and caused this fantastic dream," Arnold exclaimed.

But Beryl took no notice. She went on, speaking now as might one in a trance, one who is relating the scenes that follow each other in a vision:

"I looked, through glass walls, into spacious aisles and chambers, and saw there figures of the dead, some seated, some standing, others lying, some in groupings which, no doubt, had their meanings, had I been able to understand them. All were lighted up, though where the light came from I could not here discover; but I noticed that it had everywhere one curious quality—it seemed to throw no shadow. At last we stopped before the closed glass door of one of the smaller of these side-chambers, and, looking into it, I saw two figures only—one of a youth, the other of a young maiden, both very richly dressed, lying, as though in repose, upon separate couches. The door was opened, and our hideous attendants—I do not know what else to call them; they accompanied us throughout—entered, took up the two recumbent bodies, and brought them forth; and thereupon we all returned to the throne-room."

Beryl paused again, and wiped her face with her handkerchief. Evidently, she found the recital painful and exhausting, and Arnold begged her to rest awhile, or to defer the rest to another occasion.

"No," she answered, with a brave effort to subdue her emotion. "I have got thus far; let me finish, and then—as far as I can—try to forget it.

"We returned then to what I may call the Hall of the Fiery Serpents, where the woman who had compelled my presence there seated herself, in queen-like fashion, upon the throne, and the two dead bodies were laid upon rugs in the centre.

"Then the wild music began again, though where the sounds came from I could not perceive, and the attendants formed a ring and began a horrible, grotesque dance, going round and round, at first slowly, but gradually getting faster, throwing their legs high into the air, and convulsing their corpse-like faces with the most frightful contortions. And now, as though attracted by the sound of the music, there entered other weird beings, who, as they came in, added their numbers to the ring, and joined in the dance and song. They arrived in groups of two or three, or half-a-dozen, the total numbers increasing until the whole of the great hall was filled with whirling figures, all wildly gesticulating, dancing, singing, shouting, leaping—the maddest-looking throng, I should think, ever seen. The greater part were dressed in what I took to be the military fashions of some long-past, barbaric age, in chased and polished armour, and glittering accoutrements and throughout, the richness and splendour of the dresses, and the flashing of innumerable jewels, combined to make up a scene utterly beyond my poor efforts at description. Once, twice, thrice the 'Queen' came down from the throne, and, stopping the dance for a brief space, touched the lifeless forms with a rod or wand. Each time she did so flashes of light burst from its end and seemed to envelop the bodies with a luminous halo like that by which she herself was surrounded; but this died away again after she had stepped back to her seat. The third time, however, she first put the end of her wand into the glowing light upon the altar, which leaped out to meet it even while it was still some distance away. Thereupon the dance ceased altogether, and the whole crowd stood around as though expecting what was about to happen. And then—then—those two dead forms moved! Not only moved, but began to breathe, labouriously at first, then gradually more easily; finally, they opened their eyes, and sat up.

"I cannot tell you," Beryl went on, after another brief pause, "the feelings with which I looked on at these proceedings. Nothing but the superior power which had held me all this time in its thrall prevented my swooning or going mad with pent-up horror. But still I was constrained, by a force I could not resist, to stand there and be a helpless witness, incapable of either word or movement.

"To continue: the two erstwhile dead beings rose to their feet, and, as though first attracted by the power of the one who had brought them back to life, they both knelt at the foot of the steps of the throne and bowed profoundly three times. Thereupon the Queen' made a sign, and they rose, looked at each other, and immediately embraced rapturously, as might two lovers who meet again after a long separation.

"Then, for the first time, this mysterious woman spoke, though in what language I could not tell you. It may have been Myrvonian—which, as you know, I can now understand fairly well—or it may have been English, or, again, she may not have spoken at all; she may only have *willed* that I should understand what she wished to convey.

" 'Go, my children,' she said, addressing these two; 'you will find, without there, plenty more of your friends and comrades. Go and enjoy your new-found life, which I have given back to you after a thousand years. Go and rejoice together—till I call you again.'

"Thereupon the two went out, walking hand in hand, and as they passed me I had a better view of their faces than I had been able before to obtain. They were both very, very fair to look upon—he handsome as a god, she as beautiful as a goddess; but their faces were not flushed with the warm blood of youth or health, or even of life at all. They carried in their looks and features the proof that they were but dead automatons made to move and act by some occult power, as might persons walking in their sleep. Following upon their heels the whole motley rout rushed out also.

" 'And now,' said this terrible woman, addressing myself, 'hear why I have summoned thee hither this night. Thou hast chosen to come into this, mine own country, whereof I was to have been queen, and to steal from me the love and adoration of my affianced husband, Lyostrah! By what wicked spells, by what vile enchantments, thou hast succeeded, accursed sorceress that thou art, I know not.... But this I know, that though thy power over him seems to be greater than mine, yet it prevails nothing against myself. I have compelled thee here this night to warn thee; if it be in vain, and thou obeyest me not forthwith, then shalt thou come again in very truth, in thine own proper body, to meet and endure the punishment that I have marked out as befitting thy audacious crime. I extend to thee this offer of clemency—bring back Lyostrah to me within three days, restored to his old feelings of love and affection for me, as by thine arts thou no doubt canst do, and thou shaft be free to depart unhindered and in safety to thine own country.

" 'But if, before the end of three days he is not here, kneeling at my feet as of old, then shalt thou share the fate of another vile sorceress who, by wicked arts, hath also, some time back, endeavoured to ensnare him. Her, therefore, I have also doomed, but without offer of escape; and if thou yieldest not, then shalt thou suffer in her company. And this will be your joint doom— you will be brought hither, and here, at my feet, you will seem to die. But think not that your punishment will end there; for by my power I will give both of you such life as I have this night given, as thou hast seen, to the two who have just gone forth, such as I have given to the crowds that romp and revel without. All these are my creatures, beings of my will, dependent on me for the very life they live from day to day, having no will of their own, and knowing no queen but me, owing, offering, allegiance to no one but myself.

" 'Here, amongst this rout, shalt thou exist through countless years, while each day thou shalt be compelled to look upon Lyostrah and myself and behold our happiness, and to gnash thy teeth with rage and ever-living jealousy at the sight of our felicity. For well do I know that once thy power is finally broken he will return to me, and we shall again be happy together as we were before he looked upon thy accursed loveliness; and thou shalt be a daily witness of our joy, and a hopeless mourner, for ever, that thou hast lost him.

" 'Now come forth with me, and I will show thee the life thou wilt live, and the companions that will be thine. That other one I spoke of I cannot show thee to-night; well will it be for thee if thou never seest her.'

"During this tirade I strove in vain to speak, and to deny the foul charges of which she thus wickedly accused me. As I listened to the hateful slanders I felt ready to die of shame and humiliation; but no words could I utter, and I had to stand there dumb, like one who admits, by her silence, the truth of all that is alleged against her.

"And then she led me out into what seemed to be an open plain of immense extent, where I saw, to my great surprise, a veritable army of soldiers, some drawn up as if on parade, others marching and counter-marching as though practising field exercises and military manoeuvres. Thence we passed on into the 'Sacred Gardens'—or rather, as I should call them after what I have seen, the 'Gardens of Comus.' What I saw there, the awful sights I was compelled to look upon, the ghastly, hellish revelries, the sickening, disgusting debaucheries—of all these things I can never speak. My tongue would refuse to sully itself with such abominations; my heart would burst with shame and horror. I can only tell you that before I was allowed to turn my back upon it all I seemed to have passed a thousand years in Purgatory, and when at last it came to an end—"

But the end was not told; for overcome by the emotion aroused by the recollection of what had appeared to her so real, poor Beryl fell back in her seat and fainted.

CHAPTER XXVII

THE BLACK CANOE AGAIN

JUST AS THE moon rose above the distant heights, and her soft beams lighted up the river and the sleeping city and country around, Leslie and his friend Gaylia drew near to the temple of Dornanda. They had chosen a path that at first led through groves of trees, whose shadows favoured their desire for keeping out of sight of any chance wanderers near the river side. True, item was not much probability, in view of the tragic discovery of the morning, and the general feeling of fear that was abroad, of meeting with any of the ordinary inhabitants. But they wished to keep their investigations secret for the time being, and to avoid the chance of being seen even by anyone watching from a window. When, however, they had passed out of sight of the last house, they left the shelter of the woods, and walked along the river bank till they came nearly in view of the great temple; then Gaylia diverged a short distance inland to gain the shelter of a rocky ridge covered with trees, which came down to within a short distance of the stream. Plunging into a thicket of fir trees, they climbed a steep path and gained the summit of the ridge, where they rested upon a spot that overlooked the river.

Leslie saw at once that Gaylia had brought him to a place peculiarly suitable to their purpose. They stood upon a broad table of rock, a sort of headland, which commanded a view of the river for long distances on both sides, extending ahead of them as far as the tunnel from which it issued. The colossal temple, its face being in deep shadow, towered, dark and frowning, upward almost to the fleecy clouds above; while, at its base, the river spread itself out to the right hand so as to form a lake, extending for some distance towards the mountainous barriers which shut in the prospect in that direction. To the left, also, the water reached for some distance, but not so far as upon the other side. Beyond it, the massive front of the temple continued until it was lost in a light haze which there hung over the valley.

The rocky table on which they had halted was covered so thickly with trees that they were well in shadow, and there was just sufficient undergrowth to completely conceal them on all sides, without interfering with their view. Thus they could see all round their post of observation upon three sides, the fourth side being the continuation of the ridge, which rose steeply towards the heights beyond.

Leslie had brought his revolver; but his companion was furnished only with the sword which was part of his ordinary dress. Lyostrah did not arm his people with firearms it seemed— at least, while they were engaged in home duties. There was supposed to be nothing for which they could possibly need them, and what stock he had he kept under lock and key. So said Gaylia; but Leslie had one day heard the real reason from Lyostrah himself. It was that he regarded all ordinary firearms with contempt looking upon them as mere toys.

"I have invented," he told Arnold and his friend, "a weapon which surpasses all your modern rifles and such-like arms as completely as an ordinary rifle surpasses a bow and arrow. When the time comes I shall put it into the hands of my soldiers, and teach them how to use it."

That was all that had been said. He had vouchsafed no further explanation; but they knew enough of him to look forward to future enlightenment with lively curiosity.

Leslie and his companion sat down upon a ledge of rock well hidden in the shadow, and conversed in whispers while they waited and watched.

Gaylia had already heard a full account of Beryl's vivid dream, for Leslie, on leaving her, had sought him out and told him everything.

"It is of no use to mince matters or stop short at half-confidences," he had said to Arnold. "I believe we can trust in Gaylia; and, in the circumstances in which we are placed, we certainly have need of all the help, in the shape either of counsel or direct aid, which we can obtain."

But Gaylia, being at the time very much occupied, had made very little comment, saying he would turn it all over in his mind, and speak further of it when they met at night.

Now, however, when Leslie questioned him, he showed a disposition to still defer expressing any opinion.

"Wait, my friend Leslie;" he whispered, "until we see what our watch to-night brings forth. It may be that we may meet with something which will throw light upon the rest I would prefer, therefore, to postpone further discussion until the morning; and, in any case, it is as well to be perfectly quiet while we are here."

Leslie felt somewhat disappointed, as he was in that restless, anxious mood which inclines one to seek the solace of talking with another and listening to his opinion; but he saw the force of the warning, and without further remark lapsed into silence.

They sat there for a long time, each immersed in his own thoughts, nothing disturbing the stillness save the squeak of a bat, the hooting of an owl, or a sudden splash and plunge from the river below them as a fish leaped up and fell back into the stream.

Leslie looked at the great, dark mass that loomed up opposite to them, and speculated and wondered upon the stories it could tell of a grim, dead-and-gone past. From that his thoughts wandered to the present, and he recalled Beryl's dream, and wondered whether there was indeed anything going on within those walls in any way resembling what she had so vividly described. Then he wished he could light his pipe, but that he knew Gaylia would forbid as being altogether imprudent—though, he thought dreamily, what did it matter?—there was nothing, nobody about, they had come upon a wild-goose chase—and so—

A quiet, significant pressure of Gaylia's hand upon his shoulder awoke Leslie just as he had been falling into a doze. He started, and glanced round, but another warning squeeze called him to himself; be sat up, looked straight across the water, and saw—what was that?

It was the mouth of the tunnel, which was gradually becoming luminous with a soft, suffused radiance, as from a light that was steadily advancing but was as yet far back in its inky depths. Slowly it became brighter, and, presently, upon the dark waters, brilliant rays darted forth from a star-like light that could now be seen travelling towards them.

In a few minutes more Leslie made out the outline of a large black canoe, which gradually shaped itself against the surrounding light; yet another few minutes and it had emerged from the tunnel and come plainly into view; and this is what he then saw:

A large Indian "War" canoe, apparently black with age rather than with paint, floated towards them upon the placid stream. Its prow rose high above the bulwarks with a bold sweep, turning over at the top in a sort of curl, and upon it leaned a single dark figure, motionless and statuesque, gazing straight before it with staring eyes. Behind it were six other dark figures, facing the same way, each with a paddle which, dipping into the dark waters, turned them, at each stroke, into ripples and circles of fire. The heads and shoulders of these weird beings were bowed in attitudes that suggested, in a peculiarly strange and subtle fashion, a sense of terrible, hopeless, helpless misery. In the stern were two more dark forms, of which little could be seen, since they were muffled up in cloaks and hoods. Lastly, beside these, standing erect, was the figure of a beautiful woman, clad in shining, white robes, with fair hair hanging in luxuriant tresses around her shoulders, upon her head a golden crown in which were stones or gems which sparkled and shone with more than earthly light; while her whole body was surrounded by a luminous halo, out of which, at intervals, darted little arrows of flame.

"The Black Canoe, and the Woman of Beryl's dream!" murmured Leslie, under his breath.

"Alloyah!" Gaylia whispered, and clutched him tightly with the hand that was resting upon his shoulder, as a warning to be silent.

But it seemed as though, somehow, that low murmur had reached the ears of the stately woman standing in the stern of the mysterious craft, for her basilisk glance was now evidently fixed upon the spot where the two were hiding; and then, without any word or signal, so far as the watchers could perceive, those wielding the paddles turned noiselessly round, and began to paddle the other way. The others all retained their positions, the woman's gaze—which now seemed to have in it a look of fierce anger, as though enraged at having been spied upon— remained riveted upon the watchers. Gradually, yet with some rapidity, the canoe receded into the tunnel, the light faded, and, finally, every trace of what the two watchers had seen vanished like a dissolving view.

They waited on for some time in silence, as though expecting some further development; but nothing happened. Then Leslie drew a long breath.

"Phew! what does it all mean?" he exclaimed. "Did I really see that which our young lady dreamed last night, or have I been dreaming too?"

"It was no dream—either now or last night," returned Gaylia, in a low, awed tone. "I knew it, I was sure of it; but I hesitated to say what I believed."

"Knew what?"

"That what that maiden said she saw was no dream."

Leslie stared at him. "But what else could it be?" he asked. "She *could* not—no, it is too absurd—"

"Yet you have now, yourself, seen the black canoe, with its demon crew and the sorceress-queen Alloyah, just as she described them. How, then, can you say you do not believe?"

" 'Twas a dream, I tell you, 'twas but a dream," Gordon

returned, obstinately. " 'Tis but a coincidence. She—perhaps— had heard this strange craft talked of even as you talked of it to me."

He would not, *could* not, admit the possibility of the other's contention. It was too horrible, too Satanic—no! he *would* not admit the bare possibility of such a thing!

Gaylia remained silent, and did not argue the matter further. Presently he said, suddenly:

"Do you remember what the maiden said of great crowds, and revels going on by night in the 'Sacred Gardens'? Would you care to come with me to one of yonder heights, whence we can get a better view? We may haply there witness something further."

To this Leslie raised no objection, and Gaylia at once started off, by a path evidently familiar to him, in the direction he had indicated.

It proved to be a long, stiff climb; but the moon was now high, and very bright, and that helped them considerably. On their way they passed up a shallow valley formed by two rocky, tree-crowned ridges, running down parallel to each other towards the river. The space between was open grass-land, which sloped gently from either side towards a small stream running parallel to the ridges. High up, on the opposite side to that by which they were ascending, was what we should call a small cottage, stand-ing alone and in deep shadow under the farther ridge. From a window, a faint gleam of light travelled across the valley. Leslie asked who lived in the lonely dwelling.

"A shepherd named Tokabu, and his daughter Veta," Gaylia replied, in a low tone. "Let us pass on quietly, or we may be heard, and they may come out to see who it is."

Then they left the greensward and plunged again into the weeds, until, after half an hour's stiff walking, they came out, quite suddenly, upon the edge of a lofty precipice. Leslie then saw, half-a-mile or so away, the upper towers and spires of the great temple standing out against a lurid glare, as though there were a great fire behind them. Clouds of smoke or vapour were floating upwards, and there was a confused humming like the undefined noise made by a distant crowd, through which rose, now and again, faint yet distinct sounds of shouts and laughter.

Gaylia seemed disappointed.

"I thought we should have heard and seen better," he muttered, discontentedly. "Still—what do you make of it? Is it not even as the maiden described it to be, over there—so far, at least, as can be made out?"

"I see your meaning, my friend," Leslie assented. "God knows, it is all more than strange! I cannot understand it; it passes the powers of my poor brain to comprehend. Let us, friend Gaylia, return to the palace, where we can watch over the safety of our friends. These uncanny experiences are filling my mind with fresh fears on their behalf."

Gaylia turned and led the way, and Leslie followed. The return journey was much easier going than the ascent had been, and they soon found themselves almost in sight of the isolated dwelling they had passed on their way up, when an awful, blood-curdling scream rose upon the still air, followed by a series of piercing cries as of one in dire distress. At the sound Gaylia started off at a run, and Leslie followed closely at his heels, drawing his revolver as he went along.

CHAPTER XXVIII

DEMONS OF THE NIGHT

AS THE TWO young men burst out of the wood into the open they could just make out the shepherd's cottage standing upon the opposite side of the narrow valley. The whole of that part was buried in the deep shadow thrown by its wooded ridge; but the greater portion of the intervening space, sloping to the small rivulet which, as already described, ran down the middle of the dell, was in bright moonlight.

Looking across the dip the two could see, as they ran, that the cottage was no longer lighted up, and it was almost indistinguishable in the shade; but, in front of it, in the moonlight, a girl was running down the slope towards them screaming pitifully as she ran. Behind her, evidently in pursuit, was a dark figure—apparently, Leslie thought, one of those weird beings he had seen wielding the paddles in the black canoe. Just then the girl turned, as though either to avoid the stream in front of her, or in fear of the newcomers, whereupon Gaylia shouted to her to come straight to them, assuring her she need have no fear. At the sound of his voice her hideous pursuer stopped and turned back, disappearing, a moment after, in the shadows from which he and the girl had just emerged.

The latter, finding, by a hurried backward glance, that she was no longer pursued, dropped upon the greensward as if in a faint. Just, however, as Leslie and his companion, after scrambling across the shallow stream, came near to her, she partially raised herself, and, recognising the young officer, gasped out in terrified, trembling accents, pointing, the while, in the direction she had come from:

"Honourable sir:—my father. They have killed him. See! Oh see! They are carrying him away!"

This was said in her own language; but Leslie understood it, and, looking towards the place she had indicated, he made out, in the shadow of the ridge, a party of dark figures moving down the hill. Looking more closely, and shading his eyes with his hand, he thought he could discern that they were carrying something in their midst.

Gaylia also saw it at the same moment, and, with a loud shout, that appeared to his companion to be a sort of war-cry, started off in pursuit, Leslie running close beside him.

The whole hillside being here covered with greensward there were no obstacles to impede their progress, and they gained quickly upon the moving group. These looked round once or twice, but did not hasten their steps, or show any sign of an intention to abandon what they were carrying. Perhaps they were bolder when in company than the single one who had followed the girl; or perhaps they were beings who shunned the light, and were stronger and more confident when shielded by the darkness. In any case, they all continued steadily on their way, with the exception of one, who now hung back and kept turning with threatening gestures towards the two pursuers.

As the latter came closer they could see with sufficient clearness that the burden that was being carried away was the body of the shepherd; but as to his captors, they knew not what to make of them. They consisted of a party of seven, of whom only two were like the crew of the black canoe. The others were dressed in military fashion, with shining cuirass and helmet, and gleaming sword. One, more richly dressed than the others, with a waving plume upon his helmet, and a gold-emblazoned tunic instead of cuirass, looked like an officer in charge of the party. He it was who kept in the rear, and turned threateningly towards the two young men.

Now Leslie felt that, as matters were, he was not, so far as he himself was concerned, upon very safe ground. Here was a party of uniformed soldiers, apparently in charge of one whose resplendent dress denoted that he was in authority, and, for all he (Leslie) knew to the contrary, they might be some of Lyostrah's guards carrying out their master's orders. In that case, of course, it would be dangerous for him to interfere. In the semi-darkness he could not see the uniforms with sufficient distinctness to decide whether they were exactly like those of Lyostrah's people, so far as he knew them; nor did he, in any case, know them sufficiently well to be quite sure about it even if the light had been better. Therefore he now kept in the background a little, thinking that in the parley, which he doubted not would follow, Gaylia would naturally be spokesman rather than himself.

At the moment that Gaylia came up with this officer the whole party had to cross a patch of moonlight, and Leslie, now standing still, saw them all, for a brief space, with clearness. It was but for a moment or two, yet was it sufficient to turn his very soul sick with overwhelming horror. Every face was that of a corpse, save as to the eyes, which blazed with a ferocity more like that of a beast of prey than of a human being. Moreover, the lower part of their faces, in every case, was stained with blood, which, with some, still dribbled from their chins on to their clothes. The one they carried—now a stiff corpse, turning a face of deathly whiteness upwards towards the sky—was also dripping with blood; but with him it oozed from a terrible wound in the throat that looked as if it had been torn open by impatient claws.

Just as Leslie's sickened senses grasped all this—it passed out into the moonlight under his view, and vanished again into shadow in the space of but a moment or two—the officer in the rear turned suddenly to meet Gaylia, and stood awaiting him almost in the centre of the strip of bright moonlight; they both, therefore, saw him plainly. If those with him were demons—as Leslie now began to think must surely be the case—then truly this monstrous presentment of a human form was worthy to be "in authority" over them. He stood and faced Gaylia, with a snarl like an enraged tiger; in his eyes there was a baleful glare, that seemed to scorch the eyes of those who looked upon him, and the lips were drawn back, showing the great teeth, like a hungry wolf's. The ungloved hand that he raised in menace was dyed a deep red tint. This hand held no weapon, and it remained for a second or two poised aloft, then it descended and struck Gaylia upon the shoulder. As it touched him a bright flash seemed to leap forth like a fiery dart, and Gaylia fell to the ground without cry or sound save a heavy sigh.

Thereupon Leslie, who was standing two or three paces behind, fired at the one who had thus struck down his friend, the bullet striking him full in the chest and just over the heart. He heard the thud; but the wound seemed to produce no effect whatever, for the hideous, snarling monster, with fresh fury in his eyes, turned upon his new assailant with arm uplifted as before. In despair Leslie aimed his second shot at this arm, and felt certain that the bullet must have struck it, for it gave a backward jerk, and then fell, and swung for an instant in limp fashion as though it were broken. But directly afterwards it was raised again as its owner advanced upon him, and then it seemed to Leslie as though a flaming sword darted from it and struck him to the earth.

When he recovered consciousness he was lying out in the moonlight, his head supported by Gaylia, who, assisted by the girl from the shepherd's cottage, was bathing his head with water. For some time he was too confused to remember what had occurred, and he was suffering such pain in his head as to render him almost incapable even of thought. By degrees, however, the pain grew less, and recollection came back to him. He sat up, and looked about him.

"Keep quiet a little while," Gaylia advised. "You will be stronger in a few minutes."

"What happened to me?" Leslie feebly enquired. "I don't seem to remember—"

"Don't try to just now, friend Leslie," Gaylia urged. "You will be better by-and-by."

But memory was returning, and Leslie shuddered as he recalled the experience he had gone though.

"It was horrible! It seems like a direful nightmare!" he exclaimed. "How did you escape?"

"I should never have recovered—nor would you—but for the presence of mind of this brave little girl here. When the foul demoniacal troop had gone, she ran back to her home and brought some special cordial that her father used to make and keep always at hand, and it revived us both just when it was, as you would say, touch-and-go With us."

Leslie murmured his thanks to the young girl, but she modestly disclaimed having done anything unusual or worthy of note. She was an extremely pretty young maid, albeit she then still looked white and scared; and Leslie saw that her eyes were filled with tears.

"Her name is Veta," Gaylia explained, in an aside to Leslie.

"Her father, as I told you before tonight, was called Tokabu, and now that he is dead I know not indeed what the poor child will do. It has been a terrible shock to her to see her father thus brutally murdered and carried off. Consider, then, how plucky it was of her to watch them away, and then venture out of her hiding-place to come to our assistance. Was not that brave—wonderfully brave?"

And Leslie warmly agreed with him, and said as much to the blushing young girl Then he asked Gaylia if she had seen which way the horrible troop had gone.

"They went away," Gaylia answered, "in the black canoe—and towards the tunnel under the temple. That is all she knows."

"Ah! And the woman? Alloyah? Was she with them?"

"Apparently not," Gaylia returned. "She may have allowed them out alone; or they may possibly have come out upon their own account, as it were, without her knowledge or consent."

"It is a horrible, an inexplicable affair! My revolver was of no

more use than a popgun. I fired twice, and hit the—creature—
each time; but it had no more effect upon him than water on a
duck's back, as we say in England."

He then related to Gaylia what had occurred after he (Gaylia)
had been struck down.

"By what mysterious power," Leslie asked, in conclusion, "did
that ghastly, fiend-like creature hurl us both over as though we
had been struck by lightning? And how comes it that wounds
that would kill or disable any ordinary mortal upon the face of
the earth, affected him not at all?"

But since puzzling over it would not help them, they presently gave up the discussion, and decided to turn their steps
homeward.

"You had better come with us," said Gaylia, addressing Veta;
"after what has occurred you cannot stay here alone. Come, then,
with us, and I will put you under the protection of our people."
An offer that the young girl gladly accepted.

They wended their way down to the river, and walked along
its bank towards the palace. Their talk was for some of indifferent
subjects, chosen by Gaylia rather with the object of diverting the
girl's attention from her great grief than from any idea that they
were matters of interest at the moment. There was much which
Leslie would have liked to discuss with his friend, but which he
felt they could not very well talk about in her presence.

They kept a sharp look-out on all sides as they journeyed, but
saw no further signs of their late enemies. Everything around
them was wrapped in peaceful slumber; the stillness was unbro-
ken save by their own low tones. Even the night birds seemed
to have given themselves over to repose.

As they were drawing near to the palace a faint swish, as of
something moving quickly through the water, fell upon Leslie's
ears. He had scarcely time to draw Gaylia's attention to it, when,
round a bend of the river, they saw the "Myrvonia"—the state-
barge in which they had travelled the last stage of their journey—coming swiftly towards them.

She showed no light, no mast, and carried no banner, nor was there any sign whatever of anyone on board. She glided past them in ghost-like fashion, looking as though she were managed and steered by ghostly hands.

The two young men stared after her in surprise.

"Now I wonder what that means?" exclaimed Leslie. "Has Lyostrah returned, do you suppose?"

"No," Gaylia answered, with decision; "she would carry his banner if he were on board. It looks to me rather as though Alloyah were taking a secret midnight trip on her own account."

"But we saw her in the canoe, and she went back to the temple, you remember," said Leslie.

"True! I had for the moment forgotten that," Gaylia rejoined, thoughtfully. Then after a short pause he said suddenly, "I think I have it! She was going down the river to meet this boat when we first saw her, and she went back because she somehow became aware that someone was watching. If so, her anger against us may be something we shall have to reckon with."

"It might be, if she had known who we were," Leslie answered, confidently; "but thank goodness she doesn't know."

"I'm not so sure of that," Gaylia answered, gloomily.

Just then their attention was again specially attracted to the "Myrvonia," which was still in sight, by a loud splash.

"Someone has jumped overboard," exclaimed Leslie.

"Or something was thrown over," Gaylia suggested.

"It was something large and white," Veta declared, "and it was alive. See! Yonder it comes! It is swimming this way!"

"Someone jumped overboard and swimming to us! What can that mean?" Leslie cried. "Let us go and meet him, and see if he needs help!"

They could see in the moonlight what appeared to be a head, which was coming towards them as though partly swimming and partly drifting upon the current. But before they could get near, it had reached the shore some distance away, and there then rose out of the water the form of the great white puma so well known to Leslie. She stood and shook herself, like a big Newfoundland dog.

The other two regarded her with some misgiving, but Leslie ran forward to meet her, crying out, excitedly, "Myllio! Myllio! Myllio!"

The intelligent beast evidently knew him, for she bounded forward at once to meet him. His companions, however, drew back in evident fear.

"Do not be afraid," Leslie called out, "she hurts no one. See here;" he patted the great head—"why, what is this?"

Myllio wore a beautiful gold collar, and attached to it by a piece of cord was an india-rubber bag. Leslie eagerly detached and opened it, a dim presentiment of coming evil filling his mind. Inside, very carefully wrapped up in more india-rubber, was a note. He opened and read it by the moonlight.

And this is what he saw there, written twice over, once in Myrvonian, and once in English;—

I, Rhelma, daughter of Manzoni, the hereditary king of Myroo-nia, am a prisoner. I have been carried off in my fathers absence, to be taken, as I understand, to Alloyah in the Temple of Dornanda. Whoever shall find this note is prayed to take it to the honourable stranger who is visiting at Lyostrah's court, whose name is Leslie, and beg of him to try to find means to inform my father.

"What does it say?" inquired Gaylia, looking over Leslie's shoulder. His curiosity, as he saw Leslie open the note, had got the better of his distrust of the strange messenger, and he had ventured to come up and pat her.

"Say?" cried Leslie, between his teeth, "it says that there is more devilry afoot, more mischief brewing by that she-devil, your precious priestess, your infamous Alloyah! Poor Rhelma! Poor girl, to be carried off thus! And to think she was in that very boat as it passed us! Oh, my God! What appalling wickedness can be in the wind now! Rhelma in *her* power. At *her* mercy! Quick! Let us run after that boat and bring her back if—but she has gone—gone away out of sight. Ah, gone!"

Poor Leslie raved like one distracted, while the other two listened in mute wonder. It was some time before he was sufficiently composed to be able to explain the state of the case to Gaylia.

When, however, the young officer had mastered the facts, he put his hand to his head and exclaimed:

"I see! I see! O sorceress! Queen of wickedness! Do you not remember, friend Leslie, the 'other one,' also a woman, in the maiden's dream, who was to suffer likewise? and who was not then there but was to arrive later? That one was Rhelma! She was not there then; but she is by this time!"

CHAPTER XXIX

BERYL MISSING!

LYOSTRAH SAT UPON his throne in the great reception-hall, looking more stem and angry than he had been known to appear in the memory of any of his officers.

He had returned that morning—the third day after the events recorded in the last chapter—and had been met on the water by the priestess Alloyah and her suite. What had then passed between them was not known, but when she had left him and started to return to her temple; he had gone to his palace, called together a solemn court, and sent for Leslie and Gaylia.

"You two are accused," he said to them, coldly, "of plotting against our well-beloved and most revered Priestess, Alloyah; of spying upon her by night, and endeavouring to poison the minds of our people against her by wicked and abominable accusations and suggestions. Certain lamentable crimes have been committed during my absence, and Alloyah charges it against you that you have yourselves committed those foul deeds, or instigated their commission, in order to attempt to cast the guilt upon her. She requires at my hands that you shall both be forthwith given up to her that she may examine fully into the matter and deal with it as she may deem fitting. Do you admit the charge, or deny it?"

"It is only true so far as—" Leslie began, when, to his utter dismay, Lyostrah took him up promptly:

"You admit it! Then that ends it so far as my part is concerned. You, Leslie, came here unasked, and without your presence

254

being either required or desired. You have, nevertheless, been treated with courtesy and confidence—such confidence that you have been able to roam about wherever you chose at your own pleasure. And this is how you requite my generosity—by spying upon—"

"But, I pray you, first listen to what I have to say," poor Leslie pleaded.

"Nothing that you can say can extenuate such conduct," Lyostrah interrupted, angrily. "However, I am not going to judge you; you can say what you have to urge to the one you have so deeply offended. I advise you to throw yourselves upon her mercy; she is gracious and may show you clemency; and if she does, it will be time enough then for me to hear what you may have to urge by way of making your peace with myself. Officers, remove them; take them at once to our great temple, and deliver them into the charge of Alloyah's guards."

"They shall not go!" Arnold exclaimed, passionately, going up to Leslie and putting a hand on his arm. "Or if you send them, then send me too; for whatever they have done I have done also. If they are guilty, so am I, for I have been privy to all that they have done."

"You?" Lyostrah asked, in surprise.

"Ay, I. But what foolishness or wickedness is all this? What is it they are accused of?"

He had only just entered, and had not heard the commencement of the affair; and he now stood behind Leslie, staring at Lyostrah, bewildered and indignant Lyostrah paused and seemed to consider. Some one just then came and whispered to him, whereupon he abruptly rose and went out, saying only, "Let every one now present remain here till I return."

Leslie was as bewildered as Arnold, and was endeavouring to explain matters to him in a low tone, when he felt himself pulled by the sleeve.

He looked round, but could see no one near likely to have

touched him. He therefore turned away to resume his hurried conference, when he felt the tug again.

Amongst the crowd moving around him, the nearest person at that moment was one of the Indians, of whom several were present. Most of them, it was understood, had come back with Lyostrah in his suite. This one was a tall fellow having the appearance of a great chief, decked out with a head-dress of feathers not unlike the crest upon a gigantic cockatoo. His body was covered up in an immense cloak, and his dark features were disguised beneath a mass of paint. Once more Leslie was about to turn impatiently away, but in the very act of turning, he caught a glance from the Indian's eye which seemed to have in it some hidden meaning. Before, however, he had time for further observation, the Indian had turned on his heel and was walking slowly across the floor of the hall. Something in his bearing and manner, as he moved away, struck. Gordon as familiar; but in another moment he had mingled with a group of Indians, and thereafter but very slight glimpses of him could be obtained.

The minutes went by, and Leslie and Arnold discussed the situation from every possible point of view. Gaylia, too, assisted in the debate, but the only result of their joint council was to still further increase their alarm and bewilderment. Gaylia gloomily informed them he felt assured that there was very little hope of Lyostrah's altering his mind. He (Gaylia) knew him too well, and Alloyah too, and her influence over him.

"Alloyah must have gone to meet him this morning with some lying complaint, before anyone else could make a report," he said; "and Lyostrah, you can see, believed her. And what he has now said he will never go back upon. I told you I felt very far from assured that she had not, by some subtle art, seen and recognised us."

Leslie could not repress a shudder as he listened. The idea of being given over to Alloyah's tender mercies was a gruesome one to contemplate. But with the thought came into his mind the query, "Should he there see Rhelma?"

Just then his glance wandered to the Indian chief who had before attracted his attention. He was crossing the floor to speak to someone on the opposite side, and as Leslie again noticed his gait, a dim association of ideas between Rhelma and the Indian's bearing gave him a sudden clue.

It was Manzoni!

Leslie stared at him in utter astonishment; then, catching his eye, and noting its significant glance, he turned his own looks in another direction, and affected to be specially interested in some of the intricate decorations upon the wall before him.

Yes! He could not be mistaken! It was Manzoni—Manzoni, who had promised him that in the hour of danger he would not be far away. He had warned him, too, as if by some prophetic instinct, not to recognise him when they met until told he could do so.

His heart gave a great bound as these thoughts passed through his mind. Now, at least, there was one strong friend at hand! A minute before all had seemed so hopeless; he had felt so helpless struggling in the toils which Alloyah had evidently woven—fighting vainly against accusations in regard to which Lyostrah so coldly refused even to listen to what he had to say in his own defence.

But his spirits fell again as he remembered that Manzoni's daughter was also in Alloyah's power. If he had not been able to protect his own daughter against the craft of this woman, how could he (Leslie) hope for effective aid from him?

Thus his thoughts ran, and Arnold, who was talking eagerly all the time, wondered at his incoherent answers to his questions.

Then Lyostrah returned, and his brow looked darker even than before. He seemed to have heard something which had angered him still further; and Leslie and Neville, as they anxiously watched his face, felt they could draw no hope from what they read there.

There was a dead silence as he mounted the steps of his throne. But ere he reached it he paused to listen to a confused sound which became audible in the stillness. It was like the undefined murmur which emanates from a surging crowd where no particular cry or noise can be distinguished from the rest.

Whatever it was, Lyostrah evidently found it annoying, for he ordered Okabi to go and inquire the meaning of it As to the two prisoners, he merely waved his hand, saying curtly, in his own language:

"Ye have your orders. Take them away."

At that moment Maylion entered the hall, closely followed by his principal lieutenants. Many had remarked his previous absence, and wondered that he had not been present to take some part in proceedings which threatened the liberty, and possibly the life, of his only son. But no one seemed to be able to say where he was, or suggest a reason for his absence.

As he came up the centre of the hall, Lyostrah, still standing, looked at him, and those with him, with heavy displeasure.

"How, now, Maylion?" he asked, in a voice that was low, and yet seemed to ring all over the hall. "What means this intrusion? Hast thou not received my message saying that I do not need thy services here this morning?"

"My lord," said Maylion, "I come not so much on my own account as in the name, at the solemn request, of a number of our principal inhabitants.

"We cannot tell whether what has happened while he has been absent is known to our lord: we feel bound to believe that it is not; for only upon the ground of such ignorance can we understand our lord's apparent indifference to the occurrences of the past week, and the terrible feelings of terror, the panic of dread and horror, that are abroad in the land. Here are two young men—one of them my own son, whom I know to be innocent of any guilt in this matter—condemned without being heard in their own defence, upon the mere complaint of the Priestess Alloyah, who, if half what is now openly asserted be true, is herself—"

But at this point Lyostrah seemed to lose all patience. He

had listened thus far in silence and without moving, appearing, however, to do so rather from a feeling of overwhelming astonishment that any should dare to speak to him in such terms, than from any interest in what was being said. Maylion, on his side, had evidently but little liking for the part he was performing, and his uneasiness visibly increased under the look that was slowly growing upon Lyostrah's lowering brow, and the glances that shot from his fiery eyes. When, however, Alloyah was mentioned, Lyostrah started forward in sudden wrath.

"By Dornanda!" he exclaimed, furiously, "this is treason—rank, open treason! Mutiny amongst mine own guards! What! Dost thou dare speak against Alloyah, and accuse her to my face?"

He walked slowly down, step by step, till he stood upon the floor, when he seized Maylion by the neck with one hand, and by the thigh with the other, then, lifting him high above his head, as though he had been a child, be threw him from him upon the floor, where he lay stunned.

Without so much as a look at the unconscious man, Lyostrah turned to Okabi, who had just returned.

"What is the noise about?" he demanded.

"It is a crowd—a large crowd—my lord, and they seem in a very angry mood—"

"In angry mood!" thundered Lyostrah. "So am I! Tell them so! And, if they desire it, bid them send another spokesman! But first tell them how I have served the one they sent, the one who dared to open his rebellious lips to speak against our well-beloved Alloyah!"

He looked first at one, then at another, his eyes flashing wrath and scorn upon them all.

"What!" he continued, with a contemptuous sneer, "have ye no champion, then—no leader? Think ye to come here to dictate to me in my own palace, like a flock of silly sheep, when ye cannot even find a leader?"

He glanced round about the assembled crowd with a superb

disdain, looking like an enraged lion in his fury. Then, with a slight shrug of the shoulders, he turned to mount the steps.

"Let us have done with this," he added, more quietly. "You have not even a leader who dares—"

"Yes! a leader is here, Lyostrah," said a deep, sonorous voice; "one who will call thee and thy accomplice, Alloyah, to account!"

At the sound of these words Lyostrah, who had turned his back for a moment, faced round again, his face expressing amazement and his eyes blazing with rage.

He saw before him only one of the Indians, and stared at him for a moment without speech.

The Indian pulled off his head-dress, and a sort of mask from his face, then threw his cloak from him, appearing in a rich suit of purple and gold with a star worked in sparkling diamonds upon the front of his tunic. In one hand he held what appeared to be a sceptre, one end formed like a serpent's head with open mouth and forked tongue. Upon his left breast was a medallion of curious workmanship, in the centre of which glittered one immense diamond.

He first bent over Maylion, lifting his head tenderly and examining him to ascertain what his hurts were. Then he beckoned to two or three of the bystanders.

"Take him up gently and carry him hence, and see that his hurts are attended to," he commanded, with an air of quiet authority. Then he walked past Lyostrah, up the steps, and seated himself upon the throne. "My children," he said, in a clear, penetrating voice, which was perfectly free from any trace of excitement, but which, nevertheless, seemed to thrill the crowd more than sound of clarion or trumpet, "you are, indeed, to-day, like sheep without a shepherd, and I see ye have sore need of one to lead and guide you. For that purpose I have come amongst you once more. I hold in my hand the ancient sceptre that has been the emblem of authority in our land for countless ages, and upon my breast I have placed the sacred symbol which denotes the wearer to be the true representative of our generations of kings, and which none dare wear save he who is justly and truly entitled to assume the honourable post of Ruler amongst you. For twenty years have I locked these insignia of my office away, and renounced the place that was mine. But to-day I have opened the casket in which they have so long reposed, and I now, before you all, acclaim my intention to re-assume my lawful position. Say, my children, are ye content that I should do so, or are there any here who would dispute my right?"

But if there were indeed any inclined to so dispute with the speaker, their voices were drowned in the shouts and cheers which then broke out on all sides.

"Manzoni! Manzoni! Manzoni! A welcome to Manzoni, our lawful king! Shout for Manzoni, our lost ruler! A thousand cheers to greet Manzoni, the father of his people!"

From the interior of the hall the shouting spread along the galleries without, and was heard through the open windows and boisterously taken up by crowds outside. And from the prolonged and repeated acclamations it quickly became apparent; beyond all possibility of doubt, that Manzoni had a thorough hold over the affections of the populace, and that his return to take a position of authority amongst them was welcomed by all.

Of those present perhaps none was in a better position to understand the scene, and estimate its true character, than Leslie. In his intercourse, brief as it had been, with the man who had thus stepped forward at so critical a juncture, he had learned sufficient to enable him to feel assured that he could be trusted, and that his newly-asserted authority would count for nothing but good. He turned to speak of this to Neville, and was surprised to find he was no longer there. As a matter of fact, Arnold had already grasped the idea that this sudden change in the position of affairs meant safety for Leslie, and in the gladness of his heart he had gone off to acquaint Mrs Beresford and her niece with the good news, intending, after having just said sufficient to relieve their anxiety, to return at once to watch the further developments of the situation.

So Leslie had no one to sympathise with his feelings at the moment save Gaylia, who, on his side, was in anxiety as to the nature of the hurts his father had received at the hands of his enraged master.

The ebullition of excited feelings gradually quieted down, and presently Manzoni, by a wave of the hand, secured silence.

"My children, I thank ye. It is well!" he now said. "I see that no one amongst you is disposed to dispute my right to take up my old place. Tell me, Lyostrah, dost thou dispute it?"

Before replying to this challenge, Lyostrah cast a keen look around the hall. His glance ran along the eager faces ranged two or three deep round the room, and then he turned and faced Manzoni.

"I have no desire to dispute thy right, Manzoni," he answered, somewhat sullenly. "Thou knowest that I have never disputed thy right. I have even gone out of my way to urge upon thee to abandon thy proclaimed resolution of permanent retirement; to persuade thee to return to take thy place here amongst us. Still, I have, it seems to me, some ground for complaint that thou shouldst return in so unexpected a fashion. Surely thou didst owe it to our former friendship to give me some notice of thy intention. I do not understand this sudden irruption, upsetting our proceedings, and interfering betwixt me and my people. Surely thou couldst have given me notice, so that I could have prepared a fitting reception. I must e'en repeat, I do not understand thy object in coming in such a fashion." Here the speaker exhibited again something of that disdainful air which he could so well assume when he chose. "It seems scarcely a brilliant or a worthy idea for our esteemed Chief to creep back amongst us like a thief in the night, in mean disguise—"

"Like a thief in the night!" Manzoni exclaimed, sternly. "Ye say well; ye say well! But tell me, Lyostrah," and his tones grew each moment sterner, "why hast *thou* stolen upon *me* like a thief in the night, and robbed me of all I had in the world? Why hast thou crept upon my sleeping household—in my absence, coward that thou art—and stolen, and murdered, and destroyed? And what—aye, what"—here the speaker suddenly burst out as though unable to any longer repress the angry fire he had kept pent up for so long—"*what* hast thou done, thou coward, with my daughter, my innocent, helpless daughter!"

At the word "coward" Lyostrah had started as though he had been stung, and upon its repetition he had seemed, for a moment, as though about to rush upon his questioner to fell him to the earth; but at the last words he stared and looked bewildered.

"Thy daughter! Rhelma!" he said, in stammering fashion, as though he did not understand.

"Aye, Lyostrah, Rhelma! Where is she? What hast thou done with her?"

Lyostrah looked at him still as though only half comprehending what was said. Presently he answered, slowly:

"I know nothing of thy daughter. Surely thou art dreaming—or jesting."

"It is no jest—as thou shalt shortly find, if thou darest to trifle with a father's anxiety," returned Manzoni, with ominous emphasis. "Either thou or thy accomplice Alloyah has most foully attacked my sleeping home when I was away, destroying everything, burning my house, and leaving me not so much as a roof to shelter my head, killing and scattering my faithful servants and attendants, and murdering or carrying off my daughter. Once more I demand of thee—and take care! I will not brook much more of this trifling—what hast thou done with my daughter? Is she dead or alive? And, if alive, where? If thou hast imprisoned her, I demand her instant release. If harm happens to her, or has happened, I will make thee account to me for it with thy life!"

Manzoni's announcement created a great sensation amongst those around him. At first there was a hush of breathless astonishment, then a buzz of conversation as one talked with another in low tones, which grew gradually louder, until the indignant feelings of the crowd began to burst forth in cries of "Shame!" "Infamous!" "We will avenge thee, Manzoni!" and such like exclamations.

But, to the general surprise, none appeared to be more genuinely astonished than Lyostrah himself. He looked altogether puzzled as he exclaimed:

"Thy house burned! Thy servants killed and scattered! Thy daughter carried off or murdered! Believe me, Manzoni, I know naught about it. I can scarce credit thy statements!"

Manzoni regarded him gloomily.

"It seems to me," he answered, "there is a great deal going on that thou either knowest nothing of, or ought to be ashamed of if thou didst know it I tell thee—"

But at this moment there was a disturbance at the end of the hall near the door. Arnold had burst in, panting, his face white, and his whole manner betokening overpowering emotion. He rushed towards Manzoni, fell on his knees, and lifted his hands imploringly.

"Help me!" he cried; "help me quickly! Alloyah has carried off Beryl—my affianced wife!"

CHAPTER XXX

LYOSTRAH AND MANZONI

MANZONI LOOKED COMPASSIONATELY upon the young man kneeling, almost heartbroken, before him; and, extending his hand, spoke to him in kindly accents!

"Come hither, my son, and tell me more clearly what has happened. Or perhaps thy friend can explain better, for I imagine you are the one he has spoken of to me." He beckoned Leslie to come across to them, and upon his approach, said to him, indicating Arnold:

"This is thy friend, I take it. Explain to me what is the matter. I can scarcely understand his meaning."

In answer to Gordon's questions, Arnold told how, when he had gone but a few minutes before to speak to Beryl, he had found Mrs Beresford nearly prostrated with anxiety and fear, and all he could learn from her was that Beryl was missing. But from the attendants he heard that she had been carried off by force by a party who were known to be some of Alloyah's people.

"This is horrible! It gets worse and worse!" Leslie exclaimed. "Will Lyostrah deny this also, I wonder?" he continued, looking at him with anger and reproach in his eyes, "or will he allow Alloyah to suggest that it is my doing?"

But Lyostrah took no notice of the sarcasm. He strode up to Arnold, and putting his hand somewhat roughly upon his shoulder, gave him a slight shake as though to rouse him from the grief to which he was giving way.

"Tell me, Neville," he said, in a voice that scarcely seemed the same, it was so subdued, almost trembling, "are you sure of what you say? I—I—cannot believe it; I cannot realise it!"

Then he turned to Manzoni and added in a lower tone:

"It is all strange to me; as strange and unexpected as it is to you. That I swear! It is to me incredible that Alloyah has carried off this young lady."

"It would not appear so strange and incredible if you knew what I know—if, indeed, you are ignorant of it," Leslie retorted.

"And what may that be?" Lyostrah demanded. "On all sides I hear nothing but hints, and innuendos, and suggestions. Will no one speak out like an honest man?" he asked, fiercely, forgetful of the way in which he had, but a few minutes before, treated the man who had ventured to speak out. "What have you to say against Alloyah? How do you know she has done what you believe?" He paused, clenched his hands and muttered, as if to himself, "But if it should be so; if I should find that Alloyah has indeed deceived me, played with me, kept me supplied with false news! Then—let her look to herself! It were better she had never been born!"

Only those close to him heard the words, but for them they shed a new light upon events.

Arnold seized his hand.

"O Lyostrah!" he cried, imploringly, "you have never given me reason to believe that you were a false friend! I have received much kindness at your hands. Be true now, for the sake of God, be true to your own promises! What has my poor, innocent, helpless darling done that she should be handed over to the suffering that yonder woman will inflict upon her. I cannot tell you—"

"As I live, Neville," Lyostrah declared, "I cannot believe that Alloyah would harm her. But," he continued, his brows darkening again, "if she does, then shall punishment such as never—"

"It seems to me, friend Lyostrah," Manzoni interrupted, in a dry, severe tone, " 'twere better to help us to recover these two maidens—for I now know beyond doubt that my daughter is there too—from Alloyah's hands; than to talk about after-vengeance. While you have been speaking with our young friend, Leslie, has been talking with me. He has given me a letter from my daughter, and explained a good deal besides. It is becoming clear to me that we, amongst us, know a great deal more about what is going on in this country than you yourself do. Let us put our heads together and compare notes, and see at once what can be done. If you are sincere, and have sinned through ignorance, or through the fact that lies have been served up to you in place of the miserable truth, and if, moreover, you will honestly help us in our endeavours—"

"I will, Manzoni—if I find I have been deceived! I swear I will do my utmost to atone!"

"Ah! To atone! Who can say whether that may be possible!" Manzoni responded, shaking his head. "However, it seemeth to me that this is not a suitable place in which to discuss these matters further. Let us adjourn to another chamber."

The four, thereupon, retired to a neighbouring apartment Manzoni, on the way, spoke to Gaylia, bidding him go see after his father and bring word how he fared.

When they were closeted together, Manzoni first showed Lyostrah the note which Leslie had taken from the white puma.

"While I was away," he went on to relate, "Alloyah—I now suppose it was done by her orders, and without your knowledge—sent a party to my place, and burned or destroyed everything. When I returned there was nothing whatever left. All my machinery, my laboratory, my tame animals, even our crops, and my plantation of the Mylondos' are gone. And, as I have said of my faithful Indians and servants, some were lying dead—evidently foully murdered while defending my home—and others—amongst them my daughter—had disappeared. As to the latter, this note shows where she probably now is; and it clearly inculpates Alloyah, if not yourself."

"I can scarcely credit it! I knew nothing whatever about it!" Lyostrah again asseverated.

Then, at Arnold's suggestion, Leslie read a long statement, which he had written down, of Beryl's dream. He had taken it down just after she had related it, and had carefully set out every detail, in the belief that it might be afterwards important to have an exact account to refer to. And so it appeared it was; for Lyostrah's astonishment increased as the recital proceeded. But when, after finishing it, Leslie went on to give a narrative of the terrible events of the night upon which he had watched, in Gaylia's company, for the "black canoe," Lyostrah rose and began walking restlessly up and down the room.

Leslie sat and watched him with mingled feelings. He was naturally sore at his own treatment, and the narrow escape he had had of being handed over to the plotting priestess. Then a sickening feeling of horror came over him as he thought of the two helpless girls who were actually in that relentless being's hands, and he vaguely wondered if it were yet possible to do anything in time to save them. He was filled with doubt and perplexity at Lyostrah's avowal of ignorance of all that had been taking place, and was at a loss to understand how one so shrewd and keen, one who, in regard to everything else, had always been so well served by his agents and servants, could possibly have been so misled, as must here have been the case, if his assertions were to be believed. But as he watched the changing emotions in Lyostrah's expressive face as he paced to and fro, there grew up in his mind a feeling almost of pity in place of his former resentment. He thought of the expression which Beryl had said she had seen upon that proud face, formerly so impassive and inscrutable—as of a man who, unexpectedly, found himself upon the edge of a precipice over which he was sliding and knew that he could not save himself. Leslie saw that expression there now. It was written as plainly as though set out in print, and he fancied it was the sum, as it were, of all those shadows that had been clouding his brow during the last few months. Had his display of ungovernable anger that day, against the unoffending Maylion, been but an outward sign of a wearing struggle going on within? Leslie began to think it might be so.

Manzoni also sat and watched Lyostrah, his own features clouded over with trouble and anxiety; and Leslie, looking at him in turn, thought of the day when he had first met him as the "lord of the mountain." He had been struck then, at first sight, by his noble bearing and stately mien, even in the rough hunting dress in which he had been attired. But to-day that kingly aspect had been more marked than ever, for Manzoni's feelings of indignation and just anger had impressed his actions with a lofty dignity that exceeded anything he had seen before. "He looks every inch a king," Leslie thought to himself. "By the side of him, even Lyostrah's natural grace seems less perfect than it did."

But Manzoni had more to tell. Other dark tragedies had taken place; men, even women and children, had been seized upon and, in some cases, carried off, in others, cruelly murdered in cold blood and—

"I do not wish to seem to pile up the terrible indictment, Lyostrah," he said to him. "But the people are nearly mad, some with terror, some with rage and a desire for revenge upon—the one who is responsible. I do not wonder that they essayed to turn on thee to-day; rather is it to me almost a marvel that they did not tear thee to pieces in their frenzy. They assert that a whole army of fiends—of vampires, as some declare—has been let loose upon them. What does it all mean?"

Lyostrah turned, and looked at him. In his face there were many contending emotions, but the chief, the one that seemed to dominate all other feelings, was a look of agonised despair.

"Manzoni," he said, in a low tone, "we used to be firm, honest friends. As thou believest in a just God above us—and I know thou dost—I would now that I had more often followed thy counsel—be my friend now, once more—perhaps it may be the last time I shall ask it of thee. Come with me and listen to what I have to tell; and then, if thou still wouldst be merciful, for the love of God, advise me!"

He motioned to the other to follow him, and they went out together.

"He has some awful secret," commented Leslie, looking after them. "I wonder what it is?" He paused, and then continued thoughtfully. "A very strange story—the story of that man's life—and a story that approaches its last chapter—or I am greatly mistaken. Ending, as men's lives do, in disappointment, disgust, or despair. There is nothing new in that, you would say? No; and some men might bear up against it, and live it down—but not Lyostrah! Manzoni predicted that if he met with disappointment in the grand scheme of his life he would never survive it. And that is true; I can see it in his eye. Not a bad man, though, I do truly think; a man wonderfully, preternaturally clever, yet, methinks, not wholly wise. But an hour since I was full of rage against him; now my heart is overrunning with pity for him."

"I wish I could understand the meaning of it all," Arnold rejoined, in a weary, agonised tone. "With tragedies that will not bear the light of day going on around us, at a moment when dear friends are in danger that cannot be named, and while chasms that descend to no man knows where are yawning beside us, it boots little, it seems to me, to employ one's thoughts in philosophical reflections. Exercise thy wits, man, and tell me what I want to know—whether the last chapter of the story, as you term it, will bring us relief, or only plunge us into blacker misery! What I suffer in my anxiety upon Beryl's account seems too great a load for human nature to bear! And inaction is intolerable! Can we not take some steps, do something, towards setting her free? If the people are incensed against Lyostrah, they are more so against Alloyah. Let us put ourselves at their head and go to this accursed temple, and demand that her prisoners be given up!"

"And so, probably, hasten their death," Leslie answered, shaking his head. "No, Arnold. Difficult as I know it must seem to you, we must try to be patient yet a little while. Remember that Manzoni is not less anxious about his daughter; and whatever is possible will be done. If Lyostrah is sincere—and I believe he is—we have here the promised aid of two whose combined wisdom should be equal to mastering even so subtle an enemy as this priestess evidently is. We should be unwise, indeed, to precipitate matters by acting without their co-operation."

Thus the two talked and argued, the time dragging on heavily while Manzoni and Lyostrah were away; for they were absent a long time.

Presently Gaylia came in and told them that his father had received no hurt, and had gone out amongst the people to endeavour to pacify them.

In other respects the news he brought was very grave, not to say alarming. "It is not an easy matter to reassure them, though," he declared to Leslie. "Manzoni's presence here at such a juncture is a fortunate event indeed, for his influence is very great, and they will follow his advice implicitly as far as any overt action is concerned. But what can he do to allay their panic? They are, many of them, half mad—some are, I am told, really crazy—between dread and raging anger. The bravest of them go about in deadly fear, for no man's life is now safe. This abominable accusation against you and myself, to-day, took up all my thoughts, else I had much to tell you; and I have learned more since. Last night, I now hear, was the most terrible we have had yet. These midnight murderers are increasing both in numbers and audacity. Not only have several more of our fellow-countrymen been foully slain, but those who hastened to their aid, or tried to defend their family or their friends, have been served as you and I were; but with worse consequences, for they are now lying dead or grievously hurt. And another most extraordinary, most inexplicable, feature is that all arms are entirely useless against these assailants. We say that, you and I, that night. Since then there have been many further proofs of it. How, then, are we to defend ourselves against such enemies, who care neither for firearms, swords, daggers, nor spears? You can, therefore, understand the reign of terror which exists. They are crying out that a legion of devils—of veritable vampires—has somehow been let loose in the land, that their number is growing, and that we shall all soon be overwhelmed and exterminated by them!"

During the last part of this ominous statement Manzoni and Lyostrah, both exceedingly grave and thoughtful, had entered the apartment and had listened to it. Manzoni put a few questions to Gaylia, which drew from him a number of particulars and details of so gruesome a character that they are better, perhaps, left undescribed.

Manzoni looked at Lyostrah.

"There is no time to be lost," he said. "Let us now hasten to make our arrangements."

Lyostrah, by way of reply, only nodded slowly. He had an abstracted, almost vacant manner, and gave Leslie, who was observing him, the idea that his thoughts were far away, and were occupied less with the events of the moment, startling even as these were, than with some even more momentous catastrophe which they dimly beheld approaching.

Manzoni went up to Arnold and put his hand upon his shoulder.

"My son," he said, "thy trouble and anxiety are, I know, great; but so are mine. Whatever can be done we will do; and thou shalt presently help if thine heart be stout and fail thee not Thinkest thou that thou couldst stand, on behalf of the one thou lovest, a trial of thy courage as great as any mortal man can be put to?"

Arnold, too surprised for words, could only look back at the wondrous eyes that were gazing so searchingly into his. Manzoni seemed satisfied with that look; for, without waiting for answer, he said, "Good. We shall want thee to-night." And with that he and Lyostrah left them and went out.

CHAPTER XXXI

A NIGHT EXPEDITION

THAT EVENING NEVILLE and Leslie sat in their room waiting for an expected message from Manzoni. They were neither, of them inclined for much talk, and when, now and then, they exchanged a few words, it was in a subdued tone, almost as though afraid of being overheard.

It was not any such trifling thought, however, that hung over the two young men, and oppressed them with vague apprehensions. It was rather an idea—perhaps even a conviction—that this night was to be a critical one in their fortunes. They were swayed by a foreboding that events were impending fraught with unknown perils and hidden possibilities of evil.

"I cannot endure this suspense!" exclaimed Arnold, suddenly jumping up and beginning to pace impatiently up and down the apartment. "If it lasts much longer I shall go mad! Who can tell what may be happening in yonder hateful temple'—as they call it, forsooth!—while we sit idly here! How, if nothing is done to-night? How can I endure further days and nights of this torment?"

"I think something *will* happen to-night, Arnold," Leslie replied, in a low voice. "I know that preparations have been going on—though I confess I know not of what nature—but—they *must* do something to-night. As Gaylia said to-day, and we have since seen it for ourselves, the people are going wild with fright and terror. It is the weird mystery of the whole affair which is playing upon their nerves, I fancy, quite as much as the actual

273

happenings—and they are horrible enough, one must admit. If one could only even form a theory—make some guess as to the nature of the horrible mystery—"

"Gordon!" Arnold interrupted, suddenly stopping, looking earnestly at his friend, and speaking in an awestruck tone, "you remember Beryl's dream?"

"Certainly."

"At the time I thought it merely a nightmare, one of the most preposterous—though no doubt vivid and coherent—dreams that a human being could be bothered with. But now, in the lurid light of what has happened since, the horrible, torturing thought keeps forcing itself upon me—Was it truly only a dream?"

"How do you mean, Arnold?" Leslie asked, evading a direct answer. "In what way?"

"I hardly know; it seems so wild, so fantastic, so outrageously impossible," Arnold replied, dreamily. "And yet, there must be some unholy doings going on in that most unholy of temples. How if—somehow—by some—strange—coincidence, let us say—*how if Beryl saw what was actually happening within those unhallowed walls?* How if that terrible woman Alloyah really has the power to endow again with life—or with some impious, devilish imitation of life—the preserved bodies which repose—or should repose—in those catacombs! Would it not be then comparatively easy to understand the origin of this horde of ghouls and vampires' that—the people declare—has been turned loose in the land? Great Heavens! In such case *what* would the end of it be?" Arnold broke off, and resumed his excited pacing to and fro. Then he burst out again, impatiently: "Pshaw! What nonsense I seem to be talking!—and yet—you ask for a theory! Do you not find one ready made in Beryl's dream—one that explains everything, fits exactly the known facts? What would it be, after all, but a further development of those curious experiments which Manzoni—as you told me—showed you when he endowed mummified bodies of animals—and even a skeleton—with seeming life, by means of what he called the Red

Ray? It is a horrible, an abhorrent idea, thus to apply the powers of Manzoni's Red Ray to bring to life the dead of past ages. But once you admit the possibility in the case of mummified animals—and that you yourself saw—it is no more wonderful in the one case than in the other. It makes one shudder to think of such things!"

"I do confess, Arnold," rejoined Leslie, "that my speculations have more than once, though much against my ordinary sober judgment, carried me in the same direction. But the idea seemed too monstrous, and I refused to contemplate its possibility. Besides, I cannot think that any human mind could conceive and carry out so daring a project—"

"None on earth, perhaps—except Lyostrah's," Arnold put in. "He alone would be sufficiently daring—and—Alloyah may be a woman hardy enough to aid and abet him—"

"Or even to improve upon it by the aid of some 'Black Art Mysteries' of her own," Leslie suggested, in slow, thoughtful tones; "and if she has played him tricks, and done something of the kind without his knowledge—and we now know she has deceived him in other matters—that might explain many things—Lyostrah's troubled look during the past few months, and his present perplexity."

Here further talk was interrupted by the arrival of Manzoni and Lyostrah. The two young men were surprised to see them in person, and still more that they should appear unattended; but Manzoni's grave face, and impressive, almost solemn manner, caused them to refrain from offering any remark, even by way of greeting.

Manzoni put his band on Arnold's shoulder, and, looking at him keenly, thus addressed him:

"My son, we have to call upon you to-night for a great test of your fortitude and courage. But, in order to explain why we feel impelled to do so, it is necessary to impart to you some intelligence which I would have preferred to keep till another time, rather than divulge it now, and in so hasty a fashion. But time presses; and circumstances leave me no choice in the matter. I asked Lyostrah, to-day, what his reason was for having been so desirous that you should leave England and come with him to this country. I confess it was a puzzle which has greatly perplexed me, as I doubt not it has you also. He answered me in half-a-dozen words. They were, 'Because he is one of our race!"

Exclamations of astonishment broke from both Arnold and Leslie. Lyostrah smiled ever so slightly as Arnold's eyes sought his; but it was a smile that was sad, and even mournful, rather than mirthful. Manzoni continued:

"He went on to explain that he did not feel sufficiently assured about it while in England to care to disclose his belief—for it was then no more—to you. But he suspected it the very first time his glance fell upon your features, the chief reason being the likeness you bear to your father, my dead brother."

"Your brother!" Arnold repeated, in too much amaze for lengthier comment.

"Yes. For reasons which I will not now go into, he deserted us many years ago; and it was thought, at the time, that he had perished in the swamps which shut off our country and help to guard it from the rest of the world. After having seen you, Lyostrah commenced inquiries, but, owing to his being compelled to return here, he could not then conclude them to his satisfaction. He has, however, continued them since, and he succeeded in securing the final proofs during his last journey, and brought them back with him this morning."

Another exclamation escaped the young man; but he was still too full of wondering thoughts to express himself coherently.

"To cut a long story short—for time presses—he has shown me the proofs, and I am satisfied with them. You are undoubtedly my nephew, a descendant of the royal line of Myrvonia, and my heir. As such I recognise and welcome you."

"Arnold, I congratulate you!" Leslie cried.

"So do I," said Lyostrah, quietly taking him by the hand. "Now you know why I called you brother,' and spoke of your sharing the government with me. In Manzoni's absence it was your place, your birthright. I had hoped and intended," he went on, in the same subdued, almost mournful manner, "to have broken this news to you under happier conditions. I would prefer to have been a witness of the pride and pleasure it would, I feel sure, have given to the lady who taught me to admire and respect her beyond any woman in the world—your brave, pure-hearted, affianced wife. But fate has willed otherwise; and I am learning to-day that fate is mightier than the strongest human will."

"I must now hurry on," Manzoni resumed, "to another matter. In the religion of my country, as I told your friend Leslie, we are not atheists—far from it. We worship a supreme Being, as do the Christians; but intermingled with that fundamental tenet are many curious mysteries handed down from ancient times, which I will perhaps some day further explain to you. Amongst them, however, is one that, from time immemorial, has been a privilege of our Royal Line. We have ever been permitted to appeal, on occasions of special danger or exceptional crisis, to the special Guardian Angels of our race. The present is such an occasion; and, knowing no other way in which to avert the cataclysm, which we perceive is about to burst upon our beloved country, we have determined, after careful and anxious deliberation, to resort to this our one remaining hope. It is an act full of peril for those who take part in it; and it may, after all, fail, and end in our own terrible destruction; but we deem it our duty to attempt it. Unfortunately, it needs three participators, and they must all three be members of our dynasty. Lyostrah is one, I am another, and you would make the third, for you are, besides ourselves, the only representative of our line now living. Now you can see why we require you to join us."

"But what is it to do?" Arnold inquired, with considerable hesitation. "Is it—that is—I mean—you see, sir, I know nothing about it, and—"

"And you would refuse to participate in any profane or unholy rites? You are quite right to be cautious. But if I declare to you that I told, as my ancestors have always held, that in time of dire trouble we are justified in resorting to it; that we have always regarded it in a reverential spirit as a heaven-born privilege of our race, and part of our system of worship of the Great Eternal Being who rules the destinies of the whole human race—irrespective of religions, creeds, sects, dogmas, or schisms—then I believe that you will feel reassured as to that first and all-important point. But, as regards the personal one of danger to yourself, I must tell you again that there is serious risk, and equal risk, to each of us. Yet if we essay it not, the doom of the one so dear to you, and of my daughter, so dear to me, is sealed; while, as regards our own lives, they will not be worth an hour's purchase, and could only be saved, at the best, by an immediate, cowardly, and ignominious flight from the country, leaving my poor people to their fate. That, for me, I need not say, is an impossible alternative."

"And for me," said Lyostrah.

"And for me also!" Arnold exclaimed. "Say no more; whatever the danger, I am willing to face it with you, since you tell me that in doing so lies the only possible loophole of escape for those we love. You advise me too, Gordon, do you not?"

"I believe, Arnold, that we may safely trust our friend Manzoni with our lives, and, what is more, with our honour. Go; and may God preserve you! If I may be allowed, I will join. It seems hard that you should go to brave the danger while I stay at home idle and in comparative safety."

"Not so, friend Leslie. We have a post of danger for you also; one that will equally tax your courage. All, then, is settled. Follow us, and be silent."

Manzoni led the way down to the palace entrance, where, in the darkness outside, they found a large party quietly awaiting them. It consisted mainly of about a hundred soldiers, under the charge of Maylion, whom Lyostrah, with a few gracious words of apology and regret, had restored to his old position. All carried lanterns, which were not, however, lighted.

Gaylia came up to Leslie, and, in a low voice, asked to be

allowed to accompany him. He explained that he not been ordered to join, but came as a volunteer.

"I cannot rest at home in suspense," said the young officer. "I am too full of anxiety as to the fate of that brave and sorely-tried lady. Let me, I pray you, keep with you and try to do something to aid in her rescue. In the darkness I shall probably pass unnoticed."

To this Leslie could see no objection; indeed, he felt only too glad of the companionship of one who had already proved himself to be a true and trustworthy friend.

In a few minutes more the expedition started, walking in silence, save for a slight clank now and again from accoutrements that refused to be altogether muffled, or a word of command given in low tones.

They followed the route taken by Leslie and Gaylia on that eventful night when they had waited for the black canoe, and as, in due time, they came in view of the lake-like expanse upon which they had watched its progress, Leslie involuntarily looked across the water towards the black mouth of the tunnel, which he could dimly make out, half expecting to see it again coming to meet them.

No sign of the fateful craft, however, nor any indication of life or human presence could be seen. The massive face of Dornanda's mysterious temple rose, as ever, frowning and sombre, its upper towers lost in a mist which, to-night, overhung the whole of this part of the land.

A halt was now called, and Manzoni came to where Leslie and Maylion were standing, awaiting their further orders.

"Here we part company, Maylion," he said, in guarded accents. "Art thou certain that thou dost understand thy orders?"

"I think so, my lord. Thou canst rely alike upon my zeal and my courage."

"I am sure of it. Here is the key of the secret entrance. To make sure, let me go over again what thou hast to do. Thou wilt remain concealed till half-an-hour before midnight. At that time exactly—no sooner, no later—thou wilt unlock the secret gate, and mount the stairs to the chamber I told thee of; and there, in silence and darkness, await the result, while we are making the Appeal. Be very alert, very vigilant, very wary. Whatever thou hearest, up to midnight, stir not unless actually assailed. Just before midnight make ready for the rush. If haply we prevail, thou wilt hear those within desert the great hall. Then light thy lantern and rush in; make fast the doors and windows as thou hast been instructed, and hold them against all enemies till we arrive.

"But if, haply, we fail," Manzoni added, more slowly, "then the great God of our ancestors guard thee—help us all! We shall meet no more in this world!"

Then he turned to Leslie, saying:

"If God gives us grace, my friend, thou wilt see my daughter before I do. Befriend her, comfort and aid her, I pray thee, all thou canst, and tarry till I come. But if it is willed otherwise, then farewell. Let us put our trust in the Mighty One who shapes the destinies of us all."

Leslie, with Maylion, Gaylia, and most of the band, then went noiselessly forward in the direction of the temple, but by a roundabout route. Manzoni and Lyostrah, with Arnold and a small guard of a dozen soldiers, turned off and made for the mountain heights by the path by which Leslie and Gaylia had climbed when they had tried to oversee what was going on in the "Sacred Gardens." They passed the lonely dwelling of the shepherd Tokabu—now deserted—and presently reached the heights above. Here the guard of soldiers was left, with instructions to await the others' return; and the three continued their climb, now carrying lighted lanterns, till they reached the flat peak of a high mountain, from which, in a good light, extensive views of the surrounding country would have been obtained. To-night, however, it was so misty that, though the moon was just rising on the scene, nothing could be distinguished beyond a few hundred yards. Here they climbed down some rocks into a hollow, and halted; and Arnold looked about him. They were in a small space of three hundred yards square, perhaps, shut in on all sides by rocks that formed a wall or parapet six to seven feet high, and with a flat top which stretched around on all sides for some yards. In the middle of the well thus formed was a ring of boulders and huge blocks of stone, some standing upright in pairs with a third placed crosswise on top. The whole were arranged much after the fashion of the so-called Druidical circles at Stonehenge and other places. In the centre of all was a raised circular platform or table of level rock, five or six feet from the ground, and probably twelve feet in diameter. In one corner of the enclosure, at a short distance from this table, was a lofty watch-tower. It had a door, but no windows, and appeared to be uninhabited.

Manzoni bade Arnold mount the table of rock with one of the lanterns, while he and Lyostrah went across to the tower. Taking a key from a chain around his neck, Lyostrah unlocked the door, and the two disappeared within, but presently returned carrying curious-looking instruments, tripods, and braziers, which they handed up, one after the other, to Arnold. When they had brought out all they required, they mounted the rocky table and proceeded, with the most careful exactness, to arrange the various articles. A number of tripods were placed in a circle two or three feet from the edge, and upon these, after a while, fires were lighted, which quickly threw up brilliant blue and red flames. Within the circle thus formed was another and a larger fire, over which was suspended a crucible, and into this, from time to time, Manzoni and Lyostrah cast certain ingredients, which hissed, and bubbled, and sent up columns of many-hued vapours.

Then ensued a long interval of silence and inaction while the three, each absorbed in his own thoughts, awaited the approach of the appointed hour.

CHAPTER XXXII

MAHRIMAH THE TERRIBLE

THE THREE STOOD thus for perhaps an hour, no word being spoken amongst them. Lyostrah, with folded arms, gazed out straight before him into vacancy, his head a little bowed, his face sombre, but stern-set and resolute. The fierce passions that had contended for mastery in his bosom that day, each in its turn exerting for the moment its sway, seemed to have died out The fiery anger, the gusts of lofty pride and disdain, the gloomy, sullen despair—of these there was now no trace. He turned towards the rising moon a face that was outwardly calm as marble, and in his pose, in his manner, there was an air of kingly dignity, and in his voice, when presently he spoke, a ring of tender, sympathetic feeling, such as Arnold had never heard in it before. The mouth, too, so exquisitely chiselled, was now free from the suggestion of cynicism, and the lurking shadow of cruelty hidden beneath an iron will, which had formerly marred its otherwise perfect lines.

Manzoni showed no change from his appearance in the morning, save that he was, if possible, yet graver in his demeanour. His face, also, was set and determined, and his eye keen and piercing, but when, now and again, he turned his glance upon Arnold, it would soften at once into a look that had in it something wonderfully gentle and benevolent.

Arnold's thoughts were a medley. Grief, distress, surprise, expectation, and many other phases of emotion possessed him, one following upon the other as he, with what patience he could muster, waited the expected developments. Towards Lyostrah his feelings were a curious and somewhat incongruous mixture. He scarcely knew whether to be angry and indignant, or compassionate. Probably the latter sentiment was uppermost, for he knew that he had suffered, was suffering, cruelly, in the knowledge and contemplation of the pass to which all his soaring ambitions and daring flights had brought them all. And had he (Arnold) known *all* the thoughts that were passing through that powerful, masterful mind—then beyond doubt his pity would have chased away all other sentiments. But he did not know the actual truth till afterwards.

"Neville," presently said Manzoni, "I prefer so to call you, because it is the name which most resembles that of your father Nevillion—which you can perceive he abbreviated into Neville—tell me, my son, are you still sure of yourself in this matter? We would not that you should remain under compulsion. There is even yet time to draw back if you wish it."

Arnold shook his head. "I have no such thought," he answered, firmly. "God helping me, I will endure the trial, whatever it may be."

"It will try your fortitude sorely; but, remember, the thing you have to dread most of all is *fear*. If you give way to fear we are lost. Fear, only, is our weak point; nothing can harm you so long as you do not yield to it. Take this staff; it will lend you support." He placed in Arnold's hand what had appeared to be an ordinary walking stick; but immediately the young man grasped it he perceived it must be one similar to that which Leslie had described to him as endowed with the magic virtues of the Red Ray. He became sensible of the tingling sensation which Gordon had spoken of; it slowly pervaded his whole frame as with a grateful warmth, bringing with it an extraordinary sense of physical strength.

"I feel now as though nothing can affect my nerve!" he exclaimed.

Manzoni smiled slightly. "Let it not lead thee into the other extreme," he rejoined. "Be not rash; and, whatever happens, do not step outside our circle of fires. If you feel you need further support, lean upon me."

"The moment approaches," said Lyostrah. "Arnold, forgive me for having brought you into this trouble. If you come safely through it, think of me kindly in future years. Believe me when I declare that I had no purpose in view with regard either to yourself—or your affianced wife—which was not just and honourable."

"Truly I believe it, Lyostrah," Arnold returned. "But why do you thus speak of thinking of you in future years'? If I pass through this ordeal unscathed, so also will you, will you not? and live with us—"

Manzoni waved his hand in warning, and whispered "Silence." At the same moment Lyostrah, who was holding in his right hand a staff similar to the one Manzoni had given to Arnold, dipped the end of it into the crucible. Immediately a column of fire shot upwards, lighting the whole scene with a sudden, ruddy glare. As the staff was withdrawn, flames kept darting from its end, like fiery serpents flying off in the direction in which it was pointing.

Upon the ground, Manzoni had marked out a triangle, and they had taken their stations upon it—one at each angle. It was of such a size that, while so standing, they could join hands. Placed thus, they had a view over the surrounding parapet, and, as the moon rose higher, the haze cleared away above, and also below them, so far as to disclose the adjacent mountain summits, which became lighted up in the moon's rays, but, beneath, all was still enshrouded in mist. Lyostrah was standing in front, upon the apex of the triangle, with his back to his companions, who stood upon the base, one at each of the remaining angles. Arnold, looking at Lyostrah, now saw, to his amazement, that he was becoming luminous, as the figure of the woman in the boat had been. The fife continued to dart forth from the end of the staff he held in his right hand; but it also began to travel backward. Soon it reached the hand that held it, and crept up the arm. Thus, in a minute, it had enveloped Lyostrah's whole body, whereupon he reached out with his left arm behind him, and Manzoni, extending his own left, grasped it. The fire quickly ran along his arm and over his body in like manner, when he stretched out his right hand, took Arnold's left, and a minute later the latter found himself enshrouded, as it were, in flames, which kept flying outwards, scintillating and sparkling, but causing him no feeling of inconvenience or sense of heat. Instead, there was only a marked increase of the agreeable sensations he had already experienced from grasping Manzoni's staff.

Suddenly there came upon the brooding stillness a sullen, rolling boom, like the discharge of a piece of heavy artillery or a peal of distant thunder. Lyostrah, who was holding his staff extended straight in front of him, appeared to Arnold to point to something in the distance, and the latter perceived that the flames, which leaped forth from the tip of the wand-like rod, seemed to have grown in a long line or path of light, which extended to the horizon, and ended in a circle of light just above it. In the midst of this circle was a dark speck, which was every moment growing in size. Presently he could see that it was some flying creature winging its way with incredible velocity towards them. On it came, increasing each instant in size, till Arnold began to be able to make out something of its shape. It was like a winged human form!

On it came, cleaving the air with powerful strokes, till the listening ears could hear the sound of the mighty wings. It increased to the size of an ordinary man, and still continued to grow, till, coming quite close, it loomed up against the sky, and revealed a gigantic form of human shape, with wings that stretched for many yards from the shoulders.

This giant being stopped abruptly in mid-air and looked at the three, then threw himself upon the rocky parapet which surrounded their station, lying upon his breast, with wings expanded on either side. Extended thus, all that could be seen of him was the dark face peering over the ledge, and the two arms framed, as it were, between the great wings, the chin

supported upon the hands in an attitude of attentive and penetrating observation.

And then it was that there came to Arnold some conception,
such as had never before entered his mind, of the hidden possibilities lying behind what we term the human countenance.
Though, of course, he had in his lifetime seen many thousands
of men's faces, in the flesh, and painted, or sculptured, never had
he looked upon the like of what now met his gaze—never had
he dreamed that a cold, passionless human face could express so
much. The word "human," it is needless to explain, is here used
as a convenient term by which to indicate a face that did not
belong to a human being, and therefore can only be so called by
a figure of speech. The essential point is that the face *resembled*
the human countenance, but conveyed more in its fixed and
unchanging gaze than the most mobile, the most expressive,
features that ever belonged to mortal man. The face of a mortal
may be likened to a book, whereon or wherein is written—if
the observer is able to read it—the sum total, as it were, of that
mortal's knowledge of good and evil up to date. That is to say,
if he has lived fifty years, then will be engraven on his face, and
crystallised in his glance, the sum total of fifty years' experience
and *knowledge* of good and evil But, since men do not live for
centuries, it follows that no mortal's features can contain a larger
amount of knowledge than can be learned in a hundred years.
What sort of a face, then, would be that of a being who had lived,
not for a hundred, or even a thousand, but for untold thousands
of years? Take a single feeling—hate, for example—and imagine a glance which should convey the stored-up hate of thousands upon thousands of years! Or—what, perhaps, is even more
awful, because more difficult for mortal mind to grasp—a glance
which conveyed a *knowledge* of those thousands of years' hate!
People talk glibly of "infinite love," or "infinite hate," or "infinite
evil," but they never, probably, try to picture to themselves what
such abstract attributes would be like if they saw them looking
at themselves through eyes that had behind them the "infinite
knowledge" which the words mean. The best attempts of even

the greatest painters or sculptors that the world has known to portray the faces of angels or devils are lamentably weak and unsatisfying when judged from this point of view. A face is not necessarily that of an angel because it is beautiful, nor of a devil because it is evil-looking. The difference between the face of the most evil man and a devil is, that the one's *knowledge* of evil is confined to a few years, while the other's embraces an eternity; and between a human saint and an angel the same argument holds good. And this subtle but most tremendous distinction neither artists nor sculptors have ever succeeded in embodying in their ideals.

These words of reminder are here rendered necessary in order that Arnold's feelings under the gaze of the being before him may be understood. When it is said that the look that was thus bent upon him seemed to be the most awful experience, not only that had ever happened to him, but that he could even have dreamed or imagined—that it affected him to such a degree that he was seized with a mortal tenor, as though his whole soul were oppressed with the weight of some nightmare burden too heavy for mortal man to bear—it needs not therefore be supposed that he was very easily frightened or upset. What affected him was not really so much fear; it was not even repulsion, loathing, horror, abhorrence. It was not that the great face opposite, on a level with his own, was an evil face, or that its expression was threatening. Indeed, he was unable to quite decide whether good or evil predominated in that terrible countenance. Taken by themselves, the features were grand, sublime, in their statuesque beauty. The beauty was of a dark and sombre character; but there it undoubtedly was. It was not the face of a man—no mortal could ever look like it,—but of a god—a fallen god, perhaps— still, of a god. It was the face of one with a master-mind; of one who was endowed with immense, unimaginable power, and knew it Nor was it that the face expressed any passion in partic- ular. There was in it neither hate nor anger, neither scorn nor mockery, neither pleasure nor sorrow, neither interest nor specu- lation. It was the face of one too strong, too mighty, as compared with the puny mortals upon whom he gazed, to condescend to feel or express any such sentiment. It never altered; showed no sign of passing thought or feeling. And there was no speculation in the terrible being's gaze, because *he knew!* That was the awful, terrible, unbearable part of it; that gaze pierced the very soul through and through. Arnold felt that it searched every hole and corner of his consciousness; brought out everything into the open, and looked at it; that it knew, not merely his present thoughts, but every thought he had ever had in his life. And at the back of that glance—behind it, as it were—there was very clearly, unmistakably written, the sum of a knowledge of evil extending to thousands, millions of years. The mind of man cannot grasp the mere idea, cannot support the bare conception; human intelligence tottery and falls crushed beneath the effort, as, in a nightmare, sometimes, or in delirium, the brain seems to give way in the attempt to realise the vastness of some towering structure too colossal, for the senses to grasp its immensity. Moreover, Arnold knew that this being was not looking at him and searching his soul only, but was gazing just as searchingly, and with the same overwhelming sense of *knowledge,* at his two companions; and further, that if there had been five hundred men before him, or five millions, he would have appeared to look exclusively at each individual in just the same way.

Arnold, therefore, was neither unusually nervous nor less than ordinarily brave because he trembled and panted, with uncontrollable emotion, under the look that was bent upon him. He felt as though he must turn his eyes away, or scream out, or go mad. He broke out into a cold perspiration; the weight oppressing him grew heavier and heavier, crushing him, grinding him, down, down, into the dust.

He seemed to have lost consciousness for a space, when the sound of a voice broke the spell, and recalled him to a perception of his position. He found that Manzoni was supporting him with a grasp of iron.

He partially roused himself, by a great effort, and listened, like one in a dream, to the deep tones of the being who had so powerfully affected him.

CHAPTER XXXIII

ALESTRO, SON OF THE STARS

THEIR INSCRUTABLE VISITOR had indeed spoken. His voice was harsh, but very sonorous and deep, and by no means disagreeable. It even had in it a sort of persuasive eloquence; and it had been his instinctive perception of this quality, probably, which had roused Arnold from his state of intolerable terror, and helped him to follow Manzoni's injunction to bear up.

"Well! What is thy Appeal?" were the words that he heard.

"Our Appeal is not to thee, Mahrimah," was Lyostrah's reply, given promptly, and, as it sounded, fearlessly. "Why hast thou come hither? I summoned thee not; I want thee not."

"No; thou wantest Alestro; but him ye will not see. He hath abandoned thee. Twice; thrice before, thou hast summoned him in vain."

"Because, perhaps, I alone called upon him. To-night we have the Three."

"That is why I came instead. Perchance I can help thee. What is thy trouble?"

"I seek none of thy aid, Mahrimah. I reject and scorn thy offer."

"Alloyah has been less scornful of it She has not found my power weak, nor that I failed her in carrying out my promises."

"Ah! She has accepted thy aid! I might have known it! But I desire it not. Mighty thou art, I know; but I do not desire either thy help or thy presence."

"Thou wilt call upon Alestro in vain. And when thou hast

failed in thy Appeal to him, thou wilt come back to me in thy despair, and thou wilt find me less complaisant."

"I treat thy offers and thy threats alike with contempt, Mahrimah. In interfering between Alloyah and me, as I perceive thou hast done, thou hast already wrought mischief enough. Be content, and leave us."

"And who else, then, thinkest thou, will help thee, proud Lyostrah? Alestro cannot; even if he would; he has not my power. Why dost thou now fear to go on in the path thou hadst marked out for thyself, the one thou hast eagerly pursued so long and so perseveringly? Why this sudden change? And of what use now the greatest gift I sent thee—the elixir that hath restored thy lost youth—"

"*Thou* sentest to me!—*Thou?*"

"Truly. I showed Alloyah the secret, and she so managed that thou and she seemed to discover it together."

"Ah! Then is she worse even than I thought!"

"Nay, there is no harm in her. She is but ambitious as thou art—or wast; for I perceive the change. Thou art like a changeful child. In a few days thou wilt repent of this fit. Of what use will the elixir be to thee now, if all thy great schemes are cast away? Couldst thou endure a thousand years of such a life as thou hast passed thus far?"

"Peace, Mahrimah, peace!" Lyostrah replied, wearily. "I will talk with thee no more. Thou only tellest me, with each breath, of fresh infamies; or thinkest to dangle before me what thou believest to be some new temptations. They are none to me. I will talk with thee no more!"

Arnold at this moment gave a great jump. A weird, pallid face had just shown itself close to his own, peering into his with such a wicked, malicious leer, that he sickened with disgust at the sight of it. Involuntarily he struck at it, but it had already withdrawn beyond his reach; and he turned his glance again upon the mysterious being whom Lyostrah had addressed as Mahrimah. Spite of the suffering—for it had been nothing less than actual pain, physical and mental too—that he bore while endeavouring to support the glance of those searching eyes, Arnold was now conscious of a desire to meet that look again. Though it pained him to bear it, there was something terribly fascinating in its suggestion of fallen majesty, vast power, and immeasurable knowledge. Something, too, there was subtly attractive in the exalted indifference, the apparent inaccessibility to human emotions. For, during the whole time that he had remained facing them, this inscrutable being had shown no sign of emotion whatsoever. There had been no "mocking smile," no frowning brows, no sign of anger, no hint of displeasure at the (as Arnold thought) daringly contemptuous manner of Lyostrah's replies to him. And now, preserving the same serenity, he raised his giant form, spread his wings, and withdrew to a neighbouring mountain crest, where he remained standing, as a still attentive spectator, his chin, as before, resting upon his hand.

Arnold could not repress a sigh of relief; Manzoni alone of the three, seemed to remain absolutely impassive.

And now a strange change seemed to be taking place in their surroundings. Mountains, which Arnold knew did not exist, anywhere in the vicinity, rose around them; darkling rocks towered up and overhung them, threatening to fall and crush them; lurid lights played here and there amongst the beetling cliffs. It grew darker, and the air became heavy and sulphurous; their fires began to burn dim, and, at times, seemed to be on the point of going out altogether. Vague phantom shapes came and went about them; evil faces with jeering, hateful leers appeared suddenly out of the surrounding gloom, and as quickly vanished. A sound of thunder came rattling down from the mountain tops, reverberating through the rocky gorges and echoed and re-echoed from rock to rock. Then a plain opened out before their eyes, and by the light of some baleful glare— whence coming could not be discovered—Arnold saw a battle-field, or what had been one, now almost deserted, save by the dead and dying. About it, in the shadows, flitted ill-omened shapes; upon the air rose sighs and groans, and now and then startling, agonising shrieks. And there, amongst the prostrate forms lying prone upon the ground, flitted ghastly shapes which passed to and fro to a sort of rhythm, that seemed to correspond to the heart-beats and the pulsation of the blood in his veins. He began to be sensible of horrible odours and disgusting effluvia, which arose from the field of carnage; some of the wounded dragged themselves painfully towards them, coming quite close, as though entreating their protection, but they were followed up by the foul beings, whose measured rush backwards and forwards now began to make him feel giddy. Some of these creatures, he thought, resembled those Leslie and Gaylia had described as manning the Black Canoe, or attacking the shepherd Tokabu and his daughter. They came yet closer, and he saw their mouths dripping with blood, and great ugly fangs showing between the snarling lips; he saw them kneeling over the helpless, crawling wounded, and heard the cry of pain and horror as they bent down—

"He comes! He comes! Alestro! Radiant Son of the Stars! Bright Seraph of the Realms of Light! Hasten! Drive from us these foul phantoms, and let me look upon thy beloved face once more!"

These words were uttered by Lyostrah, and were instinct with gladness and rejoicing. They were the first sign of really strong emotion he had shown that night; and formed, Arnold thought, the most striking outburst of unaffected pleasure he had ever known him to exhibit. There was in the ringing tones a note verging on ecstasy; truly a wonderful display for the man who, of all others, was usually so self-contained, so little given to showing enthusiasm, so disdainful of human pleasures and joys.

As Arnold looked round to seek the cause of this unexpected outburst, he felt considerable curiosity as to the shape it was likely to take, and the revelation it would afford of the nature of the attraction that could thus seem to charm one so difficult to please.

At first he could discover nothing that appeared likely to afford the answer to the riddle. The hateful scenes upon which he had been gazing but a minute before were slowly growing dim like a dissolving view, though the sickening odours were still in his nostrils. The mountains, as he had seen them earlier in the night, became visible once more above the mist, and the moon, now much higher, lighted up their summits. The fires were beginning to revive; and then the form of Mahrimah could be seen winging its way back in the direction from which he had come, growing every instant smaller.

"See, Manzoni! Dost see? From yonder bright star he comes!" Lyostrah cried again, in tones of almost childish delight. "Mahrimah said he would not hear our Appeal! But he lied, he lied! Dost thou not see him? Ah! I cannot be mistaken? No! He comes!"

Arnold now followed with his eyes the direction in which Lyostrah, while indulging in this rhapsody, pointed his staff. And then he noticed that one particular distant star had become brighter than all others in the heavens, and from it there stretched a tiny thread of glowing light which reached out and joined the flame that went forth from the tip of the staff. And now the brightness of the star had visibly increased again, and something seemed travelling towards them along that narrow bridge of light, even as Mahrimah had come, only that in this case it soon became evident that no dark-winged form was approaching, but one that was in itself a centre of glowing light.

A little while more and a form in human shape could be made out, nearing them swiftly, without wings or other visible means of motion. Presently the luminous atmosphere in which the three were enveloped paled, and the lambent flames of the fires became scarcely visible in the brilliancy of the light that emanated from the radiant visitor.

The whole atmosphere became redolent with exquisite perfumes. Sounds as of distant music, warbling of birds, the plashing and bubbling of brooks, and the tender sighing of gentle zephyrs, were heard around them. A dreamy, enrapturing sense of delicious repose and delightful contentment stole over Arnold's senses, and he felt, without knowing why, strangely

attracted towards this unknown visitor. Then he fell to wondering at the distress and anxieties that had lately so troubled him,
for all trouble, all worry, all sense of danger, flew away; it was
as though some unseen Power bade him forget his griefs, and
rejoice, and be happy. A minute or two later a glorious being
alighted lightly upon the parapet, and stood before them.

Who shall describe the beauty of this radiant Son of the Stars,
or the feelings of joy and exaltation, the sense of grateful peace
and rest, that spread around him? Love, happiness, rapture,
seemed to emanate from him on all sides, like perfume from
the rose. Who could hope to succeed in picturing to another's
mind the surpassing loveliness, the ineffable beauty, of the face
that looked with smile so tender, so full of sweet sympathy, upon
the three? Who could depict that placid brow, or the charm of
the glance from those wondrous eyes?

Arnold gazed upon this vision in a very trance of wondering
delight. Now, indeed, he understood Lyostrah's emotion when
he first perceived that the being he wished to invoke was really
on his way to visit them. What god-like grace, and what a sense
of irresistible power, yet what gentleness and simplicity! What
dignity, yet how utterly free from all pride or self-assertion! The
shining raiment in which he was attired fell about his form in
graceful folds, displaying a figure in every respect perfection, as
we should judge it.

As Arnold continued to gaze, an uncontrollable impulse came
upon him to kneel down in adoring, worshipping love; but the
object of his devotion seemed to be aware of the feeling, for he
anticipated his intention by a gentle admonition:

"Nay, friend, thou doest not well. We kneel and worship but
One, the All-wise and Eternal One! As for myself—I am but
one of the lowest of the Outer Kingdom. I walk, as yet, but in
one of the farthest circles of the millions of Zones of Light, each
of them higher and better than the one I am now in. Think not,
then, of worship in connection with myself, but be my friend. I
will gladly be thy friend; faithful and true to thee in that love and

holy friendship which is a part of our very being—for without it we should cease to be what we are!"

It cannot be told how Arnold's heart bounded at these gracious words! What raptures filled his very soul at the thought of such a friendship! He dared not answer; his heart was too full for words. He could but stand and gaze like one in an ecstasy of joy.

And, in meeting the Seraph's glance, he was aware of a feeling somewhat corresponding to that which had so impressed him in the case of Mahrimah; only here the conditions were different. He was equally conscious of the immensity of the sum of the knowledge of *good* that beamed from these lustrous eyes. They knew so much of all that is good and pure! Knew so well how far beneath the lowest angel is the purest, holiest mortal! But, instead of grievously oppressing him, this thought now imbued him only with a tender sadness, and he sighed as he began to realise how very far away from him was this lovable being who had proffered his friendship.

There was that in the very voice of the stranger that could assuage a pain or heal a wound. Its silvery, melodious accents fell upon the ear like strains of delicious music, soothing the troubled spirit, and calming rebellious passions. Arnold listened rapturously to the soft, mellow tones, as the visitor addressed himself to Lyostrah:

"And thou, Lyostrah, beloved friend, what wouldst thou of me?"

"Ah I thou knowest, friend of my soul! Thou knowest even before thou didst start, but a few brief minutes ago, upon thy journey from thy home in yonder star, millions upon millions of miles away! I watched thy coming, and I saw that thou didst travel swifter even than ever before. Need I tell thee what thou knowest? How that I am in sore straits, and have urgent need of thy help, or, at least, thy advice? It is long since I have looked upon thy beloved face. I have called to thee in vain! Time was when thou wouldst come to me at my own appeal alone, and give me a brief hour of paradise in thy sweet society. But then—then—afterwards, I called to thee many times in vain."

"And why, dear friend? Thou knowest why. Thou didst become of the earth earthy. Thou couldst not be of the earth and also in the companionship of a Son of the Stars. I grieved greatly, but I could not come to thee. Lyostrah! Why didst thou wilfully undo all that I had done for thee?"

The glorious eyes looked down upon Lyostrah with a pathetic wistfulness that would have melted a heart of stone. No anger was there, no shadow of reproach; only pitying sorrow.

"I know not, Alestro. I have been mad, foolish, infatuated!"

A gentle sigh was the only answer; and Lyostrah went on:

"I see now my terrible error! I am like unto one in a mortal sickness who has lost all earthly ambitions, but would fain make atonement ere he goes forth. Tell me, Alestro, can atonement be made?"

"It is not for me to say, beloved friend. I can only carry the appeal to another—to the great Dornanda—but he is wroth at what has been done in his temple."

"Then is my case hopeless indeed?"

"Not hopeless, Lyostrah, while thou hast one to plead for thee," was the sweet response. "I had already interceded for thee ere thy Appeal was made. I will essay it now once more."

He lifted his hands on high, and pronounced some words that the listeners could not understand. Almost immediately there came a clap of thunder, and a luminous cloud descended and rested suspended in the air a short distance away. The whole outer edge of the cloud was intensely bright, as though it veiled something brighter still within. From its midst came a voice that seemed to float across the intervening space like a murmur of the distant ocean.

"I have come, Alestro, in answer to thy message! Say, favoured Son of the Stars, what wouldst thou?"

"First to greet thee and thank thee, Brother of the Realms of Light! It is a delight to me to hear thy voice again, even though

I cannot look upon thy loved face. But thou dost well to veil thyself, for there are those beside me who could not bear to look upon thy splendour. One of Three makes the Appeal."

The Voice lost its gentleness, and grew stern as it answered:

"Lyostrah! The favoured of the gods! He who, not satisfied with gifts and opportunities beyond those granted to any other upon earth, hungered yet for more, and aimed to be a King even over the Dead! My temple hath been defiled; the true worship therein distorted and abandoned, and a plague of devils hath been let loose to overrun the whole earth. How dare Lyostrah make the Appeal to me!"

"Nay, nay, O my loved Brother! Out of thy tenderness have now compassion, for he doth repent him grievously. And not by him hath thy temple been defiled, but by the act of the woman, who hath deceived him. And here are Three; and the two others are innocent; two others of thy favoured race. Shall destruction fall upon them for his sin! The one cannot be destroyed here this night without the other two. Is there not a Way? Is there not a means to atone? A means that shall not destroy the innocent with the guilty? Wilt thou not carry the Appeal to the All-wise and Eternal One? Have I not also sinned in the past? Yet I have been permitted to atone!"

"At thy intercession I will carry the Appeal, O most gentle and winning of all the Seraphs! Let them wait."

There was a heavy peal of thunder, lightnings darted athwart the cloud, which seemed to dissolve and vanish. A thick, impenetrable darkness spread suddenly over the land, amidst which nothing could be seen except the figure of the Seraph, standing motionless, in an attitude that had in it an appearance of waiting and listening in tender, anxious suspense.

Again came the sullen roll of the thunder, the darkness lifted, and there, in the moonlight, was the cloud again.

"Hear! O Alestro, the gracious Word of the All-wise and Eternal One. Atonement can be made. The store of the Red Ray can be guided to destroy this foul brood, but it will destroy also him that wields it. All others shall be safe. The Appeal is heard; the evil is already stayed, and the Woman's power is broken. As to the other two, let them see to it that my temple is cleansed from pollution and from false servers; and let the people there again worship the All-wise and Eternal One as of old. Farewell, beloved Alestro!"

"Farewell, Dornanda, Illustrious Brother of the Light!"

The cloud vanished, and Alestro spoke again in tones of saddened tenderness:—

"I have done the best I could for thee, Lyostrah. Dost thou understand?"

"Aye, most faithful and true of all friends," Lyostrah answered, in a low tone. "I understand; and I will obey!"

"In the hour of thy trial I will be near thee, beloved Lyostrah; and in ages to come thou shalt join me in my home in yonder star, and we will tread the Circles of Light together. Now, fare you all well!"

The gentle presence faded quickly away into the distance, and with it vanished the sense of tender protection and grateful rest. Then the Three turned with bowed heads and anxious hearts to go to meet the trials that lay before them.

CHAPTER XXXIV

IN ALLOYAH'S POWER

WHEN BERYL HAD been carried off by Alloyah's myrmidons, she had been taken by water, in the barge "Myrvonia," straight to the Temple of Dornanda, where she was at first placed in a room alone. Towards the evening, however, she was removed to the apartment in which Rhelma was imprisoned; and thus the two young girls met for the first time.

Sisters in misfortune, they very quickly made friends, and each endeavoured to cheer and console the other; though, it must be confessed, there was little in the situation from which comfort or encouragement could be gathered. Beryl had been brought away before Manzoni had declared himself, and she knew nothing, therefore, of the later turn which events had taken. The only thing she knew for certain was that Lyostrah had that morning returned from his recent journey, and shown himself to be in a very excited and dangerous mood, having ordered the arrest of Leslie and Gaylia upon some charge which she had not heard clearly explained.

It was likely, she told Rhelma, from what she had heard, that the two young men would be handed over to Alloyah's tender mercies; and as she made this announcement, she looked at her companion, and there was no mistaking the meaning of the flush which mantled the lovely face.

"This is evil news for me to bring you, dear friend," she went on to say. "I feel sure you take more than an ordinary interest in our friend, Gordon Leslie; is it not so? This is no time for hiding the truth from me, dear. I have watched him closely since he has been here, and I am quite sure he is in love with you. He is a changed man. He used to be studious, quiet, and easily contented; now he is restless, and very difficult to please. I feel convinced he is in love! I have many times laughingly told him so, and of late he has scarcely pretended to deny it. I am glad, dear; for he seemed so difficult to please that we began to think he would never find anyone to his taste. Well, I can tell you this;—I have known him a long time, and next to dear Arnold, there is no one in the world I admire and respect more."

Rhelma blushed, and gave no sign of contradiction, but she evaded any direct answer; and the anxiety and distress engendered by the situation in which they were placed soon led them to other less pleasant thoughts. Presently Rhelma asked her new friend if she could form any idea why they had been thus imprisoned, and what was likely to happen to them. Beryl made answer:

"In my pleasure at meeting you, Rhelma, I almost forgot for the moment where we were. I cannot think that Lyostrah will allow this mysterious woman they call Alloyah to harm us. And yet I cannot understand his permitting me to be brought here, or his unjust behaviour to poor Leslie this morning. And it is less like him than ever just now; for he, also, has seemed to me to be a changed man during these last few months."

"In what way, dear Beryl?"

"Well, you must know that during that long journey from England to this country he and I were constantly arguing, continually disputing—"

"Disputing! Did you quarrel, then?"

"Well, no; I don't mean quarrelling exactly. He was too gentlemanly, too delicately attentive and considerate in his conduct towards us to allow me to be angry; otherwise, you know, I should naturally have felt angry and indignant at the trick—as it then seemed to us—which he played upon us, in kidnapping us and bringing us away from my aunt's home against our will. No;

we did not quarrel; but we had many arguments and discussions. They were chiefly about religious subjects. I believe; you know," continued Beryl, confidentially, as though confessing something very dreadful, "I was a little rude to him in those days. He told me something of his plans and schemes, and I hurt his feelings terribly by pouring cold water upon them, and telling him that I admired the humblest man who did his duty steadily in the position and station God had assigned to him, far more than the greatest general, or the most wonderful conqueror the world had ever seen. And you know that he is very clever, do you not?"

"Wonderfully so. Of that there is no doubt."

"I saw him perform a little act of kindly courtesy one day to a poor beggar woman in Caracas, when he did not know I was in the neighbourhood. And I astonished him afterwards by telling him I admired him more for that little simple act than for all the talents he had shown himself to be gifted with, or the wonderful inventions he had discovered; more even than for the thousands—hundreds of thousands I think it was—that he gave away while he was in England to charities. That was the sort of thing we talked of and argued about; and he frequently paid me the compliment of declaring that my poor little weak arguments surprised him, and gave him much food for thought."

"I never liked him; I was afraid of him," said Rhelma, with decision. "But; then, I have not seen him for a very long time. He may, as you say, have changed since then. But, in that case, I wonder what can have changed him?"

"I have no idea," Beryl answered, simply. "But why did you not like him?"

"I had an instinctive fear of him. I used to run away when I heard he was coming to see us. Indeed, it was in that way that I—met—Mr Leslie. But, apart from my own instinctive dislike, there were rumours amongst the Indians. They are curious people, you must know, the Indians. You cannot understand them unless you have lived amongst them for many years, as I have done. Then you see them as they really are; and one thing I have learned to know, is that, though they are certainly very superstitious, and also, of course, ignorant, from our point of view, yet there is generally *some* atom of truth lying at the bottom of even the most extravagant of their tales. Things get about amongst them, too, in the most marvellous manner; that is, things that have any interest or importance for themselves. Thus their rumours and hinted tales about Lyostrah have had for me, I confess, a sort of half-doubting fascination, and their weird title of 'King of the Dead'—"

"I have heard something of that," Beryl interrupted, shivering in spite of herself. "What does it mean?"

"I do not know myself. My father has told me that the name 'Lyostrah' means, in the Myrvonian tongue, Favoured of the gods'; but the Indians aver that it is also an Indian word, signifying 'King of the Dead.' If so, it is a horribly suggestive and unfortunate name for a man to have."

"Quite enough, perhaps, as regards the Indians, to account for the wild stories you have heard."

"I do not know; I cannot tell what to think," Rhelma answered, shaking her head. "I am in the dark in every way. Why am I brought here? Why should Alloyah have an enmity against me? What is she like? Have you seen her? I have been here now several days, and have seen no one except the attendants who bring in the food, and they will not so much as speak a word."

"Like yourself, I, too, have heard wild rumours, but I know nothing certainly. I have, however, had one terrible experience which, though it was but a dream—"

"A dream!"

"Yes; it may seem strange to you to call a dream an experience; yet it was so extraordinarily vivid, and made such a deep impression on my mind, that you may like to hear it. It related to this Temple where we now are—a place I have never been to in the flesh until I was brought here to-day."

With this preface, Beryl proceeded to relate her dream, while Rhelma listened, with almost breathless attention, but without comment, until the end. Then she drew a long breath, and exclaimed:

"And you say that that was a dream?"

"Certainly; it could not have been anything else," Beryl replied, with a slight smile. "What would you call it?"

"Come to this window, Beryl, and look out over those gardens. Are they altogether strange to you, or do they seem to be like anything you have seen before?"

Beryl looked out. The window commanded a view of the "Sacred Gardens," situated at the back of the Temple. As her glance fell, now here, now there, she shuddered. Allowing for the fact that it was daylight instead of night, she perceived that they were the same gardens that she had seen in her dream.

"It is as I saw it in my dream!" she said, in a low voice.

"Ah! And let me tell you that each night I have been here, that place, by day so quiet and deserted, is full of a strange crowd who carry on just such revels as you have described. I could not understand what it all meant; but I see it now but too clearly. Whether your so-called dream was a reality, or a prophetic vision, matters, perhaps, little now. To my mind, dear friend, it speaks only too plainly; I know now what terrible fate lies before us if our friends fail to rescue us from this she-demon's clutches! May God in His mercy succour us! I almost doubt if it be within the power of man to do so!"

Beryl caught her hand, and stared into her face.

"Rhelma! You cannot mean it! You cannot believe such a thing: Oh! I cannot endure such a thought as that what I saw in that awful dream is really going to happen to us!"

"My poor sister, it is useless to delude ourselves. It will be so, I feel assured. I am that other one' she threatened in your dream. Do you not see, now? This woman is madly jealous—jealous of you and me; though why of me, God only knows—and she intends to be revenged in the fiendish manner she foreshadowed to you. You say that Lyostrah has changed of late. He has, you may be sure, changed also in his attitude towards her; and she has put the blame upon you and me."

"But why upon me?" cried Beryl, in cruel distress. "What have I done?"

"What have *I* done? The woman must, as I said, be mad; but it is a madness which has a terrible method in it! O father! father! Where are you now when your daughter is in such peril? I wonder if my letter ever reached you!"

This reminded Beryl of the incident of the puma, and the letter which Leslie had taken from its neck. She told Rhelma about it.

"It is certainly curious," said Rhelma, when the other had finished, "that my message should have gone straight into Mr Leslie's hands. It looks as though there were a fate in it. They allowed me to bring my pet puma with me, and I prepared the note, and managed to so arrange that I could fasten it on to her collar at a moment's notice. When we came out of the tunnel into the midst of the city I looked carefully about on all sides, but not a soul could I see till we had got past all the buildings; and I was giving up all hope of seeing any one about, when I discerned, in the moonlight, three figures standing on the shore watching us. There were two men and a girl, but they were too far off for me to see who they were. I reflected that I was not likely to meet with a better opportunity, so I sent the puma overboard so suddenly that she was gone before anyone could interfere. How little did I suspect that the one I saw was the very best friend, in the circumstances, to whom I could have sent the faithful messenger!"

"And if it had not happened that he was abroad that night watching for the Black Canoe, and that Alloyah somehow perceived him and turned back, she would have met you, I doubt not, at the tunnel mouth. With her jealous eye upon you, you would scarcely have been able to send your message, and we should not have known that you were here."

Thus the two captives conversed, while the shades of evening fell, and evening turned to night. After a while, a few lights appeared in the "Sacred Gardens," then they slowly increased, and, first here and then there, what appeared to be groups of people could be seen promenading or seated about in arbours and alcoves. Gradually their numbers grew, the illuminations became more brilliant, and bursts of laughter and singing came floating up to the trembling watchers. The whole extent, as far as they could see, became a blaze of lights, which shone out more or less clearly, through floating clouds of rosy-coloured haze or vapour. The noises augmented in volume till they became a tumult, and the air was filled with riot and uproar, the clash of music and sound of song, peals of ringing, hateful laughter, the din and clamour of wild carouse and unholy revel. The scene recalled to Beryl, as she sat shivering and shuddering, sick with anticipations of what was yet to come, Poe's description of the Haunted Palace, where the passing traveller sees

> "...forms that move fantastically
> To a discordant melody;
> While, like a ghastly rapid river,
> Through the pale door
> A hideous throng rush out for ever,
> And laugh—but smile no more."

As it drew on towards midnight the door of their prison chamber was unlocked, and some guards entered, who, without speaking, first bound their wrists together, and then signed to the two young girls to accompany them. Beryl trembled as she saw amongst them some she distinctly remembered to have seen in her dream. There were the hideous beings who had paddled the Black Canoe, and the corpse-like attendants who had waited upon their mistress in the Hall of Serpents. It was no surprise to her, therefore, when, a few moments later, she found herself in that same hateful hall, with the serpentine lights dancing and twisting on all sides around and above them, and the altar, with the mysterious, ever-changing fire.

And there, upon the throne, just as she had seen her in her

dream, sat the woman she now knew as Alloyah, looking like a
beautiful she-devil, with perhaps the most cruel smile of mocking triumph that ever sat upon mortal woman's lips. Beryl turned
dizzy, and all but fainted at the sight, and would have fallen had
not Rhelma, who was herself in but little better case, bravely
struggled against her own growing horror, and managed to
support her weaker sister.

Alloyah looked long and steadily at them both. She seemed
to be drinking in great draughts of gratified revenge. Her bosom
heaved, and her eyes shone and flashed with exulting delight, as
she noted their scared, white, horror-stricken faces and trembling frames. But, seeing this, Beryl, by a great effort, suddenly
controlled her emotion, and, proudly drawing herself up, gave
back glance for glance.

"Why have we been brought here?" she demanded, her voice
firm and clear, and her eyes steadily fixed upon her enemy.
"What have I done that I should be made a prisoner in a country where I have been treated till now as an honoured guest, and
whose ruler promised me protection?"

Rhelma, fired by her companion's example, also plucked up
courage, and addressed the priestess:

"I am a daughter of the Sovereigns of the Land," she cried,
haughtily, and in ringing tones. "My father is the lawful king of
this realm, *thy* lawful king, Alloyah; and he will exact a heavy
punishment for this outrage!"

The triumph in Alloyah's eyes grew, if possible, even greater as
she listened. The stronger and more defiant her victims showed
themselves, the sweeter the victory would be to one, of her
nature.

"I have brought you here by my own power," she replied,
coldly; "by my own power I shall punish you for your crimes.
You have both, by some accursed arts, interfered between me and
my betrothed, and turned away his love. But it has been revealed
to me that when you are both dead his affection will return,
and he will kneel before me and ask my pardon. Therefore, this

night—within the hour—you both die; but your punishment will not end there. Thou who art called Beryl, thou knowest thy doom, for I have already warned thee. You shall both, within the hour, die, yet live again, creatures then of my will, spectators for ever of the happiness of the two with whose destinies you have been audacious enough to interfere. Enough! Let the ceremonies begin!"

And now they brought in and laid before her several of the occupants of one of the chambers in the catacombs. Two were handsome young men, richly dressed in martial attire, and with many decorations shining and sparkling upon their breasts. They looked like officers, or nobles of high degree. But all the others were dark, miserable-faced creatures, resembling those who had manned the Black Canoe. Beryl, looking on with feelings of detestation and loathing, recognised the resemblance; and there came into her mind the idea that these poor creatures had once been slaves of the white people who had ruled the land.

Then broke out strains of wild music, and the grotesque dance commenced as she had seen it in her dream, the dancers chanting a strange, weird melody the while. By degrees the place filled, again as in her dream, with a dancing, whirling, shouting throng, which each moment grew more excited, more furious and unbridled in its mad romp. Suddenly Alloyah held up her hand, the dance and music ceased, and, in the silence which ensued, she spoke in cold, measured tones:

"My children! All is now prepared! To-night I show you a new wonder. These two mortals are anxious to join your ranks that they may afterwards become as you are, and participate in your free, happy existence, your merry gambols, and joyous revels. You shall indeed enjoy an unwonted spectacle. They will, be put to death before your eyes, and laid beside these who already lie here awaiting their awakening.

"Then will I bring them all to life together, and appoint these two nobles to be the gallants of the maidens, and the others to be their slaves. And, when that is accomplished, I charge ye all that ye take them forth with you and teach them to enjoy their new existence, even as ye have been taught in the past. Bring them hither."

The two girls were led towards the foot of the throne and made to kneel by the side of the recumbent forms upon the floor. Half-fainting with terror and abhorrence, they stood before the cruel murderess, who made no pretence of concealing her malignant jubilation. What death she had designed for them did not as yet appear, and she remained for a minute or two purposely prolonging their suspense; and enjoying their suffering.

Suddenly there was a crash of thunder—a peal that shook the hall from end to end. The lights died down, a thick darkness fell upon them all, and, in the hush that followed, a voice was plainly heard. It seemed to come from far off, but there was in its tones a dread sound of majesty and power:

> *"The Appeal is heard; the evil is already stayed, and the Woman's power is broken!"*

As the voice finished, Alloyah uttered a loud cry, which was followed by a terrible din amongst the crowd around. With screams of terror they dashed from the room, out into the gardens, where their cries could still he heard for some time, gradually becoming fainter and fainter, till they died away in the distance.

CHAPTER XXXV

THE END

FROM THE BARRED windows which overlooked the gardens a faint light crept into the darkened hall, and revealed Alloyah standing like a Fury, gazing with eyes full of evil passions at her prisoners.

"Think not to escape me!" she cried. "If it cannot be accomplished one way, it shall be another!"

She drew from her girdle a glittering poniard, and advanced slowly, but with murderous determination, upon her two bound and helpless victims. She had already raised her hand to strike Rhelma when a loud outcry caused her to turn.

At both doors there was a rush of men, and in another moment the place seemed full of soldiers. Some carried lighted lanterns, others had in their hands drawn swords. Amongst these was Leslie, who, running quickly across to where the would-be murderess stood, struck the poniard with his sword, sending it flying out of her hand.

She turned upon him, mad with rage.

"You!" she exclaimed. "*You,* again! I thought Lyostrah— Where is he? But you shall pay dearly for this!" And with that she ran swiftly from the room, and followed the others, who had gone down into the gardens. Maylion and his soldiers promptly closed the door after her, and then proceeded to bolt and bar all other doors, and to examine the bars of the windows. Meantime, Leslie, Rhelma, and Gaylia were occupied with Beryl, who had swooned.

Under Rhelma's affectionate ministrations she soon recovered, and presently sat up, and began to question her rescuers.
Leslie told her all he knew, saying that they were hoping to be
joined by Arnold and the others before long. She seemed disappointed that Leslie should have been amongst their rescuers, and
not Arnold; but as to this Leslie explained:

"I understand—so far as one can understand anything in
proceedings so full of mystery and unexpected happenings—
that our troubles are far from over yet. Arnold has gone with
Lyostrah and Manzoni—"

"Manzoni! My father!" exclaimed Rhelma. "Oh, have you
then seen him? Tell me about him!"

Leslie thereupon related to the two everything that had
occurred since Beryl left the palace; and they, in turn, told him
of the experience they had passed through.

"I was about to say, just now," Gordon presently resumed,
"that it would appear we are not yet out of the wood,' as we say
in my country. Maylion informs me that he expects we shall be
attacked and besieged by some of Alloyah's hellish rout outside.
His instructions were that in such case we must do our best till
our friends come to rescue the rescuers. Certainly, it is not a
cheerful prospect; for we are less than a hundred, all told, and, if
noise be any guide, there must be thousands of devils around us.
I suppose Alloyah has rallied her hell-hounds from their panic,
and is inciting them to come on to the attack."

"Could we not now get out of the temple on the other side,
and escape while they are forcing their way through?" Beryl
asked, anxiously.

"No; it would be useless. They would be after us, and catch us
up before we had gone half a mile," Leslie answered, with a shake
of the head. "Besides, Maylion says he had orders to remain here,
and do the best he could till other help came. So you may be sure
he will not show his back to the enemy."

The noise without, which Leslie had referred to, shortly grew
from a confused clamour into a tumult, and he went with Gaylia

to one of the windows to see what was going on. At the sight of their faces looking out between the bars, there was a still louder outburst, and such was the storm of cries and yells that greeted their ears that Leslie involuntarily drew back. A moment later, however, he looked forth again, and an extraordinary scene met his wondering gaze.

An immense crowd was surging beneath the windows, making an indescribable clamour, some rushing to and fro in an aimless sort of way, others endeavouring to force the doors and windows. It was a nondescript throng, dressed in a wonderful variety of costumes, amongst which the soldiers and the slaves were conspicuous. The soldiers were not only in the majority, but were the most active, for they gradually cleared the others out of the way, retaining only a certain number of the slaves as general assistants. They then proceeded to justify their action by taking regular measures for storming the place. Scaling ladders were brought and raised against the rocky walls, but they were not long enough to reach to the windows of the hall. A few arrows came whistling through the air, some striking the rock and falling shivered to the ground, two or three glancing off some of the iron bars, and a few actually coming through into the room, though without doing any harm. The Temple being hewn in the solid rock and not built of masonry, the outside was not smooth, as stone walls would be, but full of slight inequalities, and upon these a few adventurous assailants managed to climb and actually appeared at the windows, where they attempted to wrench out the bars by main force. Leslie fired at two or three of these with his revolver; but the shots seemed to take no effect whatever. He saw, in two cases, actual open wounds as the result, but, so far as he could see in the uncertain light, no blood flowed, and the beings thus struck certainly showed no consciousness of pain, or even any sign of inconvenience. They were afterwards pushed away from their precarious footholds by some of the soldiers with their pikes, falling heavily to the ground, but with what result could not be seen in the confusion.

The only light within, came from the lanterns, and, outside, from a number of burning braziers put about at intervals in the gardens. The greater part of the usual brilliant illuminations seemed to have been extinguished; so that what light there was was flickering and, at times, very dim and uncertain.

"It is no use firing at them, friend Leslie," said Gaylia, "we saw that that night when they carried off the shepherd."

"But what then are we to do? It is only a question of time, and they are sure to force an entrance somewhere by sheer weight of numbers. Look! Who is that yonder?"

It was Alloyah, dressed in a war costume, with shining breast-plate and helmet, carrying a standard in one hand and a drawn sword in the other, directing and urging on the attack.

"I must say she would make a superb Amazon Queen," Leslie observed. "I wish we could understand what she is saying."

She seemed to be haranguing her forces; and Leslie, looking more closely, went on:

"There would appear to be some difficulty. See! They are dividing into two parties. It can't be a mutiny?"

Something of the kind it really appeared to be. There was evidently contention going on amongst the crowd. One section looked as though trying to force their way in the direction of Alloyah, while those surrounding her seemed to oppose them, and to be trying to drive them back.

For the time, at any rate, the attack on those in the hall was suspended, and the besieged, relieved from any immediate danger, crowded to the windows to view the scene below.

A little to the right of their position, a wall of rock ran out at right angles, like a tower or bastion, and upon this, at a level a little higher than the windows from which they were looking, was a hanging terrace. There were windows and doors opening on to this terrace, but they were dark, and showed no sign of life.

The commotion below increased until it became a veritable pandemonium. The two factions were contending with each other with shouts and cries; horrible yells and fiend-like screams rose on the air, though, in the dim light, the onlookers were unable to make out what was taking place.

Then a door opened on the terrace that has just been described, and from it Lyostrah stepped forth, bearing in his hand something that shone with a dazzling red light, which at once clearly illuminated the whole scene with an intense though lurid glare. He was closely followed by Manzoni and Arnold, and all three went forward to the edge of the terrace and gazed down at the struggle below, which had now become a fierce fight.

At one of the windows of the hall a group consisting of Beryl, Rhelma, Leslie, Maylion, and Gaylia, were watching with intense interest the battling crowd, when their attention was drawn by the bright light to Lyostrah and his companions.

They saw him direct the attention of the latter to what was taking place, and at that moment Alloyah saw him too. She handed her sword and banner to an attendant, and raised her hands imploringly towards him, making frantic signs which were interpreted by the observers to be appeals for help or protection; for it could now be seen that the face she turned upwards was filled with a deadly fear. The eyes were almost starting from their sockets; and, in the space of a brief moment, while she turned them away to her surroundings and then looked back at Lyostrah, the expression had turned to ghastly, stony horror and despair. Lyostrah was making signs to her, as though urging her to retreat towards one of the entrances to the Temple, but just then there was a combined rush amongst those who had been contending with her defenders; the latter were swept away, and a troop of hideous beings, with a deafening chorus of demoniacal, blood-curdling howls, surged in upon the priestess and bore her back. She seized again the sword she had been carrying, and fought like a tigress, but in vain; the ravening fiends pressed up, seized her in their grasp, and tore her in pieces under the eyes of the horrified spectators.

Then the latter saw Lyostrah sign to Manzoni and Arnold to leave him, which they were evidently unwilling to do, and seemed only to consent to do under protest. No word that was said could be heard amidst the turmoil and the horrible chorus of shrieks and yells.

Manzoni and Arnold went in through the door from which they had issued, and Lyostrah, left alone, stood for a moment, looking first upon the awful spectacle below, and then upwards at the sky above him.

There was a great flash of blinding light, an earth-shaking roar, as rocks came tumbling down on all sides with thunderous, booming reverberations. Crash upon crash followed, like a series of loud explosions, and when, at last, they died away, clouds of dust rose, obscuring and almost shutting out the view.

But the total cessation of the cries that had but just before been so deafening told its own tale. The quiet that fell upon the scene was as the quiet of one vast grave.

Marvellous as it appeared, the witnesses of this outburst were none of them hurt. Beryl and Rhelma had been somewhat badly frightened and shaken by the terrible tragedy that had passed before their eyes, and all were temporarily blinded and deafened by the awful flash and the stunning roar. But they soon recovered sufficiently to follow Manzoni, who was now seen at one of the doors beckoning to Leslie and his companions.

He led them out on to the terrace, where they found Arnold kneeling beside Lyostrah and supporting his head with one arm, while he anxiously dashed water upon the still, white face.

It was calm and peaceful, and retained all its preternatural beauty, while upon the lips rested a smile of happiness and content. There was a faint sigh, and Arnold, bending down his ear, caught the softly-whispered words, "I have obeyed! I have atoned, Alestro!"

Thus died Lyostrah.

IT WAS about a month after the above events that Manzoni one day sent a message to Neville and Leslie, asking them to come to him in his private chamber in the palace. When they reached his room they found him sitting at the window gazing at the fair scene that lay spread out before him. The winding river was to-day alive with boats, in which richly-dressed men and women were seated under gay awnings and rowing slowly about in the sunshine, or drifting with the stream. Around were smiling meadows and shady woods; beyond, in a purple haze, soft mountain crests reached up into a sky of deepest blue.

At the sound of the young men's footsteps Manzoni turned, roused himself, with a sigh, from his reverie, and greeted them warmly and with all the stately yet quiet and sympathetic dignity that they both so well remembered, and now knew to be part of his very nature. He bade them be seated, and inquired first after Mrs Beresford and her niece.

They had scarcely seen him since that eventful night in the Gardens of the Temple, the night of Alloyah's tragic end and Lyostrah's death. He had been most of the time immersed in business connected with the government of the country, of whose affairs he had now the sole charge. And such intervals as he could snatch from these duties he had preferred to pass in meditation, either shut up in his own room, alone upon some lofty mountain-top facing the rushing winds of heaven, or in the depths of a secluded wood, listening to the sighing of the breeze among the trees, or the thrilling lay of some shy feathered songster. Even his daughter Rhelma had seen but little of him, though she had herself remained most of the time shut up in their own suite of rooms in the palace.

Both Leslie and Arnold noticed that he looked worn and ill; like a man who had received some great shock or undergone a severe mental strain, and it was evident that he had felt very much the events of those few days of stress and anxiety. But his smile was genial as ever, and it was difficult to say which of the two he seemed most pleased to see.

"I feel it to be due to you both," he began, "to give you such explanation as I can of the trouble and danger your friends have been so unfortunately subjected to in this my country, where your stay ought to have been a wholly pleasant one as honoured guests of its ruler, I have said such explanation as I can; and I am compelled to make that reservation, for I must admit that, spite of what was told me, and what I have since discovered by investigation, there is still a good deal which remains obscure. Lyostrah, on the night of"—here the speaker paused and hesitated painfully—"his heroic death, assured you, Neville, that his intentions towards you and the dear young lady who is affianced to you—that his objects and intentions in bringing you here had been of a thoroughly sincere and friendly character—"

"I remember; and I believed him, sir," Arnold interposed.

"—and I am satisfied, from what he told me, and what I now know, that no idea of any danger to you or to that young lady ever entered his mind. His trust in Alloyah was implicit; and he would have expected her to have defended and protected you in his absence. That she should, instead, have wished to harm either of you, was to him inconceivable. But it is equally inexplicable in the case of my daughter Rhelma: what could my poor innocent child have possibly done that Alloyah should plot her death? These are both puzzling points in this affair. However, let me pass on to other matters:

"I have before told you, Leslie, that there are in existence ancient prophecies predicting that one day two men of our race should arise who should rebuild the nation's fallen fortunes, and restore it to its former place on the earth as a great conquering world-power. Also that the present time would seem to be the date indicated in those predictions. Lyostrah had made these archives his special study, and it was his interpretation of them upon which we built our expectations of great things that were somehow to happen in our lifetime, and under our leadership.

"I do not know," Manzoni continued, with a slightly bitter smile, "what we two (then very young and sanguine) exactly looked for; whether a miracle, some special interposition of Providence, or what else. But this I will say: we went abroad to see the world, with the fixed intention of preparing and qualifying ourselves for the high destiny which we honestly believed would one day be ours.

"There a great and crushing grief befell me. I married an Englishwoman whom I met. I loved her passionately; and for three years I lived in Paradise with her, travelling about in Europe and Asia. Some day I may tell you the story; suffice it now to say, she was false to me; she left me, and it—all but broke my heart! When I returned here (as you, Leslie, have been already told) I determined to give up my dreams of worldly glory and devote myself to experimental research, in the hope that the outcome of my work might be of some ultimate use to the world. And, because I was averse to gaieties and to society—but even more because Lyostrah's constant talk about the ambitious schemes he was still pursuing jarred upon me,—I withdrew myself from my own people, and went out and made my home in the wilderness. I lighted upon the remains of one of our own ruined cities, the soil of which I found would grow the Mylondos—that wondrous plant which has been the innocent cause of all this trouble—and there I fixed my abode; and when I heard that my wife had died—I had taken care to keep myself informed of what happened to her—I went to England and brought back my daughter.

"In the meantime the years rolled on, and brought Lyostrah no nearer, so far as could be seen, to the fulfilment of the great dream of his life. With the unlimited wealth that was his, and his splendid natural abilities—to say nothing of our joint discoveries in science, so far in advance of the rest of the world—he could, had he chosen, have become one of the world's most prominent characters—ay, and what would be of far more value in my eyes—one of its greatest benefactors. But he still sought, thought of, lived for, nothing but the one grand idea. He would be a sort of king of the earth, or nothing. My defection, as he called it, had a little checked his enthusiasm for the moment; but this had been counterpoised by the discovery of the Red Ray, and the almost magical properties which it developed under experiment and investigation.

"I come now"—here Manzoni paused for a few moments as if in some doubt, and when he resumed spoke with a slow, hesi-

tating manner—"I come now to what I may term the parting
of the ways, his leaving the safe road of honest (even if worldly)
ambition for his country's greatness, for the dark and dangerous path that enticed him, in the event, to destruction, and
very nearly led to such a catastrophe as would have formed a
misfortune of terrible import for the whole world. It happened,
it seems, in this wise: I was the first to discover the power of the
Red Ray to endow with a semblance of life some mummified
animals which I by chance came upon in some vaults under
one of the ruins amongst which I had made my home. I think
it must once have been a sort of museum. Anyway I found in it
some preserved specimens exactly suited to my purpose. So far
as my objects were concerned, I merely saw in the matter a most
curious and interesting experiment and demonstration of the
power of what I call Will-force; but when I exhibited the results
to Lyostrah, he, it appears—though he said nothing to me at the
time to lead me to guess what was in his thoughts,—he, I say,
saw in it a possibility at once so daring, so audacious, that, even
now, I almost hesitate to declare it to you."

"We have guessed it," Arnold said, in a low tone. "Gordon,
indeed, grasped the incredible truth from the moment that he
heard Beryl's dream, though he said nothing of it to me; and
hardly liked to admit its possibility, I fancy, even to himself."

"Ah! Then you understand. He thought he saw a means here
to his hand, to raise up for himself a great army such as the world
has never seen; independent of food supplies and other difficulties that so hamper ordinary armies—the individual members
of it almost invulnerable, and absolute creatures of his will. No
other man upon the whole earth, probably, would have evolved
or dared to attempt such a mad scheme; and certainly no one
else would have found the materials so ready to his hand as
was the case here. He knew that there were immense numbers
of mummified bodies lying in our catacombs, and these he
designed to endow with this factitious semblance of life, and
convert into a conquering host, with which he could sweep the
earth and make himself a victorious war-lord such as history

has never seen. There is one other thing that helped to determine him, viz. the coincidence connected with his name. In our language it means, as I believe you have been told, Favoured of the gods'; but the Indians discovered a semblance to a word of their own, signifying 'King of the Dead.' To one of Lyostrah's mystic temperament, that of itself seemed like the finger of Destiny pointing the way. His first experiment, it appears, was with the—creature—he called Moreaz."

"Moreaz, the secretary!" exclaimed the two listeners, in amaze.

"The same. With his characteristic caution—or what used to be characteristic of him—he determined to make experiment at first with one only—one that he could utilise in such a way as to keep it—him—one scarcely knows how to designate such a monstrous creation—under close observation for two or three years. And he decided, accordingly, to have one as secretary."

Here Manzoni abruptly broke off, and remained for two or three minutes silent, evidently plunged in deep reflection.

"However any human being could endure such a companion for that time passes my understanding," he presently declared. "However, so it was. He gave me a long account of his experiences over this his first tremendous experiment. The feelings of repulsion and disgust with which the human being in him (if I may use the expression) regarded this creature were strangely mingled with the cold, calculating curiosity and gratified pride of the scientist at his own astonishing success—though—

"But I do not wish to moralise. Let me keep to the plain facts. After a time he became used to the idea, and grew even to regard his familiar' with favour. It never gave him trouble, never had a will or a wish of its own, was free from passion or appetites, showed no interest in anything or anyone—not even in its master. And Lyostrah found he could control it at a distance; by simply *willing* that it should do this or that he could prompt it to obey his unspoken wishes.

"Then followed other experiments, until he had within the Gardens of the Temple a numerous retinue, who attended in secret upon him when there, and upon Alloyah; for he had taken her into his confidence, and she entered with spirit and enthusiasm into his audacious plans. And this crowd of creatures lived upon Will-force alone. Like butterflies, they loved to sip a little at syrups or wines as luxuries; but food they did not require!

"And thus the marvel grew! Lyostrah the while becoming daily more used to the presence of his ghastly subjects, and more certain of ultimately gaining the utmost summits of his soaring ambition—certain of becoming a veritable god amongst men.

"Then there came the discovery of a wondrous medicine prepared from the Mylondos, which acted with such marvellous effect as to bring back the appearance of youth to this congenial pair. But, from what we heard that night on yonder mountain's summit, I imagine that Alloyah had, in regard to this, tried to improve upon what, up to that point, had been a purely scientific development. She accepted assistance from the Spirit of Evil, and so entered upon the road that led her, and, with her, Lyostrah, to direful consequences. At least, so I surmise; for Lyostrah himself could not tell how the mischief began, or when the evil influence first made its appearance. Probably the woman's vanity was at the bottom of the trouble; as it has been so many times before in the history of the world. She wanted youth again to keep Lyostrah to his allegiance to her. She looked with jealous eyes upon all other women, and by some subtle instinct came to know that he looked with favour upon my daughter. He has assured me that he only so regarded Rhelma because she was his kinswoman, the daughter of his old friend—myself.

"Or it may be—and to this hypothesis I am inclined to attach much weight—that creatures in this condition—so to speak, neither living nor dead—offered a temptation, an easy opportunity, for devils to enter in and take possession.

"Who can tell? We never shall know now. But, to resume. Lyostrah, by an act of his own, which had consequences he never dreamed of, became associated with the young lady you, Neville, were engaged to. With the half-serious, half-whimsical idea of forcing you to come out here without his having to persuade you by explaining everything, he carried her and her aunt off, and thus—hear what he confessed to me. For the first time in my life,' he declared, 'I passed several months in the daily society of a really good, true, pure-hearted woman. I had always, up to then, scoffed at her co-religionists, and felt nothing but contempt for their professions. I had often said that I did not believe there was one whole-hearted, sincere believer amongst them all; but in the case of this young girl I had to admit that I had been wrong! I tried her in many ways; I set for her what many would term cruel and cold-blooded traps and temptations, baited with everything that wealth and my own perverted ingenuity could suggest, to dazzle and attract her, to rouse her vanity, or create in her bosom the fire of ambition. But it was all in vain. With unfailing instinct she saw and easily avoided the most carefully-concealed snares, and turned aside from the most artfully-contrived temptations; each time, with unexhaustible gentleness, forgiving my wiles, and increasing my respect and admiration.

" 'And thus she conquered, and showed me the littleness of my earthly ambitions by the side of her lofty spiritual ideals. Under the influence of her artless teachings I grew more and more to doubt the wisdom of the path upon which I had entered, and to fear that in choosing it I had made an appalling, irrevocable blunder! I compared her innocent, modest faith and devotion with Alloyah's worldly yearnings. You can understand, from such a comparison, how it came about that my former admiration of Alloyah lessened, and with it my affection. This she quickly perceived, and put it down partly to Rhelma, and partly to this other one whom she knew I had brought into the country?'

"Such, my sons, was the true cause of the change which, as I hear, you have seen taking place in the Lyostrah you formerly knew; such the true meaning of the struggle going on in his breast, of which you saw only some outward effects."

"But he was still loyal to Alloyah; and would have remained so; but she was unworthy of either his affection or his confidence. Whether it was that the first beginnings of the awful change that stealthily took place in the creatures they had brought into existence was caused by some act or fault of hers, cannot be known; but certain it is that she feared to make it known to him. That, and her own raging jealousy, led her on to practise systematic suppression and concealment of the ugly facts, so long as concealment was possible. While he was away he always had wireless messages sent to him, keeping him informed of all that occurred, and these she managed to control and alter from the truth. Thus it was that when he came back this last time he was absolutely ignorant of the true facts, and believed genuinely that you, Leslie, had been guilty of some very shameful behaviour towards her, and so on. Still, even then, he had no idea—so false and plausible was she—that she intended to do more than give you a severe lecture, and perhaps keep you in a sort of honourable captivity for a few days."

"And Beryl," Arnold asked. "What did he think of Alloyah's carrying her off?"

"That opened his eyes more than anything. They soon became opened still further; and he realised what he had done. When, however, he knew that he had, in very truth, let loose a legion of devils, who might from here quite conceivably overrun the whole world, he never hesitated. He rose higher than he had ever risen before; and he did not hesitate to take the only course that—as we were instructed—would undo the mischief, involving, though it did (as he then well knew) the sacrifice of his own life. But better so! For now I can think kindly, lovingly, of the greatest friend I ever had in my own youth, and, whatever the faults of his later life, feel that he has nobly atoned for them with his life! Let us ever think well of him, and pray God to have mercy upon his soul!"

"Amen!" responded the two listeners; and for awhile the three lapsed into silence.

"And you think, then, that the mischief is indeed ended?" Leslie presently asked. "What has become of—Moreaz? I have not seen him for a long time."

"By some strange fellow-feeling, he seems to have been drawn to those like unto himself, and, presumably, shared their fate. He attached himself to Alloyah, and remained with her. They all now lie blasted by the stroke of the Red Ray which Lyostrah had accumulated; buried under thousands of tons of rock which the shock shivered and brought down upon their common grave."

"Alloyah's was an awful death," presently said Leslie. "Could she not have been saved?"

Manzoni slowly shook his head.

" 'Twas her own doing," he said. "And it may be that it was as well. Perhaps her terrible fate may plead for her hereafter with an offended Judge!"

"And the plantations of the Mylondos," Leslie asked. "Where are they? I have never seen them."

"They are in the Sacred Gardens,' and have been all but swept away in the general ruin. Lyostrah's great machinery and instruments and contrivances for extracting and storing the magic force have also been badly damaged; but whether beyond repair, I cannot yet decide."

THERE CAME a day, not so very long after, when Leslie led the beauteous, blushing Rhelma into Manzoni's presence, and with eloquent appeal craved his permission to make her his wife.

"My consent I freely give, and my blessing with it," was his answer. "Do you remember, Leslie," he continued, "my telling you, the first day I saw you, that I was seeking two things, and that I thought I had found one?"

"Yes," Leslie returned, slowly, "I do remember. You told me what one was—the universal medicine—but not the other—the one you said you thought you had found. May I now ask what it was?"

"You may; and I will tell you. It was some good man to whose care I could trust so precious a charge as my daughter when I should be no more. As I looked from her to you that day, I thought then that I had found him—and the sequel shows that I can sometimes prove a true prophet."

And Leslie felt a thrill of delighted pride at this avowal of confidence at first sight; but Rhelma ran to her father, and hid her red face upon his shoulder.

ARNOLD NEVILLE and his wife, and her worthy guardian, settled down for good in the country that claimed him as one of its sons, and where the two first-named are the honoured heirs to the throne of the tiny kingdom. Leslie and the charming Rhelma, however, preferred to roam, at least for a while. They therefore came down to the coast at Rio by a route through Brazil (which proved easier and shorter than the one through Guiana which they had taken coming up) intending to embark for Europe in the yacht "Alloyah." Then they discovered that she had been driven from her moorings while lying at anchor during a great storm, and had almost been wrecked. A comparison of dates revealed the curious coincidence that this storm had occurred on the same night that her namesake, the treacherous priestess, had perished in the precincts of the great Temple of Dornanda.

It is understood that Gordon Leslie and his wife will return to Myrvonia after a short interval of travel, for his father-in-law declares that he has yet several promising lines of research which he intends to take up, and in which he desires an able assistant. It is not yet known, however, whether they are connected with any further developments of the marvellous Red Ray which led Lyostrah so far towards justifying his weird Indian title of King of the Dead.